90

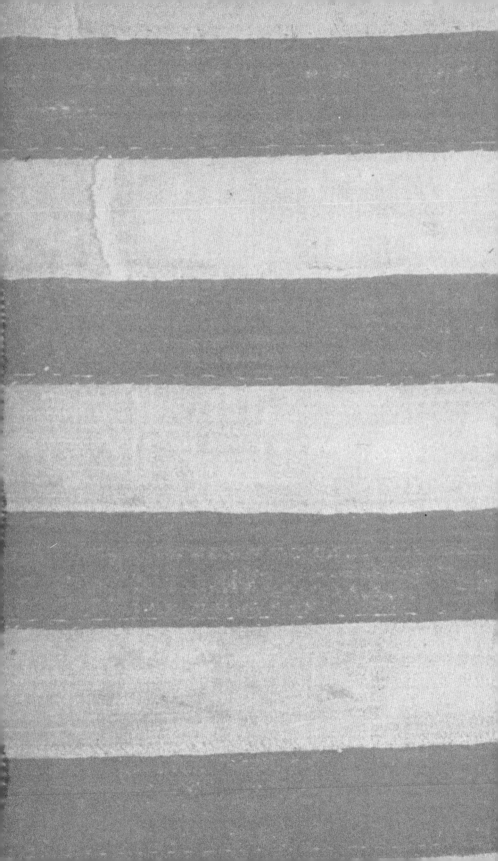

REVOLUTIONARY

Alex Myers

SIMON & SCHUSTER

NEW YORK LONDON TORONTO SYDNEY NEW DELHI

Simon & Schuster
1230 Avenue of the Americas
New York, NY 10020

First Simon & Schuster hardcover edition January 2014

Designed by Joy O'Meara

Manufactured in the United States of America

10 9 8 7 6 5 4 3 2 1

Library of Congress Cataloging-in-Publication Data

Myers, Alex.
Revolutionary / Alex Myers. —First Simon & Schuster hardcover edition.
pages cm
1. Gannett, Deborah Sampson, 1760–1827-Fiction. 2. Women soldiers—Fiction. 3. United States—History—Revolution, 1775–1783-Fiction. 4. Biographical fiction. 5. Historical fiction. I. Title.
PS3613.Y464R48 2013
813'.6-dc23
2013003204

ISBN 978-1-4516-6332-7
ISBN 978-1-4516-6335-8 (ebook)

For Ilona, now and always

REVOLUTIONARY

CHAPTER ONE

A man in a blue coat crossed the common, and Deborah craned her neck to glance through the window. No, not the recruiter; no need to worry. She turned back to her weaving; the broad room on the ground floor of Sproat Tavern was empty and silent. Another row of fabric emerged as she worked her shuttle through the wool.

With a rush of air, the front door of the tavern opened—from her workbench Deborah could just see that corner of the public room—and, pushing back her hood, Deborah's friend Jennie bustled in. Deborah gave her a little wave, then swept her gaze across the common once more: a pair of men, neither in a blue coat.

"Which man has caught your eye?" Jennie asked.

"You know me better than that." Deborah reached below her bench and handed Jennie a small bundle. "Thank you for letting me use these." Neatly covered with an old apron, the bundle contained a set of men's clothes, borrowed—without their owner's knowledge, of course—from young Master Leonard, son of the family Jennie served.

"Will you tell me now what is afoot? You've kept me curious for days," said Jennie.

"Sit close, then." They settled side by side on the loom's bench, and Deborah absentmindedly stepped on the treadles and passed her shuttle through as she whispered in Jennie's ear. "Last night, the quartermaster brought a recruiting agent to town, to Israel Wood's public room. I used those clothes and enlisted myself."

Jennie jolted back, making the bench squeak. "You did not!"

"I did. Jennie, the town is offering twenty pounds. That's far more than I'll make from years of weaving. And I've sat at this bench, or in service to a family, through seven years of this war, dreaming of leaving this town. This may well be my last chance."

"Why didn't you tell me your plans, Deborah?"

Deborah paused in her weaving. "I didn't want you to get into any trouble on my account. And I didn't want you to disapprove. Since we were little, you've been the more cautious. . . ."

"Levelheaded, you mean, and reasonable," Jennie chided.

"Fair enough." Deborah leaned against her friend's shoulder. "You are prudent and wise, then. And you would have tried to talk me out of it."

"Twenty pounds. What will you do with it?"

"Buy myself my own set of clothes, for one," Deborah said, with a meaningful glance at the bundle on Jennie's lap.

"Whatever for?"

"I intend to get away."

"But, Deborah, you cannot mean to—"

"I can. I will. I just don't wish to be seen by the recruiter before then. Hopefully he won't frequent this public room." She turned from her weaving to grip her friend's wrist, as if she might squeeze some certainty into her. "Just imagine what it will feel like to walk away."

"Is Middleborough so bad?"

Deborah heard the sadness in her friend's voice. "What is here for me? I'm twenty-two, and I have naught to offer, naught to gain."

"You're free of indenture. That's more than I can say. And you have your weaving. That is a fair trade."

"It is. I have work enough to wear my fingers to the bone and make me go cockeyed." Deborah crossed her eyes grotesquely and Jennie laughed. "I'll be a hunched crone before you know it. No. I mean to get out."

"But, Deborah . . . there's marriage and family to think of, not to mention—"

"Marriage? For you, perhaps. But carry on: list for me those men interested in the hand of Deborah Samson. I daresay there's nary a one. Or if there is one, he's lazy, and a drunkard to boot, and will expect me to weave to support him. There is a world out there, Jennie, beyond weaving, beyond housework . . ."

"Not to mention," Jennie said, plowing ahead, "how you intend to go about as a man, let alone a soldier. That scarcely seems possible."

"You should have seen the likes that were enlisting. Half-starved apprentices and stripling sixth sons. Why, I could have wrestled the lot of them and had them pinned in a trice."

Jennie gave a smile. "I don't doubt that."

"You see? That's why no man would want me."

"Never mind that. Tell me. What was it like?"

"A wonder. I felt . . . like I could go anywhere. No one to chide me, to herd me back to my proper sphere. I might have done anything I felt like and no one would have said a word against me. Wouldn't that have been a welcome change."

Another gust of cold air rushed in, and Deborah bent to her weaving, in case the wind heralded the arrival of Ezekiel, the woolens merchant who had engaged her services this spring. Standing, Jennie put on her cloak and hugged the bundle of clothing to her chest. "I should be off. Mrs. Leonard will be wondering where I am. Will you come by tonight and tell me more?"

"I will try. Thank you so much, Jennie. I hope I didn't cause you any trouble with the master's clothes."

"None at all. He did gripe about misplaced shoes. But the shirt was buried at the bottom of the young master's trunk. . . ." Jennie fell silent as a voice from the tavern intruded.

"Deborah Samson? Why, yes. She is weaving on our loom."

Both women turned as the serving girl led in two men. One, wearing an old-style horsehair wig, Deborah recognized as Israel Wood, the lawyer whose rooms were used by the recruiting agent the previous night. Deborah rose as Mr. Wood's eyes flicked between her and Jennie. "Miss Samson?"

"Yes, sir?" Deborah said.

He nodded and turned to Jennie. "And you are?"

"Jennie Newcomb. I serve the Leonards. . . ."

"Best you go serve them, then, and not idle about in a tavern."

"Yes, sir." She curtsied, casting her eyes demurely to the floor. Deborah tried to catch her gaze, wishing her friend could stay, but Jennie dashed out the door, leaving Deborah standing stock-still, feeling like a cow that has been clouted over the head before slaughter, her legs weak beneath her.

"Miss Samson," Mr. Wood said once Jennie had departed. "Let me see your hand."

"Sir, I . . ." Panic pinched her voice higher, and she had reason enough to think this a good thing, for she sounded less like the man she had impersonated the night before.

"Your hand."

She lifted her right hand slowly.

"Your left hand. The one you write with, Miss Samson." He grabbed her arm, took her forefinger—the one marked by a long scar—and pushed at it, trying to bend it toward her palm. It would not move. "Just as Mrs. Holbrook said. She noted your finger wouldn't bend when you signed the recruitment papers last night."

"Sir, I don't understand," said Deborah. She knew Mrs. Holbrook, but she hadn't seen the woman last night. It was as though she were a candlewick being dipped into tallow, such a cloying heat rose through her—fear, shame, anger.

Israel Wood narrowed his eyes. "I won't stand here to explain. I will take a deposition in my office. You'd do well to bring the bounty with you. It is best, I think, if we accompany you so you don't lose your way."

The sarcasm in his voice bedeviled her as she fetched her shawl and purse, but she could do nothing except obey. Out on Middleborough's streets, she trailed Mr. Wood by a pace, as around them shops were bustling: merchants loaded carts bound for Boston or unloaded goods brought in from New Bedford. Those ports were so close—and Rhode Island just thirty miles distant. The whole world was near about her, if only she could get away.

Mr. Wood's clerk opened the door to the public room alongside the lawyer's office, releasing a stale odor that clashed with the muddy, tumbled scents of spring. "After you, miss," the clerk said, and Deborah, ignoring the disdain in his voice, edged past. The low ceiling pressed a hush on the indifferent room—no line of young men, none of the rowdy excitement she had experienced the previous evening. At the far end, an old woman was spinning thread by the fire, accompanied by two girls carding wool. The three of them sang a little song that Deborah knew well—"With a high down Derry-o! Derry-o!"—the sort of tune to keep one's mind active during the monotony of carding or weaving. She crossed the public room to Israel Wood's office, and the singing evaporated as Deborah met the old woman's eyes. It was Mrs. Holbrook, with whom she had worked on many occasions; a woman familiar with Deborah's face, her hands, the peculiar way she held a distaff or a quill. How had Deborah not seen her yesterday? And even as she reined in her fear and anger, she salted away this lesson: how hard it was to fully disguise oneself, especially in a place where one is known, and how giddiness at her initial success had made her unaware of a crucial person's presence. Being disguised could make one blind. She would remember this, and next time—she tried to reassure herself that there *would* be a next time—she'd be on her guard.

The clerk had set up his ledger, and Mr. Wood stood by him to commence his questioning. "This is an official inquiry; a report will be given to Justice Nelson when he returns from Boston in the coming week. Do you understand?"

She nodded, eyes downcast.

"Are you Deborah Samson?"

"Yes, sir." She studied the floorboards. What could she say? What would the justice want from her?

"Place of residence?"

"I reside where I weave, sir; of late at Sproat Tavern."

"You have no permanent home? Where is your family?"

"I have not resided with my family since I was five and sent to foster with the Widow Thacher until her death." The clerk scribbled all this down.

"Weren't you servant to the Thomas family for many years? I didn't realize you'd ended your term and not married. Now, to the matter at hand. Did you don men's clothing and attempt to join the army in these premises yesterday?"

There was no way out except to confess. But she wouldn't give them the whole truth. "It was a lark," she said, the words bitter in her mouth.

"A lark, eh?"

"Aye. Here's the bounty." She presented the purse. As Israel Wood counted the money, she ran her right hand over her left forefinger, feeling the scabby ridge. She'd been chopping kindling in the yard with one of the Thomas boys, years ago. His ax had stuck in a knot, and she had gone to help him. When he yanked the blade loose, it sliced deep into her finger, almost to the bone. It served her right for trying to do a man's job, Mr. Thomas had said when he learned of the injury. But that had occurred so long ago that she felt the scar not as a mark upon her but as a part of her, essential as the finger itself; she had not thought it a distinguishing feature.

Mr. Wood returned the money to the bag. "It is entire. That's well for you." He placed the purse on the table. "Lark or no, the statutes of the Commonwealth forbid a woman to dress as a man, and I will bring this case of deception and fraud to the justice upon his return. Until then, I advise you to mind your virtue and keep close on this. It is not good for a woman to be masterless. It leads to dangerous and misguided behavior."

"Misguided indeed," came a woman's voice from behind Mr. Wood. Mrs. Holbrook had risen from her seat at the wheel and crossed the room to stand near the lawyer. "Do you know, sir, that this woman has been on her own for over a year, with no one to watch her?"

Israel Wood's brows converged as he frowned at the older woman. "This is not your matter, mistress." He turned to Deborah. "Why did you not stay on with Mr. Thomas?"

Deborah drew herself up to her full height, pleased to see that she topped the lawyer by an inch or two and could look down on the crooked part in his wig. "My term of service ended. I owe him no more of my labor, and I can find my own way in the world."

Mrs. Holbrook plucked at the lawyer's sleeve. "She left the church, too. Quite a scandal. And that young girl, there"—she pointed to the hearthside—"the one now at the wheel: she was under the tutelage of this Deborah, learning to weave. But, oh, when her parents discovered that Deborah had loosed her bonds and left the flock, they stopped that tutoring, now, didn't they?"

Deborah stared at the woman, aghast. She had never known Mrs. Holbrook held such venom against her.

"Is this true, Miss Samson? Did you leave the church?" Mr. Wood asked. His clerk's quill scratched across the page, recording this as part of the evidence against her.

"I joined the Baptist worship. There are many fine families

of this town in the congregation." She had done so as soon as her indenture to the Thomas family ended. The Baptists gave women a voice in church matters, and all sat together equally on benches, not like the divided seating in the Congregationalist meetinghouse, where the rich were separated from the poor. No, Mr. Thomas had not liked Deborah's leaving his family or his congregation, but she did so despite his disapproval.

"Few will hire a woman of such ill repute," Mrs. Holbrook continued, but Mr. Wood waved a hand at her.

"Enough, mistress. There are charges leveled against Miss Samson, and she will have to answer for them."

Deborah glowered once more at Mrs. Holbrook and then faced Mr. Wood on the verge of offering a word in defense, of pleading that she had wanted to join out of patriotism. But that, as Widow Thacher had liked to say, would be mending the coop after the fox had come visiting.

Mr. Wood's lips curled in grim displeasure, and his horsehair wig straggled low over one eyebrow. "Make yourself small about town, Miss Samson. I would not think the recruiter pleased to see you."

Deborah gave a scant curtsy and left, not wanting to view Mrs. Holbrook's gloating face. Was it not enough that women must be servants to men, drudges of the hearth and cradle and wheel? Must they also imprison each other through rumor and reputation? This was yet one more reason that she wished she could flee this town. Closing the door with a good measure of violence, Deborah hurried back to Sproat Tavern. What now? No bounty, charges soon to be brought against her, and Mrs. Holbrook doubtless already spreading vile gossip about town. *May the old hag lose every tooth in her jaw.* Deborah had wanted freedom, but she had brought down a host of trouble instead.

Two crows scrackled by a stable as Deborah walked past the common. *Two for luck,* she told herself, and she clung to that hope as she pulled open the door to Sproat Tavern. Back in 1775, Mr. Sproat had put out a sign—"Entertainment for All Sons of Liberty." Liberty; a good word, that. She could recall, even before that sign hung, the news racing like wildfire from Boston—how the British had closed the port after the colonists had defied the tea tax. She and Jennie shirked their chores to linger outside the parish hall, waiting to hear the words of Middleborough's council: the town would send twenty barrels of flour in aid of the beleaguered Bostonians. She and Jennie had whooped along with the rest, then hurried home, arguing about how the whole matter would end, both of them bursting with pride that their town supported the Bostonians' defiance.

And then, in 1776, Colonel Sproat, the tavern keeper's son and head of Middleborough's militia, had stood on the front stoop of this very tavern and read aloud the Declaration of Independence. She'd been taking care of the Thomas boys, the youngest held in her arms, another clinging to her skirts, so she could not join in the stamping and cheering as she wished to. Nor could she join in when the colonel led off the first wave of Middleborough's minutemen; she and Jennie could only stand on the roadside, kerchiefs in hand, two faces amid a flock of women. She couldn't know what the others felt then—sorrow, fear, doubt—but she knew what she felt, and it coursed through her now, six years later, as Washington sent out a call for troops that few had answered: she wanted desperately to go. To join up, yes, and serve—but more: to get away, to be free.

She thought again of the young men who also signed on the previous night, how the recruiter must be scraping the barrel's bottom if he accepted those scrawny lads. Not to mention the bounty: the town had to offer such generous money just to sign on these pitiful specimens! And though she would have liked the bounty, she'd go willingly without, just for the chance to leave behind the loom and the wheel and the tedium of her life, the endless years she saw unraveling before her.

Inside Sproat Tavern, Deborah found the Widow Wells weaving at the smaller loom, and the old woman offered a brief greeting. Settling at her own bench, Deborah wove automatically, the rows beneath her fingers growing, turning from twists of thread into a coherent whole. Usually weaving soothed her, but this afternoon her mind churned through the event of her enlistment the previous day. No one had known her. Why, she had even encountered Reverend Sayles, minister at the Congregationalist church, and almost dropped him a curtsy out of habit; but he had merely nodded his head at her, murmured a good-day, and walked on. How wonderful to tread the world anonymously, without the past lurking, with no one waiting to scold her. And now, well, the justice would hear the case, and old hens would listen, and she would be shamed back into serving a household, put under the careful watch of a master until she could be fastened to a husband and brought to heel.

Light slanted through the windows, and the room grew dim about her; Deborah fetched a taper from the tavern's public room and lit the lamps. "Supper and bed for me, then," said the Widow Wells, rising from her loom. Deborah stretched her aching hands and shoulders. She'd have her supper, too, and then go to see Jennie. It would be good to disburden herself of some of the anxiety she had felt since visiting Mr. Wood's office.

"Deborah?" Beth, who cooked and cleaned at the tavern, peered around the doorframe into the room. "Mary's taken ill. Could you serve this evening?"

"Mary's always taking ill. Particularly when her Daniel is likely to be in town."

Beth wrinkled her nose. "That may be. But she's a good girl, and as you're here and able . . ."

"Yes, then, I'll serve." *And serve, and serve.* She'd never be the good girl, never be the one courted. Always she'd be Deborah the capable, the not-quite-pleasant but at least reliable Deborah.

Men began to drift into the tavern, their day's work done. Deborah settled Widow Wells down with her supper and then ferried food and drink to the men. They stood about, ignoring her unless they wanted something, and she caught snatches of their conversation.

"... Nemasket's running high for April ..."

"He came down from Boston today ..."

"... what they say. But that price is bound to fall."

She wished she could merely resent them. But instead she envied them—the consequence of their speech, the way they conveyed importance, purpose. She was just a drudge, fetching and serving, as she had been in the Thomas household, where she'd cleaned and washed, tended fowl, and milked cows. Only yesterday, she had thought she might be among these men. No, she'd never be rich like Mr. Thomas, with servants of her own, but to be a tradesman or a farmer, to own land and a house, to be free in this sense—that was all she longed for. A bitter taste rose in her mouth as she delivered drafts of cider to three apprentices.

Full dark, and the tavern began to empty. She put a log on the fire and made her way through the remaining patrons: two old men enjoying a last pipe, and a younger man finishing his beer. She just might have time to visit Jennie. But a burst of night air, frostbitten already, heralded a new arrival, who untied his cloak and held it forth for Deborah.

"A room for the night," he said imperiously.

"Yes, sir."

"And greetings to you, Deborah." Stepping into the meek light of the fire, he handed her his hat, and she saw it was Ezekiel, the woolens merchant. She knew him well, for not only did he often hire her services as a weaver, but he was also a Baptist and joined her congregation when his business brought him to Middleborough. "Some supper, too."

She laid his cloak in a chamber and brought him bread and stew. "Are you just arrived then, Brother Ezekiel?" She used the familial to remind him that according to the doctrine of their church, in

God's eyes they were equal, even though she was serving him tonight.

He raised a spoonful of stew and blew on it. "I've been here long enough to learn the news." He turned his face to her, his eyebrows lifted. "Cavorting with soldiers? The Elders will have you out of the church for certain, Sister."

"Rumors . . ." she began, but stopped, clenching her jaw until her teeth squeaked. It would be wrong to lie, worse to tell the truth. She turned from Ezekiel to fetch his draft of cider. There had been a time when she had fancied that a match with him was possible. When, just finished with her indenture, she had looked at him and thought that she could do worse: he was fair and sturdy, ambitious, and not too domineering. He would come to survey her work, to praise the tight weave of her linen, and for some time she nurtured a hope that they might court. But in the early years of the war Ezekiel had gained a modest fortune, money enough to raise his ambitions high above a woman such as Deborah. She brought him his cider, setting it beside him. "Anything else for you, Brother?"

"No, but let me offer you a word." He tore into his bread and spoke around a mouthful. "Only a fool would join up. A fool or a woman. Or both. The time for soldiering is over. Any man worth his salt should be in business. Why, the prices of woolens! Besides, the war is done but for a few British holed up in New York." He let his eyes range over her. "Perhaps you could handle them. You're a sturdy lass. But you'd do better to spend your time at the loom, weaving my yardage, even if whoring with soldiers pays a higher wage."

Deborah blinked back her fury. If she'd had her distaff in her hand, she'd have brought it down over Ezekiel's pate without a second thought. But dignity and discretion won out. She must remember, she was an accused woman now, and it would do no good to bring yet more notoriety to her name. "Thank you, Brother, for attending to my welfare." Her words dripped with sarcasm, but Ezekiel merely sopped the bowl with his bread, ignoring her completely.

At the sound of the door latch, Deborah turned and watched two men stagger in. They seemed to be well into their cups; perhaps they had started drinking at Coomb's and been tumbled out of there. She eyed them warily as she stepped to take their coats. Only last week she'd been obliged to wield a fireplace poker to separate two brawling men. Maybe Ezekiel would rise to the occasion tonight and offer her succor. Likely, though, he wouldn't want to dirty his hands.

"What can I fetch for you, sirs?" she asked as they doffed their hats.

"Rum," said one.

But Deborah hardly attended to the rest of his order. For with the hat and cloak dispensed with, she saw that the second man was none other than Israel Wood's clerk. His eyes glittered up at her while his lips parted in a wicked grin, and she knew that within moments he'd be telling the whole tavern of the deposition he'd heard that day. Ezekiel would lap it up and carry the news straight to the Elders. Men, given the chance, were just as eager to gossip as women. She stood up straight, stiff with shame, and hung their coats from pegs before ducking into the kitchen. "Beth? There's two more just in for rum, but I fear Mary's headache is catching. . . ."

Beth rolled her eyes at Deborah. "Get you to bed, then. I'll tend to them. It'll be one round, and I'll have them out on the streets."

She took her time climbing the steep staircase, trying to let the night air leach the anger out of her. By the time she reached the attic rooms where the weavers and servants lodged, her rage had congealed like cold grease. At the door to her room, which she shared with the Widow Wells, she stood with her hand upon the latch. She had wanted to visit Jennie, but it was late, and she didn't want to appear unseemly—gallivanting about at night—before the clerk, who certainly would note her departure. Easing her way into the darkened chamber, she paused to let her eyes grow used to the dimness; the contours of the bed gradually emerged with the widow's body a mound upon it. Now and then came the soft whisper of a snoring breath. Her own breathing still came in sharp huffs of dissatisfaction, and not from climbing the stairs. She should have just brushed past the clerk and gone to see Jennie. It was within her rights. Deborah crossed to the single window of the chamber. Outside, the darkened world offered nothing. What should she do? If she left, where would she go? And how would she make her way in the world? Yet if she stayed . . .

Deborah turned back to the bed and stood awhile, combing out her hair, counting up to a hundred strokes and then counting back down again, before beginning to unbutton her dress. She could just see the widow's face, slack with sleep, mouth agape, showing barely enough teeth to chew with. A hank of white hair escaped from her cap and fell across a sunken cheek. Deborah's fingers paused. Would that be her someday? Sixty years old, used and discarded, forgotten in some attic? She didn't know what to do. But she knew that sleep would elude her if she lay down, that her mind would tumble over the day, awash with regrets. At best, she'd wring from her slumber a tortured nightmare or two. So she buttoned her dress up again and slipped out of the chamber. Jennie would have an answer for her.

She wrapped her shawl about her shoulders as she treaded lightly down the stairs and past the door to the weaving room. She glanced into the tavern. Beth had been true to her word: not a man remained therein. The flames of the fire lay banked, and everything was quiet and dim. A little imp of an idea grabbed at Deborah, and she retraced her steps to the corridor off which Ezekiel's room lay. He'd left his shoes outside his door; no doubt he hoped that she'd have them cleaned and polished by the time he broke his fast on the morrow. Well, she might. She snatched them up, clutching them to her chest, and tiptoed down the stairs.

Out the back door and into the yard she went, the night cold about her. Should she take the shoes to Jennie or hide them in the woodshed? Better not to burden her friend. Deborah crossed the darkened yard toward the shed and narrowly missed being dashed by the door to the necessary house, which swung open and slammed against the side of the privy. Deborah stumbled back in the darkness, giving a yelp of surprise as the clerk emerged, his hands still buttoning the front of his pants.

"Pardon," he slurred, and then, seeming to realize who it was that he faced, he leered up at her. "Miss Samson. I didn't expect to find you here."

"I weave and lodge here, as you may recall."

"Have you not a pot in your chamber, though?"

"It is none of your business," she said, though she dearly wished she could upend said pot over his head. "I don't have to answer your questions now that we are quit of the lawyer's office. I am free to mind my own—"

"Don't be so certain about that. Mr. Wood surely would wish to know of your nocturnal habits. Cavorting behind taverns?"

"I'm not cavorting . . ."

"And what's that in your hand, then?"

Deborah tucked the shoes behind her back. "It is none of yours to mind—"

The clerk stepped up to her, seizing her arms as if to pry them loose. "I say that it is." His face was close to hers now, rum hot on his breath. "How many soldiers have you had back here?" He pushed against her now, forcing her back against the side of the woodshed, and the jolt of her spine against the wall took her breath away for a moment, allowing him to grip her tighter.

"Let go of me," she gasped.

"Is this how you treat all your lovers?"

"I have no lovers," she grunted.

"We shall see."

Cold air slapped her legs as the clerk plunged a hand beneath her skirts, pulling them high. He tugged at her smallclothes and she heard the fabric tear, felt the rough wool of his trousers chafing against her inner thighs. She yanked an arm free. Her hand still grasped Ezekiel's shoes, and she flung them desperately at the clerk and then drove the heel of her palm into his face, catching the side of his jaw. She heard his teeth click, but before she could get away, he had grabbed both of her wrists in one hand. With the back of the other, he struck her cheek. Sparks burst across her vision, and for a moment she hung limp, supported by the clench of his hand, by the press of his body against hers. She opened her mouth to yell, but his fingers came over her lips. She bit down, feeling her teeth puncture skin, blood blossoming salty in her mouth. He jerked back in pain, and the moment of release let her push away from the woodshed. Spinning, she tried to twist free, tearing the fabric of her neckline. The clerk, thrown off balance, fell, carrying her with him. The two of them landed on the muddy ground in one tangled heap, the clerk cursing under his breath. Her feet had no purchase on the soft ground, and he regained a hold on her, his knees pinning her legs, his hands on her wrists.

Forcing her legs open, he lay heavily upon her, a forearm to her neck, the other hand pulling at her skirts. She closed her eyes against his face, felt him on her, in her. She counted, seeking refuge against the pain, waited. There; he began to thrust more wildly, his body arching above hers. Now—enough space for her to raise a knee and free an arm. She caught him in his crotch with her leg and felt him go slack. But before he could collapse, she lashed out with her fist, striking him square in the face, a blow that sent ripples down her arm, followed by a warm flush. His blood, dripping onto her wrist and her forearm, snaked toward her shoulder. She'd split open his nose.

Deborah rolled out from under him and tried to stand on quaking legs. Her skirts fell down as she stood over the clerk, watching him move to his knees, one hand cupping his nose. Her kick caught him in the back of the head. If he saw it coming, he gave no sign, and his head snapped forward like a rag doll's. He fell again to the ground, heavily, without resistance. Her chest heaved as she bent down and grabbed Ezekiel's mud-coated shoes.

Now she ran: down a narrow side lane, out to a field, over a stone wall, and into a woodlot. Trying to stifle the noise of her sobbing, she crouched on the ground. Her hand ached where she'd struck the clerk, and her cheek throbbed, too, but that was nothing to the agony between her legs. Was he still lying behind Sproat's? Or did he pursue her already? She pushed herself up and walked slowly, each step sending an arc of pain through her groin. She had to get to Jennie. Standing at the border where the trees melted away and the land became field, she could see a few houses, a track that wended to the north of town, a street that led to the common. No sounds of hoofbeats or footsteps, no men's voices calling. What had she done? One thing was clear: she had to flee, and flee now. Morning would bring the justice and additional charges; morning would bring her shame and total ruin.

Deborah skittered along the margin of the field, hewing to the stone wall. When she came to the road, she hesitated, and instead of following it to town, she cut across the lot, scrambling over walls and through freshly turned garden patches. She passed the Thomases' residence, where she had served so many years—all its windows showed black, mirrors of the night sky—and through a straggly orchard finally reached the Leonards' house.

Thank God Jennie slept on the first floor. In the utter silence, the click of the metal latch rang loud in her ears and she froze, waited, then pushed the back door open. She knew the space well; she navigated by the kindling pile and past the pie cupboard to Jennie's room. The faintest light filtered through the window—what bit of the moon could sneak inside—but it was enough to show Jennie curled beneath the covers. More than anything, Deborah wanted to lie down beside her, let Jennie hold her and tell her everything would be fine.

She sat on the edge of the bed, near where Jennie's knees were bent. Gently, she touched her friend's face. Jennie awoke with a jolt, clutching the quilt to her chest.

"Oh! Deborah . . ." she gasped, but sleep still muffled her voice. She dropped the quilt and reached out a hand to her friend, touching her exposed shoulder, looking at the muddy shoes in her lap. "What happened?"

"I was at Sproat's, and the clerk, Israel Wood's clerk, he . . ." Deborah twisted her lips against the tears, and before she could find words, Jennie had wrapped her arms about her, pulling her close.

"It'll be fine, Deborah." For such a small woman, Jennie's arms were strong, and Deborah let herself be held, rocked, crooned to as a babe. "It'll be fine." Jennie's fingers found the dried blood on Deborah's arm, and she reached over to light a candle. There came the scratch of the flint, and a small orange flicker illuminated a corner of the chamber. "Shh, shh," said Jennie, though Deborah had not made a sound. She lifted the corner of Deborah's skirts, saw the blood and the dirt streaked on her thighs, and said nothing, just held her.

At last, Deborah raised her head. "Will you help me, Jennie?"

The candle fitzed and sputtered as a moth came too close and fell in. Jennie swung her legs out of bed. "Of course. What do you need?" Ever practical.

"Just that bundle of clothes. I have a little money in my purse. I'll be on my way tonight. The justice . . ."

"Let's get you clean first." Jennie disappeared from the chamber, returning a moment later with a basin and a few rags. Setting them at the foot of the bed, she helped Deborah clean the mud and leaves from her hair and skirts, wash the blood from her legs. They leaned their heads close, and Deborah whispered the story of Israel Wood, Mrs. Holbrook, all the details from the night before, and what had happened with the clerk. Jennie sighed and shook her head. "I'll fetch what you'll need." But she didn't move; she just sat there, her arm around Deborah's waist. "Deborah?" she said at last. "Why did you do it? Why take such a terrible risk?"

Deborah shook her head. "I don't know . . . I don't know."

"But you asked for those clothes last week, or more."

"I saw the notice on the green, the offer of the bounty."

"To be a soldier, though. What were you thinking?"

"I wasn't thinking of the risk. I thought only of . . . of . . . getting free, breaking away. I thought of Elder Backus and how he went to jail rather than pay the church tax. I thought I was in line with the cause of liberty. What others call wrong, but I know to be right." She sniffled a bit.

"Oh, Deborah." Jennie passed her a kerchief and Deborah blew her nose into it.

"I suppose I've made my decision." She managed a strangled laugh. "I'll be getting out of town soon."

Jennie stroked her hair, finding in it an overlooked twig that she gently disentangled. "Why would you want to leave? We've lived almost our entire lives here. . . ."

Deborah felt a surge of guilt. "I didn't want to abandon you. I just . . . Do you see how you are treated, by Mr. Wood in the tavern today, or by young Master Leonard around the house? Or how the clerk could . . ." She trailed off, clenched her hands on her soiled skirt. "What is there for me here?"

"I think I understand. But it's no easy road for you to walk. I'll gather those things."

A few minutes later she came back, arms full, and deposited her load on the bed. First, she handed Deborah the same bundle they'd exchanged that morning.

"Will young Master Leonard miss these clothes?" Deborah asked, untying the apron that held them.

"Not for a while, anyway. It is good you found the shoes." She paused as though she would inquire about their origins, but restrained herself with a sigh. "The master would miss those." She passed Deborah a hefty package wrapped in a kerchief. "Corn bread and dried apples. There's hard bread and cheese and a knife tucked in as well." She searched in a trunk at the foot of the bed. "Here's a candle, flint, and a sewing kit. And my letter box." She pressed it into Deborah's hands. "Write to me." Her hands lingered there for a moment, both of them gripping the box. "Do you know what you will do?"

"No." It was a miserable admission. She hadn't thought this through at all. The lure of money, the thought of freedom—she was goaded by the desire to get away, to find a more promising future. "But I must go."

Deborah laid everything inside the apron and tied the garment tightly, leaving the strings long so she could carry the bundle over her shoulder. "One last favor, Jennie. Would you cut my hair?"

"Your hair? But, Deborah . . ."

"I cannot travel as a woman. By morning, the justice is certain to seek me. Besides, it will grow back."

Jennie sat on the trunk, and Deborah sank to the floor between her knees. She felt Jennie's fingers pull through her locks, hitting a snag here and there, pointlessly untangling the knots. It was as though they were young girls again, combing each other's hair and pretending to get ready for a ball. It felt so good. But this wasn't pretend, and they weren't children. Deborah pushed away the horror of the evening, focusing on Jennie's words. "It's a shame to cut . . ."

A creak sounded from above, and both women froze. *Maybe just the house shifting and settling.* Another creak, and another. One of the Leonards had woken.

Deborah leaped up. Jennie grabbed the bundle and passed it to her. "Go, be safe, Godspeed."

Deborah scurried out the back door. She took a quick look at the stars, which in the cold night air seemed even farther away than usual, then glanced down the narrow lane. Empty. She stepped into the street and hastened away—away from the green, away from town, away from all she knew.

CHAPTER TWO

Each step dragged as though thick mire clutched at her foot. Still she pressed on, stopping at times to catch her breath and listen, but the night remained silent. When she was a good distance from town, she left the road for the woods. Under the boughs, the darkness thickened and coalesced into a presence of sorts. She stumbled through some brush, never minding that her dress caught on prickly branches; a few more tears would make little difference. At last she sank to the ground, leaning against a fallen trunk.

In the darkness, she fingered her hair, wishing that Jennie had had time to cut it at the Leonards' house. The scissors in the sewing kit were meant for snipping thread; instead, she hefted the knife and, pulling her hair taut, began to saw away. The rending of the strands—a tender and terrible sound—made her shudder. Another thing torn. She sawed more ferociously, and her hair fell in disorderly clumps about her. She felt the rough edges and used the sewing scissors to even out the hair here and there. It hung just over her ears now, in a crude imitation of the hairstyle favored by the apprentices of Middleborough—off the neck but long enough to hold a curl. With a hat, it would do until she could find a looking glass and proper scissors. She pulled out her blanket and wrapped it about her shoulders. As best she could, she gathered the clumps of hair from the forest floor. There was no reason to keep it—it was dangerous even—but still, she untied her apron from her waist and carefully folded the hair within. Tonight, at least, it would serve as her pillow. She wrapped her arms around herself and, squeezing her eyes shut, whispered, "Lord God, give me strength for my journey." Chilled in the spring night, she pulled her knees to her chest and prayed: "God, don't let his seed take hold in me."

Something rustling in the woods awoke her when the sky showed the yellow-gray of first light, and she sat up, momentarily disoriented, her stomach aching like she'd eaten a raw potato—it felt empty and full all at once. She stood, knees creaking, and pulled young Master Leonard's clothes out of her bundle. Unbuttoning her dress, she drew the garment over her head. Her flesh prickled in the cold air. From the tattered remains of the dress's lining, she cut a band of muslin and wound it about her pale chest; inhaling, she tightened it until it squeezed her ribs. The pressure felt good, almost reassuring. She secured the ends and then pulled on young Master Leonard's shirt, wrapping the long tails about her thighs before stepping into the breeches, the wool sharp and itchy against her flesh. She yanked them up and belted them firmly about her hips; if she kept them low, the curve of her waist would not show. Had her mood been lighter, she might have chuckled at this. Ladies spent hours lacing up their corsets and fixing their panniers, trying to gain the most flattering curves possible . . . and here she was, hunched in the midst of a woodlot, doing her best to appear straight, flat, and boyish.

She pulled on the leggings, fixing them at the bottom of her breeches, and then reached for Ezekiel's shoes, slipping one on. Her foot felt like the clanger of a bell, knocking about in there, but better they were loose than that they pinched; she stuffed her old stockings in the toe and fastened the buckles as tightly as possible. She wished she had a looking glass. More, she wished Jennie were there to laugh and clap her hands and tell Deborah that she looked every bit the handsome young man. But Jennie wasn't there, and now the sky kindled orange. The morning might bring the justice's men to the road, and sighing over loss only frittered away time. She buttoned up the waistcoat and stared down at her front, making sure her breasts made no swell.

Folding up the dress and cap around her shoes, she stuffed them, together with the apron containing her hair, into the bundle. Carrying her old clothes invited risk, but leaving them in the woods struck her as even riskier. She settled the hat on her head, slung the bundle over her back, and picked her way out of the woods. When just two days before she had accomplished this same transformation, it had been thrilling, head-spinning. Even now, with fear scraping away at her, the feeling of the trousers and waistcoat made her grin. The sun cleared the horizon, already blazing. Putting it at her back, she set out away from Middleborough.

After a short while, though, she stopped and removed her hat. Something felt odd. She ran her hands through what remained of her hair and realized what it was: the weight. Her neck felt lighter, and it took less effort to look up toward the sky or to face what lay ahead.

The track she walked—little more than a wagon and a half wide, with ruts that ran deep in places—soon followed the course of a brook. Weeks of living at Sproat's had afforded her time to study the almanacs in the public room—there was little other reading material to be found there—so she had a general sense of the roads that wound between Middleborough and the surrounding towns. She kept her course aimed west, toward Taunton, her mind churning through the events of the past days. Like bubbles in boiling water, memories—the clerk's face, Mrs. Holbrook's words—kept rising to the surface, unbidden. She forced her thoughts into a more practical vein: a name. When she had enlisted in Middleborough, she'd signed as Timothy Thayer, two names common to the area, but with the justice alerted, she could not reuse this guise. As she walked along the banks of the brook, she wondered what name her mother would have given her if she'd been born a boy. It was a question she had asked herself before, though not so much about the name as the fate: What would her life have brought if she'd been born a boy? With a birthday so close to her mother's, she'd been given the selfsame name. Two Deborahs under one roof—as if her mother couldn't be bothered to find truer inspiration, as if she were confining her daughter to a similar destiny.

As a child, it had fallen to Deborah to watch her brother, who was three years younger. She would stand at the foot of his little cradle and rock him to and fro. In the summer of her fourth year, just before her father went away and was lost at sea, a fever raged through their house. Everyone except the little boy survived. And though his headstone in the cemetery bore, out of thrift, only the word "baby," she still carried his name with her like a treasure: Robert Shurtliff. A destiny lost by one could now be seized by another.

Robert after a favorite uncle, Shurtliff a middle name come down through the generations—she could hear the name on her mother's lips, and although Deborah had scarce seen or spared a thought for her mother in a year's time, this memory gave her comfort. She could be someone new yet carry a piece of the past. She was Robert Shurtliff, born in Plympton. This, the truth, seemed safe to her. She knew Plympton well, having lived there for five years and visited upon occasion, yet few from Middleborough would know to associate her with Plympton.

Coming to a crossroads, she picked the northerly track, thinking to aim for Taunton, but she'd barely made it a quarter of a mile when it began to rain, a drizzle that swelled into a steady patter. Puddles formed quickly in the ruts, and Deborah walked in the middle. In another half a mile she came upon a cart lodged in the muck, the rain having transformed the looser portions of the road into quagmire. The carter, wearing the wide-brimmed hat and homespun jacket of a farmer, berated his horse, but the beast couldn't make the stuck wheel budge. Deborah pulled her own hat low and made to sidle by, not wanting to talk or be seen.

But the farmer called out, "Hey, boy! Lend a hand?"

She could scarcely refuse a request for help. Tossing her bundle in the back of the cart, she and the farmer put their shoulders to the wheel. "One and two and heave . . ." the man said. With a mighty sucking sound the wheel came free, and the cart lurched forward. Deborah fell to her knee, and the farmer grabbed her arm, pulling her up.

"There's a lad," he said. "Want to ride a piece?"

She nodded, numb and muddy, and stepped to the side of the cart. For a moment, she waited for the farmer to offer a hand at her waist and push her up.

But he just said, "Well, come on," as he clambered in.

She grasped the cart, stepped onto the wheel, and swung herself aboard. It was hard to keep from grinning. The farmer's simple assumption of her competence—lend a hand, get yourself up—buoyed her spirits tremendously.

Slumping forward on the seat, she stretched her sore arches inside the sodden shoes, which still held the imprint of Ezekiel's bunions. She squinted at the overstretched leather, proof, it seemed to her, that the man was noxious down to his toenails. At least she had redeemed these shoes from their terrible fate.

"It's always this way in the spring, with the mud. But it'll be good for the crops," the farmer said as he chucked the reins and set the horse in motion.

"Yes, sir," she said, keeping her voice low.

At the next crossroads, the farmer gave her an inquiring look as he pointed the cart to the north, but Deborah just nodded; any direction but back the way she'd come suited her. At what might have been midday—the gray muzziness obscured the sun—the farmer stopped the horse under a densely needled pine. Hopping down, they took shelter under the boughs, and the farmer ate a sausage and roll while Deborah untied her bundle and broke off a piece of corn bread. Until she began to chew, Deborah didn't realize the extent of her hunger. Jennie's corn bread tasted buttery and soft, the top a thin crackle of crust. She devoured the piece and forced herself to pack away the rest, else she'd eat the entire thing.

"All right, boy?" the farmer said. Deborah nodded, put one foot on the cartwheel, and pulled herself up. She allowed herself a brief moment of satisfaction, savoring the pleasure that the word "boy" gave her—the thrill of being unbound from herself.

The farmer spoke to the horse when it balked at puddles, and Deborah settled as comfortably as she could on the cart's seat, trying to imagine what might happen next. Before she could worry about finding work, she needed to find safety. The justices of the area would be looking for a runaway weaver who matched the description of Deborah Samson. But if she went just a little farther afield, she'd be safe. She would find some farm that needed labor for the spring planting or a tradesman in need of an assistant; she could read and write and had no fear of hard work.

"I'll be going west here, lad." The farmer's voice cut across her thoughts.

She saw that they had reached another crossroads, a major one, with a cleaner, wider track headed to the north and a signpost listing nearby towns. "Thank you, sir. I'll take my leave." She took care to press her voice down and speak gruffly; it would take some practice.

Sliding down the side of the cart, she grabbed her bundle and watched as the farmer whipped the horse into motion again. Then she stepped up to the signpost to study her options. An arrow indicated that Middleborough lay twelve miles behind her already, and enough daylight remained to cover several more. Though still within the town limits of Taunton, she thought she must be on its outer edge, for the sign said Easton was two miles along the northerly track. With her bundle over her shoulder, she set out.

On the far side of Easton, she spent another night in the woods. A morning of walking left her hungry, and she ate the last of Jennie's corn bread at the foot of a bridge, weary but relieved that many miles separated her from Middleborough. She followed a small track north, then a road headed west, and she entered the town of Stoughton as dusk gathered, bringing with it a pounding rain that sent her running for the first outbuilding she could find—a farmer's barn. He found her curled up in some hay the next morning and chased her out, hurrying her on her way with oaths she never would have heard had she been wearing skirts. In Walpole and Wrentham she stopped by public rooms to warm up near the fireside and catch the news, listening for any word of a fugitive weaver who'd slipped away from the Middleborough justice, but she heard nothing.

There were clear days—the morning sun on her back, a twig of minty yellow birch in her mouth—when she could enjoy the choice that each crossroads presented. For the first time in her life she determined the course of events, day after day. She hitched another cart ride and, settling into a woodlot for the night, gathered sticks and built a fire. The flames stuttered before her, wavering in the breeze. As she gnawed the last of the cheese, the fire's depths mesmerized her. Though she was wracked by exhaustion, under the fatigue a tendril of exhilaration fed her spirit. She tried to count back over the days. Six? Or seven? In all that time, no one had seen through her disguise. She had meant to get away and now she had. No matter that she had just devoured the last of her food and had only a few coins to her name. No matter that her name was not truly her name. She reached into her bundle and pulled out the apron containing her hair. Loosening the knot, she took the strands up in great handfuls and threw them on the flames. They popped and hissed, as if in disapproval. Another handful twisted and melted, wilted and disappeared, filling the air with a cringing odor. Her old dress she tore into strips. Much as she wished to burn it, to be rid of it forever, she could hear Jennie's voice arguing prudence and frugality, to save it for rags. Still, it felt good to rip it, to burst its seams. She would find a barn or stable where she could leave her old shoes; someone would be happy to chance upon them. She let the fire burn down and imagined how the next town would provide a chance to earn her keep as a chore boy or a field hand or a shop assistant. She could be any of those things.

EIGHT MILES OF MUDDY TRACK brought Deborah to Bellingham in the late afternoon, and she gratefully pushed open the door to the only inn on the common.

"A room for the night?" Deborah asked the woman who knelt by the hearth, scooping ash.

"Five shillings, and with that you get board tonight and tomorrow morning."

Deborah extracted the coins from her belt as the woman heaved herself up. "You can have the room at the top of the stairs, on the left."

"Thank you, ma'am."

At the rear of the inn she found a small foyer with a staircase and two doors, one leading outside to the backyard. Deborah pressed her ear to the other door and heard it: the light laughter, the steady thumping of some woman's treadle, pounding out a rhythm that seemed to say, *No more! No more! No more!* She climbed the stairs, a smile on her lips.

At the very top she found her room, nestled under the eaves of the house. She gave her leggings and breeches a vigorous cleaning with the clothes brush, flaking off the mud from the previous days. She poured water from the ewer and washed her face and hands. Then she stood before the looking glass, silvered and dim, to gaze at the reflection. She barely recognized it: brown hair that curled away from the forehead and neck, a waistcoat snug against a flat chest, leggings that hugged a finely shaped calf. From her bundle, she withdrew the sewing kit Jennie had given her and used the scissors to straighten up the ragged edges of her hair. Leveling the line across her ears and—as best she could—at the nape of her neck, she thought she had done a fair job. She shook off the stray strands and then walked across the chamber, watching herself in the glass, seeing how her stride had stretched out, how her arms swung loose at her sides. She looked just like a young man. She stared and stared, trying to believe this wasn't someone else. This was her reflection. This was Robert Shurtliff.

She lay on the bed, which was inexpressibly soft after all those nights in the woods, and was pondering what she would do the next day, when noises—a scraping of chairs, a sudden upsurge of voices—broke her reverie. She drew her waistcoat on and hastened downstairs to see what caused the excitement.

"Just three years! It's a chance to fight the British, a chance to prove you're a man, red-blooded and hearty!"

Deborah emerged from the foyer at the rear of the inn to find a uniformed soldier standing on a table, trying to rally a small crowd of young men—some little more than boys. A harried-looking serving girl edged through with her hands full of tankards. Deborah wished that she could offer a word of sympathy—tell the girl that she knew how she must feel. Or better yet, lean close to whisper in her ear: *Run away! There's a world beyond serving these louts!* But first she must attend to her own destiny.

The soldier carried on: "Cut the apron strings that tie you to your mother. Kiss your sweetheart farewell. You'll get a bounty and the gratitude of General Washington." A few of the boys cheered at this, though whether on behalf of Washington or the money, Deborah couldn't tell. "And it isn't like the army of old. Why, when I joined up, we hadn't shoes or blankets, but you boys . . ." The soldier's voice disappeared in the rising hubbub. Tankards were passed hand to hand, and as Deborah pressed farther into the room, she saw a man seated at the table, his ledger open near the soldier's boots, ready to write down the names of recruits.

The woman who had taken Deborah's coin earlier came over. "You signing on, then?" She, too, carried a tray laden with mugs.

Deborah cleared her throat. "I just came down for dinner," she said lamely.

The woman gave her an appraising look. "Lad like you ought to join up. Got three sons of my own, Lord help me. If you're anything like them, you'd do better taking your wild spirits far from home. Put those handsome calves to good use." Deborah dipped her chin to hide her blush. The woman laughed and shoved into the crowd. "I'll see about your dinner once I clear away this crew of ruffians."

More of the boys, it seemed, had come as spectators than as potential recruits. They lifted their tankards and urged each other on as the soldier circulated, cajoling them to sign. Deborah pushed along the wall toward the hearth. A woman praising her calves—wait until she wrote to Jennie about that. The heat, the compliment, the noises of merriment about her suffused Deborah with happiness. It was good to be among people again; she had been lonely on the road.

"Here's a tall one!" Deborah turned toward the voice and saw the soldier wading over to her. He grabbed her upper arm. "Strong, too! What do you say, lad? For God and Country?" Deborah felt the eyes of everyone in the tavern upon her. "Come now. Sixty pounds. And by the time you return, there'll be hair on your chin." God, she hoped not. But sixty pounds? She hadn't imagined a purse that sizable. The soldier began to pull her toward the table. "One for your rolls, Mister Hewes!" he called.

"I'm not . . ." Deborah began, but the soldier raised his voice, shouting out for the benefit of the room at large.

"Fair of cheek, but bold of spirit! Here's a real patriot, a son of liberty!"

She began to protest again, but then stopped. Why not? Fate had brought her to the enlistment rolls once more. It was meant to happen. She heard the buzz of the crowd behind her, like bees swarming upon rich blossoms. Sixty pounds. Her future signed away. This flight, born of fear, brought to a triumphant end. The agent dipped his quill and gave Deborah a weary look. "At least seventeen years of age?"

"Aye." She would show them, those men in Middleborough—Ezekiel and Mr. Wood and his clerk—she wouldn't allow them to confine her, to tell her how to live.

"Name and place of origin?"

"Robert Shurtliff, from Plympton."

He pushed the book and quill toward her. "By signing you are enlisting in the Continental Army and agreeing to muster."

The rigid forefinger of her left hand jutted out as usual and she set her tongue between her teeth, forming her letters with care; this was her first time signing her new name. Fear licked at her, lapping like a wave that threatened to engulf the shore, but as it washed over her, it felt like jumping into a pond in summer: a gasping moment of cold followed by blissful relief. She lifted the quill with a flourish. Robert Shurtliff had signed on.

The soldier dragged a few other boys to the book before the crowd in the public room began to dissipate. "Now, then!" the soldier called out. "Those of you who signed, gather round." She shuffled over with a half-dozen others. "We close our books tomorrow and muster the day after, at Lothrop's place in Worcester, where you'll receive your payment."

"Why not now?" a boy asked.

"And let you piss it away at dice and drink? This way you are certain to make muster, though I remind you that you have signed and are bound by law to appear."

Those words settled in Deborah as if she had swallowed a cold stone: *bound by law*.

"A round of drinks, mistress!" Once the serving woman had furnished everyone with tankards, the soldier lifted his. "To our own Saint George, General Washington."

They clinked and drank. The rum scorched its way down and dissolved the cold stone in her stomach. Sixty pounds would be in her pocket soon. More than that, she'd have a place to go, a purpose. She would be a soldier.

"Drink up, lads, then find yourself a girl. There won't be any where you are heading," the soldier said.

Deborah buried her smile in her mug. There would be at least *one* girl.

Pie and more rum by the fire. The serving woman brought another tankard, telling Deborah a bawdy story from her own youth. The public room emptied until just the two of them remained, and the rum no longer burned Deborah's throat. The clamor of the day, the whirl of what she had done pounded at her, and it became important that she explain it to the woman. "I wanted . . . I always wanted . . ." Her tongue felt too clumsy to find the right words.

"There, there," the woman said, patting Deborah's thigh. "That's a good lad."

Deborah drew her sleeve across her face. "I should sleep."

"Yes, you should. You've quite a walk to Worcester."

Her teeth wore wooly jackets, or so it seemed when she awoke. Thick, wooly jackets. She'd taken off her shoes and her breeches and had gone to bed in just her shirt, with the door to the hall hanging open. *Lord, what was I thinking?* Hopping up from the bed made her head throb, but she dragged herself to the door, shut it, and began to pull on her trousers. A few brown spots dotted her thighs and the tails of her shirt. Her menses. Letting her trousers fall, she shuffled to the washstand and dashed handfuls of water against her face, hoping to lessen the ache at her temples, before she scrubbed at her shirt. She wondered if it augured poorly for her endeavor to have her menses come, but as she drew out a rag from her bundle and stuffed it in her crotch, she thought that something between her legs might actually help with her walk. And it meant her body had spat out the clerk's seed.

Downstairs, the tea swept the sour taste from her mouth. She blinked at the almanac as she ate her bread, trying to focus her gritty eyes on the roads to Worcester. Twenty miles. Despite her headache, despite the tightness in her stomach, happiness swam up in her, as unstoppable and satisfying as a great big yawn. She finished her tea and, stepping through the inn's front door, headed down the road toward Worcester.

CHAPTER THREE

No one stirred on Worcester's common when Deborah arrived, but it was early yet. She'd spent a sleepless night curled up in the woods, wracked with worry that the company would muster without her. In the shreds of dreams that jolted through her mind whenever sleep did overtake her, rivers of blood coursed down her thighs. Now her stomach was clenched in a ball—squeezed tight by anxiety, and tighter by hope. The sign for Lothrop's Tavern swayed in the morning breeze as Deborah pushed the door open.

Within, two men in blue Continental Army uniforms flanked a seated gentleman who scribbled away on a piece of parchment. A few boys milled about, and more entered after her. Several of them looked as haggard as she felt, and she took solace in one boy's haircut; she had feared her own locks appeared ragged, but his looked like they'd been chewed off by a ravenous goat.

At last, the seated man finished his writing and nodded to the two Continentals on either side of him. The older soldier turned to the shuffling crowd before him. "All right, lads. I'm Captain Eliphalet Thorp, muster master for the Fourth Massachusetts Regiment. And this is Sergeant Calvin Munn, who will conduct you to West Point." He indicated the other uniformed man, who was barrel-chested and had curly brown hair. "One at a time, you will come forward, confirm your enlistment, and sign a receipt for your bounty, which Mr. Taft"—here he inclined his head toward the seated man—"will properly divide. We will then proceed with muster. Now, line up."

The eager fellows pushed to the front, while Deborah worked her way into the midst of the throng. She had no zeal to go first—*Fools rush in where angels fear to tread*, Mrs. Thomas used to say—nor did she want to be last. After the initial jostling, there was the tedious business of listening to the quill scratching and the coins jingling. At last, she stepped forward to sign.

"Name?" Mr. Taft said, barely sparing her a glance.

"Robert Shurtliff."

Mr. Taft sorted his papers, marked one, and pushed a slip of parchment over. "Sign."

Deborah moved the quill carefully, sensing the men's eyes on her, but when she looked up, Mr. Taft was counting out coins, and only the barrel-chested sergeant studied her, his mouth in a somber line. The specie Mr. Taft pushed across the table made a sizable mound, and Deborah hastily scooped up the money.

"Step to the back room and wait," said Sergeant Munn, his arms folded across his massive chest. Perhaps it was just his size, but the man radiated authority.

Deborah dipped her chin, wanting to make a good first impression. "Yes, sir."

Unlike at the inn where she had signed on a few days before, no spirit of festivity ruled here. The men waiting in the back room sat at tables and spoke quietly to each other or to mothers and wives who had accompanied them. The husbands and sons passed their coins to the women and leaned in to speak in hushed voices. One mother hissed angrily at her son, looking as though she might box his ears. Deborah saw boys who appeared far too young to be soldiers; men old enough to be her father, or even grandsire; and two lads who had to be twins, with matching long necks and catfish mouths. Finding a stool in a corner far from the fireside, she took it gladly. She set her bundle by her feet and dug around, feeling past her sewing kit, pushing the spare bits of fabric to one side until she found the letter box. Narrow, with a hinged wooden lid, it held paper and quill and provided an even surface to write upon. She slipped out a sheet, carefully inked up a quill, and began to write.

My Dear Jennie,

I am now in Worcester, about to muster with the Fourth Massachusetts Regiment. They say we will be marching to West Point soon. If I count correctly, it is almost two weeks that I have been gone, but it seems like a year. This part of Massachusetts looks akin to Middleborough, but for me, it is as though I have discovered a new world. On the streets, no one knows me, and when I walk the roads, I am stopped when people need help hoisting a log or freeing a cart. These simple actions bring such pleasure. I only wish that you could travel with me, laugh with me, and tell me how marvelous this whole voyage is. What a delight to move as I wish, to be able to assert my will. You must be able to imagine how good it feels to be assumed capable and intelligent and not always to have to prove this matter.

There is so much I cannot write, but I don't want you to worry about me. I pray that the worst is behind me. I had not thought to join up, but it feels as if Providence led me thus. You will tell me of any news from town, will you not? I will write whenever I am able and report to you all the details of a soldier's life. I miss you.

With love,
Robert D. S. Shurtliff

She tapped the quill against her nose, thinking about how to express this freedom she felt, the liberty and the burden of it. She wanted to share with Jennie the horrible delight of having a serving woman call her handsome or of bedding down in a stranger's barn. She felt certain she hadn't given too much away in the event that someone else laid eyes upon her letter. Many men bore the name of Robert, and Shurtliff was a common surname in the Middleborough area, so this guise would not forge a link to her. Besides, she knew Jennie. If the justice questioned her, she would be quick to think of an excuse. When the ink had dried she carefully folded up the paper, wrote "Jennie Newcomb" and "Middleborough" in clear, bold letters on the front, and, packing up her bundle, walked to the door. Only a few men still waited to be paid. Off to the side, she saw an entryway to the kitchen and, peering in, found a woman peeling potatoes and another stoking the fire.

"Pardon," Deborah said, stepping inside, "but can I give you a letter?"

The woman stopped her peeling. "Joining up, are you?"

Deborah nodded. The woman dried her hands on her apron, took the letter and the coin Deborah offered, and tucked them in her skirt. "Running away from home, then?"

Deborah shook her head. "No, ma'am, not really."

The woman clucked her tongue, sounding disbelieving. "Boys. I can always tell when boys are lying. You can't fool me."

"No, ma'am, I guess I can't," Deborah said, and retreated quickly, before the woman wasn't fooled about something else.

When she returned to the back room, the voices had grown to a fevered pitch: an older man came in and dragged a younger one out, the two of them shouting and thrashing. Odors brought from farms and of clothes long unwashed saturated the space. She wondered if the smell of her own fear, or worse, the smell of her blood, colored the air at all.

At last, the two soldiers appeared in the doorway. "Muster on the green for roll call!" Captain Thorp shouted.

A brief cry went up, part huzzah and part groan, and the mass in the room surged forward. Caught up in the movement, Deborah realized she was bound to these men, that in the coming days and weeks they'd be at each other's sides. She bumped up against someone's shoulder as they piled out into the chilly sunshine. A few wagons, oxen sullen in the yokes, stood to the side, tended by a young Continental with a drum.

"Line up in rows of five!" the sergeant shouted.

Everyone milled about, unsure what constituted a row. Sergeant Munn moved among them, reaching out with his thick arms to push people into place. His mouth set in a grimace, he sorted out the recruits with a plodding deliberation that indicated he'd done this often. Seeing him approach, Deborah arranged herself two paces behind the man in front of her and stood as still as she could. His glance moved over her and he grabbed the fellow to her left. "Straight line, boy."

At the front, Captain Thorp cried out, "Answer to your name!" The roll went on, some thirty souls in all. Somewhere in the middle, Thorp called, "Robert Shurtliff," and Deborah felt herself twitch before saying, "Aye!" Eventually, Thorp tucked the parchment away and said, "Per orders of General Washington, you will march to West Point to join with the rest of the regiment. There you will draw equipment and be assigned to a company within the regiment. You are now soldiers and under the command of Sergeant Munn. Sergeant?"

The sergeant gave Captain Thorp a crisp salute and stepped forward. Alongside him stood two other uniformed soldiers. Neither rivaled Sergeant Munn's girth, but both were tall. Munn cleared his throat, but when he spoke, his voice came out harsh and scratchy. "This is Corporal Booth," he said, indicating the taller of the two men. A scar curved down Booth's face, forming a seam from eye to lip. Beneath his tricorn, he appeared to be bald. "And this," Munn continued, "is Corporal Shaw." The other man gave a nod. He had the slightly bulbous eyes of a frog, and his prominent gaze traveled across the rows. "As the captain said, you are soldiers now, and any failure to do your duty or to follow orders is subject to discipline. If you attempt to desert or otherwise disrupt this company, may the Lord have mercy. I certainly won't. We will set out immediately and march in an orderly fashion, three across. I'll take five men to drive the wagons. For those of you who brought your own firearms, you will . . ."

The sergeant went on, but try as she might to listen to his words, Deborah found the thoughts in her own head spoke more loudly: What would West Point bring? Looking surreptitiously at the other troops, she saw men shuffling their weight from foot to foot and one young fellow plucking at the sleeve of his coat. Around her, the corporals shifted the recruits into walking files. Sergeant Munn gave an indistinct yell, and from somewhere ahead a drum began a steady beat. "Get up there, get along," the corporals called to them, as if they were horses or cattle. She settled her bundle on her back, lifted one foot, then the next.

CHAPTER FOUR

With men on either side and the drum setting a rhythm for their march, it wasn't long before Deborah missed her solitary rambles of the previous days. There was no dodging potholes or picking out the driest path when she had to stay in a single file. Nor could she stop when she wanted a rest, though she welcomed no longer having to pause at every crossroads and wonder which way to go. The sun had fallen past its zenith when Sergeant Munn called a break, his scratchy voice barking out the command from the head of the column. They stopped by a river, and many of the recruits dropped right down on the roadside, overcome by exhaustion; a few soaked their feet in the water, while others slaked their thirst.

Deborah walked idly around the perimeter of the group, taking stock of the men she'd spend the next three years with. When she was walking the roads alone, she had believed she could easily appear to be a man. But now the truth bore down on her: this was more than a disguise, more than a masquerade. She tugged at her waistcoat self-consciously. It was a matter of strength and stamina, of keeping pace on the march, of bearing the same load as the others. And she scarcely knew what other challenges the coming days and weeks would bring. Whatever West Point might demand of her, she'd be measured against these men. Real men—who scratched wherever they itched, who did not prettify their language; in short, men who thought no womenfolk were lurking about. She cast her gaze across them, seized by worry that her chest was not flat enough, that her hands were not large enough, that her voice was too high. *Enough*, she chided herself. *Enough. You wanted this.* It was better to try to measure up as a man than subject herself to the prudishness of the Middleborough gossips.

Corporal Booth offered the men biscuits from the wagons, but Deborah noticed that many of the recruits unpacked their bundles, taking out greasy wrappings or untying kerchiefs carrying a final taste of home. She thought about the mothers and wives these men had left behind, whether others sought escape, like her, and if so, from what. She took two biscuits from Corporal Booth and sat down on a stump. As the men lounged and ate, the corporals walked among them, making introductions and general inquiries. Corporal Shaw, his round eyes popping, approached her.

"Your name, son?" Up close, Deborah saw that his wide mouth complemented his frog-like eyes. She could almost imagine him darting out his tongue to catch a fly.

"Robert Shurtliff, sir."

He nodded. "Occupation?"

"A little farming. A little weaving. And I know my letters ably."

"Good, good." He smiled and his eyes seemed to bulge even more. The effect was comic, and Deborah had to fight back a grin.

Soon enough, the rest period ended with drumbeats, the sudden report making her jump. The men around her jostled and shoved back into position and then, as if they were all oxen hooked into traces, they lurched forward.

Evening could not come too soon. All afternoon, Deborah had

watched the sun slide incrementally across the sky. She willed it to move like a lick of butter on a hot skillet, but it dropped only grudgingly as she marched on. The pace was a shade faster than she wished to walk, her body unused to any rhythm but her own. She hadn't thought she'd be giving up her newfound freedom when she enlisted, but as she reminded herself, there was more freedom in this troop than she had dared to dream of even a month ago. Each step was better than Middleborough. When she grew tired of following the sun and sky, she watched the queue of the man in front of her, the little clubbed tail of hair swinging as he walked. She was comforted by the trickle of perspiration that ran into his kerchief, grateful that others felt the same strain. Then she turned to the sun again to mark its progress, and so the afternoon wore on.

They crested a rise, and Deborah saw a river splitting the land below, reflecting back the sun. At the head of the column Sergeant Munn conferred with Corporal Booth, who had removed his hat and was mopping his bald head, and then the drum rattled out a halt.

"Form lines below!" Booth yelled, pointing to a level spot beside the river. They lined up as neatly as they were able, and Corporal Booth walked among them, shoving them into proper order. He moved with a bobbing walk, exuding an energy that Deborah could not match. Even his voice lilted as he asked her column, "What do you say, lads? Fair tomorrow? Or will it turn worse?"

Deborah squinted at the sun she'd been watching all day—the ball was still yellow, like an egg yolk, even as it inched lower, grazing the horizon. No clouds in the sky, but the breeze felt chancy; she marked how it ruffled the leaves, exposing their pale undersides.

"Rain, I say," she offered.

Booth turned to her. "Rain?"

"By the morning." She could feel a change in the air.

He nodded and gave her a careful look, as if taking her measure. "Very well, boy. We'll see if you're right."

Imagine that. A man asking her opinion and listening to it as if it had value. The breeze played across her face again. It did feel like rain. At the head of the group, Sergeant Munn called roll, pausing every six names to shout out a duty: kindling, cooking, water, wagons, and finally, watch. "This may be the safest road in all of Christendom, but good practice dictates that you always set a watch. Form that habit now; it is a serious charge. Corporal Shaw will distribute gear as you need it. Fall out." The square of parchment that held the recruits' names looked minuscule in Munn's massive hands, and Deborah stood for a moment studying him, noting that she had yet to see the sergeant smile.

Shuffling ensued as men found their work crews and collected hatchets or pots. Deborah's group was assigned to wagons, and for a while she untied bundles and passed out equipment and food. "Tend to the horses," Corporal Shaw called. Deborah stood beside an older man whose brown hair fanned gray at the temples. "Get them out of their traces and watered," Shaw said. She hadn't dealt with horses before, so she waited for the other recruit to act, hoping to follow his lead, but he'd unbuckled his horse and had it moving toward the river before she'd untangled half of the reins on hers. At last she freed the straps and left them dangling from the cart. Grabbing the bridle, she gave the horse a tug. It didn't move. She yanked again, but it would not budge. Sergeant Munn lumbered up the slope toward her. "Move, you miserable beast," she muttered to the horse and gave another desperate tug, to no avail.

"Get that horse settled before night falls. Come on now, boy," Munn said to her.

"Sir, I don't know a great deal about horses . . ." Deborah began.

The sergeant stepped closer, so that he was toe to toe with her. "What kind of fellow doesn't know how to handle a horse?"

"I worked as a weaver, sir."

"Good Lord, help me," said Munn. "What happened to all the sturdy farm lads?" With one hand he grabbed the bridle and with the other he delivered a sharp slap to the horse's flank. The animal tossed its head and then ambled forward. "You have to be firm. Don't let it drink too much."

"Thank you, sir," said Deborah, as she jogged beside the horse toward the river.

"There's one I won't be putting down for the cavalry," Munn said from behind her.

She got the horse back up from the river and led it to the makeshift corral that Corporal Shaw had set up. "Wretched creature," she said as she released the animal, though she knew the fault lay with herself and not with the horse.

When Shaw declared their work done, she and her crew dispersed and set about clearing the ground for sleeping. While Deborah kicked at a particularly pointy rock, the tall, broad-shouldered man next to her sank down, stretching himself out flat on his back.

Eyes closed, he spoke to her, "I don't know if I've ever walked for so long."

"Tired, eh?"

"My feet feel as though they've been cooked."

She laughed, then coughed, afraid her laugh sounded too light and airy.

"I'm James Snow." Still lying on his back, he held out his hand, which engulfed hers entirely when she took it.

"Robert Shurtliff. Are you from Bellingham, then?"

"Aye. Born and bred. This may be the farthest I've ever been from home."

She whistled, confident that this made her sound like a man, for so had Mr. Thomas oft complained.

"And you?" James asked.

"Plympton." She sat on the grass next to him; the ground was dry but cold through her breeches.

"Ah. So you signed for the money."

"And you for the town?"

"Worse even," James said. "It was my master who was called to serve, but as he owns my indenture, he sent me instead."

"Hey, there!" Corporal Shaw stalked toward them, his froggy eyes narrowing in anger. "You boys can't lie about while others work for you. Go help the water crew."

Deborah jumped up and hurried toward the river, but James rose slowly, ran his fingers through his thick, brown hair, and made his leisurely way down to the water. In his insouciance, with its hint of disobedience, Deborah sensed something distinctly manly. No woman would ever behave like that; it would be a quick curtsy and a dash to the kitchen to tend to the chores. Of course, in the privacy of the kitchen, the woman might cuss the man roundly. But in company, she'd maintain at least the veneer of good behavior. Deborah would have to learn.

"To what trade were you apprenticed?" Deborah asked, as the two of them joined the line of men with buckets. Standing, he topped her by an inch or two, and she noticed how everything about him seemed doubly large—his hands, his feet, his ears. She spied the beginnings of a beard about his chin.

"Blacksmith." He wrinkled his nose. "If I'm not careful, I'll be cast in the same role at West Point, sweating before a forge every day. You?"

"Weaver. But I don't intend to take that up again," she added.

"Then we're in the same lot." He heaved the buckets that another recruit handed to him, and then Deborah seized hers, and the two of them waddled, ungainly, up the slope.

Back in the clearing, men stood around the fires, some cooking meat or stirring pots, others merely warming themselves and idly chatting. Deborah looked around for Corporal Shaw, saw him standing by one of the fires, and figured they could relax now as well. They brought their buckets to a cook and joined the group. As the men exchanged information about hometowns and potential family ties, some part of her wished to stay aloof, on the margins;

this part counseled: *Don't draw attention to yourself, that is the safest course.* But another part said: *Safety comes from belonging to the group.* She would need these men, and they would need her. So she stood close to the flames, next to James, and followed the ebb and flow of the conversation.

Munn banged on a cooking pot, clanging the company to silence. "Doff those hats." Deborah heard the swish of three dozen scalps being bared, and the ensuing quiet was such that she imagined she could hear heads being lowered in prayer. "Heavenly Father," Munn intoned, his husky voice making grace sound strangely intimate. "Bless this bread and bless these men who eat it. . . ."

At last the company chanted "Amen," and as everyone settled their hats back on their heads and shuffled into line, James leaned in to whisper, "Is he a sergeant or a minister?"

Deborah looked at Munn, his hat still tucked between his elbow and his torso, his broad face solemn and placid in the lee of his prayer. "I imagine that in this company he is both, and nearly God besides."

They ate with their crews, spooning a mush of beans and salt pork out of a pot. As she watched the faces of the men around her, flickering in the firelight—the grease on their lips, the loud sound of their chewing, how they spat out the gristle or dug with their fingers to loosen a morsel stuck between their teeth—Deborah was reminded of all the adventure books she'd read about savages, the anthropophagi and the men with heads beneath their shoulders, about how ill-mannered they were, grabbing food with their bare hands and shoving it into their mouths. And this, with the same levels of behavior, was the civilized world.

THE DRUMBEAT OF REVEILLE MADE Deborah sit upright in her blanket, and it took her a moment to gather her wits. Around her, men groaned and turned over; a few rubbed their eyes, looking as confused as she felt. Out of habit, she reached up to tuck her hair behind her ears, only to find that her hair was gone. Scrambling to her feet, intent on attending to her business quickly before the others made to relieve themselves as well, she had taken only three strides toward the woods when Corporal Shaw bellowed from behind, "You, there! Tuck up that roll and stow it. Then report for morning duty. You think of the group first and then yourself, however pressing your needs are."

"Yes, sir." She folded her blanket neatly and brought it to the wagon, then went over to where the corporal stood. He handed her a bucket. Down to the river and back up, she delivered water to an old, creased recruit who had revived the fire from the ashes.

"Careful, boy, or you'll undo my work," he said as she poured the water from the bucket into a pot. He grimaced as he stood, clutching at his back, and she wondered what sort of army this was—like a forest made half of saplings and half of hollow trees. Together they hung the pot over the fire and stoked the flames, waiting for it to boil.

By the time Corporal Shaw ambled over to say, "See to your needs," they were indeed pressing. She trotted to the trees, where men stood or squatted at semidiscreet distances. She plunged past them, hoping to find a patch of plentiful undergrowth, but not wanting to go so far afield as to arouse suspicion. Crouching behind an evergreen, Deborah kept watch for any who might approach, and let the tails of her shirt fall to the ground to give her some coverage. There was no point in dwelling upon the unfairness of it—the ease with which men could drop the front fall of their breeches and let fly.

THE CORPORALS WALKED UP AND down the files as they marched, making small talk and answering questions about what awaited at West Point. Corporal Booth marched alongside Deborah for a time, now and then lifting his hat to mop at his bald head with a kerchief.

She eyed the scar that ran down his cheek; it gave him a fearsome look, but he smiled often and tried to teach them a marching song. He soon abandoned the song and told them about walking this same road years ago and having to drag artillery pieces through the spring mud. It sounded like every tale spun by old-timers, but at least it helped pass the time, and now and then useful tidbits of information emerged: unlike the ill-equipped army of yesteryear, they would receive smart, new uniforms; and Booth held the opinion that the full-scale fighting was over. The occupations of New York and Charleston would likely end in treaties, and the only action West Point still saw was small skirmishes. Though the whole of Westchester County remained a hotbed of loyalist refugees from New York City, and squads from West Point continued to patrol this area, more than a year had passed since the last pitched battles. As Corporal Booth spoke, it was clear that he missed the glory days—the gory fighting, the cannonades and fusillades—and that the relative peace disappointed him.

Miles churned by as they passed woods and fields and farms, small villages with wooden bridges, one larger town. Walking through them, Deborah remembered when Middleborough had sent out its first class of men—all the commotion, the gathered crowd, the musicians playing. How long the war had dragged on. Now, as they trudged through each village, scarcely an inhabitant waved at them.

Just before noon, the rain started—no light drizzle either, but a downpour as steady as the drum. Corporal Booth appeared at her elbow. "You called it good and proper."

"Now I wish to have been mistaken." Ezekiel's shoes had already let in water. The vile man, too cheap to visit the cobbler. Add miserliness to his list of shortcomings.

"How did you know?"

She tried to gauge whether Booth was teasing her, but he seemed sincere. "By the breeze, and the color of the sun and the sky around it."

"A watcher, eh? It's good to be alert."

Booth moved off, and James spoke from behind her. "Buttering up the corporal, are you, you dog?" He laughed.

THE CLOUDS INDUCED AN EARLY night, the mist clinging to the river, its surface dimpled by the drops. Deborah felt she carried much of the road stuck to her leggings, each step burdened by an extra pound of mud. Light-headed from the long walk and an empty stomach, she plunked one foot in front of the other. Buildings appeared through the mist, flanking the road, and Sergeant Munn called a halt, his broad figure looming at the head of the column. He and Corporal Booth strode off, while the recruits stood there, sopping statues slowing sinking into the ruts. Corporal Shaw walked up and down the lines.

"The sergeant knows you are but tender and soft, so he's finding you a dry place to stay the night." His words were pleasant enough, but Deborah heard the needling tone beneath and wondered why he saw the need to mock them.

Booth reappeared and led the group to a large building where a portly man unlocked the door and ushered them inside.

"Send over your cooks when you're ready," he was saying to Booth when Deborah walked by.

The smell of mold and some prickly scent—like hay, but not as sweet—lingered in the dim room, and she sniffed, fighting off a sneeze. "My nose itches," she said.

"Granary," said James, who'd dropped his bundle and had sunk to the floor already. "Dusty spot. And with a nose that size, you're bound to snort up some dust."

She rubbed at her nostrils, recalling how Jennie had once gently deemed her nose prominent. James wrung out the sleeves of his coat, and she could see a slight puddle of water grow around him, black on the gray floor. He shifted to a dry spot and stretched out; she couldn't decide if he was lazy or smart, resting whenever he could.

But she knew she liked him, she felt it immediately, and she didn't even mind his comment about her nose. At least he was honest and direct. There was much virtue in that.

Booth and Shaw moved among them, sending out crews to deal with the wagons, the animals, water, and supplies. Booth approached. "You two, follow me."

James rose grudgingly, and they trailed after the corporal as he collected another three fellows. Back out in the rain, they trotted across the thick mud to a smaller building. The kitchen they entered was blessedly warm, with a fire blazing in a brick hearth and a rich bed of coals ready beneath the oven. Booth set them to cooking, though the other recruits struggled to stir a pot properly, Deborah noticed. The portly miller came in with a sack of flour. "For the soldiers," he said as he clapped it on the table, raising a cloud of dust.

"Who's making cakes?" asked Booth. "Richard?" A slight boy who barely reached Deborah's shoulder shook his head. "I thought you worked for a miller."

"I know how to make flour, but not how to make anything with flour."

"I only know how to eat cakes, not make them," James added.

"I've made a few cakes in my day," said Deborah, deciding it was worth taking on this feminine chore if it meant being useful.

"There's a fine fellow," said James. "Make them sweet."

While the others tended to the pork and boiled beans, Deborah was soon up to her elbows in flour, mixing in suet and molasses. Richard, the miller's boy, helped her pour the batter into pans and set them in the brick oven. The men stood close as the food cooked, letting their rain-soaked clothes dry.

James turned to Booth and asked, "How common are those skirmishes around West Point?"

"Pretty fair, especially in autumn, when the harvest is brought in. After all, the British are as bored and hungry as we are."

"So we'll ride out to meet them?"

Booth laughed. "Nobody here will be riding anywhere. Most of you won't even march out. Only if you're picked for the light infantry. Otherwise . . ." He shrugged.

"Otherwise?" Richard asked, looking up from the pans.

"Otherwise you'll make yourself useful at the camp or fort. Repairing equipment, building fortifications. Even tending crops. And training. It might be dull now and then, but a soldier never knows when the war might pick up. And so you value the dull times."

Deborah nudged at the pans with a baker's peel, trying to cook them evenly. Nobody liked a cake burnt to charcoal on one side and all but raw on the other.

"And the light infantry, what's that like?" asked James.

"They're the best. Tough and hardworking. Alert and quick. Can't mind hunger and fatigue if you're in the lights. I might not be the fairest judge, though. I'm in our regiment's company, along with Sergeant Munn. We're the ones who head out on patrols and such. Still plenty of British irregulars in Westchester, and it's the lights' job to track them down." Booth spoke with relish. His bald head had turned pink in the warmth of the kitchen, and he launched into stories of skirmishes, rolling up a sleeve to show them where he'd taken a musket ball. "Didn't touch the bone, lucky for me," he told them. He didn't explain the scar on his face.

The cakes browned quickly, and Deborah pronounced them done. "Back across the yard, boys. Don't spill a drop," the corporal ordered. Carrying the pots and pans, they trotted to the storehouse where the rest of the recruits waited. The heat of the kitchen had taken the worst of the wet and chill from Deborah, while those who had labored outside stood wrapped in their blankets, eyeing the steaming pots with greed. Deborah tore into one of her cakes—it was good, but not as good as Jennie's. Across from her, Richard spoke while chewing a piece of meat, his words coming out thick and greasy. "No infantry for me. I think I prefer to stay safe inside the fort."

James bit back a yawn and then said, "I don't expect we'll have much choice in the matter. They'll put us where it best suits the regiment."

Neither course appeared safe to Deborah, though she imagined that her true nature might more easily go undetected on the battlefield, where the others would have more pressing concerns than Robert Shurtliff's beardless cheek. She stuffed more of the cake into her mouth. Men belched and laughed, and somewhere she heard the rattle of dice, the high squeal of a fart, and she wished that she, too, could sink so easily into this routine, trusting that all would be decided, and decided well. What must it feel like to be so certain of oneself, to be in a place and have it feel so right?

A hand on her shoulder startled her—she'd been lodged deep inside her head. "Your cakes are as good as your weather forecasts," Corporal Booth said. "When will the rain end?"

"Soon," she replied, "though that is more hope than certainty."

As he moved off, she heard Richard's high voice complaining about the hard floor and James's low reply that he was tired enough to sleep anywhere. Deborah wrapped herself in her blanket. Her breeches had dried, and her waistcoat, too. Only her shirt and the binding beneath remained damp. She lay down and closed her eyes, feeling the constriction around her chest like a snake coiled about her. *I am Robert Shurtliff,* she told herself. She wanted to measure up to these men, to find her place among them. *Lord God,* she prayed silently. *Deliver me through this trial. Grant me faith and strength.*

CHAPTER FIVE

The days flowed together until Deborah had little sense if she'd been walking a week or two—if they were marching through Connecticut or had already passed into New York. By day, she strode alongside James and Richard, learning about their lives and inventing her own stories to tell them in return. Despite his short stature and high voice, Richard claimed to be seventeen, the same age as James, and the age that Deborah had claimed for herself upon enlisting. Twice he'd tried to run from his master, whom he called a right bastard once they'd gained safe distance from Bellingham. The first time he'd fled, he'd been put in the stocks for half a day. The second time, his master clipped Richard's ears—and here Richard pulled back his hair on one side to show them the neat triangle of flesh that had been cut out. "I thought for a while that it would grow back, like a nail that's fallen out, but a year has gone by and I'm still marked."

The little notch fascinated Deborah, but Richard let his hair fall over it again. In the spirit of equal exchange, she showed him her finger with the long scar that ran across the knuckle, keeping it rigid. "From a hatchet," she said. "I also thought it would mend itself, but it's been years and it is still stiff. A marvel, isn't it, what the body can't do? For all the hair your head can sprout, you can't make a measly scrap for an ear."

James, like Deborah, had lost his father young, and both of them had been turned over to indenture by mothers who could not afford to raise them. Richard's father, though alive, was a drunkard, and so Richard had also been apprenticed at a young age. None of them had ever traveled far from home, and during their march they often noticed things they'd never seen before: Deborah spotted an orange-and-black bird, James pointed out a stone bridge, and all three of them marveled at the size of the city of Hartford. To their disappointment, they were able to view the thick cluster of buildings only from afar; Munn charted a careful course around the city, and Richard speculated that the sergeant feared that some of the company might desert.

They slept in fields, and once, when it pelted rain, they piled into a barn, where one of the soldiers tried to milk a cow; Munn had him whipped. "We don't steal from our hosts," he told them. Deborah watched the flogging with the other recruits, the sergeant delivering the blows with a measured and merciless cadence. Munn's face was impassive as Booth counted the strokes, and Deborah felt a chill run through her; Munn was not a man to be crossed. When Shaw had led the whipped man off to tend to his wounds, Munn addressed the company. "The Good Lord and General Washington have seen fit to provision this company. You'll want for nothing, if you but trust in God and your officers." He coughed to clear his throat, his eyes scanning them in the gloom of the barn. "To do otherwise borders upon treason."

On an especially cool evening, they built a large fire, and Corporal Booth passed around a bottle of rum. The others drank and sang—Booth's voice was among the loudest—and when the bottle came to Deborah, she put it to her mouth but did not let any of the liquor pass her lips. She watched as the men grew merrier, recalling the tavern in Bellingham, and she knew that to be sober and alert was safer. She clapped her hands to the music and watched some of the men dance. Once they had finished the rum, most of the recruits lurched to their blankets. A few of the more drunk ones undid their front falls and pissed out the flames of the fire, which Deborah watched with a mixture of curiosity and horror. The men laughed and fumbled with their buttons before stumbling away, but she stood by the smoldering remains. It took a while for the flames' imprints to fade from her eyes. Corporal Shaw picked his way through the men, now and then stopping to utter a word, and he stepped close to her. "What say, lad? To sleep?" His breath burned fierce with liquor, and when he laid a hand on her shoulder, she could feel him steady himself.

"Aye, it's sleep for me now."

"Good fellow," he said and gave her a look, inscrutable in the darkness, before continuing on, his steps the overcautious plodding of a drunk. She gazed after him; something about the interaction bothered her, as if he communicated in a language she did not know. But there was nothing for it now, and she gathered up her blanket and found her spot next to James. Stretching out on her back, she watched the stars tick overhead and counted the rings of the moon. All about her the snores and grunts of sleeping men interrupted the coiling darkness of the night. How easily they accepted her as another recruit, a shoulder to lean on; how quickly they would turn on her if they knew. Her clothes were like an eggshell about her, a thin layer of protection, a veneer that both kept out and held in.

Sweat coursed down their necks and backs while they marched. The hills grew into mountains as they entered the highlands, and Sergeant Munn called the halt earlier than usual. "Tomorrow we'll make it to the Hudson. But for today, there is a lake nearby. I'd suggest you take a bath. The Lord knows, no one fancies a dirty recruit." Richard snickered, but Deborah heard only the usual flat tone in Munn's voice.

Shaw distributed cakes of soap from the wagons, and the recruits made their way to the lake's rocky shore. Some stripped down immediately and ran into the water, whooping and splashing, while others waded in slowly, and a few perched on a rock, washing out their leggings or breeches. Deborah tried to think of an excuse for not disrobing. For the moment, she stood rooted to the side of the lake, transfixed, though she knew it was wrong to stare at the men as they swam and washed. She had seen her share of unclad men—the Thomas boys, her brothers—but this was different. Now she must measure her own body against these. Uncovered, their chests and legs were surprisingly thick, the dark hair standing out against the pale skin.

"Well?" Corporal Shaw, also fully dressed, sauntered over. "You need a bath as much as any, Shurtliff."

"I . . . I thought I would volunteer to gather firewood first, before I got clean."

"Then stop staring and get gathering." His wide lips stretched down in displeasure.

"Yes, sir." Without pausing, she turned and hurried into the woods. What if he had demanded that she bathe? Through the trees, she heard the sounds of the men splashing. Her skin felt close against her, her coat itchy. Breaking a dead branch over her knee, Deborah gathered up an armload of wood and brought it to the camp. A few others sat idle among the baggage, and Booth leaned against a wagon, cajoling them to get into the water.

"Not one for bathing, myself," said an older man. "Don't fancy the cold water. 'Tisn't good for a body."

"It'll make you sing high for a song or two, no lasting harm," Booth replied.

The man shook his head. "Not for me, I thank you."

How easily men could say no, how readily they did as they pleased. Hearing them, Deborah felt like a tree battered by the wind for so long that she'd just stayed bent, ready for the gale.

A few recruits trotted toward the wagons, shivering with damp hair. She went back to the shelter of the trees and gathered another armload of wood, skirting the shore of the lake, where she could see some of the men still swimming and a few standing nude in the shallows scrubbing at their clothes. Not many remained, just the hardy souls, but their voices and laughter echoed off the water's surface, making them sound myriad. She watched them, cold but at ease, naked and not minding. How soft their private parts appeared, so that even the strongest seemed tender, pale and as plucked as a chicken ready for the pot.

Bending again to the forest floor, she picked up another dead branch and was flexing it under her foot when Corporal Shaw approached.

"Still gathering, Shurtliff?" He eyed her armload of branches, then flicked his gaze to the lake. "Not just standing here, peeping? No need for mollies among us." He said this last casually, but it still held the sting of accusation.

"No, sir, no need for that. I keep my eyes where they belong and my hands busy with proper work."

"Aye. See to it," he said, and for a moment he just stood there, as if he might watch her work or say something further. She stiffened, feeling a peculiar tension in his waiting. Then, without another word, he turned and walked back toward camp. A molly? She had heard the term before, bandied about at Sproat's, an insult flung at a visiting preacher from Boston who had lectured the men about temperance. They'd found him foppish, in his velvet waistcoat and long lace cuffs. And, over their cider, they'd imitated his airy manner of speaking and his flighty laugh. Deborah picked up another branch. A molly? What had she done? What had she said? It was normal for a young woman to look at a young man, to size him up, to see in him a potential protector and lover; she and Jennie had spent many a Sunday service studying what the meeting house had to offer. But now she would have to stop looking. She risked a glance at Shaw's retreating back. She noticed that he hadn't gone for a swim either and wondered if the rest of him was as froggy as his face.

Deborah made only a pretense of eating supper. Her stomach churned sour when she thought of Shaw and how she must have appeared to him. As soon as the last light failed, she made her way into the woods, as if to relieve herself, but instead kept walking along the lip of the lake. Bats dipped through the sky—a sure sign of summer approaching. It was a romantic time, this purple hour when everything becomes dim and obscure, with softened edges. Arriving at the far shore, she crouched down over the liquid surface. It was too dark to see, even though the water waited, still as glass. She peered anyway, wishing she could catch a glimpse of her face. But the lake gave nothing back. It didn't matter. What she really wanted to know was how others saw her, and no lake or mirror could tell her that. Did she look like a molly? She picked up a rock and tossed it in; a hollow splash answered. She paused to see if anyone heard and would approach. Nothing stirred. Across the lake, flickers of orange flame, the small fires of camp, darted through the trees. She thought—fleetingly, like a cloud moving across the sun—of running away. But her life could not be one long escape.

Her hands worked her buttons and she cast off her coat, waistcoat, breeches, and shirt. A few quick tugs loosened the band around her chest. She felt the oddness of her breasts swinging free as she stepped lightly into the water. She wanted to rush, but she made herself move slowly, silently parting the water with her legs. Goose bumps rose on her skin and the cold made her gasp. It was just flesh, that's all, cold, hanging flesh, these little tags and marks. Now the water reached her stomach and she bent her knees, ducked beneath. It was a relief to float, to be buoyed up over the depths.

She scrubbed at her legs and arms with sand from the bottom and imagined the layers of dirt and skin sloughing off. By the time she emerged, shivers rushed through her. She dried herself with her coat, but she was still damp as she bound her breasts and dressed. The moon had risen while she swam and now a thin streak of silver rippled across the lake, defining a path so straight that she thought she could walk it clear into the sky.

Creeping back, her teeth chattered as she scanned the sleeping ranks for her blanket and gear. Her eyes had long since adjusted to the darkness, and at last she spotted the bundled mound that was James and the smaller molehill of Richard, with a space in between for her. Taking off only her shoes, she wound the blanket about herself and lay down.

"Is all well?" James said, his low voice gruff.

"Aye. Sorry to wake you."

"I wasn't asleep." His face, poking out of his dark blanket, shone palely, like the moon. "We were waiting for you."

She turned her head and saw Richard blinking at her, too.

"Fancied a midnight swim?" he asked, eyeing her damp hair. "Are you certain all is well? Why didn't you bathe earlier?"

She stuck as close to the truth as she dared. "I meant to. But Corporal Shaw was watching me." She took a deep breath. "He started talking to me about—"

"Let me figure it," Richard cut in. "Mollies?"

Deborah nodded.

"He had a comment to me on that topic earlier in the march when I was standing watch one evening." Even in the dark, Richard's eyes twinkled as he talked. "Told him he could go molly himself. I wager he's off rogering some poor horse."

Deborah choked back a laugh, and James snorted, then nudged

her. "He fancies every pretty boy he sees." He raised his chin to Richard. "And even some not-so-pretty ones."

Richard made a face, and Deborah laughed again. So she wasn't the only one Shaw hounded; there was nothing particular about her appearance. She shifted her bundle beneath her head and settled in her blanket.

"West Point tomorrow," James whispered. "But we'll stick together."

"Of course," Deborah murmured. They waited for Richard's reply, but he had already fallen asleep. What had she just been wondering? How others saw her? A pretty boy. One of the group. And they waited up for her, which was the best sign of all.

CHAPTER SIX

Skirting craggy slopes, by midmorning the troop had reached a point near Fort Independence, where a ferry would carry them over the Hudson. They'd crossed brooks and creeks, even the Housatonic River, but the first view of the Hudson stunned Deborah. She wished she could drink the landscape in, make it a part of her: the water dashing around a curve, the dramatic rise of the cliffs, steep mountainsides leaping straight up from the bank. As they waited for the ferry, Booth pointed out landmarks. He'd been stationed at West Point five years ago, and underwent his military initiation not far from this landing, at Fort Clinton, when the British made an attack under fog, coming up the river to the boom chain and destroying the fort. Booth had retreated to West Point with the remains of the garrison. Now the corporal bounded along the riverbank, pointing to where the cannons used to perch. "You boys aren't likely to see such a battle," he concluded, shaking his head with apparent regret. Deborah wondered if his zeal for combat made him peculiar or normal among soldiers.

The ferry pulled to, and the recruits shuffled on, followed by the wagons, the balky horses stamping their displeasure. It was hard to believe, on this cloudless spring day, that they were engaged in a war—that if they let the current take them, they would be carried down the Hudson to New York City, an enemy stronghold, where they would encounter the British Army.

Some recruits huddled toward the ferry's middle, as discomfited as the horses by the surge of water against the hull. Deborah stood at the railing with James and Richard, watching the white foam churned up by their passage, glad that this morning Corporal Shaw was keeping his distance. A molly! She would give him a wide berth now that she knew his game.

On the other side of the Hudson, a smooth, wide road led north, and they formed their normal files and headed out. It was a brutal march, with steep inclines that made Deborah's legs throb, and precipitous drops that sent her sliding down loose gravel. At any moment West Point would appear, and twin emotions struggled within her. The first was excitement at the thought of finally seeing West Point. For years that name had loomed large in the news: at Sproat Tavern she had heard about Benedict Arnold's treachery, the battles along the Hudson, and the strategic importance of the fort. But fear, too, coursed through her, a prickling doubt that she hadn't been able to shake.

"I imagine you'll be lined up right away for inspection," Booth told the recruits as they huffed up another hill; the corporal's breathing came regular and even. "Look crisp, or you'll be stuck molding musket balls for the rest of the war." He laughed, but no one else joined in.

At last they passed the pickets and the sentries and came right up to the battlements. Sergeant Munn, at the head, called out, "The spring class from Bellingham, Fourth Massachusetts Regiment."

"Bring 'em in, lads," came the cry in response, and a cheer—tepid as leftover tea—went up from the recruits as they filed inside.

Deborah swiveled her head, anxious to see what she had only imagined. Barracks, stables, a dirt parade ground—where line upon line of troops in blue coats wheeled and marched—grassy swaths between log buildings of indeterminate purpose. "Quit gaping and try to look like a soldier," Munn said as he strode past her. Deborah snapped her head back as if slapped and kept her eyes locked to the front.

Munn led them past the parade ground to a smaller drill field, where they stood in their now-familiar ranks. She watched the square set of his shoulders, the unyielding straightness of his posture, and she tried to follow his example, straightening her spine and lifting her chin. Three captains, each attended by a sergeant, emerged from one of the log buildings and walked toward their rows. Munn, Booth, and Shaw gave crisp salutes. Deborah longed to turn her head to catch James's eye, to see if he shared her awe, but she willed herself to stand tall and steady.

"March forward!" cried one of the captains, and the recruits—some stepping high and quick, others with the amble they'd employed since Massachusetts—moved across the field. "Halt!"

The sergeants began the work of winnowing, tapping men and removing them from line. A hunched fellow—the oldest of the recruits—shuffled off, as did the sturdy man who walked with a limp. He'd lost several of his toes, frozen off one winter. They marched again, making a full circuit of the drill field, and more were sloughed off—the stripling lads, shorter even than Richard, who was standing as straight as he could. The sight amused Deborah; for all his disdain, he didn't want to be cast off as feeble. When they halted once more, the sergeants came around with long sticks and held them up to each recruit. Would she make the cut? Did she want to? The stick came to Deborah's shoulder and the sergeant nodded impassively, moving on to Richard, who fell short of the mark by an inch or two and was led off; she could hear his feet scuffing against the sand.

"Open your mouths," came the order.

Another sergeant stood over her, peering in. "Shut it now," he told her.

They marched once more, a captain calling out commands—"Right, face! Double time! About, face!"—at a speed that pushed all other thoughts from her mind. She felt another recruit stumble and fall against her, and she pivoted so that she wouldn't be knocked over as well. At last, the order came to halt. Deborah watched a red-headed captain lean close to Sergeant Munn and Corporal Booth and confer with them while they pointed at the recruits. The captain, the sword of rank dangling from his belt, stepped forward and walked down the row, his eyes boring into each recruit, his thin lips pressed into a tight line. She heard the heavy breathing of those around her and took in a deep lungful of air to calm herself. An image of the clerk flashed before her, his leering face. *See me now*, she thought fiercely, as the captain's hand descended on her shoulder.

"Step forward."

Four of them marched out from the drill field behind Sergeant Munn like a peculiar line of ducklings waddling after their mother. Deborah saw—to her great relief—that James was among them. The other two were tall and lean like him, young lads. She'd shared guard duty with Tobias, and the other, Matthew, she knew only by sight. Corporal Booth had gone ahead with the captain, and Deborah spotted him tying back the flaps of a canvas pavilion that stood before a sloping field of smaller tents, perched like a flock of white birds momentarily at rest. Sergeant Munn brought them to a halt and went into the pavilion, leaving them outside with Corporal Booth. "You'll be joining me, then. The captain asked for the quickest, the strongest, the most alert. Here you are. The lights." He ducked into the tent as well.

The light infantry? How could she possibly measure up? And what cruel joke was this to put her in with the strongest and the quickest?

In a short while, the captain emerged from the tent, along with Sergeant Munn and Corporal Booth, who set up a field desk. High cheekbones and a thin nose gave the captain the look of an aristocrat, but the skin of his face and hands appeared rough and reddened. "I am Captain George Webb, commander of the Fourth Massachusetts Regiment's company of light infantry. If you conduct yourself properly, you will have little intercourse with me. Corporal Booth will see to your equipment and Sergeant Munn to your training. Sergeant, enroll the men and carry on." The captain received Munn's salute and turned to walk back across the parade ground.

Munn watched Booth enter their names in the register. "West Point is a big place, lads. Our company's numbers are low right now, but we'll be bringing in recruits over the next month. By the start of summer, we will be at full strength, a company of fifty men." He placed his hands on his hips as Booth's quill skittered across the register. "Captain Webb means what he says. There's a hierarchy to this company. The captain's at the top, and you needn't bother him about anything, just do what he says and be quick about it. His lieutenants are under him, the sergeants under them, and the corporals below that. Which means you're at the bottom. Do what you're told. Corporal, take them to their quarters."

"Yes, sir." The four of them followed Booth away from the captain's tent and down the slope. As they passed by rows of tents, Deborah saw laundry hanging from lines, neat circles of stone with metal spits and hooks for cooking, and here and there a soldier cleaning his musket.

Booth pointed to the east. "Necessaries over yonder. There are troughs for cleaning as well. Mark that you're tidy for roll."

Down a slight incline, he lifted the flap of a tent and ushered them in. The light that came through the thick canvas glowed pale and translucent like undercooked fish. The smell was similar, too.

Small debris, a broken flint, and scraps of leather and flannel littered the packed dirt floor, indicating that this tent had recently been used by others.

"You'll bunk here. For tonight, I'll send someone with your dinner provisions. Keep your noses clean, do what you're told, and you'll be fine. I'll fetch you at reveille and we will proceed with training tomorrow."

Without further word, he left. Tobias dropped his bundle and began to unpack, but the smell of the tent and the concomitant realities of army life were closing in on Deborah, so she lifted the flap and made her way outside. Matthew and James followed soon after, and the three of them sat, talking and surveying their surroundings.

Matthew, it turned out, had run away from his family's farm in Mendon. "The agent who signed me didn't ask too many questions," he explained to Deborah. "I'm glad of it, too. I'm not really seventeen as I said, more like fifteen and a couple of months."

Deborah found this hard to believe: Matthew stood even taller than James, who topped her by several inches. And whiskers already flecked Matthew's cheeks. "Won't your mother be upset that you've run off?" she asked.

"I'm more worried about my father. My mother might forgive me, but my father will still be angry in three years' time."

"Better save some of that bounty for him," said James, stretching out on the ground.

Matthew unbuckled his shoes and rubbed at his feet. "I'll earn that money and I intend to keep it."

Tobias emerged from the tent. With skin as soft and white as biscuit dough, he wore his long, blond hair tied in a clubbed queue that fell past his collar. Sinking to the ground next to Deborah, he pulled at a shoot of grass. "The light infantry. I can scarcely believe it."

"Why do you think we were picked? You heard what the corporal said—the lights are the best," Deborah said. She wondered if she ought not to voice her doubts, but she couldn't restrain her curiosity.

James lifted his head on one arm. "We're all tall. That stick was the height of a firelock, and to load properly you've got to be a sight taller than the gun."

"Aye. And we've got enough teeth to load, too," said Matthew. Deborah gave him a puzzled look. "To tear the cartridge open, see? If you've only a couple of teeth left in your jaw, it won't be so easy."

She nodded. Tall and with teeth. Those hardly seemed like stringent qualifications.

"I'm for some rest myself," said James, yawning prodigiously. "Wake me for dinner."

Matthew was engrossed in paring his toenails with his belt knife, and Tobias was chewing the stalk of grass while gazing around at the other tents. James's snores bubbled up softly. Watching the others, Deborah thought of the Thomas boys. There had been five sons, ranging from two to ten years her junior. She had loved romping with them when she could get away to do so, but they had been devils, too: wild and prone to fighting. Now, at twenty-two, she felt herself to be much older than these youthful tentmates, who struck her as overgrown boys.

"Hop to!" came a shout, and a man in regimentals strode past, pushed her back, and kicked James in the side. James jerked awake and jumped to his feet, surprisingly quick given his normal inclination to torpor.

"What's the idea—" he started.

"You want to eat," the man cut him off, "then you fetch the wood." He pointed down the slope. "And the rest of you get water."

The four of them exchanged glances, silently decided it was best not to argue or ask questions, and loped off. James and Deborah found a queue of soldiers by a stack of wood and joined the line.

"What do you reckon Richard is doing?" asked Deborah.

James rubbed his ribs where the kick had landed. "Nothing with a gun. He's several inches too short. But I'm sorry he's not with us."

Deborah nodded. "At least we're rid of Shaw."

"Aye. An almost fair exchange."

As they walked back up the slope with their arms full of kindling and logs, Deborah wanted to ask James what he thought tomorrow would bring, but she held her tongue. Men, she was learning, took what came to them and—at most—complained about it afterward. Women liked to dream about it beforehand, to dress up the shadows of their imaginings.

Back at their tent, they kindled the fire. Soon enough, the others returned with buckets of water. The soldier, too, came back, this time carrying a pot of dried peas and salted beef, which he placed without ceremony on the ground. The four of them cooked in silence, and when the peas softened, they spooned out even helpings. Around them, the white roofs of the tents drooped in the evening stillness.

James prodded the ground. "I wonder if I can get a straw tick to sleep on. . . ."

"Missing your bed at home?" said Tobias.

"And how. It wasn't a feather bed, but it was more comfortable than dirt and rocks."

"I think I miss the food more than the bed," said Tobias.

From down the slope came bursts of shouting. Heads poked out from the surrounding tents, and men flocked toward the noise. Deborah and James nodded to each other and hurried along, with Matthew trailing close behind. By another cooking fire, a ring of men had gathered around two soldiers, one reeling—whether from drink or a clout to the head, Deborah could not tell.

"That bastard stole my rum!" one soldier cried. The other roared back insensibly. The encircling crowd hooted and jeered, their faces indistinct in the flickering firelight. She saw Matthew laughing, delighted by the spectacle. The drunken soldier made a rude gesture, hand to crotch, and the other charged him, landing a blow to his face and then felling him easily with a shove. The crowd shouted with derision as the man toppled over. Just as his opponent lined up to kick him, two sergeants pushed through the crowd. Deborah leaped aside to let them pass, and they jumped on the man still standing, dragging him away.

The other lay on the ground, groaning, his lips bloody where he'd been struck. Seeing the source of entertainment dry up, the crowd dispersed, and another sergeant elbowed through. "You there," he said, pointing at Deborah and James. "Lend a hand." They each took a leg while the sergeant took the arms, leading them along the paths between the tents. They wound their way up the slope to a larger tent lit by a lantern on a pole. Inside, cots stood in rows, and they set the man down.

The sergeant squinted at them in the lantern light. "I wager that you two are fresh recruits."

"Aye," they said.

"A good lesson to you, then. Mind your drink and mind your mates."

They nodded and took their leave. Outside, James seemed more concerned about finding his way in the growing darkness than with the fight they had just witnessed. "Left here, Robert, you think? All these tents look the same."

When they found their spot, Matthew was regaling Tobias with an account of the fight. "Knocked him right down, fell like a sack of flour. . . ."

Deborah saw the feral glint in his eyes, the firelight catching them and setting them ablaze, wolflike. How did she dare to live with these men, to become a soldier? She wrenched her gaze from Matthew's face and searched the sky instead, where the smoke from a dozen fires twined up, dissipated, and became lost in the greater blackness.

CHAPTER SEVEN

Corporal Booth delivered a pot of cornmeal mush for their breakfast. "You'll get sick of this soon enough," he said as they spooned up steaming bowls. "Eat quick. You need to wash and be tidy for muster." The corporal paced in front of the tent as he watched them eat; the man seemed to possess boundless energy. Deborah shoveled the porridge down, hoping it would revive her—she hadn't slept well. As she finished her bowl, James crept out of the tent and walked to the rear to relieve himself.

"You there, Snow," Booth called. "Use the necessary." James buttoned up and trotted past. "Hygiene in camp is critical. Von Steuben's zealous about it. Inoculated everyone who hadn't had the pox last winter, and he insists on clean hands at inspection and nobody using the woods as a privy."

Deborah wiped her bowl with her fingers, weighing Booth's words with regret: it would be easier to avoid detection if she could relieve herself in the undergrowth. Making her way to the latrines, she found dozens of soldiers milling about. The necessary houses were long sheds where five or six men sat, cheek by jowl, to relieve themselves. She might get away with it if she was careful, dropping her trousers and sitting hastily. But luckily, this morning her need wasn't yet pressing. She would wait until she could use the woods, or return when the morning crowd had dispersed, or when it grew dark. For now, she washed at a trough, splashing cold water on her face and scrubbing her hands, mindful of Booth's words. Hustling back to the tent, she saw Tobias yawning, his blond hair tousled, as if he'd gotten as little rest as she.

Booth instructed them in shaving—though only James and Matthew needed to be concerned—chided Tobias about combing his hair, and encouraged them to clean up. Once Booth deemed them presentable, he led them to the parade ground. The rows of troops already stood at attention, and the four of them took their place at the rear, the only brown- and gray-clad bodies on the periphery of a blue mass, like boats tossed upon the sea. Sergeants strode up and down the lines, stopping to address torn uniforms or to peer at fingernails.

One sergeant stalked by the recruits and leveled a glare at Tobias. "See the barber today, boy. Your hair is a rat's nest."

His fair skin became flushed, and he choked out, "Aye, sir."

The sergeant didn't seem to hear as he turned to Deborah. "And you. Get some proper shoes. Those aren't fit for a fiddler's bitch." She dropped her gaze to the cracked and scuffed leather. "Look at me when I talk to you." She snapped her eyes up and the sergeant moved on. From the front Captain Webb called names, and soldiers responded. As Munn had said, it was hardly a full roster, maybe thirty-five in all. The other troops fell out as ordered, and Sergeant Munn approached the recruits, with Corporal Shaw a step behind him. Deborah registered Shaw's presence with shock. She thought she had seen the last of him yesterday—how had he ended up in this company?

"You'll have a week to get yourself equipped with uniforms and gear," Munn said. "The corporals will lead you through the basics of drill and fatigue training. Then you'll join as regular members of the company. Let's get them looking sharp, Corporal Shaw."

After a long march through the whole encampment—from the banks of the Hudson, with its batteries and chains, to the far picket lines and out into the fields where the regiment's horses grazed—Shaw brought them back, sweat-soaked, to the parade ground. From there, Booth took them to the commissary. The barber clipped Tobias's queue cleanly off, trimmed Matthew's shaggy mane, and straightened up the ragged edges of her own hair. "Stop frowning," James said to Tobias. "It'll be easier to keep your hair tidy if it's shorter. Besides, there are no ladies about to impress with your flowing locks."

Deborah swallowed a grin at this comment. The one lady about was unlikely to be impressed by well-styled hair.

"Next, uniforms," Booth said, as he ushered them inside a dusky room where a disinterested soldier stood at a table, ledger ready. Despite her fatigue, Deborah perked up as she drew near. She'd been admiring the uniforms since Middleborough's Colonel Sproat had first appeared in his so many years ago.

Booth took the stack of coats the soldier passed him. "Think of the lasses in Massachusetts weaving and sewing these garments for you," he said. The words caught Deborah short; she had been such a lass, weaving cloth at Sproat's, listening to other girls talk of their brothers and husbands gone to be soldiers. She had woven and envied and wished, and now here she was, on the other side—on the inside—of that same fabric. Abruptly, Booth boxed Matthew lightly on the side of his head. "Don't think of them like that, you lout." James guffawed, and Booth laughed, too. His pleasant humor made a welcome change from Shaw. As the soldier jotted notes in his ledger, Booth passed the garments around: coat, waistcoat, trousers, and shirt. "Each piece is a loose fit. Now step lively to the tailors, lads."

In the next room, double doors were thrown open, allowing better light, and a soldier with a measuring tape, pincushion, and chalk awaited them.

"All right. Put 'em on, and I'll take your sizing," he said.

James began to strip out of his coat and waistcoat. Deborah clutched the uniform to her, panicked by the realization that they were to disrobe, that the tailor would have to wrap his tape around her chest and measure up her leg.

"Sir, I can do my own tailoring," said Tobias, stepping close to Booth. "Save some time."

"As you wish," the corporal replied.

"Likewise," Deborah added. "I can fix my own uniform."

Booth nodded, scratching at the scar on his cheek. "Quick fingers then, lads. Let's get you shoes and hats."

He led the two of them across a small courtyard and into another workroom, where cobblers sat at their benches, tapping away. She tried on several pairs of the half boots the light infantry wore, finding a pair that fit her well. The leather creaked as she walked, and though she knew the new boots would raise blisters in short order, she turned her old shoes over to the cobbler with delight. Ezekiel would never know the lengths they had traveled.

At last, Booth procured for them hats with a cockade on one side and a plume on the other. "Now, back to your tent and sew. We'll get your equipment tomorrow."

Deborah retrieved her sewing kit from her bundle, and sat down to the chore with a groan of gratitude—that she could rest for a moment, that she had escaped having to strip, and that she was rid of those awful shoes. Tobias had secured his own needle and thread, and the two of them sat outside the tent holding shirtsleeves against their arms, measuring and pinning. Every so often, Tobias ran his hands through his hair as if surprised by the missing locks. She recognized the gesture—she had often caught herself trying to tuck her missing hair around her ear—and it pleased her to see that a man might do the same.

In the sunshine, Deborah marveled at the day's events. Camp life didn't yet make sense to her, but she drew comfort from the uniform in her hands. Shaking out the coat, she admired the white lining and the sharp, white facing on the lapels, and she wished that simply donning the uniform would make her a soldier. The uniform would make her blend in: one more blue coat in a field of blue coats. But what really mattered was not blending in, but belonging. And that—as she'd felt in her first days as a recruit and even more so as she now sat next to Tobias—had nothing to do with what she wore on the outside and everything to do with what lay within herself.

As she worked on the seam of the shirt, she occasionally cast glances at Tobias, who sat cross-legged and hummed as he drew the needle through the cloth. She bit off her thread and took the measure of the cuff. Letting the shirt drop for a second, she studied Tobias's work, the flat and even trail of his stitches.

"Where'd you learn to sew like that?"

His blue eyes flicked up to meet hers. "My father's a tailor." He looked at her stitches, and if he noted the wayward line of her own effort, he was polite enough to withhold judgment. "And you?"

"I was trained as a weaver, and one seldom learns to weave without learning to sew." The statement was not quite true, but true enough, a liminal quality that she was appreciating more and more.

She knotted her thread tightly and stuck the needle into the cloth as Tobias said, "I can't say I miss sewing all the time. But it's a sight better than what Shaw had us at this morning."

"Indeed. How much of that do we have in store?"

"Judging from the soldiers I've seen, I would say not much. Idleness appears to be the rule of the day, except for recruits."

She dared to raise a topic that nagged at her. "I'm sorry to see Shaw join the regiment. He was a bastard on the march over here." The vulgarity felt awkward on her tongue, but she needed to practice. Soldiers didn't stumble over curses. "I didn't think he was in the lights."

"He wasn't, but he transferred in, I suppose."

"So, tailoring did not suit?" Deborah asked. "You're more for soldiering?"

"I didn't mind tailoring, but my brother was called in this class, and he's more of a delicate sort, so I went in his stead."

Deborah knew enough to understand what Tobias left unsaid—that his family couldn't afford to pay for a substitute and that, likely, he felt less treasured than his brother. She wished she could tell him her own story and that she knew how it felt to be unwanted. Even now, she could feel a swell of resentment toward her mother, the way she had cast her off so young. She swallowed, her throat suddenly tight; best to leave that grief alone. "It is noble of you to serve on his behalf."

"It's no great matter." Tobias gave an exaggerated shrug, then examined the coat's cuff and folded it carefully. "I thought you might be a weaver or a tailor or something of the sort."

"Why would you say that?"

"You seem contemplative, a bit more mild than the others."

The words surprised Deborah. They weren't insulting, exactly, but she had never before been called mild—quite the contrary, in fact. Perhaps she'd discovered the corollary of her transformation: a cantankerous woman equaled a mild man. "You think so?"

"I do. You are always watchful. You watched Shaw with a critical eye this morning, and you learned to march faster than the rest of us. I bet that weaving forces you to pay attention to detail and leaves you lots of time to ponder."

"That it does. I liked it best when I could get someone to read to me, or even to sing."

"My brother would read in our workshop. But he likes religious tracts, and I favor chapbooks. Nothing like a good adventure story."

"Exactly," Deborah said. She and Jennie had spent many an hour reading to each other, delighting in *Gulliver's Travels* or reading *The Pilgrim's Progress* aloud to Widow Thacher. She seldom passed Leach's store without stopping to examine the texts on offer. "Was your brother employed as a tailor as well?"

"No. My parents sent him early to school. He showed good aptitude and so they continued his education. He is studying now to be a minister." Tobias bit the end of his thread and tied it off. Though he tried to speak moderately, Deborah heard the bitterness in his voice. She had thought just women were pushed aside so that men might pursue their grander destinies, but now she saw that men, too, could be held back.

"I often wished for more schooling," she replied, once again filtering the truth. "Though not to become a member of the clergy."

Tobias held pins clamped between his teeth now, and mumbled around them. "What did you . . ."

"Oh . . ." Deborah felt herself flush, caught between revealing the truth—her love of adventure novels and her desire to go to sea—and sounding convincing. "Childish things, I suppose."

Tobias dislodged the pins. "Go on. . . . I once fancied I could write poetry." He lifted an eyebrow, as if daring her to top that.

"Well, I suppose I wanted what most boys do, to become an explorer. I recall reading an account of land surveyors once, how they traversed into lands only heathens had known, how they discovered wild forests and great mountains. So I asked my master what it would take to become a land surveyor."

"What did he reply?"

"He laughed."

"I suppose it takes a good bit of arithmetic and a lot of daring."

Deborah nodded, caught in the memory of reading the book, of talking it over with Jennie and realizing the impossibility of it, even before asking Mr. Thomas. Custom and habit could be just as confining as a harsh master.

That afternoon passed in idle conversation, telling stories of their hometowns, and speculating about what, if anything, they'd see of the war. Tobias helped her measure the shoulders of her coat, and by the time the light drifted to downy gray, Matthew and James had returned, covered in some sort of white dust and looking like ghosts.

"Lucky fellows," said Matthew, plunking himself on the grass in a poof of powder, "sitting about with your needlework." He spoke in a mocking, simpering tone as James shook out his coat.

"What brought on this pallor?" Deborah asked.

"Carrying bags of flour. At least we know we'll be well fed," James replied.

Once they had finished dinner, Tobias took out a wooden flute and began to play. They sang along to "Highland Lass," with Matthew adding a few raunchy verses. Then Tobias switched to a hornpipe.

"I've seen this danced before," cried James and stood up, clapping his hands. He stumbled through the steps at first, tapping his heels and toes, and then leaping in time to the music. The notes stopped abruptly, and James sank back to the ground as Tobias began a slower air. "An old sea captain taught me that dance," James said.

"Sailed through Bellingham and taught you, did he? I didn't realize the town sat on the ocean," Matthew joked.

James let the jibe slide past. His face glowed in the firelight, and Deborah wondered what he was thinking about as she saw the edges of a smile touch his lips. Tobias's melody draped itself over the night air, its notes in tune with the hope she held.

CHAPTER EIGHT

Two soldiers stood on a platform at the head of the parade ground, stripped to the waist. Their chests were fish-belly pale, in marked contrast to their tan faces and necks. Sergeant Munn waited to the side while Captain Webb, his scabbard polished and gleaming in the morning sun, addressed the company.

"For drunkenness and brawling, six lashes will be administered to Private Cook." His voice sounded sharp and thin, a perfect match to his narrow features.

One of the stripped men turned his head, and Deborah, who stood in the ranks below the platform, saw that his face was swollen and bruised.

"I reckon that's the man we carried to the infirmary the other night," James whispered.

"For drunkenness and brawling and disobedience to an officer, ten lashes will be administered to Private Pratt." Webb folded the paper and tucked it in his coat before turning to Munn. "Sergeant, you will deliver the punishment."

"Yes, sir."

A corporal secured the men's hands to a post, and Munn raised the whip, meting out the blows in a steady measure. By the third lash, blood flowed freely down the first man's back, and on the fifth, he let out a groan of anguish. Deborah winced as she watched; Munn's barrel chest and thick arms meant that each blow bore tremendous force. With the second man, she focused on the sergeant's face, not wanting to see more blood. Munn's mouth, a flat line, betrayed neither disgust nor pleasure. When he was finished, the flogged men were untied and led away.

Tobias let out his breath in a rush. "I wonder if that happens often."

"Likely. My father was always beating us. Only way to keep order," Matthew said.

Deborah repressed a shiver at the thought of being whipped. Widow Thacher had employed a switch on occasion, but Mr. Thomas, though he threatened, had never struck her.

Captain Webb stood on the platform once more. "Let this be a reminder. In the camp, in the field, in the evening, and in the morning, you are soldiers. Now fall out."

As the other troops dispersed to their assignments, Shaw marched them out of camp to a steep incline, where he ran them up and down the slope until James nearly collapsed with fatigue. "Wait until we do that with bayonets," the corporal told them as he led them back to a storeroom in the commissary where they received their equipment: knapsack, cartridge box, canteen, musket, bayonet, and thirty cartridges of blank rounds for practice. Shaw and Booth showed them how to put the pieces together and how to strap everything on, and then instructed them in the all-important lesson of making their own cartridges.

"There are times it feels I've spent years of my life making cartridges," Booth said as he watched their work. "But then I've put them all to good use, now, haven't I?" He pointed at Deborah and Tobias. "How far along is your sewing?"

"I am near to done on the coat, and the trousers won't take long," said Tobias.

"Aye, the same," said Deborah.

"Then finish the work today. Tomorrow will be your first day as full members of the light infantry." He turned to the others. "As for you lot, I'll sort you out."

Back at the tent, they tied the flaps open and Tobias brought in some pine boughs, hoping to freshen the air.

"Next you know, you'll be sewing curtains," she chided him, delighted that it was not feminine delicacy that had made the smell objectionable to her.

A light drizzle fell, and the two of them sat just inside the flaps on their blankets. Deborah took up her needle and thread and set to work on the trousers. Few men she knew wore these long pants; most favored breeches and leggings. But from the exercises at West Point she could see how a legging would not hold up under such conditions. Alas, she thought, there would be no more showing off her shapely calves.

"Penny for your thoughts," Tobias said.

"Ah . . . thinking of a lady who praised my figure."

"Missing womenfolk already, Robert?"

"In a manner of speaking," she replied.

They lapsed into silence, and Tobias finished well before she did; his needle seemed to fly through the fabric. "Shall I play you some tunes to speed the sewing? Or I could read you something."

"I would enjoy a story."

Tobias rooted around in his blankets and came out with a battered copy of *Robinson Crusoe*. "My brother sent me off with this. I think he meant for me to absorb the religious teachings. But I like the adventure better."

Tobias read, his tenor voice slow and careful. Deborah stitched and listened and thought of Jennie. The two of them had read this volume years and years ago. But more than the story, she remembered how they liked to imagine being marooned on an island of their own and how they would arrange their days without anyone to order them about. Jennie . . . She'd have to write her again soon.

Deborah pulled the final stitches as Matthew and James came down the slope, fully decked out in their new regimentals. The uniform transformed them, turning Matthew from a lanky farm lad into a true soldier. And the sharp lapels made James's chest seem even broader. They approached with a noticeable swagger. She tied off the thread as they stowed their muskets and knapsacks in the tent and dropped the evening's rations by the fire circle. Matthew went to get water, Tobias and James to get wood, and Deborah offered to clean out the pot, which was begrimed by Matthew's attempt to make porridge that morning. Once the others had gone, she shucked off her old clothes in the tent, letting them fall in a heap onto her blanket. She stood for an instant in the cool air—just the binding around her chest and the breeches hanging low and loose on her hips—before thrusting her arms through the new shirt, which felt as refreshing as if she'd plunged into clear water. Then she let her breeches drop and pulled on the trousers, stuffing the long tails of her shirt inside. The waistcoat came next; her fingers worked at the buttons, and by the time she stepped outside and tugged the coat on, James had reappeared with an armload of wood.

"You lost no time in donning that. You're a proper Continental now," he said, letting the wood fall with a clatter.

Deborah did up the last button on the coat. "It is no exaggeration," she said, "to claim that I feel like a new man."

James nodded, intent on brushing the wood chips from his sleeves. "Don't we all," he muttered.

Booth stopped by to see how the sewing had gone. As he surveyed the four of them in their uniforms, he rubbed at the scar on his cheek and gave them a satisfied nod. "You sure look like soldiers. Tomorrow we'll see if you can fight like soldiers." He sat down by the fire with them and launched into a long-winded story about how ill-equipped and poorly prepared the army had been when he was a recruit. Deborah wished he'd tell a story about Yorktown. She'd read the newspaper accounts, but they were short and terse, and didn't disclose the gory details. Never before had she had a chance to speak with a veteran of such a major battle. But a deeply ingrained reticence, a reluctance to speak that Mr. Thomas had inculcated in her, held her back.

"What battle gave you that scar?" Matthew asked Booth. The question made Deborah pay attention to the conversation again; it struck her as rude, but she reminded herself that men were often so direct.

The corporal ran his finger along his cheek. "I got on the wrong side of a bull when I was twelve. Not the war story you were hoping for, eh?" They all laughed, and Booth continued. "I had that feeling that every young boy gets, around twelve, that he owns the world and can do anything, and never mind what he is told. So when my father told me not to go into the bull's pasture one spring day, I decided that that very pasture would make a fine shortcut." He touched the scar again. "Learned my lesson. Watch out for bulls in springtime."

The others chuckled, and Deborah remembered feeling the same way at twelve. At that age, she was helping Mrs. Thomas tend to the youngest of her brood, mending and sewing for a pack of boys who outgrew or tore through clothing at an alarming rate. Scrubbing laundry, feeding hens—chores filled every moment of the day. She remembered pinning sheets up to dry and imagining that they were the billowing sails of a ship that would carry her away, and that she could be a powder monkey or a cabin boy.

"But I have plenty of battle scars, too," Booth continued. "I'll save those stories for another night." He pushed himself up from the ground. "Get some rest, fellows."

"There," said Tobias, "is a man who loves being a soldier."

"A rare breed, you think?" asked James.

"It isn't the life I would choose," Tobias said.

"Better here than my father's farm," said Matthew. "If I'd been older, I'd have joined up six years ago. When the first call came out."

Deborah remembered that moment well: the news rushing through Middleborough—the need for men, for boys, for anyone with a musket.

"Not I," murmured Tobias. "I hope this all ends soon."

Matthew blew air through his lips. "Those bastards will sit in New York for as long as they please. You mark my words. . . ."

Leaving them to talk, Deborah slipped inside the tent and carefully set her hat next to her musket and haversack. Rolling up her old clothes to use as a pillow, she lay there with her eyes open to the darkness, thinking of the torn strips from her old dress, which were still in her bundle, the roll of young Master Leonard's clothes beneath her head, and the crisp uniform enclosing her now. Which one was she? Could she be Robert only, and do away with Deborah? Or would she always be both? Would the dress always be there as a reminder and a source of fear? She ran her hands along the fabric of her trousers, feeling the tight muscles of her legs beneath. She had created Robert Shurtliff, and now she had to believe in him, to become this man.

All four of them brushed the facings on their new coats as they prepared for roll call, and Matthew puffed out his chest, clearly delighted in his uniform. The morning air enveloped them in its damp warmth, a sign that spring had run its course. As Deborah stowed her gear in the tent, she heard a familiar voice through the canvas.

"Suited up and ready, are you?"

She stepped out to see Corporal Shaw. "Ah, Shurtliff. There you are." He nodded at her. "A small tip for you new recruits. Put a little more polish on those buckles. The captain likes to see the brass shine. Now, don't be late for muster."

After roll call, Sergeant Munn led the four of them through the steps of cleaning their pieces. Rags and oil, the names of each bit: muzzle, pan, lock, and barrel. Munn handled the gun with a curious mixture of tenderness and brutality, with loving care but also with an apparent awareness of its capacity for violence. The weapon looked small in his meaty hands. Deborah watched fervently, trying to imprint the process on her memory; it couldn't be more intricate than learning to thread a heddle on a loom. After demonstrating each step, Munn watched them manage on their own, nodding and offering advice or warnings.

"Just remember, lads, it's a weapon. Care for it, and it will care for you. But don't forget the danger. Too much powder in the pan, and it will flash up and burn you." He paced as he spoke. "Don't brace properly, and the butt will kick you and break a rib or worse. And never pull the trigger without considering where it is pointed. Even if you think there's no load in the muzzle. Goodness knows the stories I could tell you. Why, I've seen a man set to cleaning, certain there was no shot in his piece, and then, when he worked the trigger, it sent that shot flying into his barracks—through a wall, through a man's arm, and right into the chimney."

James cleaned his gun as if it might bite him, Deborah noted, but she just leaned closer to her work. With the musket in her hands, much about the light infantry became clearer. With its butt on the ground, the gun reached as high as her shoulder, and it weighed at least as much as a tub of wet laundry. Little wonder they needed tall and sturdy soldiers.

That afternoon, Deborah's group learned the drill, with Sergeant Munn standing before them to demonstrate. The commands came sharp:

"Poise your firelocks!"

She raised the musket perpendicular to the ground, left hand above the lock, height equal to the eyes. Munn insisted that everyone, even those who were left-handed, as she and Tobias were, learn with the same hands. "It's a company. You can't choose whichever hand you please," he'd shouted at them. "Otherwise, every lad in the line would be bumping into each other. In this army, everyone is right-handed." She had felt her stomach sink at the time, but then she realized that she would scarcely be able to do the movements with her left hand anyway, scarred and rigid as her finger was. Besides, the need to learn it right-handed might provide her with a ready excuse should she prove less dexterous than her fellows.

"Cock your firelocks!"

Keeping her head steady, she drew the lock and set it back.

"Present!"

She stepped her right foot six inches to the rear and raised the butt end to her shoulder.

Munn walked them through all twenty-seven maneuvers of the manual exercise twice, slowly, and then he picked up the pace. By the third iteration, Deborah's palms were slick with sweat and slipped on the stock. The musket struck her foot and fell to the dirt.

"You oaf! Can't even hold on to wood!" Before she could reach for the gun, Munn had swiped it up and thrust it hard against her chest. The blow pushed the air out of her. "Do I need to nail it to your hands? Quit gaping at me like fool! Stand up straight!"

He pushed her again, and she swayed. Steadying herself, she bit down on the inside of her cheek. The pain would focus her, help her look him in the eyes. She held the musket firm. "Yes, sir."

"Shall we start again?"

"Yes, sir," they all chorused.

"Cock your firelocks!"

Within moments Matthew became fuddled, stepping forward instead of back, and by the sixth order—"Handle your cartridge!"—James had fallen behind, unable to snag the pouch and bite the top clear off the cartridge. They all fumbled along, and when, at last, Munn cried out, "Charge bayonet!" only Tobias and Deborah lurched forward, and he didn't even have the blade affixed to his muzzle.

Munn shook his head and turned to James to ask him how it was that he couldn't bite through paper. Deborah breathed through her nose to keep from gulping at the air. She had been yelled at before, but never like that. *Be a man*, she told herself. Munn left James and began to berate Matthew for his clumsiness. "Do you know right from left?"

"Of course."

"What did you say?"

"Yes, sir."

Munn narrowed his eyes at Matthew. "Mind your mouth as well as your feet."

Deborah shot a glance at Matthew, and Munn spun to face her. "And you. Keep your eyes to the front. Let's try it again, and endeavor to do it correctly this time around."

Again and again and again. Munn shouted the commands, his voice growing ever more harsh, shaking his head at each mistake. Finally, when James mishandled his ramrod and sent his musket crashing to the ground, the sergeant reached over and grabbed him by the coat. "Get it together, boy!" He yanked him closer, making James's head wobble. "Brace that musket and draw the rammer in two motions. Drop a loaded musket, and you could kill someone. You're a buffoon." He released the coat. "Let that musket fall once more, and you can spend three years cleaning stables." Munn turned to the rest of them. "Heaven help us all. Now do it again!"

When they had run through it perfectly—or at least, not terribly—they marched to the larger parade ground, where the rest of the company was practicing drill: wheeling and breaking off, quick steps and sudden halts. Deborah thought of the militia she'd watched from her loom at Sproat's Tavern. That she'd ever thought of them as soldiers, with their rough homespun and ancient blunderbusses, amazed her. The ranks before her arched with precision, turning and stopping without a wasted movement. She gripped her musket, wanting to be among them, in step with them, a part of something larger than herself.

Captain Webb dismissed the company as the sun began its decline. Munn held the recruits back, his hands clasped behind him, his chest swelling expansively. "All right, then. You have your pieces, and now it is your job to keep them clean for inspection." He gave them a sharp little nod as though to underscore the importance of this point. "Tomorrow being Sunday, you are free of camp duties. There's chapel if you wish it." He waved toward the north. "Sunday, after all, is the Lord's day." He gave them a scowl in case they might claim otherwise. "But I'll turn you over to Corporal Booth, and he'll explain the rules." Munn nodded at Booth's salute and strode off across the parade ground.

"The sergeant is not one for such diversions, but you'll find that many soldiers take part in games of chance. This is allowed, but mind that you pay your debts and avoid quarrels." Booth's voice sounded light and pleasant after hours of Munn's harsh barking. "Others take this time to launder their uniforms, or other such, ah, domestic enterprises. Now, then. Let's fetch your food."

At the commissary, they picked up the normal ration of pork and peas, along with a gill of rum each, which Booth handed over with mock solemnity. "Welcome to a soldier's life."

By the fire, after they had cooked and eaten, Matthew prodded a blister on his heel.

"Better burst it," James said.

"Feels hot enough to cook on," complained Matthew.

"Relief is but a sip away," said Tobias, raising his flask of rum.

James hoisted himself on an elbow and did the same. The two of them drank. "No spirits for you?" he asked, lifting his flask to Matthew.

"A moment," said Matthew, who was ministering to his blister with one of Tobias's sewing needles. "There now. A toast to blisters!" They drank.

Robert stood and stretched his shoulders. "It isn't my feet so much as my arms. That musket's no toothpick."

Matthew looked up. "Not as heavy as a sledge. I'd take a day of carrying a musket to a day of raking hay. That's enough to make your arms fall off."

James's voice was muffled, for he had placed his hat over his face and lay flat on the ground. "I just don't fancy remembering all those moves. Present this, cock that. I'll show him how to cock it." He sat up and, taking another slug of rum, dug an elbow into Tobias's side. "Wasn't that what Booth was talking about, cocking it?"

Tobias grinned, though Deborah had lost the thread of the conversation. "What did he call it, now . . ."

"Domestic duties?" Matthew chimed in.

"That's right. I'm all for domesticity."

"I'll drink to that," said Matthew. And they did.

Deborah, who had been lifting the rum to her lips without pouring it down her throat, smiled along with them, not certain what they meant.

"I hear that on the other side of the woodlot, well behind the lines, is where they keep them," Tobias continued.

"On a Sunday?" Matthew asked.

"If it's the only day we are free from obligations . . ."

Now Robert caught their meaning. The women—wives of soldiers, some mothers and sweethearts—who traveled with the soldiers kept their own camp. He'd heard others mention having laundry done there or getting better food. Thinking he had cottoned on to their meaning, he added, "I think I'll do my own laundry, save a shilling."

The others guffawed, and Matthew said between laughs, "I've been doing my own laundry all week, Robert. Time for someone else to hang me out to dry."

She was lost again but tried not to show her embarrassment. Tobias, perhaps tired of their silliness, stood up next to her and said, "They're talking about whores, Robert. Though I suspect that come tomorrow, they, like you, will prefer to save a shilling."

The others drank steadily without offering up toasts. Matthew put another log on the fire, sending a shower of sparks into the air, swaying as he spoke. "Now I understand why everyone in Mendon would hide their women when the British passed through. Let me loose in a town right now, and I'd steer for someone's daughter."

His words sent fear rushing through Deborah. She fought back thoughts of the clerk, of the way young Master Leonard leered at Jennie. The waves of her memories rocked her, threatening to capsize her. *Let it go*, she counseled herself, knowing that she could no longer be Deborah, rooted in the past. She had to sail these waters in this moment.

"What do you say to a contest?" asked Tobias, setting the cooking pot at the far margin of the firelight. "Pitching pebbles."

Matthew tossed a stone, and it landed in the center of the pot with a clang. "Make it a real game. Spitting."

The others all lobbed neat balls of phlegm at the pot, although Tobias's fell short—the only one not to hit at least the outside of the mark. Then Deborah cleared her throat and spat out a glob, half of which dribbled dispiritedly down her chin; the other half made it only as far as Matthew's boot. James and Tobias hooted with laughter as Deborah winced at her performance; she'd seen men spit her whole life and always assumed it would be easy, but she'd never had the occasion to try before. Little seemed to be going right this evening.

Matthew wiped his toe against the grass and said, "What, were you raised by maiden aunts?"

"No," she said, conscious of the heat coming off her face.

"You certainly spit like one," he said, and the others guffawed even louder.

"You going to let him call you that?" asked Tobias when his laughter had subsided.

"Of course he is," said Matthew, giving Deborah's shoulder a shove. "Robert doesn't want a fight."

"I'll save my fighting for the British," Deborah replied. Matthew pushed her once more, but Deborah ignored him. She'd seen this behavior with the Thomas boys, even at Sproat's now and then—how boys or men goaded each other into blows over petty matters. Any fight here would lead to a flogging, and that was no petty matter. There was a time, she knew, when she would have risen to the bait, when her anger lurked right below the surface, but those days of evil temper had subsided now that she was in the company of men.

"Let it be, Matthew," said James, who had returned to pitching pebbles.

"Come on, Tobias," said Matthew. "There must be better games afield."

The two of them walked down the slope, and Deborah watched James toss stones, listening to them ping off the pot. "Want to learn how to spit?" he asked. Without waiting for an answer, he explained. "It is better if you clear your nose, thus." He gave a big snort and then spoke thickly through the phlegm. "It's heavier, you see."

Deborah watched with mild disgust as James moved his tongue about his mouth and explained how to form the phlegm into a ball. He launched it at the pot, landing it square in the center. "Now you try."

She did her best to imitate him and managed to propel a glob most of the way toward the target.

"Practice," said James, lowering his voice to a harsh pitch like Munn's. "We can't have weak spitters in this company."

Robert spat until his mouth went dry. His last effort had hit the pot's rim—better than Tobias had managed, though not as good as Matthew or James.

"That's the spirit. You may have been raised by maiden aunts, but we'll send you back to them a changed man."

True enough, Robert thought, *true enough*.

CHAPTER NINE

Tobias, the remains of his blond hair crumpled from sleep, had started a fire and set a pot to boil by the time Deborah crawled out of the tent the next morning, her letter box under her arm. From the undergrowth, a few birds called—one of them a gurgling, watery cry that she did not recognize—and homesickness tugged at her, as a goat will tug at an apron, relentless and demanding. Tobias sat cross-legged near the fire, picking at his coat. "Fleas," he said, holding up his pinched fingers. He tossed the pest into the flames and set about searching the wool for others.

Deborah opened the lid of her box and brought out the quill, ink, and paper. With a last glance at Tobias, she began to write.

My Dear Jennie:

Why would any woman want to marry a man? I am at West Point, sharing a tent with three other recruits, and I must ask you this. As I sit here, I can hear the snores of two of my fellows busily sleeping off last night's rum. And across from me the third sits, pick-

ing fleas off his coat and tossing the vermin into the flames. He seems to delight in consigning these pestilential mites to hell.

But I count myself among the ranks of these men and have been wielding a musket and running up hills along with them. Let me tell you about our uniform: buff trousers, a plumed cap, and a blue coat with white facing. Jennie, I am in the light infantry! I do not need to tell you how strange this uniform feels, that one such as me should wear the clothes of this regiment. Best of all, I have some new shoes to wear.

I would not want you to think that my companions are a sorry lot. They are fine boys. I have spoken most with Tobias, formerly a tailor, and he seems observant and quick to learn. He likes to read and can play the flute. I think that if he were not forced to be a soldier, he would be a most gentle fellow, one you might like very much. He is certainly much quicker than James, who is a great bear. James can fall asleep at a moment's notice and takes much joy in simple pleasures, like a good tune or a fresh loaf of bread. He is more jovial than Tobias, and often makes me laugh. For both of them, I feel pity, as they did not enter the army of their own free will. James's master sent him, and Tobias came in his weaker brother's stead. Despite this, they work hard and are amiable. The third, Matthew, ran away from home to join up. He is a coarser sort, though I have had no trouble with him, and he does work hard and is pleasant enough.

I wish I could say the same of the officers and drill practice. Jennie, I have never felt like such a fool! We spent much of yesterday learning to walk in a straight line, and the sergeant barked at any who fell behind, as I did. But life here begins to make sense. There are rules and orders and all seems fair, even though it is harsh at times. I like our Corporal Booth. He reminds me a bit of Mister Leach, with his round, bald head and his stock of stories.

I have just now read over my words at the start of the letter and find myself thinking that apart from you, there is no one I would rather share a tent with than these fellows. There is no one else in

Middleborough that I miss in the least. Was I such an ornery sort? Others called me cold or thought me severe. I know that when I was at my loom, I brooked no idle chatter. But here I am mostly at ease with my fellows. Perhaps, as it was so often with the two of us, it is that we share a common task. More, I am now appreciated for my capabilities, while at home they were regarded as failings. My severity is an asset at drill, and my cold reserve befits a soldier who might be called on to kill. But when we are not on guard or on parade, I can let this rigidity in me soften and be at leisure as I never was in Middleborough. Many in Middleborough wished to send me to the cooper's and have me safely secured by iron hoops. Here, though, I feel no such constraints. There are not rules so much as expectations, a code by which I am pleased to abide.

I think of you every day, Jennie. Send me word when you are able.

With Love,
Robert Shurtliff

Robert put down the quill and flexed his fingers, which were stiff from writing. He read the letter through once more, making sure that he hadn't said anything that might arouse suspicion if an officer or someone from Middleborough read it. Assured that the contents were innocuous, he looked up to find Tobias watching him. "To your mother? Or a sweetheart?" Robert blushed but didn't deny it. Tobias prodded him again. "Think she'll stay true?"

"I hope so."

Certain the ink was dry, Robert folded his letter and addressed it. Matthew emerged from the tent, rubbing his eyes and releasing a gargantuan yawn. Tobias offered to cook porridge, and Robert put the letter in his coat and the letter box by his blanket. James was still snoring away, unmindful of the noise and the sunlight.

Back outside, Robert poured molasses into his porridge and

washed it down with tea. Matthew had heard that good card games could be found in another company, while Tobias argued for getting his laundry done early. Deborah was unsure if he meant that literally or not but didn't want to inquire further. She'd made fool enough of herself the previous night.

As the others debated the order of the day, Robert stood up. "I'm going to attend the chapel service. Care to join me?"

"No, but offer up a prayer on my behalf," said Tobias.

"He'll need it," added Matthew.

Tobias rolled his eyes and waved good-bye.

Robert squared his hat and set out across the parade ground. Chapel ought to provide a chance to sit in quiet, and he craved a moment alone. It hadn't dawned on Deborah how much solitude she had had at the loom, and how she would miss the hours spent alone with her thoughts. Sergeant Munn hadn't been specific in his directions, so Robert wandered over to the edge of the camp, doubled back, and then walked past the officers' houses. Eventually he reached a clearing with rows of benches and a rough lectern at the front, where a preacher waited for the congregation to assemble.

Robert chose a bench in the middle and studied the preacher; he was a short man, older than most of the troops, with mottled skin. His flesh hung slack at his throat like a turkey's wattle, but his bones jutted like a scarecrow beneath his simple, black garments. He offered a smile, giving Deborah hope that his sermon wouldn't be like the preaching at Mr. Thomas's congregation, full of hellfire and the lurking presence of sin. Soon after Robert sat down, Sergeant Munn arrived, taking the bench behind him. They began with a hymn and Robert joined in on a verse, singing gruffly. All around, the trees' leaves dappled green and blue above him, the forest inviting his mind to wander. It reminded her of the services she had attended when she first joined the Baptist congregation. They had not yet built a church and often worshipped outdoors, or as Elder Backus said, in the full of God's creation. She liked the simplicity of it. There was none of the status and hierarchy of a Congregational service, just pure spirit and a close attunement to the inner light.

The sermon contained a patchwork of aphorisms, Bible verses, and quaint advice to avoid drink, stay virtuous, and keep clean. When he had concluded, the preacher called for them to pray together, and Robert bowed his head and spoke aloud the Lord's Prayer. "Let this be a time of quiet reflection," the minister intoned.

Deborah formed silent words. *Lord, take care of Jennie in my absence. Provide someone to look after her while I am not there. And, Lord, thank you for bringing me safely to this day.* She paused, keeping her eyes closed. *Keep me strong and steadfast, Lord. Amen.*

Another hymn, and then everyone stood to offer the peace around. When he went to shake Sergeant Munn's hand, Robert hesitated, thinking he should salute, but Munn extended one of his massive palms. "We're all equal in God's eyes," he said. And even though his hand engulfed Robert's, Munn's grip didn't crush Robert's fingers. "It is good to see you here, Robert, but you didn't manage to bring any of your mates."

"No, sir. They were still abed or eating breakfast when I left."

"No matter."

The minister offered a benediction, and the congregation began to disperse.

"Are you headed back toward your tent?" Munn asked.

"Yes, sir."

"I'll show you a shortcut."

They took a narrow path that skirted the cluster of officers' houses that Robert had bungled through earlier, and soon emerged near the commissary. After the shade of the woods, the sunlight made him squint.

"On a morning such as this," Munn said, "one sees God's glory. We need such mornings. It is hard work we do here. And I don't mean the training. For all the importance of drill—don't question that, Robert—it is harder yet to go into battle, to shoot, to kill."

Robert looked up at the sergeant, taking in the bulk of his shoulders and chest. He was built like an ox; it was difficult to imagine that he found anything hard. "Do you think, sir, that we'll be called into battle soon?"

"In my years, I have found it best not to anticipate the Lord's will but to let it come. I imagine life as a road. We must walk it, to be sure. It will not advance on its own beneath our feet. But it will bend and twist as it wishes, as God wishes it to."

"Yes, sir," Robert said, but did not agree. If he had held that belief, then he would still be in Middleborough, at the loom or worse. No, he had to believe that one worked with Providence to forge one's own fate. That on the path of one's life there could be a crossroads—a moment of decision for the daring to seize.

Munn pursed his lips, staring at Robert, and seemed to read his mind. "You disagree? It is fine if you do. I suspect that most lads disagree with the thoughts of their elders. Certainly, I did when I was seventeen. Here, at least, you may state your disputes. Not on the drill field."

Robert weighed his words carefully, still unused to superiors asking his opinion. "I was thinking, sir, of Jacob wrestling the angel at the Jabbok River; how sometimes we might win something, as Jacob wins a new name, if we have the boldness to fight on our own behalf. It seems to me that the future and one's fate might work this way."

Munn nodded. "Perhaps when this war is done you will become a preacher, Robert. Those are wise words."

She tried to hold in a laugh, but couldn't. The thought of herself as a minister was beyond ridiculous. "Thank you, sir," she said, not wanting to offend the sergeant, but Munn was gazing off into the distance, as if still mulling Robert's words.

"Yes, I would agree. There are causes worth fighting for. Causes greater than one's self or one's name. I believe all of us soldiers are knitted together in one now."

Their conversation had carried them across the sun-splashed

drill fields to the top of the slope where the company's tents were aligned.

Robert took the letter from his coat. "I'd like to post this, sir."

"I'll take it to the captain's tent, then." Robert passed the letter over. "You've a tidy hand, Shurtliff."

"Yes, sir. I had a meticulous teacher." Her knuckles smarted at the memory of Widow Thacher's instruction on the alphabet.

"That's the best sort," Munn said. "God bless, Robert; I bid you good day."

"Thank you, sir."

HE FOUND THE OTHERS ALREADY back from their adventure, such as it was. The prices were high, the lines were long, the ladies were diseased; they each had an excuse for why they had not completed their mission.

"Did you see a pasture on the way to chapel, Robert?" Matthew asked.

"Not a sheep in sight," Robert said, with mock solemnity. "I imagine they've scampered off in fear long ago."

"Eaten or buggered. What a fate," added Tobias.

"Might I borrow your copy of *Robinson Crusoe*?" Robert asked.

"Of course. I'm going to try my luck at fishing."

"And I'll try my luck at dice or cards, if I can find a game," said Matthew.

The two of them headed off, and Robert opened up Tobias's book, skipping to his favorite section, where Crusoe begins domesticating the goats of the island. He had read only a few pages when James interrupted.

"Robert, could I ask a favor?"

"Certainly."

"I saw you have a writing box. Can you take down a letter to my mother?"

"I would be happy to do so."

As Robert set up his ink and paper again, James sat beside him. He watched Robert's movements keenly and said, "I learned my letters and my numbers, but they never held my interest. Not of much use to a blacksmith."

"What would you like to tell your mother?"

James scratched at the stubble on his jaw, making a rough noise that Deborah envied. "Tell her I am fine and healthy and fed well."

"Do you think so?" Robert asked as he dipped the quill and began to write.

"Better than I got from my master."

She supposed that was one advantage to working in the kitchen, as she had at the Thomases' and at Sproat's on occasion: it was easier to sneak a bit of food for oneself. "What else should I write?"

"Tell her the march was long and tiresome and that the Hudson is a grand river. She has never seen its like." He tapped his teeth, as if waiting for inspiration. "What would you write to your mother, Robert?"

"I wouldn't," Robert replied. "I doubt my mother knows I'm gone." That was, perhaps, untrue. Word of the scandal and her flight had in all likelihood reached her relatives in Plympton. But she was certain that her mother didn't care. "I seldom have much to say to her."

"Then we are alike in that," James said. "I know one should honor one's mother and father. And I know she has done her best by me. But when my father died, she remarried, and I don't care for her new husband." James pushed his finger through the dirt, tracing loops and lines. "It is hard to be free of resentment."

"Because she apprenticed you so young?" Deborah said, thinking of her own life as well. "Or because of her choice of a second husband?"

"He is a hard man and stingy. Did I tell you that he turned me in to my master once? I'd gone home for a Sunday dinner and complained to my mother about how cold my master kept my sleeping quarters. When I returned to the shop, I had a beating waiting for me."

"There must be some secret league of misers that makes them honor-bound to report complaints."

"No secret league could abide having him as a member. Besides, he wouldn't pay the dues." James waved a hand, as if fending off flies. "Ah, I should put it from my mind. He's far away."

"Is there anything else I should write?"

"Could you tell her something of our company? How it is a special group of infantry and we were selected . . ." Pride edged James's voice, and Robert bent to the task, describing the lights and the honor of being in their ranks. "And a word on our tent. Write that I'm staying with good lads, not as quarrelsome a group as frequented the tavern in Bellingham. Except Matthew, but you needn't mention that. Say that my mates are fair and kind and chapel-going."

Robert feared the letter veered into the terrain of fiction, but he wrote what James requested. When he had finished, he read it back to James, and James clapped his approval. "Just right," he said. "Do folks at home call you Bob or Robert?"

"A little of both," Deborah said, amused at the thought of Mr. Thomas referring to her as Bob. "Call me as you please." She felt comfortable around James. He was open and trusting and that, in turn, made it easy for her to trust *him*. She liked the nickname, too.

Robert wrote the address as James instructed, and offered to post it; she needed to acquire more thread, as her recent tailoring had depleted her supply. At the regimental tent, Corporal Shaw took the letter from him.

"Writing to a lass at home, Shurtliff?"

"No, sir."

"I didn't think so." Shaw stared at the name and town.

"It's for James, sir." She made to step away, but Shaw leaned close.

"I hope you are staying out of trouble, Shurtliff. I wouldn't want to hear any . . . ill reports."

"No sir," she said, and turned from him, wondering whether he spoke this way to all the soldiers, or whether he had singled her out for some reason.

Puzzling this over, she walked to the commissary and obtained the thread she needed, then returned to her tent, where she found James sleeping and the others still off at games or fishing. She returned to her spot in *Robinson Crusoe* and sat down to read.

Tobias's arrival with a string of fish stirred James from his slumber, and the three of them set to cleaning and scaling. The alewives he had caught looked much like what the Thomas boys brought in from the Nemasket River. Robert and James listened to Tobias's reports of British movements in the area, and Robert marveled that Tobias had managed to get such information so quickly. Matthew brought food from the commissary when he returned, and James went to gather wood. Matthew produced a flask of rum after the meal—for he had been successful at dice—and they passed it around. When it reached her, Deborah handed it off without a drink.

"Come now, Bob," said James. "Not a drop?"

Tobias clapped her on the shoulder. "Have a taste, Robert." He pressed the flask back into her hand. Deborah weighed the possibilities, the flask warm in her hand. Should she let go of her aloofness, trading safety for the chance to belong? Or would she also be letting go of some strand of herself?

"A sip, Bob, raise it up!"

"I'll get my flute and we can have a proper night of it, if Bob'll stay outside with us."

Robert lifted the flask to his lips and tilted it, letting the rum flow cool across his tongue, then hot down his throat. Tobias's flute piped out the notes of "The Mason's Delight" and then switched to a jig. James clapped his hands. "I can't sit still through such a tune," he cried. "If only there was a woman to dance with." He pushed himself up from the ground and offered a hand to Matthew, who shook his head. He turned to Robert. "Come on, Bob, dance this jig with me. I'll even do the woman's part."

The rum had settled in Robert's stomach, spreading a pleasant muzziness throughout his chest and limbs. He let James pull him to his feet. "That's fine," he said. "You dance the man's part. I'll follow." Tobias played on while Matthew clapped the beat. James spun Robert, and it seemed to him that the stars above spun, too, as if the whole world had joined them in this dance.

THEIR LIFE AS REGULAR COMPANY members began, and the days and weeks took on a reassuring consistency. As the day's first business, they cleaned their muskets and uniforms and then presented themselves for roll call and inspection. The rest of the morning passed in drill or parade—except when a visiting dignitary or military figure, such as Baron von Steuben, received a special presentation and salute. Otherwise, they spent the afternoons engaged in a variety of chores: target practice or hauling wood, sentry duty or road clearing. Munn rounded them up for fatigues occasionally, sending them off on long, double-time marches or making them charge up embankments with their muskets fixed. Some nights were spent on guard duty—sleepless shifts in the woods beyond West Point. On his first such assignment, Robert had been especially watchful in the darkness, jumping at the wind or the flight of an owl. But gradually he learned that guard duty was mostly a matter of staying awake for the corporals or sergeants who came by at intervals to inspect. Of course, word would come of shots fired or sightings of loyalist riders in the area, but these were few and far between. Some duties spanned the whole day, like grass guard, when they took the regiment's horses out to some far pasture to graze. These chores brought him in contact with soldiers outside of his company, and at times he would work alongside Richard, the former miller's boy with whom he'd marched to West Point. Richard served in the officers' quarters and he always had good rumors to share, and sometimes good food, too.

Less enjoyable was Corporal Shaw, whose presence Robert could not seem to shake. Their paths crossed with some frequency: he would supervise them as they chopped firewood or unloaded supply wagons. He seemed to lurk about, appearing by their tent at odd hours. He tried to make conversation, inquiring about what chores they'd done that day or how guard duty had gone. Though the corporal presented a friendly demeanor, offering advice or even helping with a task, his presence made Robert uneasy.

Sergeant Munn was the other one who gave them grief. Daily, he yelled at James on the parade ground, and it was a rare session when the whole lot of them could escape his wrath at their sloppy turns or incorrect maneuvers. Robert saw Munn weekly at chapel, and the sergeant always paused for a kind word or to discuss a verse from the Bible. But this kindness disappeared during drill, when the sergeant would bark commands at them and scream in their faces whenever they made an error.

They all gradually improved at the manual exercise, and James turned out to be a good marksman. On the mornings when they practiced on wooden targets, he was often the first to shoot the nose off the figure. Robert learned to aim his piece, though he didn't care much for the shooting; the kick of the musket made his shoulder ache terribly. He preferred the deft movements of drill, the wheeling and turning, fluid and unified. Soon enough, new recruits joined the lights. Tobias pointed them out one afternoon, making their way through the tents in their civilian clothes. At last, the four of them no longer comprised the butt end of the company.

CHAPTER TEN

Sergeant Munn, in good spirits ahead of the Independence Day celebrations, had granted them an easy afternoon, and so the four of them sat cleaning their muskets in front of the tent. The bright sunshine made Robert sleepy, and he gave a start when Corporal Booth approached with a letter in his hand.

"Something for you, Shurtliff," he said.

The handwriting was plainly Jennie's, her letters formed just like Deborah's own, as they'd learned on the same slate. She touched a hand to the missive, as if she could feel the woman who wrote these words, and she was overwhelmed by the desire to be near her. She looked up at Booth. "Thank you, sir."

"Nothing for you fellows," Booth told the others. "Glad to see you tending to your pieces."

"Is there action expected?" Tobias asked from where he sat on the ground.

"You can never be sure," Booth said, scratching at the scar on his cheek. "The word is out that there is a spy in the regiment, someone passing word to the British or their supporters hereabouts. Keep your eyes open, your ears, too, and let me know if you see or hear anything."

Robert, thoughts focused on the letter in his hand, scarcely registered Booth's words. A spy had nothing to do with him or his mates. That was for officers to worry about. "Yes, sir," he mumbled.

"I hope your sweetheart sends good tidings, Shurtliff," Booth said. "Keep at those guns, boys." Whistling merrily, the corporal walked away.

Tobias rose and stretched his arms. "My gear is spotless, so I'm off. There must be a game of cards somewhere."

"Cards, now, is it?" said James. "Soldierly life has made you a gambling man?"

"Just what my mother feared," Tobias said with a half grin.

"I bet that's not all she feared."

"No harm in a game of cards," Tobias said. "I've found good fortune lately."

Matthew shot him a jealous look. "I'd like to join you and see if some of that good fortune rubs off. But there's still rust on my plate. I'm going to have to scrub it with sand."

"You should have kept it better covered in oilcloth," Tobias chided.

"Wish your mouth would rust shut," Matthew said, but Tobias had already set off down the slope.

James continued to polish the barrel of his musket, and Robert unfolded the letter.

My Dear Robert,

What a month has passed. The apple trees have bloomed. The yard is full of little peepers. I know you liked the tiny chicks.

I received your letter, and you asked about news. The town is quiet as always. There was one stir, concerning a woman that ran away. The justice sent out men and they put up signs asking for her whereabouts, but no one has heard a thing since. There are rumors, of course. Some say she had a man in another town. Others say she ran off to Boston. I even heard that she went to New Bedford and signed on a ship. I don't think any of these are true.

When I happened to be at Leach's store last week, I heard a young man from the Baptist congregation say that his church had lately met to vote on an excommunication. It was of this same fugitive woman. I tried my best to overhear the tale, but all I know is that she was voted out of the church for some conduct about town. Mister Leach said he knew the woman and remembered her fondly as a great patron of his chapbooks, and he found it hard to believe that she would engage in immoral behavior. But the Baptist man said the elders had put the matter to vote and removed her from their fellowship. As for me, I side with Mister Leach.

No doubt you have exciting news of your own, but this is all the talk in town. A clerk to the lawyer Mister Israel Wood was attacked the night that this woman fled. You know how rare any violence is in Middleborough. Rumors spread that perhaps the woman had attacked him, but the clerk says that is not so. He says two men robbed him and beat him senseless. Our town has never known the like.

You must tell me more about how you are. Your health and your thoughts. It is not easy to be a soldier, and I do worry about you. I pray that you are safe.

It is late afternoon here. I want to send this off before Mister Leonard comes home. I cannot write all that I feel. Have courage and be strong.

Your Loving Friend,
Jennie

As Deborah read the letter, the world around her gradually faded away; she saw nothing but the words on the page. When she reached the end, she read it again. How like Jennie the letter was:

full of words of reassurance, gentle thoughts and prayers, honest reports, and the quotidian matters of life. Even the bad news, that of her excommunication, was salved by the kind comments from Mr. Leach and Jennie.

"Is everything well at home, Bob?" James's voice startled Deborah.

"Aye. Just remembering."

"I know," said James with a sigh. "Sometimes it is possible for happy news to make one somber if you are not there to share it."

Deborah turned back to Jennie's words. They conjured up a familiar scene before her eyes: Jennie with feed in her apron pocket, the chicks little balls of fluff, tumbling one over the other, clumsy with greed. Mr. Leach . . . The image of his face wavered in Deborah's mind, his bald head merging with Booth's bald head, but the visage remained distant and out of focus. She couldn't recall it. Loneliness settled upon her like a heavy blanket, a weight to be borne. And the Baptists. She imagined it had been Ezekiel who had raised the matter; she could hear their scathing words about the morals of Deborah Samson. It was not sorrow so much as regret that she felt. *Regret? About leaving? Never. About not being there. About abandoning Jennie. About, in some sense, abandoning Deborah, and not being able to stand up for her.* Robert felt himself torn asunder and wished that he could be so in a physical sense—rent like a thin garment, a piece of him still there, a piece of him here. That he could lead two lives. *But aren't I?* He closed his eyes and rubbed at them with the heels of his palms. Maybe he could keep this feeling at bay, hold himself together by writing. He pulled out his letter box and inked the quill.

Dearest Jennie,

Do you recall the fair that came to Middleborough years ago? I could not have been more than fifteen at the time. I am thinking of how we set the Thomas boys to watching a mummers' play and sneaked off, the two of us, to the prognosticator's tent. What an odd man. He haunts my dreams still, with those dark eyes. I am thinking of him now because of your letter. That day I was bold enough to ask him how it was that he came to know the future. Do you remember that he leaned close and said that the spirits told him? I wish I had such a spirit now. I wish I could be like Saul and bid some witch of Endor to summon up a Samuel for me. Not so much to know the future, though perhaps I wouldn't mind that, as to see the present, and to be shown that you fare well. To know the details of what transpires while I am away. It feels as though Middleborough is frozen in place, turned to rock in my absence. I imagine that if I were to return, I would find it exactly as it was when I stepped away. But your letters tell me that life goes on. And I am not there. I am sad about this. At the same time, I am not sad. I am divided, apart from myself in so many ways. This is why I wish I could have that spirit—to float between these selves and keep them whole.

The beat of the drum made Robert set down the quill, and he had barely cleaned the ink from the nib when Tobias came running back to the tent.

"Inspection," he panted. "Look sharp." Robert stowed his letter box in the tent and then hurried to get in line. Munn stood at the top of the slope, his arms crossed over his massive chest, rocking back and forth on his heels. Corporals fanned out into tents, with Booth ducking into the one across the path and Shaw coming to a halt in front of them. "Stay here," he ordered, and slipped inside their tent. Robert could hear him rummaging about—a clatter of metal, the shuffling of cloth and paper. He emerged with a stack of papers tied up in leather and a letter box that Robert recognized as his own. Squatting before them, Shaw sorted through the papers, examining the contents and squinting at the letters. Then he stood and shoved the jumbled sheaf into Tobias's arms. "Your mother seems to think highly of you, Hall. You had best quit your drawing and find something else to occupy yourself. Can't have details of the fort lying about." Robert saw the crimson of Tobias's cheek, and then Shaw pushed the letter box into Robert's chest. "And mind what you are writing to your sweetheart, Shurtliff." Now it was his turn to blush as Shaw walked away.

Robert turned to his fellows, wondering if they thought he was the spy. He could offer to let them read his letter to Jennie so they could see there was no harm, but before he could speak, James cut in. "What a bastard. If anyone is guilty of spying, I say it's Shaw. Sneaking around at all hours, trying to catch a peek of anything he can."

"That's the truth," said Matthew, who glared after the corporal.

"With eyes like that, I imagine he can catch a glimpse of everything," muttered Robert. "Even what's behind him."

"Besides, what would one of us have to tell the British?" James continued. "That the wagons of flour come every other week, or that the best dice games are over with the Third Connecticut Regiment? Who is he trying to fool?"

Sergeant Munn came down the row, and they fell silent. He paused in front of them. "Clean your kits and wait for the call to the parade ground." He pointed at Matthew. "Get every whisker off your face, or I'll shave you in front of the company." Then he turned to James and grabbed his sleeve. "Torn along the seam. Sew it up or the whole thing will be in shreds." He poked Robert in the chest. "You've got ink smeared on your cheek. You aren't fresh recruits anymore. If you don't present yourselves in proper order, I'll have the lot of you flogged."

"Yes, sir," Robert said, but Munn had already moved down the line. Robert resisted the temptation to rub at his cheek.

"You're going to get us all whipped for your laziness, Snow," said Matthew.

"He was just as angry about your whiskers," James replied. "You'd best get shaving."

"I don't need you telling me what to do." Matthew gave James a shove.

"Don't lay your hands on me again," said James.

The two stared at each other for a moment and then Matthew grabbed his shaving kit from the tent. "I'm off," he said.

Tobias, ignoring the tension, examined his musket. "I think all is in order. Time for a wash." And he headed in the same direction as Matthew.

James was breathing heavily as he shrugged off his coat to examine the seam Munn had pointed out. "Sometimes . . . that Matthew . . ."

Robert rubbed at his cheek with his coat sleeve. "He is quick to anger," he said. "Is the ink gone?"

James caught hold of his breath. "Yes, your cheeks are as clean and smooth as ever. At least you don't have to bother with shaving." He peered at the hole in his sleeve. "I should have tended better to my uniform." He sat on the ground next to Robert, who marveled at James's ability to find equilibrium so quickly, to let his anger and resentment go. "Will you show me how to sew this, Bob?"

Robert leaned over and looked at the seam. "Tobias is much the better tailor."

"I'd just as soon learn from you. He may be the better tailor, but I wager you are the better teacher."

James's praise pleased him. "Go fetch needle and thread, then. My sewing kit is next to my letter box, unless Shaw has tossed it about in his searching."

"Shaw . . ." James let the rest of the sentiment go unuttered as he picked out a needle and some dark thread from the sewing kit. Then he sat cross-legged by Robert's side. He licked the thread and, with some effort, passed it through the needle's eye. Fixing the end with a knot, he pushed the needle into the wool of his coat.

"Don't pull the fabric so," Robert said, leaning over. "But don't let it bunch either. Keep a steady pressure, else you'll sew in a wrinkle." He watched James's thick fingers push the needle down and draw the thread through. "That's it. Now keep the stitch small and line it up straight with the one before." His words echoed those spoken by Widow Thacher so many years ago, and the memory caught Deborah by surprise. Those had been, in many ways, the happiest years of her life. The three of them in a house together, an all-female sphere. She hadn't minded it then. Maybe it became a problem only when men were introduced. She watched James fumble the needle. A world without men. What would that be like? Fine, as long as the women were more like Jennie and less like Mrs. Holbrook. Deborah released a sigh through her nose. Perhaps the problem lay not with men or women, but with herself. She was ill-content. Restless, she had often been called. Her eye was always on the next pasture, the further horizon.

They sat side by side, Robert leaning over now and then to survey James's progress or to offer advice. By the time Matthew returned, freshly shaven, James had closed up the hole in his sleeve with stitches in a tidy, if not perfectly straight, row. "Thank you, Bob," he said. "Now I ought to tend to the rest of my equipment."

JULY FOURTH ROLLED AROUND, AND Robert found himself almost too exhausted from all the extra guard duty and drill to join in the festivities. But with the whole regiment gathered on the parade ground, Colonel Meigs read the Declaration of Independence, and Robert had to blink back tears. A quick glance told him that James was weeping as well. Then a throaty huzzah went up, along with a few hats, and the spirit of the day captured him. In all the drill and duty, he could lose sight of the larger purpose, but those words reminded him of what they were fighting for.

After boat races on the Hudson, a veritable battalion of drums and fifes led in the visiting dignitaries, and then the parade began.

His company did little more than the standard maneuvers and marching in formation, which he thought might be disappointing, but he tried to imagine how it would appear from the outside, from a visitor's viewpoint. The company surely looked numerous and precise, the very standard of militarism. They wheeled and split, faced left, and then marched off, turning the grounds over to the cavalry's demonstration.

In the evening, fusillade after fusillade of cannon and rocket fire filled the air, popping and booming. In the relative silence after each report, Robert could hear the squawk of disturbed geese and the lesser pop of a musket as some soldier tried to bring down dinner for tomorrow. Afterward, sergeants dispensed a double ration of rum, and a band tuned up, the scratchy sound of a fiddle floating across the parade ground.

James grabbed Robert's elbow. "Come on, Bob!" The two of them jogged over to the music. To their surprise, men in regimentals were dancing with women, their skirts snapping. The mothers and wives and sweethearts of Laundrytown had been allowed into camp for the celebration and displays, and it was a proper dance—what the folks here called a cotillion but what was known in Middleborough as a longways. There weren't enough women to go around, of course, but everyone formed up in two lines. There were circle turns and handoffs, partners passed left and spun right. The fiddles and flutes played tune after tune, and Robert found himself clasping hands with Richard, the miller's boy, and the two of them leaned back and whooped as they spun. Then he passed the boy down the line and gave a courtesy turn to a woman old enough to be his grandmother, one hand in the small of her back. "Don't twirl me too fast," the woman said. "I'm not a young chicken anymore." She laughed, displaying what few teeth still lodged in her gums. Robert gave her a gentle rotation and handed her down the line with a half bow. He'd never danced the man's part before, but the moves were simple enough, and goodness knows he had watched many times from the side of someone's barn as Jennie spun in a young man's arms.

It was a shock to see the women, the younger ones clustered together between songs, whispering and laughing. With their hair done up in curls and lace cuffs dangling from their wrists, they seemed a separate species. He watched how they moved, the slight steps, the sway of their hips—he knew he had walked like that once. But the movements of parade and drill already felt more natural and comfortable to him; in them he knew a grace and dignity he'd never possessed as a woman. A gentle elbow in his ribs caught his attention, and he turned to find James at his side. "I bet they'd dance if you asked. . . ." The band had started a reel, and groups of six were forming across the grounds.

Robert shook his head. "I'm certain they're all spoken for."

"For a handsome lad, they could be unspoken." James offered him a flask, but he waved it off. "Well, then, will you partner me, Bob?"

"Of course," Robert said, and the two of them joined up with two other couples and began the dance. With James's arm around his back, they slip-stepped up and spun off, turning around the others. Then they wove back up the center, this time with Robert's arm around James, and Robert turned him out and around. James laughed, kicking up his heels, and they spun each other before making way for the next couple. Dizzy and giddy, Robert thought it was better than any dance in Middleborough. James's arms were stronger and more graceful than those of any other partner—and best of all, they traded off the lead with every turn, neither one possessing or controlling the other.

After that dance, Corporal Booth came over, his bald head slick with sweat, and offered them both a drink of his rum. "My throat is dry from all the singing." Robert declined his offer. He was already weary, and the rum would only make him drowsier. "If you're not going to drink, then I'll volunteer you for grass guard tomorrow, Shurtliff," Booth said with mock severity.

"Now there's punishment for being sober?"

"Tonight there is. Report at dawn." He waggled the flask.

Robert clapped James on the back. "Enjoy the dancing without me, then. I should get some sleep." He headed away from the parade ground, the music fading behind him. As he walked toward his tent, he hummed the tune of the reel, feeling James's arms around his shoulders, drawing him close.

CHAPTER ELEVEN

Mist from the Hudson brooded over West Point as Robert walked from his tent to the stables, where he found a sergeant and three other privates, two of whom, Luther and Charles, he recognized from Sunday services. For the rest of the regiment, the fifth of July would be a half holiday, a chance to sleep in. It would all balance out, Robert thought; the others would spend the afternoon in drill, but grass guard was never as taxing as those maneuvers. The sergeant, haggard after what must have been a long night's duty, led them west.

"Down this road to the far pasture," he said, biting back a yawn.

The sergeant watched as the four of them wrangled the regiment's horses, hitching them onto lines for the walk out to the pasture, and Robert marveled at how easy this task now seemed to him. Each private took a line of five horses in one hand, their muskets in the other, and with the sergeant in the lead, they headed down the road, which was bordered by cleared land used for crops or grazing. Indeed, Robert had spent several afternoons hauling stumps out of such fields to ready them for sowing. But he had never been this far along the road before. In the meadows on either side he could see the horses of other regiments already out to pasture. He flicked the lead line idly; it was early, it was hot. In the hour since he had arisen, the mist had already gone to tatters and burned away.

Luther, walking ahead, called to Robert, "I suppose this is our reward for being sober."

"Aye," he said back, "and it might be better than a pounding headache."

Within another mile, the road petered out into scrub, with a large, lush meadow on one side. The tired sergeant was helping Luther affix leather thongs to the horses' forelegs—hobbles to keep them from straying too far—when Robert came up with his string of beasts. The sergeant handed him some thongs as well, and he worked patiently with the horses, who seemed as weary as he was, lazily swinging their tails, occasionally snuffling at each other. When he had finished, he unclipped the lead and let them into the meadow. The grass, heavy with dew, bowed over, reaching only to Robert's knees as he waded in after the horses; by noon it would be dry and standing straight, tall enough to reach his waist.

The soldiers dispersed to the corners of the field, and the sergeant stood on the road. He would stay until another sergeant or corporal replaced him, or, judging by the prodigious size and quantity of his yawns, he might walk down the road and meet his replacement halfway. The rules of grass guard were simple: spread out, mind the horses enough that they don't wander off, look somewhat alert, and keep your musket close at hand.

Robert perused the edge of the meadow, where he found a little rivulet and washed his hands and face. He liked the tranquillity of grass guard—the meadow smelled fresh and clean, and there was space about him, a feeling he seldom enjoyed in camp. For a while, he sat at the edge of the water, listening to its playful sound and the swishing of the horses through the grass. He took a deep drink and then eyed the sun, so bright it seemed to have burned a hole in the sky, before he rose to count the horses. Their glossy backs were clearly visible over the grass, though he couldn't see any of his fellow guards. As he walked, he stirred a grouse from its lair, and it rose up, corkscrewing, in a whirl of feathers. The suddenness of it, right there under his feet, set his heart leaping; he wished he'd had his gun ready. Robert shifted his musket from left hand to right. Next time, he'd be prepared.

At noon he leaned his musket against a tree and sat by the creek to eat, drinking from his canteen and filling it again, and wondering whether some sergeant had rousted James from his blanket and how much headache powder had been dispensed that morning. He thought about soaking his feet in the water, but it wouldn't do to be caught like that. Though he hadn't seen him yet, there was some corporal or sergeant who had drawn the unfortunate duty of overseeing them, and it would mean extra work or even lashes to be caught sleeping, reading, or otherwise unobservant. Grasshoppers reveled in their clicking din, and swallows dipped low to scoop them up. The sun seemed to resist its slide toward the horizon, content to linger and wallow in its warmth.

Stepping out of the meadow into the woods, he took a few paces into the shade of the trees, where he unbuttoned his pants and relieved himself near a blueberry bush. He was doing up the flap when he heard a voice behind him.

"Odd way for a lad to make water."

He grabbed his musket and spun around. It was Corporal Shaw, chewing on a long strand of grass, which bounced up and down when he spoke. "In fact, you squat more than any other soldier I know. And I doubt you have the runs, Robert Shurtliff."

Robert swallowed, throat dry. Did Shaw know, or was he just guessing? This was not a contest he could win: at some point, proof would be demanded, and he had no proof to offer.

"Well, Robert? What have you to say?" Shaw stepped closer, a smile lifting the corners of his mouth. Robert gripped the stock of his gun, sun-warm under his hands. After a month of training, he was stronger than this man; he knew it. But what would violence gain him? Shaw's wide mouth stretched further up, as if he were enjoying this, the lids of his buggy eyes half-closed in a gaze that mixed close scrutiny with a sort of pleasure. Idly, the corporal reached one hand toward the pistol at his waist, toward the buttons on his trousers.

A hawk's cry, sharp and close, sounded overhead, and both of them looked up. In that instant, Robert had to choose: confront Shaw or run. Just as he took a step back—better a deserter than face total humiliation—a shot rang through the woods. He thought for an instant that Shaw had fired, but he couldn't possibly have loaded in that narrow split of time. Spinning to face the noise, Robert saw three or four men moving through the meadow low and fast, like swimmers in a lake. The report of another shot, this one closer, snapped his eyes back to Shaw, and he saw the corporal clutch his shoulder and fall to his knees. Robert stepped away. With a shower of bark, a man dropped from the tree they'd been standing by, let go of his spent musket, and reached for his sidearm. In one smooth motion, Robert fixed the bayonet on his muzzle and charged before the man could aim. His blade caught the man in the chest and neck, and Robert felt flicks of heat as the man's sidearm discharged near his face. Lifting his blade from the man's body, he drew back, stabbed again.

More shots rang out from the grass; he turned from the body to see a brown-coated man mounting a horse—he must have cut the hobbles—and Robert snatched a cartridge from his box, ripped open the corner, and primed and loaded his musket. Counseling himself to calm, he raised the gun and took aim. The kick made him step back and steady himself against a tree trunk, but his shot went true enough to catch the rider in the upper arm. He lurched forward on the horse's neck and disappeared into the woods before Robert could reload. He heard another shot from the direction of the road, then silence.

Robert faced Shaw, who knelt, one hand clenched near his collarbone, where his shoulder met his chest. Blood had soaked through the wool of his coat, spreading toward the line of buttons. As Robert watched, he slumped down, his forehead coming to rest on the ground. Robert's ears rang from the close-range shots, but over this he could hear a keening noise and now and then a mew of pain.

Still holding his musket, he squatted near Shaw's head and put a hand on his unwounded shoulder. "Here, sit against the tree." He pushed him back against the trunk. Shaw's eyes flickered, his face paler than milk. Turning to the body of the man he'd stabbed, Robert used his bayonet to cut a strip off the dead man's coat, pulled Shaw's hand away from the wound, and wrapped the wool around his shoulder. He helped Shaw press the wool against the wound, and then studied the body of the attacker. A few day's growth of stubble flecked a square chin and broad cheeks. His eyes stared, red-rimmed, already gone glassy; Robert held their gaze for an instant. He could almost believe the man was looking at something far off, something only he could see. If the attacker were clothed in regimentals, he would be indistinguishable from any Continental soldier. Nothing marked him as an enemy. Robert took a deep breath and reloaded his musket. "I'll return," he said to Shaw.

He hurried to the margin of the woods and then stalked the perimeter of the meadow, musket at the ready. Two other soldiers, Charles and the one he did not know, crouched near the road's terminus. Charles leaned against a boulder, musket in his lap, a wound in his leg showing through his breeches, and the other had his gun aimed at two black-coated men, one with a bloody head. All of them swiveled their heads as Robert approached, and Charles raised his musket before recognizing him.

"What should we do?" said the soldier guarding the men, his voice wavering. He clenched his musket in a brittle grip, the muzzle shaking as he kept it trained on the two prisoners.

"Steady," said Robert. "Are you injured?" The boy shook his head. He looked too young to be a soldier. Robert thought of all the drill that Munn had put them through and, watching the other's arms quake, he felt strength in his own. He was in the lights; he bore a confidence earned through all the exercises, the rude awakenings, the constant strain of daily chores. "Keep your weapon on these two. I'll bind them." He took some of the leather thongs they used to hobble the horses and wrapped them around the men's ankles and wrists, knotting the straps tightly.

Once he had finished, Robert turned to Charles. He could do little for the wound except tie a strip of cloth over it to stanch the bleeding. It did not look mortal, but he was no surgeon.

"Luther rode back for help," said Charles after Robert had finished his ministrations.

"What happened?" asked the other soldier. He'd let the barrel of his musket droop, as if he could not afford the effort to keep it level.

"Stand straight," Robert snapped, surprised by how much like Munn he sounded. "I don't know all that passed, but there are two men on the far side. One of them jumped out of a tree, he's dead. And the other . . . our corporal. Shaw. He's wounded." His own candor startled him but he took it in stride, realizing how he had been trained for this moment. It had become, since his arrival at West Point, almost a birthright, and now he was grown into it.

The other soldier's mouth gaped like a landed fish. "I heard the shots. My name is Jeremiah."

"Robert," he said. "I'll count the horses. You stand guard here. Keep that musket level and ready."

Six horses were missing, not including the one that Luther was riding for help. Robert glanced at the sun's arc, wondering what would happen next. A wave of guilt came over him that he hadn't been alert on guard, that he had allowed horses to be stolen and injury to come to his fellows. But Shaw had been in charge; Shaw had kept him from his duty. And now the corporal lay wounded and knew his secret. Robert puffed out his cheeks in a sigh. At least they had captured prisoners and therefore might gain information. How many attackers had swooped down? Would they come back for the two captured men? Charles had closed his eyes, but Robert could see him clench and unclench his jaw, his hands pressing the cloth tight against his leg. The other soldier, Jeremiah, stood with the butt of his musket on the ground and his eyes wide, staring off into the woods, as if at any moment they might explode with enemies.

"Get that musket level," he barked, and watched Jeremiah give a startled jolt, lift the gun to ready position.

The moment of authority faded against a chorus of doubt. Should he go back to Shaw? Would he tell what he had seen? Robert's first responsibility went to the safety of the troops, not his own reputation. He swallowed, his throat dry, and stayed where he was.

Hoofbeats came from the road; Robert kept his musket ready. Jeremiah held his gun close to his chest as if trying to wring comfort from it, and two sergeants appeared, trotting at the head of a squad of soldiers. One of the sergeants dismounted, while the other led the men across the meadow and into the woods.

"You there," the sergeant said to Jeremiah, "what happened?"

The boy stammered, "I was here, and then I heard shots, but I don't know . . ."

The sergeant frowned and turned to Robert. "What did you see?"

He gave a brief account of the shots across the meadow, the man in the tree, how Corporal Shaw had been shot, how he had stabbed his attacker and then fired at the man who'd ridden away. The sergeant nodded. "We ought to aid Shaw."

They left the horse with Jeremiah and crossed the meadow. Shaw still slumped against the tree, clenching the cloth, now blood-soaked, that Robert had given him. The sergeant knelt at his side, muttering, "Keep it from bleeding so much." Robert cut another strip from the dead man's coat and handed it to Shaw. The sergeant stood up to examine the corpse.

"Who do you think he is, sir?"

"A Tory. Or maybe just a bandit, thinking we're an easy mark after last night's celebration. It's a good thing not everyone was sleeping off their drink this morning."

"Aye. I am sorry for the loss of our regiment's horses, sir. More sorry for the injury. . . ."

The sergeant shook his head. "What matters now is that we salvage what we can and catch this rabble. The losses cannot be assigned to you." He pointed to the corpse. "You were alert. You did what you could. Now, we haven't men or time to spare. Haul this body in. Then come back for the corporal."

Robert nodded, his guilt partly assuaged.

The sergeant waded out into the grass, his head swiveling, surveying every direction. Shade still dappled the forest floor, and the brook still gurgled in the background. But true tranquillity had fled. Robert pulled his canteen from his belt, squatted by Shaw, and offered him a drink. The corporal did not open his eyes, but he swallowed and licked his lips, and water ran down his neck and collarbone, setting the dried blood on his coat flowing again, rivers within rivers. His lips moved, a nearly soundless effort. Robert leaned close. "Help . . . back . . ."

"Yes," Robert said, standing upright. "I'll come back to get you." He felt no tenderness for Shaw's crumpled form—even felt a twinge of cruelty welling up in him, and the desire to yank the corporal to his feet and make him walk on his own.

He swiveled away—letting Shaw stew there would have to be punishment enough—and went to the body; hefting a foot in each hand, he pulled it out to the grass, tugging it through the meadow. It weighed more than he thought it would, a weight that dragged on his shoulders. He had killed a man. He had driven his bayonet through him. His gorge rose, and he tasted vomit, slimy as an oyster;

he forced it back down. He had taken the life of another, and by what right? He was a soldier; he had to do his job. It had been the only course of action. At last he reached the edge of the meadow, laid the body where Charles and Jeremiah waited with the prisoners, and returned to Shaw.

Approaching, Robert saw Shaw's eyes, though glassy with pain, fixed on his. His look, knowing and sharp, cut through him. If only Shaw had been killed too. Robert leaned in. "What do you want, Shaw?" he asked, his lips next to his ear. "Do you want to ruin me?"

Shaw shook his head, his eyes closing again.

"What would it gain you, to expose me?" This close to him, he smelled his blood, the metal tang of it, felt the heat of the corporal's body, heard the short, shallow breaths. "I could have killed you or let you be killed. But I saved you. And now I'm going to help you again. Stand up."

Robert put an arm under Shaw's shoulder, and the corporal howled in pain. Robert put his other arm across Shaw's waist, seizing the cloth of his pants and coat, and pulled. Shaw levered himself against the tree trunk, the motion scraping bark loose; Robert smelled the rich sharpness of pine and hoped this would prove to be the right course of action. "Let's go, Shaw."

Shaw stumbled often and leaned heavily on Robert. Halfway across the meadow, he paused and used his hand to wipe his chin, where spit and snot had gathered. Robert offered him his kerchief. "Thank you," he said.

The feeling of Shaw's body made Robert shudder. He wanted to push him off and be free of the hot weight of his flesh, the dampness of his breath. More, he wanted to shake him, to grab him by his coat and rattle him until he promised not to tell. But he kept his arm around the corporal's waist and led him across the field.

Eventually the road came into sight, with the orderly line of trees and the blue of regimental coats. The sergeant helped Shaw and Charles onto horses and placed the two corpses across the back of another. As he turned to give orders to Robert, a clutch of mounted horses burst forth from the woods. Robert raised his gun, waiting. But he spotted the blue coats and saw they were Continentals leading another of the attackers, perhaps the one he had shot; blood matted the horse's coat, and the prisoner listed, swaying in the saddle.

A soldier cantered over to them and gave the sergeant a salute. "No sign of the other two," he said.

The sergeant signaled the men from the meadow, where they had corralled the last of the horses. The animals snorted and shied, eyes rolling after the sights and sounds of the afternoon, but the soldiers managed to hitch the horses together to lead them back to camp. As they hoisted the prisoners onto saddles, the angle of light shifted subtly, the sun gave up on the day, and, as if on cue, crickets began their chorusing.

The sergeant looked down the road, then at Robert and Jeremiah. "You two stand guard. I'll return to West Point with the prisoners. Some of our men are still in the woods. They'll be out before dark." He pointed to the other soldiers. "You four, set a perimeter on the far side. I'll see that you're relieved by midnight. Sharp eyes, lads."

Twilight bunched up beneath the trees and spread out along the road. Robert paced the edge of the meadow, thinking of Shaw's voice, how he leered. The hawk's cry, the musket's report, the bayonet. Each moment fixed, distilled, lodged in his mind like a splinter in flesh: inescapable, reverberating with every motion. He felt his face where the shot had flown by, searing a streak. The hot skin reminded him of how close he'd been and how close he still remained to danger, to death, or worse.

Even in the dark the heat lingered, and Robert kept himself alert by moving around and sipping cool water from his canteen. Jeremiah had long ago sat down on a stump, and now his musket fell from his hands, and his head drooped to his chest. Robert watched the circle of the moon grow smaller as it rose—hard and clear, no rain tomorrow—enjoying the shadows it cast onto the meadow, the way its wan light transformed the landscape, changing brown to silver, making the world more precious. Gently, Robert nudged Jeremiah with a toe. "The captain won't like it if you're dozing," he said. Jeremiah half-lifted his head before letting his chin loll to his chest again. The moon had dipped low when at last Robert heard footsteps on the road.

He stood poised with his musket across his chest, bayonet ready. "Who goes?"

"Sergeant Munn, with a squad to relieve you."

He did not lower the musket until the sergeant's face came into view, his bulky form unmistakable even in the poor light. The squad behind Munn stood at rest, and Robert set the gun against his shoulder at attention. Munn peered closely at him and then at Jeremiah asleep on the stump.

He strode over and said, "You there. Get up." He poked him with his boot, and Jeremiah jerked awake. The sergeant leaned over and picked up the fallen musket, shook it lightly. "Loaded. You could have killed someone by dropping this. Now stand up." Munn's lips twisted with displeasure, a look Robert knew well.

Jeremiah rubbed at his face. "I'm tired, sir. I've been out here since dawn." Robert could have told him that was the wrong thing to say.

The sergeant stepped close, gripped Jeremiah's coat—so tight the stitches seemed to groan—and tugged him to his feet, giving him an abrupt shake. "So has this soldier," Munn said, pointing at Robert. "And you don't see him complaining. That soldier is a man."

Robert pulled himself up straighter; the fatigue that had lurked in his legs and back vanished when he heard Munn's words. All the weeks of drill, the yelling he'd endured, the danger present in Shaw's knowledge—all of that vanished.

Munn slammed the musket against Jeremiah's chest and then stepped back to give the squad orders. He sent some of them to the far side of the meadow to relieve the other guards and set two in place of Jeremiah and Robert. He laid a hand on Robert's shoulder. "Get back to camp; get some well-deserved rest. You've done the lights proud."

"Aye, sir. Thank you, sir."

The other soldiers came across the meadow, and they all headed back to West Point, Robert and Jeremiah walking in the rear. The road ahead lay in darkness, and it was hard to imagine that they had walked down it just this morning; it felt as though days had passed. Jeremiah seemed to have nothing except sleep on his mind. But Robert could scarcely keep himself from turning around to look once more at the meadow, the site of his first battle. Over and over, he heard the same phrase in his mind: *that soldier is a man.*

CHAPTER TWELVE

"We heard about an attack—some soldiers came whooping through here with Munn," said Tobias as he gave his shoes a halfhearted polish.

"Aye," Robert said, "an ambush." He spooned out the story while they cleaned their uniforms and ate breakfast. He found it easier in the telling—leaving out certain details, such as how Shaw had encountered him, but describing the shots, the surprise, the bayonet. Speaking made it real again but also let him control it.

The others exulted over his killing of a raider and pressed him for details of the attack—about whether he'd been nervous. "Do you think Shaw will live?" James asked when Robert had finished his recounting.

"He took a ball to the shoulder, near to the collarbone," Robert replied. "One never knows how these things might heal." Putting his bowl down, he picked up his bayonet and began to clean the blade. Crimson blooms spread over the damp rag as he scrubbed.

Matthew let out a low whistle. "You really did it. I didn't think you could kill a man, Bob."

Robert ignored the barb in Matthew's comment and dried the blade. He hadn't thought he could either. Yet he had done so.

When they stood for roll and inspection, Munn paused for words. "I've passed a good report on to the captain, Shurtliff."

Booth waxed more effusive. "Your first live fire, eh? Did you piss your breeches?" He laughed. "I heard the other guard did. But he's not in the lights, eh?" He cuffed Robert on the shoulder before moving down the line to accost James about the lousy job of shaving he'd done. "You look like a monkey . . ." Robert heard, and then lost the drift, listened instead to those remembered words—*that soldier is a man*—the sense of rightness that had suffused him at that moment, that lingered still.

Then the manual exercise began, and the sun beat down, and another day charted its familiar course.

After the drill, Robert and his mates waited for the supply wagons to arrive. Robert stepped up to Munn as the sergeant tamped tobacco into his pipe. "Sir, might I see to Corporal Shaw? Last night . . ."

The sergeant's eyes flicked up. "Get you gone, now, Shurtliff." He turned his attention back to the pipe.

Robert hurried away, not wanting to hear the calls of his peers, who no doubt thought he was shirking his work. He crossed the parade ground and entered the infirmary, where he and James had carried a man their first night in West Point. A line of cots, most empty, stretched the length of the tent. Near the entrance, a soldier Robert didn't recognize sprawled unconscious or asleep, no wound visible. He walked to the next occupied bed, and there lay Shaw. The corporal's froggy eyes darted over Robert, his blue irises circumscribed by red rims, his lips crimson in comparison with the pallor of his cheeks.

"Truce?" Shaw said.

Robert nodded. He did not trust him.

Shaw licked his lips. "Who are you?"

"Robert Shurtliff."

"What are you running from?"

"I'm not here to tell stories. I'm as good as any man in this regiment, and you know it."

Shaw pushed with his good hand in an effort to sit up straight, wincing as he jarred his shoulder in the process. "There was a woman . . . joined up . . . years ago. She came to follow her sweetheart into the service. She didn't last but a day, and we found her out, hardly made it to muster . . . but here you are . . ." He reached to the other side of the bed where a stool held a tin mug, lifted it, sniffed the contents, and took a swallow.

"I saved your life," Robert said.

"I know it. I called truce."

"If you tell anyone, I'll . . ." Robert let the words hang there, unable to finish the sentence.

"What is it worth to you?"

What was it worth? The words were a fist to his stomach.

"Think on it," said the corporal, and waved his hand dismissively.

When he returned to his own tent, Robert found the others had been discharged from their duties as well. Tobias had already sought out a game of cards, and Matthew was off hunting. Only James remained by the tent, whittling at a stick. Robert retrieved his letter box and settled himself a short distance from James.

"What's that you're fashioning?"

"A spoon. Can't you tell?" He brandished the stick, which was yet an unshaped mass, slightly bulbous at one end. He gave Robert a wink. "And what love letters are you writing today?"

"It's as much a love letter as that's a spoon. Just writing to a girl

I miss." He busied himself sharpening a quill. For a time, he read over Jennie's letter to him and his own truncated reply, and listened to the sound of James's knife on the wood, patiently shaving away. Pushing aside worries about Shaw—he couldn't commit any of that to paper—Robert thought of the previous day, the grasses of the meadow, the sudden rupture of the noontime, the burn of powder in his nose. How quickly it all transpired. It left not a mark on him, and yet he felt . . . changed. What could he say? He thought of the warning he'd been given, the knowledge that someone was passing information, that perhaps even the attack on the grass guard had been a product of that spying. But the ambush had already happened, and he didn't see how this material could be harmful.

Dear Jennie,

My writing before was interrupted by a sudden inspection. Such is military life. We are afforded little in the way of privacy and free time, but in this manner I know our lives are similar.

I have been under fire for the first time. Before I tell you the story, I assure you that I am unharmed. It happened while I was guarding the regiment's horses. I still do not know who the attackers were. One dropped from a tree by my head, shooting a corporal, but I stabbed him with my bayonet.

You would not want me to write all of what happened next, Jennie. It took only a few moments. At the end of it, I killed one man and wounded another. The others on guard duty captured two prisoners. When additional soldiers came to our aid, they searched for the rest of the attackers.

Do you remember, Jennie, how we used to laugh at the swagger of men who had returned from serving in the militia? How these fellows, who had been boys fresh off the farm, came back like conquering heroes, and we could not fathom the alteration? To us, they were the same as always. Now I know why they carried themselves in that manner. There is a heavy weight on me, Jennie, and it takes all that swagger and bluff to hold it steady.

Yet, even as this new weight has settled, another has lifted. It is like the psalm says, I have passed through the Valley of the Shadow of Death. Now I stand on the other side and I feel that I stand taller and surer. I am more certain of who I am than I ever was before. Whatever the Elders or church leaders might say, I know that this is what God wants me to do. I know that this is how I am meant to serve.

I wonder how soon it will be before the whole company is called to action. There seems to be unrest hereabouts, and with our celebration of independence passed, we may be called to fight.

I enjoyed so much the news from town in your last letter. No doubt the clerk has recovered from his injuries, and I hope you will watch out for this band of robbers plaguing Middleborough. Though of late I struggle under heavy burdens, I daily rejoice at where I find myself. When I left you, it seemed as though fate had me in the straits; there was nowhere I could turn. Yet now I am through those narrows. Jennie—I never imagined how freedom would feel.

I send you all my love,
Robert

He wanted to write more about Shaw, to give voice to his fears and doubts, to disburden some of his anxiety. But he didn't dare. James stood up, brushing curls of wood from his lap, and walked over to squat by Robert's side. He put an arm about Robert's shoulders, and with his other hand he held out the wood he had been whittling. It was a fair spoon now, with a sturdy handle and well-shaped ladle. "For you," he said, and Robert took the spoon.

"Thank you, James," he said, surprised by the intimacy of the gesture.

"To honor the first in our band to be tested on the field of battle."

He spoke with mock solemnity. "You may not know how to spit, but you can kill."

Robert gave him a playful shove. "All those hours of drill paid off. Do you know, when I first arrived here and I was chosen for the lights, I thought they had made a mistake."

"I had the same thoughts about myself," James said. "Some days I still do."

"Nonsense. You're ten times as strong as I am, and a good shot besides."

"Strength isn't everything. I spend half the drill trying to tell my left foot from my right."

"Yet you're a fine dancer, James."

"What would Munn say to that? Robert Shurtliff suggests I think of the manual drill as a dance. . . ." He interrupted his words with laughter and then said, "Do you know, my birthday came a few days ago? Eighteen years old." He scratched at his nose. "That ends my indenture. If I were yet in Bellingham, I'd be a free man."

"But you still have three years to serve in the army. It's unjust that your master could send you in his stead when you had so short a term remaining."

"Perhaps," said James. "But I wouldn't trade. I'd rather be here."

"As would I," Robert said.

"I hope Matthew catches a grouse," said James. "I'm hungry."

"No surprise there," Robert said and pushed himself off the ground. "I'm going to post this letter with the captain."

The humid air muffled the drumbeats of reveille as Robert joined the lines at the latrine area. He washed his face, relishing the cold water, then dipped his whole head into the trough and let the water drip down his neck and wet his collar. It brought relief from the heat, albeit temporary.

Looking up from his ablutions, Robert noticed that the drum had not stopped, that the slow roll continued through the heat-charged air. Around him, others whispered and scurried off. Robert jogged back to his tent and buttoned on his coat. "What's astir?" he asked Tobias, who only shrugged. At last, Sergeant Munn came down the slope, but for once he was not barking orders. "Neat lines," he said in a measured tone, "right along the edge here. Stand at attention. Don't move until you are told." The four of them formed a row, and on the opposite side of the path, the inhabitants of the other tents did the same, until, up and down the slope, blue-coated soldiers bordered the road.

From the top, a cart began its descent, pulled by two chestnut horses. Robert saw captains he didn't know walking alongside the horses, hands on the halters, keeping the pace slow and steady. Atop the cart sat a flag-draped casket, and Robert could not pull his eyes from it. Who lay within? In the weeks that he had been at West Point, he had not seen such a ceremony, though many had died—a few from battle wounds but more from accidents or illness. The news whispered down. "Colonel Meigs, shot on the road into camp last night." Then quiet. Colonel Meigs. Robert had heard the name, though he knew little about the officer, one of the distant commanders of their regiment. But if he had been shot, and on the road into camp, too, the British were bold to be sure. The picket line had been pushed out for miles approaching West Point; how could someone have made it past all the sentries? The men who had attacked Robert on grass guard had penetrated only the farthest corner of West Point, the pastures on the perimeter; a colonel shot on the road revealed a far more serious breach.

The cart rolled past, and in the silence of its wake, Robert could hear the chirp of songbirds. Men around him began to shuffle their feet, waiting for the order that would release them and start their day. Tobias leaned forward and craned his neck up the slope, then down, to follow the cart's passage.

Soon the company's corporals spread out along the path, inspecting uniforms and sending men off to the parade ground. Robert shifted uncomfortably: he hadn't had time to clean and polish as meticulously as full inspection demanded, and he didn't want to spend the day at fatigue labor. Yet the others appeared just as disheveled as him and the men were being sent to the grounds without being made to clean up. Before he could puzzle this out, Booth stepped in front of them.

"Take off your coats." His voice bore none of its normal joviality.

One by one, Booth took their coats, reached into the pockets, felt along the seams. He turned out tobacco pouches, flints, bits of string. Tobias's coat produced five guilders, sewn into the bottom seam. He turned red when Booth ripped them out, holding the coins in his palm, where they glinted in the morning sun. "My winnings from cards," said Tobias.

"You'll have to find a new hiding place, Hall," Booth said as he handed them back. "Now, take off your boots." He felt in these as well, turning up nothing. "We'll search the tents while you're at drill. Grab your muskets and fall out."

Pausing only to fasten their boots and button their coats, the four of them headed up the hill. "You've done mighty well at cards, Tobias," said Matthew.

"Aye. My luck has held."

"Show me where the games are richer. I've won only rum and shillings."

Tobias laughed. "I'll take you tonight, but you have to be prepared to lose the same as you'd win."

"Too rich for my blood, then."

Robert half-listened to their banter. Nothing in the tent would implicate him; thank goodness he'd already posted the letter to Jennie.

James nudged Robert in the ribs, waking him from his thoughts. "What do you think they were searching for, anyway?"

"Notes, I suppose."

"Aye, back when André was captured, he had the plans to West Point secreted in his boot," Tobias added.

"I remember," Robert said. "What could any of us report on?"

"Schedules, locations of guards," James said.

They passed other tents whose residents were hastening to put their few possessions in order; the breeze stirred the detritus of letters and cartridge papers. Who could hope to find evidence of treason in this mess?

"You owe me three shillings, Mills!" a soldier called from one of the tents.

"No such thing, Briggs," Matthew shot back. "I owe you nothing."

An older man, dark hair streaked with gray, barreled out of the tent. "Three shillings, and you'll pay up."

"Go hang yourself," Matthew said, and continued up the slope.

The man grabbed his shoulder, swinging him about. "I'll not take your lip, you little whelp. You've gotten away with too much around here if you ask me. Walking around like you're the rooster . . ." His hand clenched around the fabric of Matthew's coat, yanking at him, and Matthew tossed a punch that caught the side of the man's head. Then the two were grappling, and Robert instinctively backed away. James rushed in to pull them apart, caught someone's fist on his chin, and then began swinging himself. Just as other soldiers crowded around, jostling, Booth appeared, wading into the thick of it, shouting, "Enough, enough." He pulled them apart and dragged all three to the captain's tent. Robert glanced after them, then turned to Tobias. Without a word, they hurried to the parade ground for roll call.

When Matthew and James were flogged that afternoon, along with the other soldier, Briggs, Robert stood to the back, not wanting to see his friends bloodied. He stared at the shoulders of the man in front of him and tried not to listen. After the lashing, the company ran through a shortened drill and then were assigned to work groups. Robert and Tobias slathered grease on the axles of carts, sharpened saws, and hauled wood to the smithies until Booth finally dismissed them. When Tobias said he would collect the evening's rations, Robert trotted to the infirmary, where the sergeant grudgingly let him in. Matthew and James lay opposite each other, a few beds down from Shaw. Robert sat next to James, who was stretched out on his stomach, his arms dangling down and his feet hanging off the end of the cot.

"Ah, Bob. Pass me water. . . ."

Robert held the canteen, tilting it awkwardly so James could drink sideways from it. "Do you want a drink as well, Matthew?"

"Yes, please," came the muffled reply. "Good thing they moved that bastard Briggs to another tent, or I'd beat him senseless right now."

Robert ignored his words. Matthew couldn't turn down a fight; anger and violence were just part of his nature, and there was no sense trying to reason with him. After helping Matthew drink, Robert asked James, "How do you feel?"

"I regret every rabbit I ever skinned, but at least they were dead. Lord, does it burn."

"They say we'll be out in two days," Matthew added.

"Mind, they didn't say we would be better by then, but that we would be out."

From a few beds away, Shaw chimed in. "That's what you get for fighting. You might think it harsh, but imagine how the regiment would fare without such discipline." Robert saw that his arm had been bound up across his chest; he remained pale and his cheeks were sunken. "We should all strive to get along. It isn't worth it to fight. Isn't that right, Shurtliff?"

"I reckon it is." He hadn't missed the emphasis Shaw settled on that word: *worth*. He longed to stuff Shaw's mockingly sanctimonious language down his throat. Rage, coupled with a sense of futility—a sense he hadn't had for weeks and weeks—rushed through him, and he turned back to James and Matthew, trying to calm himself. "I'll come again tomorrow if I can." With that, he stood and walked out, not sparing a glance at Shaw. As he walked down the aisle of the tent, he heard the corporal behind him: "I heard the drums roll, Snow. What was that all about?"

"A colonel shot on the road. Meigs was his name. . . ."

The voices faded as Robert left. Worth . . . would Shaw try to wring some money from him? Or other favors? And now the corporal was alone in the tent with two of his mates. If he told them . . . Robert rolled his shoulders back, stood straight. There was nothing to do but hope the corporal would keep his secret, though he had little faith in that.

THE NEXT AFTERNOON, MATTHEW AND James were released from the infirmary and told to rest in their tent for another day. The sight of their flayed backs pained Robert; the wounds were still weeping through the scabs. The sergeant at the infirmary instructed them to keep the wounds covered with a healing salve and a light dressing. After a morning of guard duty, Robert came back to check on them and, finding them reasonably well, offered to fetch more bandages from the infirmary. There was no sergeant about, so Robert walked into the dusky light of the tent. While his own lodging smelled of sweat, woolens, and woodsmoke, the infirmary had about it the odor of something too sweet, of fruit overripe and turning to decay. No one lay within except Shaw. He sat up and wiped his mouth on his sleeve as Robert approached.

"Shurtliff. I'm glad you're here. Do me a favor, as my writing hand is in terrible shape." Reaching into his coat, he drew out a thin sheet of paper and a stub of pencil. The effort of sitting up and talking seemed to tax Shaw, whose already pale face drained further as he fumbled with the sheet.

"Of course," Robert said, determined to hold his temper, and took the proffered paper and utensil and settled them on the surface of a stool.

"Good. It is a note to a fellow corporal." He paused. "In another regiment." Shaw drew breath as if he sucked through a straw, fretful and needy. "Write this. M gone and I am confined. I cannot meet with you and ask you not to send those two. I haven't been out to the field in days, so be cautious. The north corner is always the safest." The corporal paused and licked his lips. "Send me the day by the old path. Take care."

"Shall I write your name beneath?"

"No," the corporal said. "No need."

Robert read over the note. Strange—it was disjointed and made little sense. He asked, "Do you want me to read it back to make certain I have it right?" Perhaps Shaw's wound had led to fever and confusion.

"No," the corporal snapped. "Keep quiet." He'd pushed himself up with his good arm, his shoulder trembling visibly with the effort, craning to look around Robert toward the source of a noise from near the entrance to the tent. Though Robert dropped his eyes back to the note, Shaw seemed to notice that he'd been watching him curiously. "I thought it might be the person the note is for . . . but it seems not. I thought he might visit," Shaw temporized, settling back on his blanket.

Robert longed to be out of the tent, away from Shaw's presence, though he knew it was better—knew he was obliged—to humor the corporal. "To which regiment's office shall I deliver this?"

Shaw had slumped down again, but a familiar sneer played on his face. "You're likely to get lost before you locate the proper tent.

Just leave it within the tree stump behind the second set of latrines. The biggest stump. There's a hollow there. You'll be able to find it. You should be able to handle that, even though you're a woman."

The emphasis on the last word rang in Robert's ear, as if he'd been in a bell tower at noon: deafening, enough to make him shiver. "Very well." He stood and tucked the note into his coat pocket.

"Oh, and put this in the stump, too," Shaw said, passing a folded and grubby scrap of paper over. Robert took it, and before he'd stepped past the cot, Shaw called to him, "Get it there within the hour, Shurtliff." It was the call of a master, an owner, and Robert could feel the cord of servitude and obligation already chafing.

Outside in the sunshine Robert walked slowly through the pathways of the camp. The pages in his pocket itched. He turned toward the latrines, affecting a nonchalance he did not feel. Why had Shaw not appended his name? Why not disclose the intended recipient?

The long shed of the necessaries loomed, and Robert pushed open a door, marking—as he always did—whether it was safe for him to drop his trousers quickly and take a seat. It was; positioning himself by one of the windows cut for ventilation, he took out the two sheets from Shaw. He glanced at the one he'd written—something about it galled him, though he couldn't say what. Then he unfolded the second sheet. Thick, uneven lines seemed to mark some sort of tally. The first came under the heading *tosday*, the next, *wedsday*, and so on. Here five marks, followed by the letter *E*, there four and a triangle. Robert shook his head; something seemed wrong. He longed to drop the two notes into the latrine and be rid of them, but doing so wouldn't free him from the hold Shaw had on him.

The door to the necessaries swung open, a sudden flash of light, and Robert hastened to hide the pages from view as he puzzled over the contents. M gone. Meigs? The colonel? It could be. But anyone in West Point would know that. He finished folding the pages, gave a quick look around, and buttoned himself up. The second stump behind the latrine . . . M gone. Robert washed his hands in the trough, then lifted his hat and ran damp fingers through his hair. Shaw had seemed so insistent—suffused with urgency—and nervous. The pallor of his skin, the sudden flush of it as he'd dictated the note, the hesitancy of his words—Robert recognized these as familiar marks: the corporal was hiding something. How well Robert should know what secrecy looked like. After all, he himself had been wary of disclosure, living on the edge of his nerves, for the last few months. Dipping his hands into the trough again, he went over the words of the note, the strange marks, his own instinct to hide the material or throw it away from his person. It all stank, and the stench was one of treason. As a corporal, Shaw knew the rotation of the regiment's pickets and guards; perhaps that corresponded to the marks he'd made. Even Shaw's presence on grass guard now took on a sinister air—had he been complicit in the attack? Had he been heading into the woods to meet the attackers and only happened upon Robert?

A string of possibilities unspooled in Robert's mind, and he pushed them aside to dwell on the more urgent matter: What to do with the notes? Instinct, base animal instinct, told him to burn them immediately, destroy the evidence of his own involvement. But that would spell his own end as well. Robert could see it now. Shaw had asked him to write the note hoping that Robert wouldn't figure the puzzle out but knowing that even if he did, Shaw retained the upper hand. He knew that Robert was a woman and could therefore destroy his reputation. Should he deliver the note and be done with it? That would not release him from Shaw's grip. He imagined it as though he and Shaw held blades to each other's throats: one's demise would spell the other's, and they had not enough trust to lower their weapons. Though he loathed keeping the pages upon him, knowing that another inspection might occur at any time, he saw no way around it. He turned to walk back to his tent.

Tobias squatted near the fire, spitting two birds for supper. "Good hunting," he said as Robert approached.

Robert nodded. It seemed strange that the afternoon had passed, that life had gone on for others while he remained stuck in the hospital tent with Shaw in the tepid light and the damp smell of canvas, the air a miasma of sickness and sweat.

From within the tent, James called, "It's Bob at last! Bring in our dressings!"

Robert put a hand to his head. He hadn't fulfilled his errand, that simple chore he'd set out so long ago to do. He lifted the flap of the tent and saw the two of them lying on their stomachs, and a rush of guilt fell upon him. "My apologies. I was . . . waylaid. I'll get your dressings right now." He ducked back out, but not before he heard a groan from Matthew and some remark about flies gathering.

A sergeant now perched on a stool at the entrance to the hospital tent. When Robert approached, he held up a hand. "What's your business, then?"

"I need clean dressings, perhaps a little ointment for the two who were flogged."

The sergeant waved his hand. "Back of the tent, left, you'll find what you need."

Robert drew himself up to his full height, keeping his back as straight as a ramrod—one of Munn's favorite phrases—and walked down the aisle of the infirmary. He hoped that Shaw might be asleep, but no such luck. The corporal called out softly as he passed. "Back so soon, Miss Shurtliff? Did you do as instructed?"

Miss. That word, the susurration, made him flinch. Robert walked past and did not turn his head. At the far end of the tent, he found the stack of dressings, gathered an armful, anger making his hands shake, and headed back up the aisle. He paused at the foot of Shaw's cot and decided to take a risk. After all, he was close to lost already. "I'll not be your scribe again, Shaw. I'll see you condemned first."

"Condemned? For what?" he sneered.

"Don't play the innocent." Robert leaned in. "I may be a woman, but I'm not a fool. Those notes you gave me are treasonous."

"Scant evidence," Shaw sneered. But crimson rose in his cheeks as he pushed himself closer to Robert to hiss, "Say anything and I will bring down ruin upon you."

"So be it."

Shaw attempted to smile, a grimace on his pale face. "Think it over tonight. I could make the venture profitable. . . ."

Robert shook his head. "There's no profit in being a traitor."

"You scarcely have a choice in the matter."

Shaw would not hold this over his head; he would not grasp the reins to Robert's life. He had to get those notes to Sergeant Munn before Shaw spoke up, before he could lay the blame at Robert's feet. He ran to his tent, where he set the dressings next to Tobias and called out loud enough for James and Matthew to hear, "I must be off. Sorry. I'll be back to help in short order."

Then he sprinted toward the sergeant's tent, stopping as he came to the parade ground and taking a more measured pace. To appear haggard and panting might convey guilt.

Corporal Booth sat at the front of Munn's tent, trimming his fingernails with a knife, when Robert approached. "What're you about, Shurtliff?"

"An urgent matter for the sergeant, sir."

"Should I send him in, Sergeant?" Booth bellowed.

"No, I'll come out." Munn pushed through the tent flaps. It seemed to Robert that the sergeant's stare crushed him; he could barely hold eye contact. "Well?"

"Sir. I came to possess these documents today from Corporal Shaw. I can explain the circumstances."

Munn took the sheets that Robert held out and examined them carefully, holding them close to his nose. "Well?" he said, his mouth a grim line.

"Sir, I went to see Corporal Shaw in the infirmary. He asked me to write a note for him. Those words are in my hand." He pointed to the sheet, paused, swallowed. "Shaw asked me to deposit these notes for him, and I took them, not realizing what they were. But when I looked at them, they seemed to be suspicious. The markings are Shaw's. I brought them to you. I think . . ." He faltered, broke off, not wanting to condemn himself but not knowing what else to say.

Munn passed the notes to Booth without breaking eye contact with Robert. "I know Shaw's hand, such as it is. But do you understand what these notes mean?"

"I am not certain, but I doubt they bode well." Robert forced himself to hold his gaze steady.

"Booth. Go alert Captain Webb. Take the notes with you. Shurtliff and I will see what Shaw has to say on this matter."

"Yes, sir."

The sergeant paused to button up his coat, and Robert fell silent, closing his eyes briefly. His whole being stretched taut, as if they'd put him on the rack. His guts quivered. He remembered Munn yelling at him during their early days of training, his brusque dismissal, calling him a fool, a buffoon; he thought of how hard he had worked to learn the drill, to fit in, to be a good soldier. He had wanted so much to do well. Should he reveal the full truth and make an end of himself? Or should he wait for Shaw to denounce him? Better to be honest and forthright, but every fiber in him resisted the confession.

"This is treason," Munn said quietly, all but to himself. "God help us."

The walk from the sergeant's tent to the infirmary seemed to span miles. Smoke curled up from cooking fires, filling the air with a piquant odor. Robert felt like a ghost: there but not there. He steeled himself, imagining what Shaw might speak against him. What would Munn say? What would happen to Robert Shurtliff?

At the infirmary, the sergeant on duty eyed them curiously. "We've come to see Corporal Shaw," Munn said.

"You'll find him within."

As Munn stepped into the tent, a few words of a psalm sprang unbidden into Robert's mind: *Keep thy tongue from evil, and thy lips from speaking guile, depart from evil, and do good; seek peace, and pursue it.* He followed the sergeant into the gloom.

They passed the cot where Shaw had been, at least where Robert thought he'd been. They walked to the end of the tent. All the beds lay empty. "Where is he?" Munn spun around.

"I'll get a lantern," said Robert.

At the tent's entrance he nearly collided with Booth, who had arrived with Captain Webb. The infirmary sergeant lit a lantern and carried it within, casting spindly shadows on the tent walls. "He was here, right here," the infirmary sergeant said, pointing to a cot. They searched under each bed, found nothing. "I didn't see him leave . . ." the sergeant murmured.

"There's any number of places where he could have slipped through," said Webb. "I'll inform the colonel, and we'll send men out to find him." The captain turned to face Robert. "You're Shurtliff."

It wasn't a question, but Robert responded, "Yes, sir." He stood straight, surprised that the captain knew his name—Webb had been nothing but a distant presence, just as he'd promised on the day they'd arrived at West Point.

"I had a good report of you concerning the ambush in which Shaw was injured."

"Thank you, sir."

"Well, Munn, you can deal with this soldier." The captain headed up the aisle of the infirmary, and the rest of them trailed after.

Deal with him? What more did they want? Was he to be punished for taking the notes down? The captain strode out of the tent, and Robert followed Munn at a slower pace. When they emerged into the twilight, Munn put a hand on Robert's shoulder. "We won't send you out on this hunt, lad. You've done enough today. Now, just one more matter. Where did Shaw tell you to secret this note?"

"A hollow tree stump, sir, down behind the second latrine."

"Very good. We'll see what we can find by watching this stump for a while." Munn thumped him on the back. "Thanks to God that you were the one to find this note. Now, off you go."

Tobias's blond hair shone golden in the firelight as he sat reading from a volume, trying to entertain the invalids. Robert, quaking with relief, came down the slope, and Tobias, spotting him, snapped the book shut to ask, "Well, what's the story?"

"Yes, tell it loudly, so we can hear!" came James's voice from within the tent.

Robert settled himself by the fire and took the slice of meat that Tobias offered him, along with some corn. He bit into the kernels, letting the sweetness explode in his mouth. Why did it seem so long since he had tasted anything? He closed his eyes. Shaw had disappeared—with any luck, for good. When he opened his eyes, he saw Tobias staring at him.

"Well?"

"When I went to the infirmary, Shaw was there and he gave me a note to deliver." Robert took a bite of the fowl and, licking the salty grease from his fingers, thought of how he could tell the truth, just not all of it. "But I read the note and saw that he was passing along troop positions. So I turned it in to Munn."

"My God!" Tobias exclaimed.

"So Shaw was the traitor?"

"What's to happen to him?"

"Did he name others involved?"

The questions came all at once, and Robert threw a hand up, as if to deflect them.

"Quiet," bellowed James. "Let the man speak!"

"When we got to the infirmary, Shaw had fled. They are sending men out to find him now."

"What I want to know"—Matthew's voice came from within the tent, sounding sepulchral—"is why Shaw asked you?"

Robert's mind tumbled over a plausible explanation. "Shaw thought that, as I'd saved his life, we had some manner of bond between us. When I went to see how he fared, he took it as a sign that he could trust me not to betray him. But I've no mercy for traitors."

"Here, here," said James.

"A drink!" cried Tobias. "For Bob." He entered the tent and uncorked a bottle of rum. They passed it around, and Robert settled by the flaps and took a swallow.

"So the bastard deserted," said Matthew. "Where do you think he'll go?"

Robert let the others trail off into speculation and conjecture. The tightness he'd held in his chest ever since Shaw learned his secret had slackened now; the night sky blinked sweetly at him, confirming his place in the world. Shaw was gone. Would he melt back into civilian society? Would he go to the British? Robert wiped his mouth on his coat sleeve. A bit of pride spread out within him: Shaw had fled from his fate, refusing to face the consequences, but Robert had been willing to take responsibility for what he was.

He helped Tobias boil water, and the two of them washed Matthew's and James's backs, gently rubbing ointment on the wounds. James twitched a little as Robert spread the salve, which smelled sharply of mint. The scabs formed thick ridges, and when James flexed his shoulders, the scabs tore a little. But the doctor had said he needed to move, or else the scars would bind too tight. So Robert helped him roll his arms and twist his back, even though this made the wounds weep and bleed. As he rubbed his friend's skin, he realized that he hadn't ever touched a man like this. The gesture meant nothing to James, he knew, but as his fingers ran along James's flesh, he heard a gentle murmur inside himself, a buzz, like a honeybee flying in his stomach. His hands rested on James's bare back, a gesture so intimate that it seemed as though it should be forbidden. He thought it strange that it was simpler for him to kill a man than to touch one.

When he had finished, he and Tobias lingered by the embers of the fire.

"Were you scared when you brought the notes to Munn?" Tobias asked.

The question slashed across Robert's thoughts. It had been so long since someone sincerely asked him what he felt. Relief flooded him, a cool drink. "Yes," he said, glad he could be honest with his friend. "I was terrified."

"I would have been, too," said Tobias. "But Shaw . . . what was that bastard telling the British?"

"The guard rotation, troop movement. It was hard to tell exactly what."

Tobias placed his hand on Robert's shoulder. "I'm glad you caught him. Did he ask you to deliver the note to someone?"

"Not to someone, but, if you can believe it, to leave it in a secret spot behind the latrine!"

Tobias laughed. "That's the sort of place for a traitor." He let his hand drop from Robert's shoulder, and the two of them doused the fire and went to sleep.

CHAPTER THIRTEEN

In the wake of Shaw's desertion, Robert's company drilled and trained constantly, stood guard with increased vigilance, and zealously undertook their chores as if eager to prove themselves. Captain Webb set them to building boats on the Hudson's banks, sweating in the full summer sun on a succession of flat-bottomed barges. On guard duty, two or three would take a post that one used to hold, and at roll call, squads of more experienced men were summoned for four- or five-day expeditions. "Foraging," Munn would say, or "On patrol" whenever Tobias or anyone else inquired as to the nature of these voyages. One afternoon, as they were lugging boats down the steep road to the river's edge, Booth finally gave more detail.

"General Washington's sent orders," he said, bracing the gunwale with one hand. "We'll be heading out soon to a field camp—the whole company."

"What for?" asked Matthew, who strained at the stern.

"To keep the area neat and clean. That's what the lights are good at," Booth replied.

Tobias piped up. "It must be an attack on New York City. Is that what Washington has planned?"

"If I knew, I wouldn't be jabbering about it with you. My only word is that we are to move out soon. And I doubt these boats are for a summer cruise." Booth spoke lightly, and Robert could hear teasing in his voice, but the fear of treason, of information too freely spread, still swirled, an undercurrent in the company; they let the matter drop.

On a count of three, they eased the boat onto the ground and walked back up the rise, rubbing shoulders and forearms. Ever since the start of August, the heat had vented its aggression on West Point, and the river glinted, tantalizingly cool below. Robert looked back at the boat; that anything so heavy could float was baffling.

"Robert's the only one of you to have faced any true fighting. The rest of you lassies had better pack an extra pair of breeches." Booth laughed, and after a moment Tobias and James joined in.

Matthew was not amused. "My balls are just as big as his, I wager."

Robert held back his own laughter, thinking that, for Matthew's sake, he very much hoped they were bigger. Instead, he sought to placate. "I think we're all ready, Corporal."

Booth nodded. "We'll see soon enough," he said, and moved off to another group.

"He's right, though," Tobias said. "Our company's rolls are brimful, and something is afoot."

James emptied his nose, wiped his fingers on his sleeve. "About time, too. I can't stand much more of this drill."

"Tell me that again after a month in the field," said Tobias. "The word is that Washington's planning an attack, and he wants to run through the stages up here." He looked at the group. "And DeLancey's British raiders are more active than ever."

"How d'you know all this, anyway?" James asked.

Tobias shrugged. "I listen closely."

"You're a little sneak, more like," said Matthew, and then smiled, as if to say he meant no harm.

Robert picked up the pace, wanting to put a bit of distance between himself and Matthew, whose moods had worsened with the rising temperature. Munn himself had stopped by their tent the previous week to warn Matthew to behave himself. Nights of drinking were followed by sloppy drill and a few scuffles with other soldiers. Munn had even drawn Robert aside and asked if he could try to bring Matthew to chapel. "It might be good for him, offer some rest for his soul," the sergeant had said.

"I'll try," had been Robert's reply. "But I doubt he'll have much interest, unless they replace hymns with dicing."

Indeed, Matthew had laughed at Robert's cajoling the next Sunday. But Robert took consolation in the flattery of Munn's request nonetheless. In a moment they crested the hill to the makeshift shipyard, where another flat-bottomed boat waited for them. Robert rolled his shoulders, and James counted, "One, two, three, hup!" As they seized the gunwales and hoisted the boat over their heads, Robert felt a knee almost buckle under the weight. A quarter of a mile to go. His shoulder already screamed in protest. Just a quarter of a mile.

A WEEK LATER, CAPTAIN WEBB made an announcement to the lights. "By order of General Paterson, commander of West Point, this entire company shall be put into rotation on the lines for the end of the summer and the start of the autumn. We move out this day. Draw your rations and muster in full gear in two hours' time."

The troops complied in a flurry of action. Robert stood in line to receive his share of cartridges and rations. Then he hurried back to the tent, his arms full. Into his knapsack he placed an extra shirt, leggings, and the breeches he had taken—so long ago, it seemed—from Master Leonard. Sewing kit, candle box, horn cup and spoon, and letter box all rested below the rasher of corned beef, the bag of beans, and the sack of hard biscuits the commissary had issued. To the outside of the knapsack he lashed a hatchet, strapped on his blanket, and affixed a small cooking pot, though first he carefully cleaned off all the soot and char so that the pot would not dirty everything it touched. Fully loading his cartridge box, he suspended it from one of the white belts that crossed over his chest; from the second belt he hung his canteen and bayonet. Stepping outside the tent and shouldering his knapsack, he found he could scarcely stand straight, and James laughed.

"You look like an overloaded donkey," he said, guffawing. He had just finished a rather more haphazard stowing of his own gear.

"And you sound like an ass," Robert replied.

"Well said!" Tobias called from within the tent. He emerged and hoisted his own knapsack. "This is a considerable load."

Matthew strapped on his pack as well. "On the move," he said. "Do you imagine there will be any women where we're heading?" He elbowed Robert in the ribs. "What d'you think, Bob?"

"No more than you have here," Robert replied.

They made their way to the parade ground, straps creaking under the new weight and James's pot clanking at every step.

"Lord, lad," cried Booth as they joined the ranks. "You look like a tinker!" He pulled at James's pot and ordered him to tie it up securely. Webb called roll, and then, with considerably less clanking, they set out south toward Peekskill.

IT FELT GOOD TO MARCH again. The prospect of a new vista spurred Robert on, but the novelty wore off within a couple of hours, and he began to wonder why they couldn't just float down the Hudson in some of those boats they'd spent weeks laboring over. The very idea of drifting on water only made his feet ache more, and when Captain Webb finally called a halt, Robert could scarcely struggle out of the knapsack's straps before sinking to the dirt. James didn't bother to take off his pack but lay against it on the ground, like a tipped-over tortoise.

Robert surveyed the scenery with dismay. Hills and steep inclines all around. Here earth thrust and jutted, rocky escarpments broke forth from the soil, and the only level plain was the river itself.

In no time, the order came to form up; it took the combined efforts of Tobias and Robert to set James on his feet again. After several hours more of marching, Webb called a halt again. Corporal Booth came down the line and shouted names, saying, "March ahead, march ahead." The four of them were called, and they moved around the other soldiers to where the company's sergeants and officers stood at the head of the line. Sergeant Munn stepped forward and rattled off names, which included Robert and his tent mates. "Form up, ranks of three!" Munn called. As they complied, Robert thought of the first time he'd heard Munn say this—on the road out of Worcester—and how they had stumbled over each other like a litter of puppies seeking a teat. Now they accomplished the command in a matter of seconds.

"Move out!"

They had detached as a squad of fifteen, about a third of the company, Robert guessed, though it was hard to tell without turning around, and Munn would have his head if he did so. They marched on quietly until Booth made his way back to them.

"Are we not headed to Peekskill?" Tobias asked.

"Eventually," replied Booth, who seemed at ease despite his stuffed knapsack and the extra sidearm he was entitled to as a corporal. "Those we left will cross by Bear Mountain while we venture farther south to cross at King's Ferry. Better tactics to move in smaller groups. Divide and conquer, eh?"

The river widened as they marched; the farther they got from West Point, the thicker the forest grew on the slopes. Eventually, the track veered from the river and led them to a pass between two tall peaks, and Robert rejoiced that they wouldn't scale the summit of either of them. The mountains loomed above, providing a rich shade for the squad.

At the far end of the pass, they stopped for the night. Munn set out guards and a rotation of duty. Those not on the first shift attended to the evening chores that Robert thought of—wryly—as soldiers' domestic duties: gathering wood for the fires, clearing the ground of twigs and pebbles, finding a place without gnarly roots to lay a blanket. Soon three campfires blazed, and groups of men crouched around their pots, boiling water for the evening mess of beans and meat. It was no housekeeping that Mrs. Thomas would recognize, this scruffy crew readying stew and rough bedding, but it struck Robert as oddly comforting; the stars above and the snoring of men by his side seemed as normal as the walls and roof of a house once seemed.

They resumed the march at first light and soon followed the river, walking the path above its banks until they reached King's Ferry. This coveted crossing, where the river ran gently but not too broad, was a tightly armed post, and when their squad approached, a sentry called out a greeting that Munn answered. Marching below the guns poking out over the river, Robert realized that he had yet to hear cannon fired in anything but celebration. The muzzles of the artillery bristled from the slopes of the fort like porcupine quills, and under their careful watch the squad crowded onto flat-bottomed boats that ferried them over. The other side looked much the same to Robert, but Munn paused to set his crew straight.

"Most of you men are spring recruits—never been far from West Point. But you're in Westchester now, and the Good Lord knows the alliances in this county aren't as straightforward as they seem." He pointed east, where the sun steadily worked its way up the sky. "There's a large French camp over there, place called Crom Pond. They don't dress like us or talk like us, but we're on the same side."

He scanned their faces. "As far as the Croton River is our ground—south of that is neutral territory. And most of the landowners of the region use both sides of their mouth to talk. You step lively in this place and keep your wits about you. All sorts of folk are hereabout, all manner of British regulars and irregulars, farmers who want only to protect their stock but will shoot you without much worry. And this summer, the generals are counting on us, so mind yourselves." He swung about, pointed north. "Now to Peekskill."

They reached camp in a couple of hours and found that Webb and the rest of the company had already arrived. Peek's Kill itself ran to the north, and the surrounding land contained more stumps than trees, the result of years of army activity in the vicinity. For quarters, Peekskill boasted five lean-tos and a more substantial hut for the officers. Rough-hewn logs formed the walls and floor, and the lean-tos gaped open at one end, with slanted roofs to shunt off the rain. The company's numbers stood at about fifty men, so they'd be ten to a shelter, and they'd sleep head to foot, fitted together like kernels on an ear of corn. Surveying the shelters, Robert took a deep breath, then let it out slowly between pursed lips.

"All well, Bob?" asked James.

"Aye. Just tired from the march."

"Well, drop your sack and rest until they tell you to get up. That's what I'm going to do." He eased himself out of the belts and straps of his equipment, and lay down on a platform. Tobias came and sat down next to James, thumping the mossy logs with a hand.

"Home, sweet home," he said.

Robert lifted the pack off his shoulders, set it on the platform, and then lay down, leaning his head against it. He had to admit that James had the right idea: rest until they told you not to.

Matthew soon materialized and tossed his gear down. As usual, he was full of complaints: a new blister, an insult from one of the corporals. "I'll see about firewood," Robert said, eager to escape his bile.

Tobias hopped up as well. "I'll join you."

Close to the camp the woods were largely denuded of branches and twigs, and Tobias and Robert soon went their separate ways in search of kindling. Robert gathered up an armload and returned to camp. As he dropped the branches by a fire circle, Sergeant Munn approached.

"Shurtliff. Here you are." The sergeant withdrew some papers from his coat and handed them to Robert. "I've got one for Hall as well. Is he about?"

"He must be gathering wood," said Robert, distracted by the sight of Jennie's handwriting on the top fold. He scarcely waited for the sergeant to turn away before he settled himself on a log and opened the letter.

Dear Robert,

The sermon this week in the meeting house was on the "The Lilies of the Field," and it made me think of you—they neither spin nor weave, yet God cares for them. I know you seldom fancied the Congregationalist preaching, but you would have enjoyed this piece of the gospel. I do pray for you.

I am in receipt of a letter from you in which you described your uniform. You were quite detailed, but I cannot imagine you in these garments. You'll just have to come here and show me once the war is ended. Folks say it will end soon.

In the heat of summer, rumors grow like crops. I went visiting with Missus Leonard to one of her sick friends, up near Easton. Missus Leonard, when she thought I could not hear, told the ailing woman of the "scandal" within our town, of the woman who slipped free from the justice's snare. The two of them sat about, speculating on where she could have gone. Missus Leonard's friend opined that the woman likely had a lover and had run away to be with him. But Missus Leonard insisted she knew the missing party better and thought that she might have tried a more zealous course, perhaps going to the sea or serving in the war. I bit my lip and said nothing. We stayed in Easton a few nights and Missus Leonard was afire with these conversations, even asking what I thought. I demurred, of course, but I think she is quite delighted by the idea and secretly may even be proud if a woman were to have become a soldier. She certainly talked until my ears ached.

Young Master Leonard has yet to miss those garments. In truth, I think his old clothes have now seen more of the world than he has.

Oh, Robert. I hope there will be another letter from you to let me know you are well and safe.

All my love,
Jennie

The clanking of cooking pots, the calls of one soldier to another—sounds from another sphere. Everything Jennie spoke about in her letter seemed no more than a dream, a shadow of the past momentarily falling across the present. This was the real world now, this company, by this river. This place, these people, the demands of each day created and defined him. He was strong or smart, naïve or helpful, because of what the corporals or sergeants asked of him, because of what his fellows thought of him. He didn't know how he looked except through their eyes. He folded Jennie's letter and placed it in his pocket. Someone called for buckets of water and another yelled for wood; if he wasn't mistaken, in the distance, that was James, calling his name.

CHAPTER FOURTEEN

To the delight of Matthew and the dismay of Robert, Peekskill provided little of West Point's regularity: no drill, no fatigue exercises, and fewer chores. When they were in camp, mornings began with inspection, and then Robert might scour an area with a squad, go out to cut firewood, or do nothing at all. The idleness made the men restless and lent an edge to the banter, so Robert often volunteered for patrols or to stand sentry duty, even though James chided him and encouraged him to take his ease. Matthew was generally to be found playing cards or other improvised games, or off throwing knives or pitching pebbles. James, for his part, slept and whittled, carving spoons and buttons. Some afternoons, when the card games turned sour or when he had tired of reading, Tobias rambled about as much as Robert and returned to the cooking fire full of news: DeLancey's troops had raided north of Tarrytown; the sentries had seen Cow-Boys—the local term for British irregulars—passing by at dawn.

But nothing of significance took place. Once or twice, guards reported sounds in the woods. The company combed the trees and back pathways, but found nothing. No one had been fired upon, though Robert heard the corporals grumbling that the British were one step ahead and were aware of whatever plans the Americans made.

As the surrounding farms began their harvest, Webb increased the number of patrols on the road. He sent boats down the Hudson to search the shores and dispatched squads to the French camp, trying to gather as much information as he could. In turn, messengers came to Webb with news of what had transpired at the other American camps south of the Croton River. So far as Robert could tell, the reconnoitering came to naught: Peekskill remained a sleepy spot.

"Hall, Shurtliff, Snow, and Mills, draw rations and report to Corporal Booth," Webb said at roll call one late September morning. "The following men will fall in with . . ." he continued, but Robert didn't bother to listen. Drawing rations could only mean one thing: a jaunt away from Peekskill at last.

They set out, marching east on well-packed dirt roads. As they crested a tall hill, they saw the land unfurled below, dotted here and there with farms, the silver blade of a river, thick woodlands sprouting up like a patchy beard. Though summer had scarcely ended, leaves already fluttered yellow and orange.

"Be alert, lads, we're off to forage" were Booth's only instructions. As a company, they hunted and fished to supplement the meat and beans that came from the army's stores. But foraging parties regularly sought extra supplies—as well as information—from farmers. Robert had heard Munn complain that many locals, especially those in the neutral zone, had ceased to plant their full acreage, knowing that the spoils of their labor would likely go to one army or the other and not their own larders. Near to Peekskill, Booth assured them they'd find some farmers appreciative of the American effort.

The first farm they approached, however, offered nothing except a drink of water, and Booth moved them on quickly—"Good family. They've offered in the past. Now, up to der Groot's place. We'll see about him." Over the next hill, they found Mr. der Groot, an older man with a full, round belly; clearly, he hired others to work his fields and orchard. He spoke to Booth with his arms crossed over his chest. "Ney, ney." His words seemed stretched and strange to Robert. "Noothing. We're starving oorselves here."

Booth nodded and scratched idly at the scar on his cheek. "We'll billet in your barn then, since you can surely spare the shelter."

The farmer's face grew red, but he said nothing. Billeting, Robert soon discovered, meant more than sleeping. First, they searched the whole barn, and Tobias found a loose plank behind which a pouch of gold had been secreted. Booth examined the contents and passed the pouch back to Tobias. "Bring these in and suggest the farmer find a more secure spot for his treasure. Perhaps that'll gain his better nature toward us."

Matthew gave Tobias a poke in the ribs. "You're a fool not to pocket that for yourself."

The rest of them proceeded to milk the cow, gather eggs, and corner a nice young pullet. By the time Tobias returned with a report of the farmer's grudging thanks, they had assembled the makings of a fine dinner. Robert plucked the pullet while the others built up a fire; their cookery was observed by the farmer, who stood at his back door, face stony. Booth rubbed his stomach with satisfaction. "Poor fool. He could have bought my goodwill with a sack of potatoes and saved himself a chicken."

"I'm glad he didn't," said James, who watched the grease drip from the roasting chicken into a waiting pan. When the corporal turned his back, James ran a finger through the pan and put it into his mouth, grinning with satisfaction like a babe sucking at its thumb.

Around the fire, they tore strips of meat from the steaming carcass, and within minutes only bones remained. Robert thought James might be eyeing even these.

The next morning, they whistled and sang as they walked down the road. Robert attributed their fine spirits to the good meal: even Matthew had lost his surly look. They rounded a curve in the road, and a farmhouse appeared in the distance, a thin curl of smoke rising from its chimney.

"The Widow Chester," said Booth, pointing. "She'll be good for something."

"Aye, for this thing?" asked Matthew, grabbing at his crotch.

Booth caught him across the cheek with the back of his hand. "Watch yourself, man. These are our allies."

Matthew nearly dropped his musket and stood flat-footed for a second before touching his hand to his mouth, as if checking for blood. He lifted his arm as if to strike back, but Tobias put a hand on his shoulder. "Steady now," he said.

They cut across from the road to the widow's yard, and when the door opened at their knock, Robert saw a woman with a frowsy white cap and gaunt cheeks.

"Mr. Booth!" she cried upon seeing the corporal, and opened the door wider.

It was the first woman's voice Robert had heard in months, and it sounded shrill, tremulous, otherworldly. "Come in, come in," she urged. The corporal removed his hat, revealing his bald pate, and turned to the squad. "I'll be but a minute, lads. Keep watch and touch nothing."

Matthew counted off the seconds, muttering about how quick Booth could get it up and off. At length, he tired of his tally and leaned over to Robert. "What do you think, Bob? Is Booth going from the front or the back?"

From where he leaned against the house, James reached out a leg and kicked Matthew. "Leave him be."

Robert took in the easy beauty of the valley, the bright colors of early autumn mixed with the deep greens of summer, and thought of the widow's lined face. How could Booth desire that? Perhaps the loneliness of being a soldier fed his desire, the need for physical comfort. Robert could understand. He missed casual caresses—how he and Jennie used to scrub each other's backs on bathing day or hold each other's elbows when they walked into town. In the past months, touch had been rare and therefore precious—James's arms around him when they had danced, or the feel of James's skin when Robert had tended to his wounds.

It scarcely seemed an adequate span of time to Robert before Booth pulled open the door. The widow followed him out to the lawn, where the squad quickly stood at the ready.

"I've three sacks of meal for you, but you'll have to find a wagon elsewhere." Her cap sat primly in place, not a hair askew, and she pointed the men to the sacks. "There'll be more after I get the boys to bring the north field in."

"Better to leave those here, lads," said Booth. "We'll come back when we have a means to carry them." He turned to the widow and gave a slight bow. "We thank you, ma'am." She dropped a curtsy and shut the door.

So it went. On the next day, a farmer offered them a cart; he complained that a bunch of Cow-Boys had taken his stock, so he had no use for the cart, and besides, its axle needed repair. Booth listened to his story with interest as Robert and the others made the repairs and promised to pursue the plunderers. Without mules or a horse, the soldiers became beasts of burden, and Robert took the first turn in the traces, grateful the wagon was empty. Up and down the hilly road they visited farms, collecting flour, vegetables, sometimes chickens. Booth preferred to take what a farmer offered and not press for more—"Keeps them generous," he said—but if the landowner was stingy, Booth turned ruthless; he requisitioned several fine hams from one farmer's smokehouse and had the foresight to requisition the flints from the farmer's guns as well. At an orchard whose trees sagged heavy with apples, a farmer gave them an ornery donkey, which James and Matthew wrestled into service, but they soon agreed that the beast was more a nuisance than a blessing; Robert had two fingers nipped by the animal, and James took a kick to the rear. At last, Booth declared that only one place remained to visit before they cut back to the widow's.

Coming around a curve, Booth led them off the track. "Snow, you'll stay here to mind the cart and provisions. The rest of you, carry only muskets, cartridge, and canteen."

"Where are we headed, sir?" asked Tobias.

"Up this ridge. We'll see what we see. Use caution now."

They walked in a silence broken only by their huffing breath; Booth set a wicked pace. Cresting the ridge, he led them down the slope, urging them to crouch until they found shelter against a stone wall. "Now," the corporal said, his voice hushed but urgent. "Hall, you count the horses. Mills, you tally the other livestock. Shurtliff and I will survey the house."

Robert raised his head, peering over the wall in the direction that Booth indicated. A mansion perched below them; with a grape arbor and flagged terrace, it seemed every bit the house of a country lord. Robert counted the glazed and mullioned windows of the house—manor, rather—and took in the stables, the storehouses, the outbuildings. There came a clatter of hooves and wheels as a coach-and-four pulled into the crescent drive below.

"Mark this closely," Booth hissed, and tugged Matthew's sleeve to redirect his attention.

A footman, trim in green velvet tailcoat, planted the box steps and opened the coach's door. A froth of gown emerged first, held aloft by a slender hand, then a tucked bodice, bosom overspilling, all capped by a porcelain-pale face with a flounce of hat set on brown curls.

"My God," Matthew breathed.

"Shush," said Booth, but he, too, sat transfixed, as if he beheld the Second Coming. The woman rustled her skirts about her, setting them straight, and pulled at her gloves as another woman descended from the coach. The second woman was older than the first, and less fashionably dressed; her bodice did not hug her as tightly, and her bosom swelled behind a lace modesty piece. A man stepped forth from the house to escort them within. Robert noted on his shoulder an epaulet designating rank.

"Is he a loyalist? Is that a colonel's fringe?" he whispered to Booth.

"A what, now?"

"On the man's shoulder, there."

"Who's watching the man?" said Matthew.

Booth tore his gaze away from the women. "Yes, he's a colonel. Those were certainly officers' ladies. And they're all loyalists."

"Officers' whores," said Matthew. "Any chance of going in for a raid, Corporal?"

"Have you lost your reason? Let's head back. We've seen what there is to see. Hall, did you get a count?"

"Yes, sir."

Robert picked up his musket and, staying low, scampered to the ridgeline, Tobias at his side. Behind him, he heard Matthew muttering, "I'm like to lose my reason if I go much longer without a girl. Booth's got the widow. If the British can fetch ladies to them, I don't see why we can't."

"What sort of woman could abide staying at Peekskill, I ask you?" said Tobias.

"That's true," said Booth. "It would take a well-paid wench to put up with that. Better than you could afford."

"There would surely be some women who could handle the harshness of weather and quarters," said Robert.

"Some bunch-backed scullery maid, that's all," Matthew said. "I don't need that sort."

"I expect the feeling is mutual," Robert replied.

But Matthew seemed not to hear. "Rough hands and chapped lips, and the tongue's the sharpest thing about them."

"A fair tally of yourself, I'd say," Robert said, knowing full well that the description could, and might well have been, applied to Deborah in Middleborough.

"Looking for a fight, Robert? Or will you shut your mouth now?"

Turn the other cheek, Robert urged himself, feeling his temper swell within him like a loaf in the oven. "Mind your own mouth," he said, clamping his lips shut to hold in what he truly wished to say.

"What do you know about women anyhow, Bob?" Matthew continued.

"A good deal more than you," Robert replied.

"Ha. I meant women other than your mother or sisters. Slept with any? Even touched hands?"

He knew he shouldn't rise to his bait, but . . . "And if I have? Shared their beds, exchanged embraces?" He thought of Jennie, the two of them warming each other's feet under their quilt. Not what Matthew meant, but still, Robert certainly knew more of women than any of these men.

"If you said as much, I'd call you a liar."

"Bob is the one receiving letters from a lady friend," Tobias said. "Can't say that I've seen any come your way, Matthew."

"You're a sad lot of fools and mollies, why, I've—"

"That's enough." Booth cut Matthew off. "None of you boys knows a thing about women, and none of you is going to find some lady in the woods of Westchester. Try to be soldiers and focus on the matter at hand."

"The matter is too much at hand, I'd say," Matthew muttered.

They rejoined James and coerced the donkey into plodding along. As they walked, Tobias prodded Booth to tell them what he knew of the house they'd spied upon, and the corporal, reluctantly at first and then with relish, unspooled the story. "A family of Tories owns that house. Fled from New York, not because they fear the British, of course, but because they didn't want to lose this property. One of the daughters is said to be betrothed to a British officer. I'd say we saw some proof of that. How many horses out there, Hall?"

"I counted a dozen."

Booth sucked his teeth. "We'll see, we'll see. Could be trouble."

The next night they reached the widow's; the four privates stayed in the barn while Booth retired to the house. In the loft, they shuffled about in the straw, making nests to sleep on. For once, James did not drift off immediately but lay back, chewing a stalk.

"Is this like your farm, Matthew?" he asked.

"Not half. We've got orchards. But they're all to my brothers now. Nothing left for me but a woodlot."

"Then what will you do when your service is ended?" Robert asked.

"There's talk they may open the Ohio valley. The farmland there is said to have soil rich for growing."

From the widow's house, they heard the sound of Booth singing, his pleasant baritone rising to their perch. "I don't suppose you brought your flute, Tobias?" James inquired.

"No, I left it at Peekskill."

"I'd welcome a chance to dance. Even with the widow," James said.

"Have you a sweetheart at home?" Tobias asked. "Is that why you like dancing?"

Matthew stood up. "If we are to talk of females, then I'll take the first watch. I don't need to hear you maundering about your sweethearts. Enough of that."

They heard his steps down the rungs of the ladder and then a few more notes from Booth. Robert turned his head to breathe in the sweet scent of the straw. "Maybe Matthew has it right in wanting to strike out for new territories," Robert said.

"You don't wish to go home, Bob?" asked Tobias.

"No, you've heard me speak of my family. I have no wish to return to them." And the town where he had lived would hardly welcome him back, at least not that he could imagine, even with the news from Jennie's letter. Besides, if they did, what sort of life would it offer? Only one as constrained as before. "What about you, Tobias?"

"I used to fancy going to Boston or Philadelphia and working as a tailor in a big city shop. But now, perhaps the sea. I could sign on with a ship. Get away . . ."

"Not for me," said Robert. "That is how my father was lost. You've read too many adventure stories. I imagine that being a sailor is a worse lot than being a soldier."

"Those ferries across the Hudson are enough of a ship's ride for me. I'll take a farm over the sea," said James. "Or do you think this war will go on for years and years?"

"And we will be soldiers like Booth and Munn, with long tales of service with which to bore the new recruits . . ." Robert said.

The three of them sank back into the piles of hay. Somewhere in the barn a cricket's solitary chirrup replaced Booth's singing. The straw tickled Robert's nose and poked at the soft spot behind his ear. He was full—for the widow had made them pudding—and sleepy; the world smelled sweet, rich with the harvest. Just as his eyelids began to droop, James's voice floated out of the darkness. "We could share a farm, we three. Go out to Ohio together and try our luck. Maybe bring Matthew along. He may be a lout, but he knows more of farming than we do. What do you say, Bob, Tobias?"

There was no answer from Tobias, and Robert, voice heavy with sleep, slurred, "That sounds fine." He didn't know if James heard him or not.

BACK AT PEEKSKILL, ROBERT GRATEFULLY passed the donkey into other soldiers' care; taking his letter box, he walked down to the edge of the kill. He settled in the shade of a boulder and arranged his paper and ink.

Dear Jennie,

I am sorry it has taken me so long to respond to your last letter. I admit that your news stirred me. I cannot imagine that Missus Leonard would ever be proud of a runaway such as you speak of, but if you say so, it must be true. From what I can recall, Missus Leonard employed harsh words for the most part. I never, in all the years I toiled, received praise from any, save perhaps a time or two when I wove an especially fine piece of linen. In learning the drill, and even here in the field, I succeed more often. The officers recognize my worth. Do not think me prideful to write such things. I mean only to explain why I am content, happy even, though a soldier's lot may seem a hard one. Always, in the past, I felt that I must be measured by the tape of another, conforming to inches and driblets. Here, though, the tape is my own. My desires match its markings; I stretch myself along its length willingly.

I am well and have been billeted to a field camp, but you needn't worry that I am in danger. Our days are filled with routine tasks of the most boring sort. One of my fellows recently noted that this camp is no place for womenfolk. It affords us a rough life. You possess a head as clear and a sense of duty as fine as any soldier in the camp, but you would find unaccustomed hardships here. I suppose I count myself an odd duck, content to call it home.

I have read and reread your letter. The fall weather puts me in mind of Middleborough and the maples that grew behind the Thomases' house. Have they turned red yet? Have you been to a husking party? With whom did you dance?

Of late, I have wondered what I will do when the war is over. It may be a long time yet, but still, my thoughts wander in this direction. There are some in my company who speak with longing of returning to their homes. I don't know where home is for me. Sometimes it's easier not to think of it. But if I do, I think home is with you, with a person who knows me and cares for me, and whom I care for, too. Yet I worry now that I am someone else, a someone you might not know. It is not that I am taller or skinnier or bearing some new scar, but that the way I had, of moving and even of thinking—being a soldier has changed all that. It is something larger than me, something that matters more, and I am part of it. Oh, this is no good; I cannot write well what I feel of this.

I do miss you so.

Love,
Robert

He let the ink dry, reading his words over. He didn't want to go back to Middleborough, but how else could he see Jennie again? Could he and James and Tobias go out to Ohio? A new territory . . . On the very edges of his memory, he could recall his father telling stories of their ancestors coming to Plymouth aboard the *Mayflower*—tales of a wild and untamed land, full of Indians and animals. He had loved to hear about it and, even then, had wished he had been the one to discover this new world. Well, now he could. He and James and Tobias could start anew, all three of them fleeing the disappointments of their early years, ready to try their hands in new and fertile ground. He didn't dare to write such dreams to Jennie, but he would dwell on them, turn them over in his mind, let them bring him comfort as he stood guard or toiled in the woods. Yet even as he turned the quill in his hand, drafting out sentences in his mind, he realized that if he went off to farm with James and Tobias, he would be Robert forever. Deborah would be lost. No great loss, he tried to tell himself. Indeed, Deborah seemed far distant, and he would happily relegate her to the past. But if that was true, why keep writing to Jennie? Why not be rid of that old life altogether?

He folded up the letter with careful creases and thought of the conversation he'd had so long ago with Munn, about fate and the path through life. The road he had traveled, whatever decisions he had made at the junctions—it was his road. It had brought him to this point and to this person. Deborah was part of Robert; she would always be so. It was just that, for now, and for the future he could imagine, Deborah was an inconvenience, like a boil on one's buttocks—unpleasant and unlikely to go away. If he could . . . it was impossible, but if he could, he would burst that boil, let all of it drain out. Even then, he thought, standing and stretching his back, there'd be a scar.

CHAPTER FIFTEEN

Two days after Matthew received his third flogging at Peekskill—it seemed he could scarcely pass an evening without starting a fight—Booth came to their lean-to and delivered orders. "Full packs, load your cartridge boxes, and fall in." Matthew groaned. He lay on his stomach, his back covered in damp dressings. Robert and James packed up their kits, and then James sorted out cartridges. "I'll tend to this if you'll see to Matthew," he told Robert.

"And I'll get rations," said Tobias.

Robert peeled back the fabric and rubbed salve into Matthew's stripes. Somehow, he'd become the nurse of the squad. "That's my flesh you're tearing," Matthew grumbled.

"Be still or you'll make it worse," Robert replied. "Why do you always end up in fights?"

"Other fellows don't know how to keep their mouths shut, that's why. And unlike you, I'm no good at turning the other cheek."

Robert offered Matthew a bandage, saying, "Wind that tight and I'll fasten it for you." As Matthew wrapped his torso, Robert stared at the bare limbs on the trees, the frost biting the ground. The cool autumn air felt refreshing, but it would soon take on the sting of winter. October had a way of passing quickly. He tucked in the ends of the dressing and then left Matthew to gather his gear. Tobias had piled rations by Robert's bag, and Robert packed these away before mustering.

Munn ordered everyone into columns, and Booth walked through, examining packs and muskets.

"Where are we headed, Corporal?" asked James.

Booth barely spared him a glance. "The captain will inform you when you need to know."

"Tarrytown, I hear," said Tobias.

"You hear a lot," said Booth.

Tobias shrugged. "There's been action down there, I'm told."

The corporal moved off to upbraid some lagging soldiers, and James leaned in to ask Tobias, "What sort of action?"

"The British reminding us that they aren't gone yet. Lots of little raiding parties."

From the front of the column came the order to march. The road followed the banks of the Hudson closely, and they could watch the water rolling along, slow and patient. They walked through wooded passes below steep hillsides that gave way to farmland. More than once, Webb sent a sergeant or lieutenant to inquire at houses. By evening, the company reached Sing Sing, a post much like Peekskill but already occupied by another regiment's detachment of light infantry. They piled in nonetheless, while Webb conferred with the other officers.

Just as daylight faded, the captain gathered the company. "The British have been active in these parts, and the landholders are complaining," he told them. "It's not only Cow-Boys out to steal livestock, either. This company has encountered regulars and even cavalry."

Tobias leaned close and whispered, "What did I tell you? DeLancey's light horse."

"Tomorrow," Webb continued, "I'll split the company into squads, and we'll scour the countryside. We will rout out these Royalists. I don't doubt that some of us will draw fire. Be patient. Follow orders. Take care of your fellows."

When Webb divided the company just after dawn the next day, Robert fell in with James and Tobias, along with a dozen others, under Munn and Booth. They said good-bye to Matthew; he, with Webb, was setting out in a small flotilla of boats rowing down the Hudson. The captain, renowned for his tight discipline, had taken the recalcitrant members of the company in his squad. A third group assembled separately under Lieutenant Gilbert, an officer Robert knew only by sight.

"All right, lads," Munn told them. "The captain and his crew will be cleaning out the river and keeping an eye on the banks, and the others will cover the high ground, so it is up to us to mind the roads in between."

"They are the vise and we are to be squeezed in the middle. Like a nut in a cracker," Robert said.

Tobias winced. "I wish you'd summoned a more pleasant image."

At the head of the squad, Munn conversed with Booth for a moment. Then the corporal called out, "Snow, Shurtliff, Hall, and Diston, with me."

Rejoicing that he had been placed with James and Tobias, and that Matthew had been sent in another group, Robert stepped closer to Corporal Booth. William Diston stepped forward as well; he was a lanky private who sometimes frequented Tobias's card games. They set out down the road, and where it split, Munn and his men took the eastern track; Robert, with the others, followed Booth on the road closer to the river. They did not march in file, nor did they sing or whistle. This in itself conveyed the gravity of the mission. Soon, the sound of splashing oars from Webb's boats subsided as the track veered from the river. They walked with their muskets crosswise to their chests, ears pricked for footsteps, for rustling, for anything out of the ordinary. To his right, Tobias gripped his musket so tightly that Robert thought he might well squeeze sap from its wooden stock.

After some hours of steady marching, they came to a small creek; Booth signaled a halt. "Quick, lads, a drink," he said, and tilted his head to study the sky. Robert followed his glance and tried to ascertain how much time had passed since they had left camp. "Not far from Tarrytown," Booth murmured to himself. Robert drank from his canteen before bending to refill it; just then, the water still a cool trickle down his throat, he heard hooves pounding up the road, followed by a volley of shots. He looked to James, then back to the horses, and tried to summon Munn's words as he dropped his canteen and lifted his musket—*cartridge, pan, lock*. Before he could even load, Booth grabbed him and yelled, "To the woods!"

A second volley of shot; Robert could feel it whistling past him. His legs seized up, going heavy and numb, and he couldn't manage to lift his feet. If not for Booth's hand tugging his coat, he might have stayed there until a shot felled him. But the corporal half-pulled him into the woods before releasing him, and Robert forced a stride, then another, plunging through undergrowth, heedless of thorns and branches. A blue coat loomed ahead of him, and he followed blindly, taking shelter behind a thick tree as musket balls hit wood, raising pulpy explosions. From his vantage he saw Booth ripping open a cartridge. Robert turned back toward the road: horses plunged, a blue coat in their midst, or was it two coats? Booth rammed the cartridge down the muzzle of his piece, screaming, "Load and fire, damn it!"

If Robert didn't shoot, they'd find him and kill him. But he was unable to move with anything more than underwater slowness; the world about him seemed thick and cloying. Booth fired. The noise ripped across the woods. Then the corporal ducked down, ran to

Robert, and seized his shoulder. Shaking him, he put his face up to Robert's. "Load and fire!" He tore open Robert's cartridge box and shoved the charge into his hand. "Do it now!"

Robert closed his eyes, sank his teeth into the paper of the cartridge, and tasted the bitterness of the powder. The curl of it on his tongue set his hands to the well-practiced motions of the drill. He put the musket to his shoulder, aimed for a horse, and fired. Shots came back, a neat volley, and in the silence that followed, Booth called out, "Run, take the ridge, spread out, and seek cover." Robert turned and scrambled up the hill, chased by the whine of small shot.

A little below the ridgeline, he threw himself behind a fallen log and peered over the top. From this spot he could glimpse the road through the trees, the horses there, someone in a brown coat holding the reins. That meant the riders had dismounted. "Load up, load up, and fire, boys." That was Booth, his voice sounding close, though Robert could not see him. Robert rammed another load into his musket even as shot splintered a tree to his left, sending bits of wood into his face. He lifted himself on his elbows, quickly took sight—a man in a brown coat at the bottom of the slope—and fired, then dropped flat to the ground again. His scan of the forest below had shown perhaps a dozen men approaching the ridge. A dozen. He should run. But if he stood, they'd shoot. No, stay low, load and fire, load and fire. He got one more shot off, saw the attackers were already halfway up the slope. He buried his face in the leaves, breathed in the rot of them, praying that the shots would cease.

Musket fire exploded from behind him, then a gurgle of screaming; the sounds seemed to emanate from above him, higher on the ridge. Were more British charging from that direction? With a quaking hand, he sprinkled powder in the pan and pushed himself up to shoot, only to register blue-coated figures running down the slope beside him, below him. The flash of a saber caught his eye—Sergeant Munn thundering down, hacking at a man. Relief burst through him; the sergeant must have heard the shots and come to aid Booth's squad. Steadier, Robert again sighted over the fallen log and aimed carefully, fearful of shooting a fellow American. Below him, brown-coated figures grappled with blue-coated men, so Robert leveled his piece at the horses on the road. They were far enough away to be out of range, but he knew he needed to provide covering fire to keep anyone from coming closer. He squeezed the trigger, and sparks flew; the powder sizzled and cinders brushed his cheeks, pinpricks of heat on his flesh.

"Form up! To me, Massachusetts!" Munn's harsh voice rattled up the ridge, and Robert's body obeyed. He rose from behind the log, musket in one hand, the other flung out for balance as he skidded down the slope, the ground slick beneath his feet. Joining the ragged line, he followed the sergeant's commands: Ram! Take aim! Fire! When the smoke from the muskets drifted away, he saw brown coats ahead, some running, a few on horseback, others fallen.

"Fix bayonets!" Munn screamed. The line charged into the chaos. Underfoot, Robert felt the change from leaf-strewn forest floor to hard-packed road and increased his speed. The brown coats scattered before he reached them. To his right, Booth ran his bayonet through a Cow-Boy trying to mount a horse. The beast plunged and reared, dragging the corpse. Someone knocked into Robert, and he fell, catching himself awkwardly on his hand. He rolled away and got to his knees. Confusion reigned—two horses, one riderless, galloped down the road, musket fire pursuing them; another horse thrashed on the ground, its legs churning uselessly. But all around him were men in blue coats, blue, only blue. From behind him came Munn's voice: "Form up on the road, square!" Gratitude for the command, for the restoration of order, rendered Robert limp with relief, but he pulled himself straight as the two squads fell in.

"Watch the woods," the sergeant barked, pointing at Booth. "Mind the road north!" He pointed to another soldier. "South!" He jabbed his finger at Robert, who nodded and took a few strides down the road. All was quiet, a quiet all the more profound for the wealth of noise and confusion it had replaced. His mind churned as he scanned the trees and listened for hooves, for footsteps.

He heard splashes from the riverbank, but kept his eyes pointed south, afraid of what the road or woods could yet hold. Then Captain Webb's voice called, "All fall in!"

Robert pivoted and saw that the captain had landed his boats. The men disembarked and scrambled up the banks to the road, where they assembled in lines. Robert ran his eyes over the ranks, then stepped in beside James, who stared blankly ahead, lips slightly parted, chest heaving as though he had just been running. At the front of the company, Webb gave orders for pursuit to a handful of men, sent a messenger and scout ahead to Tarrytown and another scout to inform Lieutenant Gilbert's squad, and then turned to Munn. "Sergeant, count the men."

Munn called, "Shurtliff." It took a second for Robert to find himself, reply.

"Snow."

"Here," James said.

"Hall."

Nothing.

"Hall?"

Nothing.

"Tobias!" James cried.

"Shut up," said Booth.

"Diston."

"Here."

And again, "Hall."

Nothing.

Munn called the rest of the names, and most replied. A few cried out from the woods, seemingly too injured to move, and other names garnered only silence. "Sergeant," Webb said, turning to Munn, "tend to the wounded. Corporal Booth, fetch the dead."

"Yes, sir. My squad!" Robert stood in front of the corporal, whose face bore gray streaks from the musket smoke. Next to him, Robert could feel James's arm shaking. "Matthew, Paul," said the corporal, and summoned a few more of the men who had arrived in the boats. "In pairs, search the woods, bring any bodies to the road."

Robert tugged James's shoulder and the two of them plunged into the underbrush. Not far from the road Robert found a body, one of the enemy. "I'll take the arms," he said. James nodded, his eyes averted from both Robert and the dead man. They lifted the corpse and carried it to the road. He didn't want to look, but found he couldn't help it. The man's chest gaped wide, a red ruin, his blood-soaked shirt still wet and glistening. Eyes open. Robert had hoped the eyes wouldn't be open.

They went back into the woods, pushing aside brambles, peering behind rocks and stumps. Robert felt suddenly dizzy and reached for his canteen, but it was not on his belt. He took a few deep breaths and walked on, scouring the bushes and fallen branches at the bottom of the ridge.

"Bob!" James called, and Robert hurried over; James had found another brown-coated body. Whatever had killed this man left nary a trace: no blood, no wounds. The two of them paused for a long minute, reluctant to move the body. Gazing at the corpse, its limbs thrown out as if he'd been trying to fly, Robert wanted nothing more than to lie down like this man and sleep. "Bob? Do you think Tobias is . . ."

Robert shook his head. "I don't know, James."

"He didn't run up the ridge. I called to him, but he didn't run."

Pine needles and little twigs were tangled in James's hair; his brown eyes seemed twice as wide as they'd ever been. Robert laid a hand on James's shoulder. "I don't know."

They lifted the body and carried it to the road. Robert counted six brown-clad corpses. He swiveled his head and saw a sergeant kneeling over a few wounded men, one lying down—he couldn't tell who, except that the man had dark hair—not Tobias. The other wounded leaned against trees or rocks. A few soldiers still combed the woods, but most clustered a little way down the road, and though he knew he should obey orders and continue searching for corpses, Robert went over to the group.

Pushing his way between two men, he saw him stretched out on the ground. Blue coat, blond hair. Tobias. Captain Webb knelt beside the body, his hands pulling at the coat, the shirt. With each tug, Tobias's head wobbled, flopping so far as to touch his shoulder. Tobias's throat had been shot away, the front of his neck a yawning hole, so large, so black, it was a miracle his head remained attached at all. Robert's gorge rose at the sight, yet he couldn't force his eyes away. Webb stood, gripped Tobias's feet, and yanked his boots off. "Strip that coat—pull it apart!" he barked. Two men leapt to obey, tugging savagely at the coat. Tobias's head lifted from the ground, fresh blood leaking out from his neck, mouth in the dust.

"Stop!" It was James. "Leave him be!" He pushed through the crowd to the body and tried to pull the men off the corpse. "Let him alone!"

Two men grabbed James from behind, and he thrashed in their grasp. Booth came running up. "Quiet, Snow. This needs to be done." Robert barely heard the corporal's words over James's incomprehensible yelling. Then Booth drew his hand back and slapped James across the cheek. Robert hurried to James's side.

"Corporal—that's Tobias. I don't understand . . . why are they . . ." Robert said.

"Stand aside." Booth looked at James. "Are you steady now?" James nodded, and the corporal led them a few yards away from the others. "I know he was your friend. But he was serving the other side. He ran toward them, and in the confusion of the melee he was shot. It could have been a shot from our side or from theirs. But he was serving them."

"How do you mean?" James began, belligerence rising in his voice.

"Steady. I'll show you." The corporal walked them toward the river, where Munn crouched by a stump covered with tightly rolled squares of parchment, each no larger than a man's finger. He had one unrolled before him, and his lips moved as he studied the words. He paused when Booth approached, his eyes glancing over at James and Robert. "Sergeant," said Booth, "they need to know."

Munn stood, sighed. "Yes, I suppose so." He lifted a musket. "This was Hall's." Robert nodded; he could see *TH* etched into the trigger plate. But the stock of the gun had been shattered by a musket ball. Munn pointed to the splintered wood. "See there?" A narrow hole had been drilled within the stock, and the shot that blasted away the surrounding wood had revealed the chamber. "He'd covered it with a plug. You'd have never noticed it." The sergeant put the gun down. "These were inside." He gestured to the curled parchments on the stump. "Notes, maps, questions. Lists of passwords and names. Your friend was gathering information for the British." Robert blinked in disbelief. Tobias a spy? "He had a list of all the farmers who gave us food, a drawing showing the layout of Peekskill, another numbering the boats we built at West Point. We are lucky he did not get this information to the Cow-Boys."

"I can't believe it," Robert said.

Munn reached out his hand, placed it on Robert's shoulder. "Only God can fathom the souls of men."

Booth cleared his throat. "Thank you, Sergeant. I'll take these lads to help with the wounded."

Robert let himself be led across the road. He took the canteen the corporal offered him and drank deeply.

Booth pointed to the creek. "Wash your face. You'll feel better—and look better, too."

The water sank heavily into Robert's stomach. He wanted to apologize to Booth for not firing sooner, for freezing like that. He opened his mouth. "Sir, about shooting there, in the skirmish—I'm sorry I couldn't—"

But Booth raised a hand. "It happens to everyone. You did better than most, Shurtliff."

As others brought in bodies, Robert helped tend to the wounded. One soldier's calf had been run through with a bayonet, another's face had been burned by a powder flash, and one private had a broken arm. Seeing the row of wounded men stretched out on the road, Robert offered a quick prayer of thanks that he had emerged intact. He had a few small burns on his cheeks where sparks had singed him, and one hand was scratched and bruised where he had fallen. But these were minor injuries. The pain he dared not dwell on too long he owed to Tobias. Just a day or two ago they had talked about the future, about what they would do once the war had ended. Had he been a turncoat then? He must have been. Had Tobias worked with Shaw? He rocked back on his heels, not wanting to believe it, but seeing the possibility nonetheless.

Webb called for the company to form up. As Robert gathered his gear and stood, he found the road clear—just a few patches dark with dampness showed where the bodies had lain. "We'll send a squad back to bury them," Webb said from the head of the troop. "Bring the wounded to the boats. We'll make Tarrytown by sunset."

Robert's squad arrived at the Tarrytown field camp just before dark, finding lean-tos and tents, with a tumbled-down barn the only remaining vestige of the farm that once flourished there. Robert stared at its weathered clapboards and tried to picture the scene as it must have appeared before the war: the orchards, the sheepfold, the henhouse—all gone. In a short while, even the barn might disappear, leaving no trace of what the land had once held. And some years hence, perhaps all signs of war would fade away, too. This land would be farm again, and these soldiers farmers. But some marks, some scars, would not fade. There was that which had been truly lost, forever changed. The last patches of sunset—red-gold flames—flared against the side of the barn, and Robert watched them soberly, caught by a sudden melancholy.

"Look sharp there, Shurtliff. There's work to be done," Munn said. "Unload your gear and get supper cooked. You're mooning about like a little girl."

"Yes, sir." Robert shook his head to clear it. He'd never been one for mooning, not even as a little girl, but today had rattled his foundation. He gave Munn a salute and sought out a lean-to for the night.

Sinking onto the mossy platform, James, still dusty and soot-streaked, settled next to him. "Bob. Do you think it's true, that Tobias was a spy?"

The unwelcome image—Tobias, throat gone, blue eyes staring—rose up before him. He had held it at bay during the march, but the panic surged up in him again, an echo of the afternoon's bald fear. "It must be, James. He always had rumors to share, and he always asked questions about what we'd seen on guard duty or where we'd been placed."

"But why?"

In front of the lean-to Matthew laid the fire, and Robert thought back to Tobias, the conversations they'd had about his family—how they put their resources toward the education of his elder brother—and his desire to go to Boston. He recalled how he always sought card games. "Money. It must be." Robert stood up. "I'm going to fetch water."

Down at the riverside, he knelt, watched the swirling water fill up the pots that he carried. Robert could imagine it: a night at cards, losing money, winning money, losing more. Drinking rum and walking back to the tent in the dark, some veteran offering a coin or two, a word of advice to listen carefully, tell him what he heard. The approval and gratitude when he produced a useful tidbit, how good that might have felt to Tobias, how easy to offer more. Robert shuddered, picked up the pots, and made his way back to the fire.

Matthew cut up the meat, and the three of them sat about the pot, waiting for the beans to cook. "All well, Bob?" Matthew asked. "You are uninjured?"

"Aye. Safe and sound."

"You were in the thick of it?"

"Quite. And you?"

"I never discharged my piece. By the time our boats landed, the fighting was all but over."

Robert hoped Matthew wouldn't ask for details. Now that he thought about the skirmish, the action muddled together, a tangled skein of running, falling, the smell of damp leaves, the crack of muskets.

"I can't believe he was a spy," said Matthew.

"I will still miss his friendship," said James as he stared into the fire.

"Those coins," Matthew said, "the ones they found in Tobias's coat . . . do you reckon those were payment?"

Robert nodded. "I think you're right."

"Sold us out, he did." Matthew lifted the lid of the pot, and a cloud of steam escaped. "Beans are done."

Doubleness. A true face and a false one. Robert ladled beans into his bowl, spooned them into his mouth, and chewed. He wondered what Tobias truly believed in, what motivated his actions. But his thoughts kept drifting back to himself, like a snake biting its tail. Robert Shurtliff—his name, someone else's name. Were the lies he told so very different from Tobias's? Misleading, gaining trust, being two people at once? The beans clotted in his mouth, and he struggled to choke them down.

After dinner, they laid out their blankets in the lean-to. Robert unbuttoned his coat and scraped at some mud and bark matted to the wool. As he pulled away the filth, he saw a neat hole through the cuff, in the extra fold of fabric around the wrist and forearm. He stuck his finger in the hole, marveling at it. Too large to have been caused by a snag on a tree, it must have been from a musket ball or a blade sliding through. So close. But he hadn't been harmed. He had loaded his gun and fired it. He pulled the coat back on; tomorrow he would mend it, else the whole piece would unravel from that one small hole.

Booth moved about the camp, setting up a rotation of sentries for the night. He came by their circle of flickering light and told Matthew to stand third watch on the southeast side. The corporal brought out a flask. "A drink, then? For Snow's first true skirmish and fight." He reached around to pour. Robert raised his mug to take the proffered rum, and they lifted their draughts in a silent toast.

The fire burned down, and Robert stood, stretched, and headed toward his blanket. Matthew decided to join another campfire rather than sleep before his turn at guard. He drifted off through shadows, and Robert watched him emerge in the next pool of orange light. Now it was just him and James. He stood in silence for a while, thinking of the right words to offer his friend. None came. Instead, Robert knelt by the lean-to, as he had done during many nights this autumn. To his surprise, James knelt by his side, and the two of them rested there for a while. Robert prayed silently at first, *Thank you, Lord God, for keeping me safe during the fight. For keeping James safe, too. Thank you for protecting me from Shaw's treachery.* Robert reached out and took James's hand. "May God have mercy on Tobias's soul," he said aloud.

"Amen," said James.

With the fire gone out, the night chill rushed in, and Robert swaddled himself in his blanket. James did the same, then lay down next to Robert. "I ran," James said, and Robert could hear the quiver in his voice. "I could have fixed my bayonet, but I ran."

"We all ran," Robert said. "We were told to run."

"I am a coward."

"You are no coward, James," he said.

"I could have . . ."

"James. It is a war. You acquitted yourself ably. Any one of us might have died."

"Might die tomorrow," he mumbled.

"Aye. But you'd never sell your friends out."

"Not for all the gold the British have. Never."

They lay in silence for a while and James's breathing leveled out. Robert turned onto his back; bits of sky sneaked through the branches, and he was surprised that enough leaves had fallen to allow him to see the constellations reeling above.

He pulled the blanket tightly about his shoulders and rolled over, but James reached an arm across Robert's torso, drawing him close. Robert could feel the weight of him, knew he needed comfort. And so he let James's arm settle, enjoying the warmth of him. James's breath tickled his neck, and some feeling stirred in Robert's chest—deeper, in his stomach, as if he'd swallowed a fish that yet darted about inside him. He wanted to roll over, to face James, he wanted to . . . he leaned back against James, savoring the sturdiness of him. Something slight and tender swept through him, as though someone were stroking the soles of his feet with the softest feather. James's arm lay across his breasts, and he lifted his own hand, placed it over James's. For a moment, he felt safe. The wind stirred the branches overhead, and Robert's pulse was slow in resuming its normal rhythm, even as he told himself this was not love or desire, this was clinging to life after confronting death.

Webb ordered a close inspection of muskets, and many—James among them—were told to clean their pieces again. "Load up your store of cartridges—a full box," the captain commanded the company.

Robert opened his box and counted; he was six short, though he didn't remember shooting that many times. He sat down with his powder horn, stock of shot, and papers to begin the tedious process of wrapping cartridges. "Do you need any, James?"

James shook his head but sat to help Robert, and so the task went quickly. When he had replenished his stock, Robert mended the cuff of his coat. It felt strange not to have Tobias at his side, and he caught himself looking about for his blond hair more than once that day. In the afternoon, Webb assembled the company again and announced that they would be stationed here at Tarrytown for the rest of October. Crops had been brought in, and farmers wanted sentries to watch over the harvest at mills and storehouses as well as to hunt down raiding parties.

Robert took the duties assigned to him: escorting a foraging party, guarding an orchard. By the end of October, they were all but idle on many days and filled their time with fishing on the Hudson or hacking up firewood. Just as it had earlier, the stillness began to grate on him. Occasionally, he had the prickling sensation that someone was watching him, as though Shaw might be lurking in the trees or the ghost of Tobias was haunting the company. Thinking of Widow Thacher's favorite adage, that idle hands—and idle minds, for that matter—are the devil's tools, Robert volunteered for duties, seeking out Munn to ask for a place on scouting parties. To his great surprise, James always asked to join as well, though whether he was driven by guilt, a desire to prove himself, or a certain destructive melancholy, Robert could not ascertain. Sometimes he thought that James stuck close out of a need for comfort; since Tobias's death he had been a constant presence at Robert's side.

Most often, squads of three or four went out for a few nights at a time, carrying as little in the way of gear and provisions as they dared—moving quickly down to the British lines, slipping through the pickets, skulking in the trees and caves, for Westchester abounded with such, to discover where the troops collected, how many boats they had, whether they appeared to be massing for attack or raid.

Skirmishes came infrequently, though on a few occasions they were able to lay ambush to raiders and chase down some Cow-Boys.

Fear rose in Robert whenever the shots flew around him or he took a stand to aim his own piece, and it was later, trembling with exhaustion and the outflow of excitement as his squad made its way back to Tarrytown, that he would wonder at this world he found himself in. Other men, brave men, were content to pass the days in games of cards or dull sentry posts. But he felt safest in the thick of danger. He had not known he was capable of stealth or accuracy or daring until called to action. Cleaning his musket and thinking over what had transpired, he marveled that he might have spent his life at a loom or spinning wheel and considered that the extent of his universe.

When there were no raids to take part in, Robert took out his letter box and wrote to Jennie. It began to feel more like a diary than a letter—he had written a paragraph one day, another the next week, and so on, creating a patchwork missive. There hadn't been a chance to post it, and who knew when he might get a letter from her. But still, one chilly afternoon in November, when they already had fires roaring, Robert sat with his back to the flames and finished the rambling account.

Dear Jennie,

I am in Westchester now, the region south of West Point. More than that is not prudent to say. My squad was ambushed by some cavalry. It was all so confused that I still haven't sorted it out in my mind. I am unharmed. I shot when told to shoot, I charged when told to charge. But I am not that brave. When the fellows sit around the fire in the evening, they recount the grisly details, but I don't like to talk about it. To have death so near is to know that one is no more than skin and bones and blood.

The days in camp are not quite as dull as a day at the loom. And the life of the soldier, though constrained, is not nearly as restricted as the life of servant, especially one who serves as we did. At least I am permitted to move around, unless I am on guard duty and must stand by a piece of road. It is a peculiar difference, though; when you're at a loom, you get to produce, to make something new, something that did not exist before your hands crafted it. But what do I make as a soldier? Neither war nor peace. These would happen without me. I mold musket balls and sew them into cartridges, and then I destroy these when I shoot. But what I really make is a new self—every skirmish shapes me, as sure as your fingers shape the cloth on the loom. Never before did I believe I had the power to influence events, to form a life according to my desires, but now something more than a commonplace fate seems possible.

I long for a letter from you—for news from Middleborough, news of your health. The world seems not to exist here, just camp and soldiers and commands from the officers. At least the weather has been dry and pleasant, even though it's getting colder now that we are in the midst of autumn. I dreamed of you last night, dreamed that you were telling me a bedtime story, and in my dream I looked other than I look now. But you looked the same, and you told me a story about a horse that ran away, but I don't remember much of that.

The past has become a dream to me—that I lived in Middleborough, that you and I were young together. It seems to me that I am now a person without a past, as if I had grown, like a plant, straight from the soil of West Point. Who knows what fruit I will bear?

Do not be angry if I say that as much as I want to return to you, I can't imagine coming back to Middleborough. Jennie, I do not know what there is, apart from you, that would welcome me there. And all that I had there, well, that is a life I do not wish to return to. Now that I have tasted freedom and the world beyond, my stomach clamors for nothing else. But know that I miss you, that I think of you daily.

Love,
Robert

CHAPTER SIXTEEN

The company returned north to Peekskill with the intent to hold the line of the Croton River as full winter approached. With the advent of December, the weather grew ever more bitter. Webb presented the company with heavier coats, and James sat by Robert's side as the two of them tailored the seams: James let his shoulders out, Robert took his in. Matthew wheedled both of them, begging, then bribing them to do his sewing for him. "Have a seat. Bob will tutor you proper," said James. Matthew assented at last—he could only find one soldier willing to tailor for him, and that at exorbitant rates—and Robert loaned him a needle and instructed him in stitching.

"Gah. This thing's a menace," said Matthew as he pricked his thumb again. None of the thimbles that Jennie had packed for Robert would fit Matthew's spatulate fingers. He jabbed the needle in again, leaving a blot of red-brown on the fabric.

"You've sewn up a bit of the sleeve to the chest," Robert said when he investigated the work. "If you tear out these stitches, you can mend that. . . ."

"I'm not doing it over. My fingers shouldn't have to serve as pincushions."

"Suit yourself," said Robert.

"Imagine that. The average seamstress has tougher thumbs than you . . ." James said.

"Watch your words, Snow. I'm in no mood for your cheek."

Good fortune brought Corporal Booth by their fire at that moment. "Stand to, boys. You're up for guard duty." The three of them drew on their coats, plucking at stray threads and testing the newly mended seams. Matthew's shoulders hunched unevenly, constrained by the missewn sleeve. Booth frowned at him and yanked the fabric. "You've stitched that too tight by far. You won't be able to use your bayonet. Sit here and fix it. Any good soldier should know how to sew."

James gave Robert a broad smile, as satisfied as a cat with an overturned jug of milk. "Shall we, Bob?"

THE SMOKE OF COOKING FIRES hung low and blue in the cold air when an officer in a uniform unlike any Robert had seen before—a black coat with red facing and red slashes running up the arms—rode into camp. He was shown to Captain Webb's quarters and soon emerged in the company of Sergeant Munn, who ordered all to assemble. "Major Vernier has come from the French division camped near Crom Pond. Much of his regiment has gone to winter cantonment, and he needs our aid in intercepting a band of sympathizers who are providing supplies to the British." Sergeant Munn scanned the assembled company. "Anyone for it?"

Robert hardly paused before calling out, "Aye!"

Two beats later, James said, "Aye!" as well.

A few more voices responded, Corporal Booth's among them. "Step forward, you dogs," said Munn. Fifteen of the company moved to the front. "These are the best, sir," he said to Major Vernier, and Robert blushed with pleasure. Munn offered the major a salute and said, "Yours to command, sir."

"*Allons-y*. We go."

THEY TARRIED ONLY LONG ENOUGH to draw two days of rations, mostly in the form of biscuits and hard cheese, for they would risk no fires on the mission. In tight ranks, they marched on the southerly road, heading to the ferry across the Croton River. There, massed at the ferry landing, the French squad waited, their numbers as sparse as teeth in an old man's jaw. Robert could see why Vernier had asked for American reinforcements.

"You've never fought with the French, eh?" Booth asked, and Robert shook his head. "Good fighters. Not as quick as the British, but better with a blade." He turned and spat. "I fought with them at Yorktown. Learned some French then. Nothing useful except in a brothel." He laughed at his own joke, then quickened his pace to catch up with the front. As they drew close, Robert was surprised to see how old the French soldiers appeared; they were poorly shaven and some of them were going gray. He was long accustomed to being in an army of boys. At the same time, the Americans towered over the Frenchmen. Robert himself overtopped all but one of them.

As the ferry carried troops across the water, Munn conferred with Vernier; the major held a map and traced a route with his finger as Munn nodded along. Once everyone had arrived on the far riverbank, the sergeant called the Americans together. "All right, lads. The French scout—I think they have some spy or turncoat, but he's not saying—reports that a party of Tories is planning to provision a barn or cave tonight, and the British will cross over and collect the supplies, likely right at dawn." His gaze moved over the group. "So we're going to march quickly down to the area—there are three possible spots—and lay ambuscades at each." He licked his lips. "Is that clear?" Silence. James shifted his feet, grunted, like a cow impatient to be milked. "Good enough," said Munn, and the squad formed up in tight ranks behind the French.

Vernier set a fast pace, and they flew across Westchester County, passing farms that Robert had guarded in the autumn and orchards whose limbs now rattled bare. At one such spot, where they paused to consult a map, an obliging farmer offered apples to the troops. Vernier shouted, "*Un! Un!*" and held up a thin finger for the benefit of the Americans. Robert had learned long ago the danger of eating too many apples after a seemingly endless evening of stomach cramps and mad dashes to the privy. Long ago—had he been living with his mother then? Had he been a little girl? The burst of juice, tart and puckering, released from the tight skin flooded Robert's mouth and for an instant brought him back to Middleborough and a memory of carrying home an apron full of apples; he pictured himself in a dress and bonnet, as if in a dream. Then, with a jolt, he heard Vernier call out in French, and Munn shouted, "Up, you louts!" And they were under way. The road carried them along the Croton and away from the Hudson in a direction unfamiliar to Robert. The slant of light and the soreness of his feet told him that they'd covered well over ten miles since the ferry.

At last, with the sun casting long shadows, Vernier motioned the men off the road, and they scampered up the side of a well-wooded hill. At the top, outcroppings of rock rose high enough to give a broad view of the land below, but when a French soldier clambered up a tree for a better look, Booth—not to be outdone—found another trunk and did the same.

He returned to the ground in a flurry of bark and reported to the squad, "A big farm down there . . ."

"Called Von Hoite," Munn interposed.

"Lots of little hillocks too," Booth continued.

"That's where the caves are," Munn said.

"I don't like it," said Booth, working to remove a sticky glob of tree sap from his coat sleeve. "To cover every place we'll be spread thin as jam on a poor man's toast."

Munn tilted his head as if considering this point. "We've hours to set up the ambuscade, and they don't know of our presence. Surprise can give us considerable advantage, God willing."

Robert rested on a rock that was still warm from the day's sun, as the leaders conferred again. Munn came over and divided the group. "Shurtliff, Snow, you're with Booth. Diston, you as well."

Then, before daylight fled, they slithered down the steep hillside. "Right," said Booth when they reached the midpoint of the slope. "We're to cross the far pasture and watch that last hillock there." He gestured through the trees to a landscape only partially visible. "Give the road and barn a wide berth. If the Tories drop at our spot, we'll send a runner to alert the rest of our squad and do our best to capture the Tories. Once they've been handled, we will all await the British. Cautious now."

James, with his bearish lumbering, drew evil glares from Booth as they ventured down the hill. "Try not to step on every branch," the corporal hissed. Eventually they reached the pasture and ran, crouched over, along the hedge to the low hillock. They did indeed find a cave in the hillside, a shallow indent that they explored only far enough to ascertain that it stood empty. Then the four of them took spots above and beside it, cloaking themselves in underbrush and leaves. Robert crouched at the base of a tree, hidden behind the leafy branches of a holly bush, curled up against the cold. Just when he felt he must move or suffer a cramp in every muscle, a rustling sound came from below. A French soldier—his black-and-red uniform barely visible in the echoing twilight—ran up to their position, and Booth stepped out to meet him. The Frenchman spoke rapidly at first, but then, seeing their confused faces, he left off and gesticulated forcefully toward the road. They followed him up to a little ridge and then over. On the hillside below, Robert could see the darkened opening of another cave, and he pointed at it. The Frenchman nodded and then put a finger to his lips.

Even the forest hushed. Then someone clucked, as one would to a horse, and Robert heard the creak of leather traces and the groan of wagon wheels. He held himself in tense immobility, searching the dimness for movement. Soon enough, figures—mere shadows, really—appeared on the hillside below them: an unevenly matched pair, a man and a boy, carrying a crate between them. They stooped to clear logs and leaves from the mouth of the cave, and just as they bent to pick up their load again, a rush of French soldiers swept out of the cave like a bevy of bats, and Booth urged Robert and James on, down the ridge to the track where the wagons stood. Munn's soldiers rose from the shadows and tackled the two other Tories who had waited with the wagons. By the time Robert and James had arrived, running behind the corporal, all of the Tories had been subdued. No one had let off a shot, and the prisoners were tied and gagged, tossed in the back of the wagons, and led away by Major Vernier and his troops.

Munn gathered the squad. "Well, boys, I imagine the British will arrive by dawn to gather their supplies. We'll be ready to give them a surprise, Lord help us. I'll set you in pairs—one asleep and one awake—you can exchange duties. Eat now, that's my advice." Robert and James formed a pair, and Munn placed them midway between the track and the cave. "Take sight now while there's a little light—mark how you see the path and line of travel." Robert nodded and Munn continued, "Booth will caw like a crow when he spots them."

Robert ate a biscuit and drank water as night slowly settled around them; eventually he was able to tell that James was near only by his rustling noises as he gathered armloads of leaves for a bed. James insisted that Robert take first watch and wake James whenever he grew tired. Robert watched the moon rise through the trees, large and low at first, then higher and growing ever smaller. By its light, he could see James asleep under his heavy coat, his mouth open, his shaggy hair straggled over his forehead. Robert wanted to reach out and touch him, stroke his cheek, brush away the loneliness of this night, of these weeks.

He gauged the time by the moon's passage, and when he thought four hours had elapsed, he shook James, who roused himself in a stir of leaves, and rubbed his eyes. "You awake?" Robert whispered.

"Aye."

"Have some water." He passed his canteen over.

"Thanks, Bob." Then, settling under his own coat, Robert lay down where the ground yet held the heat of James's body and fell asleep, safely watched over.

The cry of a crow woke Robert, woke James too, for he had drifted off, leaning against his musket. The caw came again, just as he realized, blinking rapidly, that the dead of night had passed. A scant ribbon of gray lit the horizon, the scarcest mark of the coming dawn.

"The British," Robert said in a hushed tone, and quickly sprinkled powder on the pan and brought his musket to bear on the road. He had no sooner done this than a shot rang out, followed by a clatter of hooves. Robert could see little of the woods around him, but the sounds came from above, not from the track. Another shot, and Robert pivoted in time to see horses crashing down the slope toward them. He fired his musket without truly aiming it; James fired off his piece too, and then the horses were past them. Robert, grappling with confusion—he had expected the British to come by the track—made haste to reload and ready his bayonet. All around them shots rang out, from below, from above, and Robert's instinct urged him to lie low, but though there might be safety in this course, he could hear the struggles of his fellow soldiers and knew he had to help them. He tugged James's sleeve and pointed downhill toward the track. The two of them darted from tree to tree and emerged on the edge of a melee. In the chaos of shadowy undergrowth, horses, a swirl of black coats, blue coats, cries and screams rising up in the ragged darkness, Robert could scarcely tell friend from foe, and he knew only to shoot at the mounted soldiers, for his squad had no cavalry. He managed two rounds before a horseman swung about and charged, lashing out with a saber. Robert lunged, then tumbled among rocks and roots. Sparks of light burst behind his eyes as he hit his head on something, but he stood up, swaying, and managed to load and fire again.

"Massachusetts, to me!" He heard Munn's voice, but far away, on the other side of the massed enemy. A steep, brush-filled slope, where the British had taken cover, separated him from the other Continentals. Just as Robert despaired of getting to that voice, a volley of shots rang out, then another. Munn had organized enough men to give heavy fire. Robert turned left and right, looking for James, but saw nothing. He only hoped that James had made it to Munn and had joined the line now firing off their muskets again. Only a few pistol shots answered; horses whinnied, and Robert moved up the slope, trying to make a circuit around the British. Another volley, and he heard the call from the British. "To horse! Take the road!" Shots came at random, as did screams—of horses and of men. He dashed from a tree to a boulder, now moving along the crest of the slope, trying to get to the other side of the British line. Just as he crossed that invisible boundary and began to descend, he felt something slam into his leg, hot and liquid all at once. He grabbed his thigh and felt the slickness of blood there. God, Lord Almighty. He braced against the rock to load, then fired his own musket at the ragged rank of horses before trying to run toward the Continental line, but his leg couldn't support him, and he dropped to the ground.

"Massachusetts!" Munn's voice. Robert crawled down the slope. At last he had reached the rear of his own squad; a few men pivoted as if to shoot, but then recognized him. Munn had a sword in one hand, a pistol in another, and called out commands. "Load and shoot! Forward to the road!" Robert staggered to his feet, and the others rushed by. He limped along, trying to keep pace. The forest swam before him, wavering, refusing to stay still. His ears rang, a sound that swelled and shrank. A dark figure appeared straight ahead. Robert raised his musket and, with a cry, thrust desperately with his bayonet. He felt the soft satisfaction of the blade striking, entering, but as he tried to pull out, his whole body pivoted, unable to break free. His shoulder wrenched, stretching impossibly back. The bayonet was stuck, in what he could not tell; he pulled at it with his right arm, but his left hung slack and useless. The weapon would not budge. He heard his name—or perhaps just imagined it—before his vision exploded in a cloud of white.

Robert lifted his head, raising himself on his right elbow. Leaves clung to his hair; his hat was gone. The sun had cleared the horizon and bore down on him. He blinked, trying to fend it off.

"Ah, Bob, you've come awake. You were senseless for a little while." It was Corporal Booth who, seeing him stir, came to his side. "The Frenchies are bringing the wagon. How do you feel?"

His head ached terribly, as though his mind was clogged with grit and pebbles. He tried to raise himself but could not; his left arm hung useless. "I cannot move this arm," he said, wriggling his shoulder.

Booth reached for it before Robert could prevent him. His hand gently turned Robert's limb. "I see no holes in the coat, no blood, so you must not be shot." He lifted the arm an inch at a time. Robert howled, felt bone grate against bone. "Ah. It's out of joint. I've done this a dozen times." With a quick, deft movement, he lifted Robert's arm up and back. A sickening grind and slither, followed by a pop. "Better?"

Robert gasped; the shoulder burned, and though he could now raise his arm, it felt stiff and heavy.

"It will ache for a spell, that's true. But it's better than a broken bone. Now, Bob, your head is a pretty mess. Can you walk?"

Robert touched his right hand to his forehead; it felt sticky, and his fingers came away red. "I shall try." Booth helped him up, and he swayed with dizziness for a moment; each motion made his shoulder throb, but he staggered a few steps. Right foot, left foot. He walked. Nothing broken. But pain—in every step of his left leg, pain, lancing high up in his thigh. He bit his lip, took another step. "I can walk."

"Good man," said Booth, turning as the wagon wheels groaned down the track. He was down the road before Robert could ask about James. Though he turned his head—a maneuver that brought on a lurching vertigo—he saw no sign of his friend, and he didn't trust his leg to walk on. Dizzy and thirsty, he settled back against a tree trunk.

In the end, Major Vernier ordered Robert into one of the wagons. The prisoners from the previous night, plus two soldiers captured in the morning skirmish, were bound tightly about the wrists and made to march in the midst of the troops. The arrangement gave room in the wagons for the captured supplies and, in addition to Robert, another half a dozen wounded soldiers. He ended up in the wagon with French soldiers; the only other American was a corporal, Plummer, who had taken a saber to his hand and rode on the wagon's seat. Robert lay at the back near two French soldiers, one little better than a corpse, his coat soaked through with blood from a gaping stomach wound. The other had a mangled mess of an arm; it looked as if curs had chewed it. But for all that, he seemed cheerful, which Robert wondered at until he noticed the soldier had broached a captured cask and was dipping his horn cup into some liquor.

As to the other wagon, which followed after them, Robert could see nothing but the driver, a Frenchman. They took the road back past Von Hoite's farm and then a different track, crossing the Croton farther east, at a shallow and sandy bend where all could ford.

After the crossing, Booth came back to walk alongside the wagon. "How fares the shoulder?" Robert lifted and rolled his left arm tentatively. "Quite sore. But usable." In truth, it ached, rigid and swollen, but he'd be damned if he'd let some surgeon in for a closer look.

"And the head?" pressed Booth.

"Can't say as it hurts a bit." This rang closer to fact, for though he felt light-headed, the wound itself gave only an occasional throb of pain.

Booth peered in. "Still. It's a bloody mess. The Frenchies have a surgeon, they say, up at Crom Pond, and he'll sort you out."

"Why Crom Pond? I'd rather go back to Peekskill."

"Not with that head."

"Then West Point."

"Crom Pond is a sight closer. Besides, all West Point will be in disarray—they are half moved to winter quarters in New Windsor." Booth gave him a nod, as if to close the conversation, and only then did Robert think beyond himself.

"Where is James? Is he wounded?"

"Worry about your own trouble for now, Shurtliff. Snow will manage without you." With that, Booth trudged off to the second wagon.

Robert lifted his left leg, shifting it to a more comfortable position. Every bump in the road sent an agonizing shiver from his hip to his knee. Blood coated his trousers, damp and clammy against his skin. Booth must have assumed all the gore came from the gash on his scalp, but Robert could feel, now and then, a trickle seep down his thigh. He'd been lucky—very lucky—with the shoulder. That Booth hadn't insisted on looking at the flesh, that a shot hadn't torn into him there, a wound that would require him to disrobe and be examined. Robert clenched his fists as the wagon rumbled over the pockmarked road, fighting to conceal the pain.

The sun offered its full afternoon glow, but Robert grew cold despite it. The wagon lurched over a large rock, jarring his shoulder and leg, and drew to a shuddering stop; he could not keep himself from crying out. The drunken soldier across from him raised a bleary head. Robert bit down on his cheek to hold the tears at bay as Booth came up alongside the wagon. "The road splits here for Crom Pond. I'll be going back to Captain Webb at Peekskill." He lifted his chin to the west. "But there are others from our company with you—Plummer here, and in the other wagon Diston, and Sergeant Munn, and Snow as well."

Robert tried to sit up. "James is injured?"

"Aye, the surgeon will be seeing him too." Abruptly, Booth gave a short salute, and Robert, aching to know more, replied in kind.

"I'll see you in West Point," he said.

"New Windsor, more like," the corporal replied.

"Farewell."

The Americans took the road headed to the west and the wagons followed the winding track to the north; Robert closed his eyes as the horses strained up an incline. He drifted toward sleep, but sparks flew behind his lids, red in the black, little flashes of pain that startled him. Opening his eyes, he saw the sky had grown overcast, pewter gray, and as he stared, a few flakes fell, darting, sticking to the cold ground. So James lay in the other wagon. Robert looked again at the Frenchman across from him with the shattered arm, riding to what was certainly life as a cripple. He braced his own leg between his hands and prayed for a better fate for himself and for James as well.

CHAPTER SEVENTEEN

The wagon rounded the bend, and the French camp came into view. Roofs sagged, blankets hung in place of doors, the fetid smell of necessaries and neglect radiated from the site. A taste, sour and metallic, flooded Robert's mouth. The wagon rolled to a stop, and he leaned over the side, mouth gaping as his gorge rose. A thick rope of saliva dangled from his lips, and he spat, then dragged a sleeve across his face. "Need a hand, there?" Plummer asked. Robert shook his head, regretting the movement, which set the world blinking before him.

He swung his legs down and walked slowly, trying not to wince. French soldiers already swarmed about the other wagon, and one came to usher Robert inside. Within, he saw a surgeon readying an array of equipment—needles and probes, a devastating saw, vials and bottles. Another soldier walked by carrying a stretcher. Robert and Plummer were seated on a bench, and an assistant examined their wounds. He came back with a basin of water and a bottle of rum. Handing the bottle to Plummer, he urged him to drink. "It will go better," he said, and began to wash the wound on Robert's head. He dipped a rag in water, scrubbed lightly, rinsed, washed again—the water in the basin soon turned pink, and Robert could feel the man's finger now on his flesh, pulling at his skin. Something stung. Plummer drank deeply, then turned to face him. "Quite a gash, Shurtliff," he said, and lifted the bottle again.

"You feel nothing?" the assistant asked.

"No," said Robert, holding himself rigid.

At last, he ceased his scrubbing, placed a wad of cloth on the wound, and told Robert to hold it there. Then he turned his attention to Plummer's hand. From the window behind him, Robert could hear men talking and swiveled to observe, but the assistant snapped, "Sit still or you make it bleed more." Plummer groaned as the man rinsed the wound and pulled on his fingers; with his good hand, the corporal raised his rum bottle. From the other end of the building, they heard a scream, and Plummer slurred, "Poor bastard."

The assistant withdrew, and for a while they sat in silence, Robert itching to find James, and Plummer working assiduously to finish the bottle. He did so a short while before the surgeon entered. The surgeon reached only middling height, but his broad shoulders made him imposing. He held Plummer's hand, took a long needle from a tray, and worked to dislodge the gravel and debris from within the wound. Plummer grunted and groaned, but the rum seemed to serve him well, for he didn't flinch. "Nothing broken. It is good," said the surgeon. He coated the gashes with thick salve and black sticking plaster.

"No other wounds?" the surgeon inquired.

"Fine, fine," said Plummer, and the surgeon gestured for the assistant to help the corporal to a room; he turned to Robert and began to probe his head wound. After his skull was bound, the surgeon looked at him. "What other injury?"

Robert shook his head. "None."

The surgeon pointed to his leg, where the blood on his pants had dried, matted puddles of red-brown, with several spots still damp. "From this," Robert said, pointing to his head, hoping the surgeon would believe him.

"Not possible," the surgeon said.

Flustered, Robert began to stammer out an excuse, but just then a prolonged scream came from the other end of the hospital. The surgeon pivoted toward the noise and hurried down the hall, turning back only to say, "I check later." Robert slumped, his relief suppressed by the thought that it could have been James screaming. Before he could worry too much, the assistant returned and took Robert to a side room with several bunks; Plummer lay in one, snoring already. The assistant opened a trunk by the door, removed a clean shirt and trousers, and placed them on a bunk. "Change," he said, pointing to the clothes, "I'll wash yours." With that, he left the room.

Outside the room's window, the sunset barely eked through the clouds that streaked the horizon. With a deep breath, Robert pulled down his trousers. His thighs were smeared with blood. He lowered himself onto the edge of the bunk, careful to keep his back to the door, and prodded his left leg; it felt fine near the knee, tender farther up and then—ah—the sudden pain higher, perhaps three inches below his crotch. Blood flowed, a thick trickle, when he pressed. Nudging around, the blood running over his fingers, his flesh hot beneath, he felt it, something hard lodged within his thigh. Not a full musket ball, but perhaps the ball from a pistol or from a weapon loaded with a scatter of shot. He had to get it out.

Buttoning up his trousers again, he stuck his head out of the room. Noise—some talking, intermittent clatters, a near-constant groaning—came from the other end of the hospital; he hoped no one would bother him for some time, perhaps until the assistant brought dinner. He steeled himself to act now, while Plummer slept off his rum. Sidling from the doorway into the chamber where the doctor had treated him, he took a probe, a needle, and two bottles from the table. Then, spying the pile of dressings, he grabbed a wad and hobbled back to his room. Placing the already bloody coat beneath him, he removed his trousers and sat down, his back against the door to delay entry.

He washed the wound with the liquid from the bottle, which smelled like especially noxious rum and burned wickedly. With the blood cleared away, he could see that the ball had left a ragged entry hole. Holding the probe, a thin skewer like a knitting needle, with his right hand, he stretched the gash open with his left. He slipped the probe inside—its shaft lancing cold. He pushed it in an inch, another, and it struck the ball, a metallic tinge he registered in his jaw. Blood, warm as tea, flowed out around the probe. Gently pushing, he moved the ball a bit, fearful of lodging it deeper. He slid it gradually along, working it toward the opening. His leg jerked as if he'd been scalded, and he stuck his tongue out, panting like a dog. Breathe, breathe. He twitched the probe, desperate to get the shot out, but the ball slipped away, rolling off the end. Robert cursed and plunged the metal rod in again. It clicked against the ball. Slide it, pause, slide it; the shot budged an inch, slipped back, and Robert could stand the agony no more. He pulled the probe to the side, opening the wound up, and slid a finger in. The edge of the hole strained, tore, but he pushed his finger farther. Once he felt the ball, pinning it between his finger and the probe, he worked it up, holding his breath until the piece of metal dribbled out.

The blood ran freely then, and he stanched it with his coat and trousers, for, bloodstained as these already were, they would conceal this secret surgery. Waiting for the flow to stem, he picked up the ball. It seemed a puny thing to have caused so much anguish, about half the size of a normal musket charge, an irregular lump of lead. He wondered if there might be more in there, smaller pieces, but he couldn't bring himself to explore the hole further. Pouring water over the tails of his shirt, he scrubbed at his thighs, getting much of the blood and dirt off. He doused the wound again, letting out a hiss of air at the sting, then wrapped it with bandages. Stripping out of the rest of his clothes—all save the binding about his chest—he put on the shirt and trousers the assistant had given him, piling his dirty uniform on the floor. The instruments he had used he placed in the trunk by the door, carefully tucking them under a stack of clothing before settling onto a bunk. The pain gave way to dizziness as he lay down, the room spinning about him. While Plummer snored away on the other side of the room, Robert closed his eyes and let sleep carry him away.

He didn't wake until the next morning, when the surgeon appeared in his room, holding out the still-stained trousers.

"These were soaked in blood," he said. "You have another wound." It was not a question, for the surgeon pointed to the hole in the leg of the pants.

Robert, light-headed and sleepy, struggled to sit up. Disoriented, he rubbed at his eyes, felt the dressing swaddling his head, and tried to focus on the doctor. "I do not know how I gained that hole," he said, feigning confusion, "maybe a nail in the wagon?" A weak excuse, but the best he could summon. "As to the blood, the wound on my head ran freely for a time, and there were many other injured who lay alongside me. The blood may well be theirs."

The surgeon's bushy eyebrows bunched in a V of disdain. "I would examine your leg."

"I assure you, I am fine," said Robert, defensively drawing his legs up to his chest, though even this small movement caused pain—he could feel the wound flex and open, blood seep out.

The surgeon put the trousers on the bed, crossed his arms over his chest. "Then up and walk."

Robert threw the blanket back, swung his legs to the floor. As he put his weight on his feet, he did not know what to expect. But he managed to stand upright. His left leg trembled and he put his hand to his head, as if he were woozy, quickly took a step, and another. Each step sounded a drumbeat in his head, making his eyes tremble.

"Enough. Lie down."

Robert and Plummer lay abed for another two days. The assistant brought them food—"fit for invalids," Plummer complained, though Robert thought he was upset about the lack of additional rum—and returned Robert's freshly washed uniform. For his part, Robert ate without comment and occupied himself with sewing up the many rents and tears his trousers and coat had sustained in the skirmish. At first, he pressed the assistant for news of James, to be allowed to see him, but the doctor ordered complete rest and no contact with anyone.

So he watched the sun make its way across the floor, the light rendered watery by the dingy glass of the windows. He closed his eyes when his head ached and tried to ignore the throbbing from his leg and not to worry about James. His shoulder remained tender, and he could see a purple bruise blossoming above the binding around his breasts. His only movement was in trips to the latrine, when he shuffled along, feigning dizziness in an attempt to cover for the unsteadiness of his left leg. He had not dared to examine the wound again but was content that it had not bled through the bandage. At night, lying in his bunk, he would place his hands upon the wrappings, gently pressing to discern if it grew bloated, and though the wound radiated warmth, it did not seem to be getting worse. Often he jolted from sleep, overcome by the idea that James lay nearby, disfigured and suffering, and Robert could offer no comfort.

A few days later, the surgeon examined their injuries. Plummer's hand was mending nicely; the wound had been deep, but he could move his fingers and thumb. The surgeon cleaned it again, stretched the fingers, watched Plummer move all his joints, and declared himself satisfied as he replaced the bandages. He then unwrapped the dressing from Robert's head and swabbed at it with some liquid. Apart from the sting, Robert felt little pain, and the doctor covered it again. Robert thanked him for his attentions, and the surgeon nodded and withdrew. No sooner had he pulled the door shut behind him than Sergeant Munn entered. His left arm hung in a sling across his barrel chest, but he already wore his regimentals.

"Plummer, Shurtliff. The good doctor says you are both healing well."

"Aye, sir, and you?"

"Well enough, thanks to God." He lifted his arm a bit. "A shot to the arm, but the ball passed clean through and broke nothing." He pointed with his right hand to where the wound was, in the flesh above the elbow. "It will take a while to mend completely, but winter is upon us, and none of us will be much needed in the field." He sat on the edge of Plummer's bunk. "The French are keen to move out before the worst of winter. We need to vacate the hospital."

Robert could see the sergeant wiggle his fingers in the sling as he spoke and wondered if Munn felt the same nervous tension he did. These days of idleness had been agony for Robert—not just the physical pain, which came and went, but the questions that churned ceaselessly: What would happen if his leg began to bleed again? Or the French surgeon demanded to investigate? Or, worse, the wound began to fester? Even the best possible outcome—that he'd soon be dismissed and commanded back to lines—seemed grim, for he was scarcely able to walk but couldn't well reveal this without expecting some sort of physical examination. He had hoped for another week of rest before having to move. And beneath all of these pressing fears, he worried for James.

Munn continued. "So, we march back to Peekskill." Robert tried not to let the despair, the utter nausea that beset him, appear on his face; the thought of a march was laughable. The sergeant continued, "I expect the regiment will go from there to New Windsor before

Christmas." He looked from Plummer to Robert. "The French have been good enough to give us a wagon, as there are yet some fellows who cannot walk. And he says that you"—he lifted his chin toward Robert—"are to ride as well. Light-headed, are you? He says you lost a hogshead of blood." Munn laughed, a rare occurrence. "I picked you out as a tough nut from the start, Shurtliff."

That was not the beginning he remembered at all, though he wasn't going to challenge the sergeant on this point, so he said, "Sir, what about James?"

"Snow? He'll be riding in the cart with you." Munn turned to Plummer, began to talk routes and equipment, and Robert knew he had been dismissed, though he had questions aplenty on his tongue.

The next morning, French soldiers packed up what remained in the hospital, tucking all the equipment into trunks and carrying these out to a string of carts. Robert helped Plummer with the buttons on his waistcoat and then, when only he remained in the room, dressed himself, once again taking care to block the door while he did so. The binding around his breasts bore rusty stains of dried blood and stank to high heaven, but he saw no way to change it now, and so, gingerly—for his shoulder often cramped up—he pulled on his shirt and coat. He folded the loose-fitting shirt and trousers the assistant had given him and left them on the bed. If he walked slowly, pausing under the pretense of a headache, he could manage without a pronounced limp. In this way, he staggered to the wagon, where two soldiers already rested in back. The first had his head swaddled in wrappings. But getting close, Robert could make out the features of William Diston, another soldier who had volunteered for the raid. Beneath the bandages he seemed happy enough; he hailed Robert, tucking up his legs to make room for him. The other was James, whose legs were splinted with wood and leather. He grinned broadly when he saw Robert, though he didn't lift himself up. "Bob," he called, "I am glad to see you."

"And I as well," said Robert, taking his place in the wagon with caution, not wanting to bend or tax his leg too much. "How do you fare?"

"As well as a man can with one leg broken and one knee out of joint. But it could be worse. Frenchie didn't cut anything off," James said.

"Do you heal well?"

"How is one to know? It hurts like hellfire." His tone sounded light but forced—Robert could hear the strain beneath it. "And you?"

"I think I have the better of it, James," he replied. "Just a cut to the head. And my shoulder wrenched. I confess I am still faint sometimes, but there is not much pain." He would have liked to tell James of the other wound, but he turned to William instead. "Your head's a fair piece worse, I wager."

William gave an exaggerated shrug. "It looks worse than it is. A ball grazed the front of my head, and a saber sliced some from the back." He fingered the bandage. "This is just the surgeon's laziness. It is easier to swaddle me like a babe than to dress the two properly."

Robert guessed that he, too, was belittling his wounds. Still, looking at James and noticing the effort with which he kept himself alert and upright, the pain that seemed to lance through him as the wagon bumped along, Robert wanted to draw him close and offer him comfort, even if he couldn't fix his wounds.

As they listed and swayed in the wagon, they swapped stories from the ambush and the hospital; each of them had different memories of what had occurred, and they argued over how steep the slope had been, how many British had attacked. The banter reminded Robert how good it was to be among comrades again, for Plummer had been a surly companion intent only on finding spirits to drink, and every day had been a horror of imagined disasters. Now it seemed life might yet return to normal. With a little time for everyone to heal, all would be well.

In the week they'd rested indoors, winter had truly arrived;

patches of snow huddled in shady nooks, and only the oaks clung to their shabby brown leaves. Robert's breath emerged in clouds of vapor as he spoke, the wagon passed puddles rimed with ice, and all three of them chafed their hands to keep warm. Still, this ride was a great improvement over the one that had brought him to the hospital; he hadn't realized how much he missed his fellow soldiers. Moreover, his leg no longer hurt at every bump. James, however, didn't seem to be faring as well. Robert could see his jaw clench and flex against the jarring of the road, and his fingers gripped at the rails of the wagon. As William and Robert bantered, James's eyelids fluttered; he seemed to hover on the brink of consciousness.

After some time, the sun made an effort to break through the clouds, and Munn brought the wagon to a halt and encouraged the men to eat. "What a band of invalids we are." The sergeant laughed. "Better hope the Cow-Boys are home for the winter." It was true. The whole lot of them were swaddled, splinted, and slung, a sorry show of soldiery. Robert found a renewed appetite—it had ebbed to nothing at the hospital—and he ate his way through some cold fowl, bread, and apples. James chewed a piece of bread and drank thirstily from the jug of cider that Plummer passed around. When the wagon stood still he seemed better, pulling himself upright and attending to the conversation around him.

A few hours lurched past before they arrived at Peekskill. As the wagons rolled in, the company sent up a great cheer. Many hands reached to help James to a lean-to, and everyone crowded around to hear stories. The uninjured troops, having returned earlier, had given a report of the encounter, but Munn and others relished rehashing the details. Robert, once he had seen James comfortably settled, hobbled over to the fire and listened to the sergeant telling of the ambush, hearing with surprise his own name mentioned. "Shurtliff came a-charging down the hill, as though he could skewer a whole squad of cavalry," said Munn. The others laughed.

"They skewered me," said Robert, pointing to his head.

"Aye, but you dispatched a few as well," replied Munn. "And Diston here . . ."

The stories went on as the sun set and men cooked the evening meal. Everyone huddled close for warmth as much as to hear the tales. Matthew returned to camp at around the time the food was ready; he'd been on guard duty, a numbing job in this weather. However, when he saw Robert, he hurried over, barely casting aside his musket before pounding him on the back in welcome.

"For a day or two, we feared we had lost you, Bob," said Matthew. "When Munn didn't return either, I figured that it was surely a fierce fight."

"I can't say as I remember it well . . ." temporized Robert, but Matthew insisted on a recounting of the skirmish as they ate. He made it as hasty as possible and, before Matthew could ask questions, said, "James is back too, but still recovering. I should bring him dinner."

"I'll get some soup and find something to drink," said Matthew. "I really did worry about both of you."

Robert walked slowly after him, surprised to find that he had missed Matthew as well. Surly and moody though he was, Robert had come to feel a grudging fondness for him.

The two of them sat in the lean-to with James, who had propped himself up against his knapsack. He ate a little, drank a little, and asked Matthew what had transpired in their absence. The answer was: not much—just patrols in the area and the preparations for moving out to New Windsor.

"The captain says that winter comes fast here. One day it is like this, and the next you're snowed in. So he is keen to depart quickly," Matthew said, and then put a finger to his lips, for James had fallen asleep. Robert pulled another blanket over James, and then Robert and Matthew joined others around a fire. Robert stretched his fingers toward the flame, feeling tired and unsettled, as if nagged by some forgotten matter. The guards for the night went out, the fires burned down, and the two of them returned to the lean-to where James was sleeping. As Robert lay down between James and Matthew, he thought back to the very first night at West Point and the three of them together. Only Tobias missing. And James sorely injured. Robert arranged his blanket around his head; his leg ached from standing and walking, but the pain ebbed now that he'd lain down. *Tomorrow will be better,* he told himself. Tomorrow and the next day . . . but he couldn't let the future run away from him.

Robert fixed porridge, leaning close to the cooking fire. The frigid air had stiffened the wound in his leg, and he gently shifted his weight as he stirred, trying to loosen the muscles. After Webb called roll, each name emerging from his lips in a puff of steam, Munn summoned Robert. The others went about their assigned chores as Robert stepped aside to speak with the sergeant.

"The captain has said that tomorrow we leave the field for the winter. Snow is not well enough to travel. I'd say he worsened during the wagon ride here."

"That is true, sir."

"Lord knows he couldn't bear the longer ride to New Windsor. Besides, the camp is still largely being built, and the hospital not yet set up. He must recover before making such a trip."

"Here, sir? It hardly seems suitable."

"No, no. There is a nearby farmer, Van Tassel, who has agreed to quarter a wounded soldier. But he has no wife or daughter, so there must be a person provided to serve as attendant. Are you willing?"

"Aye," said Robert, relief rushing through him.

"Good lad. I'll tell the captain. Pack up your things."

When Munn found him again later, Robert was cleaning his musket; the sergeant drew him aside. "The captain says you'll leave tomorrow, and there's some wisdom I need to impart. The French doctor gave me plenty of advice, so listen close. Snow's right leg is broken and needs to stay splinted for two months, but that leg has a gash that must be cleaned. On the left, his knee went out of joint. Lord, it looked a mess at first." The sergeant shook his head as if to dislodge the memory. "When I picked him up on the field, his knee was on the side of his leg. It should bear no weight until the swelling passes. He needs to move, to turn over, even if it pains him, else his muscles will wither and he will get sores." Munn ticked these items off on his fingers and then stared at Robert. "Understood?"

"Yes, sir."

"He should be glad Frenchie didn't cut that leg off. But with time and good care, Lord willing, he should heal."

"Yes, sir."

Munn clapped Robert on the shoulder, luckily on his good shoulder. "I'll see you both in New Windsor. There's a trunk to travel with you—spirits and extra blankets and clothes. Any other soldier I'd tell to mind his manners, but you aren't the sort to go chasing after the nearest farmer's daughter."

"No, sir."

"Good lad. If I had a daughter of my own, I'd make sure to save her for you. Once your enlistment is up, you'll make someone a fine husband."

"Thank you, sir," Robert managed. "That's an office I don't expect soon to occupy."

"I suppose not. But you will. It comes in due course to most men. Wholesome as you may be, you'll never convince me that your mind doesn't now and then turn to women."

Robert found he could not hold Munn's eyes, and the sergeant loosed his rare bark of a laugh. "I knew it, Shurtliff. You're as lusty as the rest of us. You just hide it well. Now, gather your gear, and I'll see you and Snow off."

"Yes, sir," Robert said, glad the conference was over. It had been hard to keep his face composed. Marry Munn's daughter? Be a husband? His leg gave a twinge as he put too much weight on it, and he slowed his pace as he approached the lean-to. Likely, though, he'd make a better husband than wife.

He finished packing his gear and James's as well, thinking how odd it was to consider marrying his sergeant's daughter, to have Munn as a father-in-law. Munn would have been a good match for the Widow Thacher; both of them had a fierceness that now and then gave way to fondness. Except for his friendship with Jennie, the widow's affection was the closest to love that he—Robert or Deborah—had known. Both Munn and the widow had shown affection through the standards they set: they were almost impossible to please, demanding in the details, yet admirable. Still, Robert thought, as he carefully walked back to James, love must be something more than this. It must be not so one-sided, based not just on the respect earned, the admiration deeply sought by one party from the other. It must be mutual, shared, a union where each wanted what the other had to offer and granted it willingly. That would be love, and he had not seen much of it.

CHAPTER EIGHTEEN

Matthew and Corporal Booth escorted James and Robert to the farmhouse. They set out from Peekskill not long after dawn, with James in the bed of the wagon, wrapped in blankets, and Robert next to him, a hand on his shoulder, as if that alone could steady him against the bumps of the journey. They had loaded the trunk of supplies as well as all their standard gear—knapsacks, muskets, cartridge boxes—though Robert couldn't imagine either one of them putting these to use any time soon. As they jolted along the frozen ruts, Booth turned back frequently to address Robert and James. "Got your first scars, then, eh? How's that head feel, Shurtliff?"

"Fine, sir."

"Fine, he says." Booth elbowed Matthew. "Bet you wish you had joined our crew. Ladies like scars." He ran a finger down the seam on his cheek. "Still, there's time for you to earn a badge of honor."

"Do you think we'll see more fighting, Corporal?" Matthew asked.

"Not at New Windsor. But you never know. The British grow desperate and might try a raid."

Robert felt a stab of guilt that he would be leaving his company and not able to help with any fighting. But then, in his current shape, he'd be of no use in a skirmish or even a patrol. Still, he listened to Booth's speculations with regret.

Heading north and east, they reached a small farmhouse by midmorning. The neat lines of trees in the orchard, the small, dilapidated barn to the side of the house, and the scratched-up poultry yard summoned up memories of Middleborough, a world that seemed impossibly distant.

Booth hopped down from the seat and knocked on the door of the farmhouse, which was opened by a short man with a great round head. He seemed in all ways disproportioned: his stubby legs bowed out, as if he'd spent decades on a horse, his long, gangly arms reached to his knees, and he boasted a lush and thick set of whiskers above his lip, while the pate of his head was bald as a babe's.

"Good morning, Mr. Van Tassel."

"Corporal," he said in the rich voice of a man who often takes a pipe. "Come in, come in."

"I thank you. We'll be leaving these two with you."

Matthew moved to the back of the wagon, and Robert carefully stepped down.

"This here is Bob Shurtliff," said Booth, laying a hand on Robert's shoulder. "He's on the mend himself and will be nursing James there."

They picked up James in his blanket. Matthew and Robert managed his feet and legs, holding the splints with care, Booth took his arms, and they made their way through the door. "I thought to set you in the garret, but getting him up there would be a mean feat." Van Tassel shook his head, mustache waving.

"Not a worry," Booth blustered, examining the opening to the garret and the ladder leading up. "I wouldn't want to inconvenience you, sir, being the master of the house." He turned to Matthew and Robert. "Up you go, lads." Matthew scurried up the ladder, and Robert trailed behind, trying not to put much weight on his wounded leg. Once they were both secure, Booth removed the ladder from the hole, laying it flat on the floor of the house, and bent close to James. "Look here. Hold on to this." James gripped a rung. Booth nodded at Van Tassel. "Hup!" They hoisted the ladder, Booth's face growing crimson with the strain—it appeared Van Tassel didn't provide much assistance. Robert and Matthew peered down from the garret, and Booth angled the ladder to the opening in the ceiling while James held the middle part of the rungs. Matthew and Robert reached down and grabbed the top, slowly lifting the ladder through the hole. Matthew did the bulk of the work, as Robert could only pull hard with one arm. When James's torso emerged inside the garret, they lifted him off and set the ladder back in its proper place.

Van Tassel watched the procedure, shifting his weight from one bowed leg to the other. "I'd offer you my chamber, lad, but these legs of mine are not made for climbing, no, no."

"No matter, sir, we've got him up," Robert called from the garret.

"'Twill be hard to get him down, but he can practice his walking up there for a while." Booth tapped his nose, as if in speculation. "I'll go fetch the trunk from the wagon."

There were several pallets in the garret, and they stacked two on top of each other, then set James down on these. He groaned when they moved him but soon made himself comfortable. Booth returned with the trunk, and with more groaning and fuss, they managed to get that into the garret as well.

"Best of luck, Snow," said Booth, calling up from below. "We'll be taking our leave."

"Thank you, Corporal," said James.

Matthew offered James his hand. "I hope you heal quickly."

"And I hope you find New Windsor more pleasing than Peekskill."

"Anything would be better. . . ."

"I'll be back in a moment, James," said Robert, and clambered down the ladder.

Booth stood in the yard when Robert emerged from the house and paused in his checking of the horses to return Robert's salute. "We'll meet again soon, I expect, with you restored to good health." The corporal reached inside his coat. "I almost forgot. These arrived for you at Peekskill while you were recuperating." He handed over several letters. "Your lady is a faithful correspondent."

"Yes, sir. Thank you."

Matthew had already vaulted up to the wagon seat, so Robert waved good-bye to him. He watched as Booth climbed up and took the reins. The day was bright and clear, sharp and cold, with a wind racing down the valley, making Robert's eyes sting. He shoved the letters inside his coat and went back to the farmhouse, favoring his right leg freely now, no longer needing to dissemble.

Inside, Van Tassel stood by the fire. "Ah, there now," he said when Robert came in. "I am sorry I have so little space." He spread his hands in apology. Indeed, the whole of the house comprised one large room, with a bed in an alcove to the side. "But my home is yours, so welcome."

"Thank you," said Robert. "I'm pleased to help with chores, but first let me see to the invalid."

Van Tassel put a hand behind his ear. "What's that? You can't be soft of voice with me. . . ."

Robert cleared his throat. "I'll help with the chores, but let me check on James first."

"Of course, of course," said Van Tassel. "I have some knowledge of remedies. I will boil water for you and then consult my almanac."

Stiff in both leg and shoulder, Robert laboriously climbed the ladder and found James asleep on the pallet. He reviewed the instructions that Munn had given him. Keep the splints on, wash the wound, make James move and turn over. Stepping close to the bed, he touched a hand to James's face; the cheek was warm, the stubble rough. James's eyelids fluttered, stilled. Robert wanted to tell him that everything would be fine, that he would care for him, but it was better not to disturb his rest.

"Well, laddie?" Van Tassel said when Robert came down. His host stood before the fire, fiddling with a large kettle on the pot-hook.

"Could you give me some hot water, strips of cloth, and nourishing food?" Robert was careful to speak loudly.

"What symptoms does he show?" said Van Tassel as he moved from the fire to the table, where his almanac lay open to the medical section.

"A broken leg, a gash that I must keep clean, and a knee out of its joint."

"Hmmm." Van Tassel licked a finger and turned a page. "For broken bones, it here suggests apples boiled in milk, but for cuts and infections, now, hmmm . . . it indicates clear wine is to be drunk. My, my."

"First, I ought to clean the wound, sir," said Robert.

"Yes, yes, I will get the water to a boil and find some cloth."

"I'll fetch more firewood."

Soon, Robert climbed back to the garret and helped James sit up to drink the broth Van Tassel had prepared. "I am so tired, Bob."

"Well, rest, James. That is why we are here."

"I feel like a maiden with a swooning fit."

"I can assure you, you don't look the part," Robert said.

"Oh, good." He lay back down and closed his eyes.

"Just rest. I will tend to your legs."

When James seemed more deeply asleep, Robert untied one splint and carefully cut away the bandages. The last layer of cloth carried a crust of yellow and red, and when he pulled this away, he exposed a large gash. The edges of the wound were rimmed black with dried blood, but the surgeon had cleaned it out well; Robert could see no sign of pus, no dirt or debris. The cut reached almost to the bone, a wedge of flesh so neatly excised that Robert thought a sword or a bayonet and not a musket ball must have produced such a furrow. He dipped a cloth in water and gently washed away the dried blood. Then he soaked the cloth in rum and wiped the wound. At the first touch of the spirits, James jolted up, wrenched his leg, and howled in pain.

"Steady, steady, James." Robert reached out, touched his arm. "Lie still. It needs cleaning."

The rum made the flesh of the wound pink, and new blood, bright and red, flowed at the edges. Robert could hear the hissing intake of breath through James's gritted teeth. As lightly as he could, Robert covered the wound and strapped on the splint, making sure the leg lay straight. He unwrapped the other leg and surveyed the knee, so swollen that the whole joint looked like a large sausage, puffy and round and purple-red. He could see no cuts to clean, so he simply replaced the splint.

"I'll let you rest now, James, but later we should move your legs a bit. The doctor said it would be good."

James, his eyes closed, managed a faint "Yes."

Robert walked to a window overlooking the orchard, where tree limbs impoverished by winter clacked against the afternoon sky. He could scarcely believe, seeing a wound so large, that it would ever heal. Things broke, things tore, but, God willing, they could heal and be made whole. He gathered up the soiled dressings and went downstairs to ask his host to boil yet more water for washing.

Robert drew buckets of water from the well, and Van Tassel heated up a vast caldron of it. With the first pot, Robert washed all the dressings, kneeling in the backyard, bent over the tub. His groin ached in this position, but he took comfort in the steam that swathed his face. With the next pot, the two of them contrived a system by which Robert could raise buckets of the steaming water to the garret, where he then filled a tub. To Robert's delight, Van Tassel labored under the illusion that the invalid needed bathing, for it afforded Robert the privacy of the garret in which to wash himself. James, though perhaps in need of a bath, could in no way manage to get into a tub, and he lay asleep on the pallet across the room.

Outside, the afternoon light struck a golden chord, the garret grew dusky, and Robert cast one more look at the sleeping figure before disrobing completely, unwrapping even the binding about his chest, which had grown as rancid and stained as James's bandages. With care, he took off the dressing around his thigh. The hole had shriveled a little, and the edges were red and puckered. He eased himself into the tub and ladled water over his head. Van Tassel had given him a cake of soap, and Robert scrubbed his skin fiercely, standing from time to time and then submerging himself. The water turned gray, and he used the last bucket to rinse, then let the air dry him, naked and clean.

James sprawled on the pallet, his arms thrown out over the blankets, eyes closed and mouth open. Robert turned his gaze from him to look down at his own body. Some time ago he had lost a sense of what he looked like, but now he saw his breasts, the slight rounding of his stomach, the pale smoothness of his thighs—this strange flesh. Drying his hair, he thought of all the nights he'd slept curled up with James, all the ways this body of his had felt stirrings of desire, how he had bitten them back. But what was he, what was anyone, but flesh, a vulnerable body? He felt his skin prickle in the cold, the wounds he bore, and the tiredness of his leg, his shoulder. How could he not be this body? He marveled that such intimacy and distance could coincide.

In the privacy of the garret—a chamber that felt inviolate, tucked away—his limbs hung looser, his body more open, and Robert picked up the bottle of rum he'd used on James and dabbed at the wound on his thigh. It stung, and as he worked the liquid into the recesses of the hole, below the film of scab, he gave a gasp of pain.

"Robert?" James had awoken and struggled to sit upright.

"I'm here, James," he said, grabbing a shirt and pulling it over his head. As he stepped to the pile of clothing, he scolded himself—how could he have been so foolish as not to dress?

James had worked his way up onto an elbow and now reached for his leg. "It hurts. . . ." He grabbed at the splint, and Robert hurried to the bedside without pausing to put on breeches.

"James. Don't touch it."

"Like fire."

Robert gently moved James's hands from the splint. "Leave it be, James."

"Where are we?"

"At a farmhouse," said Robert, reaching for his trousers. He stepped into the shadows under the eaves and pulled them on. "Not far from Peekskill."

"Yes, I remember."

As he stuffed his shirttails into the breeches and buttoned them up, he realized he hadn't bound his chest and hoped that James's preoccupation with his legs would keep him from noticing. "There is water and some soup, too, if you are hungry. You should eat."

James lifted the mug and drank, then wiped his mouth, squinting up at Robert as if befuddled. "Why d'you think I'm so tired, Bob?"

"It is work for the body to heal."

James nodded, his eyelids already half-shut. Standing there, warm and clean, watching his broken friend, Robert felt as if he had dissolved. Perhaps the strangeness of being in a house, at once familiar and peculiar, slackened him. Or maybe it was being unbound, his breasts loose under his shirt, as though some mooring line had been cast off. There were no officers here, no rules and regulations, none of the expectations that had constrained him but also created and defined him. He looked at the uniform coat, its white facings now gone to gray, its sleeves stitched and stained. The army had formed him, taught him how to stand and act, when to speak, and how to behave. Here in this house, there was no need to hold those standards, and he wondered what he would do and who he would be without them.

James's eyes were closed and he seemed calm, without pain. Robert took the luxury of studying his face, the round chin and sharp nose, the stubble and the sharp jut of his Adam's apple that Robert envied. Out of his uniform, James looked younger. Robert tried to imagine him on the streets of Middleborough, what he would have thought of James if he had known him there. But it was impossible. He had never known a man so patient and kind, who spoke without condescension or arrogance, and he wondered whether James would behave this way with women or only with fellow soldiers. Robert shook his head as if to loosen these thoughts—what had come over him? Was it just his separation from the rest of the company? Was it the sight of his own naked body? He felt like the molasses candy he used to make with Jennie, stirred and stretched out in ribbons so thin as to be translucent, needing the pan to make him solid and thick again.

Robert emptied the bathwater bucket by bucket out the garret window, flinging it in dirty, gray arcs over the farmyard. Then he searched among the pieces of cloth that lay in trunks along the wall. Dresses of an old style were stacked within one trunk. Robert shook out a pale blue apron, thin from much use, and tore it into strips. Pulling off his shirt, he wrapped the pieces round his chest, feeling the comforting constriction as if it held him together. He covered the wound on his thigh with a new bandage as well. He rubbed the cut on his head with spirits, glad that Munn had packed an ample supply in the trunk, but could not see to clean his scalp; he'd have to ask Van Tassel for a looking glass. He smiled, imagining that his host might think him an inebriate for smelling so much of alcohol. Then he stretched out on a pallet, his leg grateful for the support, and stared up at the timbers of the roof. James's breathing rumbled softly; below him he could hear Van Tassel hum, clang pots, now and then break into snatches of song. He lay still, until he could no longer sense his body, until he might be naught but a pair of eyes, and maybe not even these.

When darkness overtook the house, and the circle of firelight seemed the only illumination in the world, Robert sat down to dinner, eager to discover if Van Tassel could cook well. His host served mutton and baked apples, and he had set aside meat and broth for James as well as a mush of sweetened apples. After asking after James's health, he inquired, "And what are your own ailments, lad?"

"By comparison, I am quite well. But I did sustain a cut to the head, and my shoulder went out of its joint."

Van Tassel gave the wound on Robert's scalp a careful examination, holding a candle so close that Robert feared for his eyebrows. "You two are young and will heal right up. But beware of old age. Why, I could tell you two days in advance when it will rain, my knees swell up so tight. . . ."

Robert offered clucks of sympathy as Van Tassel listed his ailments.

"And now that winter is here, I must be wary of draughts. Last cold snap I got a cough, oh, for weeks, it lasted. . . ."

Robert simply nodded along and ate as much as he could hold—the supper tasted delicious. At last, he seized upon a pause in the conversation and excused himself. He brought food up to James, who ate some but spoke little, only to ask Robert for help in using the pot. It took much effort to roll him onto his side, with Robert pushing on James's shoulders while gently supporting his broken leg. His friend moaned and gave a loud grunt of frustration when he shifted too much weight to his swollen knee, but managed to relieve himself. It was an awkward transaction, but Robert held James's leg steady and kept his eyes averted. That done, Robert rolled James back and helped him settle on the pillows.

"I'll get a mug of water for you," Robert said, and went down the ladder to empty the pot in the necessary.

"Is all well up there, lad?" Van Tassel asked as Robert returned. "Have a seat by the fire."

"As well as can be. Thank you for your generosity, sir." Robert sat and stretched out his feet toward the hearth.

"'Tis nothing. I owe the army much for all their protection and aid."

"Were you attacked?"

"Oh, aye, several times. Run over by the British and made to quarter them, then rescued, and the following spring swamped by refugees. It has been all topsy-turvy here. And there's men who were once loyalists and now say they are not, and some who stand only for themselves and shoot all who come close." He poked at the fire. "And now another winter sets in. I hope it is the last one of this war." With a sigh, he tossed a log on the fire. "For all your height, you look young to be a soldier. I see that scar on your forehead, but not a whisker on those cheeks."

"I'm seventeen," said Robert, automatically.

"You're that age as surely as I'm twenty-nine." He cackled. "No one in this world is what they seem."

They lapsed into silence again. The old man must have talked himself out over dinner. The longer they sat staring into the fire, the more the room seemed to shrink into darkness, and Robert thought about Van Tassel's words. A creak sounded above them, and he thought it might be James stirring, but the sound came again, just the timbers sighing in the night. At length, his eyelids grew heavy; he rose, poured a mug of water, and bid his host good night. Climbing the ladder to the garret, he pulled a pallet close to James, near the bricks of the chimney. He took off his boots and set them beside his musket; he would not need his weapon here, he thought, but he ought to have it ready nonetheless. For Van Tassel's words rang true: nothing was as it seemed, and no person either.

For quite a while he lay there in the dark, feeling the plumpness of a mattress beneath him for the first time in months, and thought of all he had been and was: daughter, servant, weaver, woman, friend, soldier, nurse, man. From the ground floor, he heard Van Tassel's footsteps and his humming of a tune. James's breath whistled through his nose. On the brink of sleep, his mind teetering between this world and dreams, Robert wondered if it really could be the last winter of the war, and what that meant for him.

Somewhere in the middle of the night—Robert had fallen into sleep fathoms deep—James woke him with a muffled curse. "Lord Almighty . . ."

"James! What's wrong?"

His breath came in panting gasps. "I must have rolled over on my leg."

Robert got up and knelt next to him. "Hush, now, let it be." He gently pushed James's shoulders, making him lie down again. "Fussing won't help. Just wait, and the pain will go away." He felt about for the bottle of rum he'd used earlier that day. Putting his hand on it, he brought the bottle to James, who tilted it against his lips. "Feels like fire," he said, and drank again, then lay back. "Bob. Do you think these legs will heal?"

The despair in James's voice yanked at Robert. "Of course." He struggled to find words of comfort. "You'll heal up in a couple of weeks, and we'll be limping back to West Point."

James sighed and drank again, and Robert could see the liquor relax him, the tension drain from his brow. "You redressed my wound. Tell me, how did it look?"

"The cut is large," Robert said, not wanting to lie. "But it is clean. If you keep the splint on, it will heal straight. As for the other, it is swollen and I cannot tell how it is."

James lifted the bottle, drinking long swallows of the rum, and then let it fall to the floor with a hollow thud that resounded in the night. "I saw you bathe today."

"What?" A flush of panic crept up Robert's neck. Perhaps he had misheard James's speech, slurred as it was by liquor and fatigue.

"I saw you. In the tub. You looked to be . . . I can't . . ." James grabbed his hair and rubbed his head, as if trying to loosen a thought. "All evening, I've lain up here thinking I might be feverish. Am I feverish, Bob?"

Robert laid his hand on James's forehead, felt his friend flinch. "I don't feel much heat."

"Then I saw what I saw. Are you a woman?"

Robert took his hand from James's forehead. Just this question spurred within him the impulse to run, though he knew it was impossible. He was broken, his friend was broken. He would not abandon him. But perhaps James would no longer want his care? Teetering on the edge of despair, Robert choked out, "I am. Or I was. I'm sorry."

"Sorry? For what are you sorry?"

"For deceiving you. I'm no better than Tobias, or . . ."

"Hush. That's nonsense."

He heard the rustle of blankets as James shifted, the heavy drag of his splint across the mattress, and then the grind of his teeth. "Gah. I forget I can't move my leg. It's gone all heavy and numb."

"Let me help," Robert said, rising to gently lift and settle his friend's limb. The floorboards pushed a chill up through his feet, making him shiver. "Are you angry, James?"

"I was, a bit. Angry and unsure. But maybe the lonesome evening did me some good. I couldn't believe what I saw at first. And then, when I believed what I saw, I couldn't understand how you managed it. No woman should do what you've done, Bob."

Robert sat back on his mattress, pulling the covers over himself and hugging his knees to his chest, feeling the jump of his own heart. He tried to form words, but he felt his tongue go dry, shriveled up in his mouth as if someone had salted it.

James continued, "I'm not angry now. I got to thinking I should have known before. When I was flogged, you cared for me as well as my mother would have. And I have sat by you so many afternoons and studied your face and never seen the barest shadow of a whisker. But it never occurred to me . . ."

"Do you think the others suspect?"

"Who would guess? You seem more like a soldier than a wife."

"I am glad to hear it," Robert said, and despite himself, he laughed.

"Is there more rum?"

"I'll fetch you more in the morning. For now you should have water." He found the mug, offered it to James, who drank a swallow or two and handed it back. "Now sleep."

"First, tell me your name."

"Deborah Samson." The words dangled, ungainly on his lips, and he wondered that he had spoken the name at all.

"A good name, though Bob is better." His voice sounded drowsy and thick, and he leaned back. "Deborah." Somehow the name seemed sweeter when James said it.

"Good night." The husks in his mattress rattled as he shifted. James knew—and the world had not ended. James knew—and did not turn away from him. Robert felt as though a door within him had opened, some internal passageway he hadn't known existed, and he could feel himself walking down it. And to his own surprise, he felt delight to be known as a woman, to have his secret lifted from him. Sometime in the night, James reached for Robert's hand. Robert gave James's fingers a gentle squeeze, and they both slept on.

After breakfast downstairs with Van Tassel, Robert brought bread and tea to James. He sat on the edge of the pallet and watched his friend eat. The bread, spread with apple butter, had been freshly baked that morning, and James devoured the pieces in a few gulps. "Tell our host he is a fine cook," James said.

"And an even better conversationalist," Robert said sarcastically, and began to gather the dishes.

"Robert, before you go, I need to use the pot."

Robert set the dishes down and turned to help James. Blood rushed to his cheeks as he brought the pot close and braced James's legs; he could barely manage to support James's thigh.

"Are you all right, Bob? You're all atremble."

Robert shook his head, looked away. "I shouldn't be. I'm the same as I was yesterday . . . aren't I?"

"You're the same Robert I have known. Now, let a man do his business."

Once James was settled again, Robert poured him a mug of water from the pitcher. "Drink plenty," he chided.

"I will," James replied.

"And sleep."

"Yes, but don't leave me shut up here alone all day." He smiled and reached for Robert's hand.

"Of course not," Robert said. "Later I'll clean your wound, and we'll move your legs."

James brought Robert's hand to his lips and Robert shut his eyes, his head reeling as if he had just consumed a jug of rum. He drew his hand back, moved to the garret entrance, and clambered down the rungs of the ladder; already the ladder was easier to climb than it had been yesterday, as if a bath and a good night's sleep had started to heal his wounds, or as if James's discovery had somehow aided in mending him. At the bottom of the ladder, Van Tassel approached him, turning the pages of a tattered volume, his nose close to the text.

"Now, then, is the skin around your friend's wound livid? Or duskish?"

Robert poured himself some tea and took a sip. "Both, I should say."

"Tense or flabby?"

"I suppose it is tense." He didn't want to think of anything except the midnight revelation, the fact that James knew and still . . . loved him.

Van Tassel clucked his tongue, ran a tobacco-stained finger down the margin, and then, finding the right spot, read aloud, sounding the words out with deliberate slowness, "Dress with treacle or a cataplasm of lixivium and bran. I know not what these are. Do you?"

Robert shook his head.

"Clean with vinegar and administer warm oil of turpentine," he continued reading. "That I have. And purge often." He shut the volume. "You should bleed him too. Shall I fetch the turpentine oil?"

"Sir," said Robert, "no doubt your text is learned, but we are neither of us surgeons to let blood safely, and I could not abide the vapors of turpentine in that small garret."

"Will you at least take some vinegar?"

"Certainly," Robert replied. At worst, James would smell like a pickle. "And I hope we did not disturb your sleep last night. My friend awoke in pain. . . ."

Van Tassel waved his hand dismissively. "Lad, little can disturb my slumber."

Robert nodded, relieved that their speech had not been overheard. "What chores can I aid you with this morning?"

Van Tassel tugged at his mustache. "The stalls need to be cleaned, and if you could split some wood . . ."

"I'll see to it."

CHAPTER NINETEEN

Through air speckled with motes, Robert surveyed the horses' stalls. Hay was stored haphazardly, bridles and saddles were splayed about, and everything festered in dusty dishevelment: work enough to keep ten men busy. When his shoulder began to ache after a few hours of labor, he traded the dust of the barn for the stinging cold of the yard. The sun offered trembling light, and the air nipped only when the wind blew. Hunching his shoulders, he watched the smoke rise from Van Tassel's chimney, how it curled and turned, twisting up to the sky. He felt like that, like the smoke. The instinct to rise, to push ever upward. But he knew, too, the insubstantiality, and the way that a tiny breeze could affect the course.

Turning his back on the house, he set out along the margin of Van Tassel's orchard, enjoying the orderly lines of trees, their bare yet sturdy limbs. At the far reach of the orchard stood a stone wall, half-toppled, and he huddled in the lee of it, glad to be out of the wind. Even though his nose stung with the cold air, he sat and pulled out the letters from Jennie that Booth had handed over to him just yesterday. How much longer it seemed. He didn't want to read them in front of Van Tassel or James; they were for him alone. Three letters, two from October and one from November. And now it was December. . . . He wiped his nose on his sleeve and opened the first.

Dear Robert,

I have read and reread your letter and try to assure myself that you are safe. It is hard, knowing that you are fighting, that the war rages on. Here all is quiet. The talk is of peace coming soon. I pray for it. And I pray for you to come home safe. Your letter worries me when you say you are changed. Do not be hard, Robert. You are a soldier and must act as a soldier. But when the war is done, you will no longer be a soldier. You can be yourself again.

There is to be a husking party soon, but it will not be the same without you. It has been busy lately; young Master Leonard is courting a girl from Taunton, and there have been dinners here for the family, and shirts and pants need to be fresh and clean. Missus Leonard's friend in Easton is still ailing, and we have traveled there several times.

These trips have been to my advantage, for I have met a man, Charles, and he is sweet and doting and kind and loves me. He owns a farm in Easton and saw me visiting with Missus. Can you believe he traveled all the way to Middleborough to make inquiries about me? Don't be upset. I know we said marriage was for fools or those willing to be slaves, but I love him. I think you would too.

Be careful, Robert.

Love,
Jennie

In love and thinking of marriage! Robert blew on his fingers, then opened the next letter.

Dear Robert,

I write in haste, only to tell you to send your letters not to Middleborough, but to Easton to Jennie Howe. Robert, I am married! Be happy for me, and hurry home to meet my husband. I will write and tell you all, but now, everything is turned upside down.

With love,
Jennie

He unfolded the final missive.

Dear Robert,

It is months now since I have heard from you. I do not chide, only worry. But perhaps you have written and the letters haven't made it through, or my letters to you have been lost. No matter. There is nothing to do about it but keep writing and hoping.

I want to tell you how my marriage happened. Charles had come over, quite by chance, to the Hamiltons' house when I was visiting there with Missus Leonard (Missus Hamilton is the friend who had taken ill). Mister Hamilton had a horse that had gone lame in one leg, and Charles is quite good with animals. He has a touch, and not just with horses. He says that he saw me there that day and asked a dozen servants before he found out who I was and where I lived. Once he did, he visited and brought me sweets, and asked Missus Leonard's permission to sit with me awhile. She had no objection as long as my chores were done, and to my delight, that meant Charles came into the kitchen and helped me with my labor. We fed the ducks and chickens together, we kneaded bread dough together—it quite reminded me of working with you, we kept up such a pace of chatter and laughter. I have never known a man willing to roll up his sleeves and help with a woman's work. He won me over in that instant.

I could go on for pages. He has dark hair and he wears it rather long for my taste, but I think I can persuade him to trim it. And he is tall, taller than you, and cuts such a figure when he is on his horse. It makes me giddy to watch him ride. And though he is of modest means himself, when he found out I was indentured, he paid off my papers to Mister Leonard, gave me money for a coach to my sister's house, and then courted me properly there before asking me to marry him.

Now I am Missus Howe. Charles has a small farm, a tidy little house to the north of Easton, just south of the town of Stoughton. It is as rocky and rough as our Middleborough farms, but I love it.

Don't think I have forgotten you in all of this. I think of you every day. Charles served a year in the militia, and he has told me of the marching and the battles and the biting cold of winter in a tent. I can't imagine how you can do it. Write and tell me you are well.

Love,
Jennie

Robert folded the letters and stowed them away. He stood and crossed his arms, warming his hands in his armpits, and began to walk along the stone wall. Jennie in love, Jennie married. Jennie free from the Leonards. She'd be a mother soon, no doubt. Robert blinked his eyes against the cold gusts. He was happy, he was sad, he was angry, he was jealous. Jennie, Jennie. He thought of the years they had teased each other, whispered secrets to each other long into the night, slept in each other's arms. How young they had been, both almost orphans, thrown together under Widow Thacher's roof. But they were girls no longer. She had a life to live, and he, well, he had chosen this course; he had gotten his wish for freedom and escape. He turned back toward Van Tassel's house, a shiver running through him that had nothing to do with the winter wind.

When he entered, Van Tassel pressed a bottle of vinegar into

Robert's hands. "I'll see to supper, my boy. That vinegar should help draw the bile from your friend's wound."

Robert ascended the ladder, found James awake, sitting up on the bed.

"At last! I thought you had forgotten me."

"Not in the least. . . . I've been tending to chores all day."

"Look—I can raise this one up." James carefully pressed his hands around the wrenched knee and lifted the leg.

"Well done," Robert said, and James smiled, the grin of a little boy. "How about the other leg?"

"Not as easy." He gingerly put his hands under the knee, grimaced. "I can't do it."

"Let me help." Robert put his hands beneath the leg, raised it slowly, lowered it, raised it again. "The doctor said you should move as much as you are able. I'll look at the wound, and then maybe you can rest on your side."

He unwrapped the dressings and washed the cut in vinegar. James wrinkled his nose at the smell. The other leg appeared less puffy, or maybe Robert only wished it so. When he had retied both splints, Robert helped James onto his side and then sat next to him on the mattress. "I am sorry, James. I wish there were more I could do. . . . Van Tassel would have me bathe you in turpentine and subject you to regular purges."

"Good heavens."

"That was my thought as well. But I cannot fathom the best course of action."

"Sleep and good company, I suppose. Tell me a story."

"What story?"

"Yours." With great care, James inched up on the mattress, put his arm around Robert's waist.

The feeling of James so near pushed all thought from his mind. What had he just asked? It was as though some part of him had come loose and now rattled about. He licked his lips, gathering his senses. "It isn't much of a story," Robert said, but James cocked his head. "It is like I told you. I come from south of Boston, I was a weaver, I didn't like it, so I joined up."

"Bob Shurtliff. You are the worst storyteller ever." The two of them burst out laughing.

"The past is not a story I like to tell," said Robert.

James leaned back. "So tell me the future. What will you do after the war?"

"I might go west, settle on fresh land, farm . . . But I've told you all this."

"I mean, will you live again as a woman?"

"I'm afraid I wouldn't remember how. And I don't think I would want to." He thought about it, the question put starkly before him. Could he live as a woman again? All the traits that had been sources of complaint—willfulness, ambition, independence—when he lived as a woman had led to his success as a soldier. Munn praised him for his powers of observation, for his persistence, for his physical stamina. None of that would matter if he returned to live as Deborah Samson.

"Is it so bad to be a woman?" James's eyes were closed now.

"Not for most, perhaps. But it was for me. I cannot abide being told that I cannot do something, cannot handle serious matters, cannot be my own person. I thought for a long while that once I was free of indenture, once I wasn't serving a family, it would be better. I fought for years to gain that freedom. And then, when I obtained it and began to support myself through weaving, it was no better. There were those who thought I was a danger to the community, that I needed a man—father, master, brother, husband—to watch over me." Robert stopped to catch his breath, blinded by once-familiar anger and resentment rising up in him.

"I can see why you do not like to speak of the past. But I think you do a fine job of watching over yourself. And others, too," said James.

James's words barely registered as Robert struggled against a tide of memories. Mr. Thomas berating Deborah on the last night of her indenture, telling her she walked the path to hell. The families who would no longer hire her to weave for them once it became known that she was masterless, as if the cloth her fingers made was unclean. The injustice of it, the utter unfairness. There had been nothing she could say or do.

Robert put a hand to James's face and felt the rapid flutter of a pulse at his temple. He brushed James's hair back from his forehead and allowed himself a moment to think of this man, and of himself, as a woman. He watched the movement of James's eyes beneath his lids.

Then he lifted his hand and ran his fingers through his own hair, touching the small pucker of scar on his scalp where the sword had caught him. The skin felt smooth and glossy; already little prickles of hair grew around it. In a month, he knew, it would be covered over, a small badge only he knew about, a token of a battle fought and survived. How easy it was to hide some things, to tuck them away beneath clothes and hair. Only they didn't disappear, did they? Standing, he ran his hands over his hips, then crossed his arms over his bound chest. How much of him was still a woman? Was it like a scar, a reminder of something past, over and done? James's question dug at him—could he go back? Where was Deborah Samson now?

Van Tassel had fixed a dish of potato dumplings and mutton cooked with dried fruit, sweet and rich at once. Robert ate two platefuls. "This is the best fare I have had in months, sir."

Van Tassel patted his round stomach. "I like to eat well. Had to learn to cook after my wife died." On and on the man talked, of his wife, of the wasting illness that took her, of how she loved to bake, how she made butter sweeter than any he had tasted. When at last his host took a bite to eat, Robert cleared his throat, careful to speak loudly. "I should take James his food, then I'll return and help with the washing."

"Of course, of course." Van Tassel loaded a plate with dumplings and mutton, and Robert carried it to the garret, watched James eat, and cast about for a safe topic of conversation.

"Do you recall how you broke your leg?" he asked.

James shook his head. "I charged with my bayonet. I remember I saw you fall, and I wanted to get over and help you. . . ." He took a big bite of potato and chewed. "But it seemed I stepped in a hole. My foot was trapped and I couldn't free it. That's when my knee twisted. The broken leg—I don't know how it happened."

"It seems so long ago."

James nodded. "A lifetime."

"I'll help with washing and then come up. You should try to move your legs a bit."

James leaned close, "Robert, do you . . ."

"What?"

"Nothing."

When Robert came upstairs, the garret sighed, shrouded in shadow; Van Tassel had pressed a cordial on him, bade him sit by the fire and talk awhile. The sweet liqueur made Robert's tongue wooly. Now he steadied himself against the chimney, the bricks warm under his hand. James, a lump under his blanket, softly snored. Robert unclasped his belt, tugged his trousers down, and folded them on top of a trunk where he'd set his coat earlier. What a pleasure to sleep on a mattress, to have a soft quilt. But what a true joy to undress and know that the man on the other mattress did not mind, that Robert had nothing to hide. He had held the secret of his nature so long and so tightly that he had forgotten the tension it created. Only now, stretched out on his back, his legs bare under the quilt, did he feel the strands fall loose, the knot begin to unravel. Here, in this space, he could be Robert and Deborah both.

He had been dreaming of Jennie, a dream in which he brushed her hair. Long and soft, it felt so good in his hands. He woke from the dream momentarily disoriented, his mouth still sticky from the cordial, and he reached out for the mug of water and took a sip.

"Robert? Will you pass me the mug?"

"Here."

James drank, and when Robert leaned over to take the mug away, James placed his arm around Robert's waist, pulled him to his side.

"Will you stay close to me, Bob?"

"Do you hurt, James?"

"No . . . yes . . ." His hand moved from Robert's waist, tracing his thigh, pausing where his shirttail ended, pushing underneath. The skin of his hand felt rough against the softness of Robert's leg—a roughness like the tongue of a cat when it licks a bit of milk from a finger, a scratchy sort of touch that seemed to set loose sparks in Robert's flesh.

Robert lay still, pressed against James, his body tensing against his will, an involuntarily flinch and shiver, and he fought against himself: Should he pull away or not? He closed his eyes and felt James's hands along the inside of his leg and the rising response of his own body, as if James's fingers were melting something within him.

"Bob . . ."

"Perhaps it's better if we . . ." He trailed off, certain and unsure all at once.

"I can't move much. So come here." James reached for Robert's hand and placed it gently on his stomach. Slowly, Robert pulled up James's shirt, let his hand rest against the bare flesh of James's stomach. Should he . . . ? He pressed his legs together, stopping the motion of James's hand for a moment. He shouldn't have had that cordial, it made his temples pound, the blood ringing in his ears. James gave a grunt as he shifted, and Robert knew it wasn't truly the cordial to blame.

"I don't want to hurt you," Robert said.

"You won't." He took Robert's hand, slid it lower, and with his other, still wrapped around Robert's waist, James ran his fingers across the skin of Robert's thigh, the crest of his hip.

James's back arched, up and down, and Robert leaned over him, kissed him on the chest, came up on a knee so that he could kiss his neck, his chin, his lips. Smelled on him the lingering scent of sweat, woolens, woodsmoke, the smell of West Point and Peekskill, a smell that spoke of the world they shared, their bodies in it, of it. A smell that almost stopped him—he was a soldier. What would this mean? How would it change him? But he felt a growing sense of urgency, as if everything within him were moving at a faster pace while the world dragged on slowly. His tongue was in his mouth. Robert lifted a leg and straddled James's hips, holding himself poised above. The wood of the splints touched his bare feet as James moved under him.

"I don't want to hurt you. . . ."

But James put one hand on Robert's waist, and with his other, guided himself into Robert. A gasp, James's hands gentle upon him, supporting and holding. The two of them joined, slowly moving together, until Robert couldn't tell where his flesh stopped and James's began.

CHAPTER TWENTY

Frost webbed the garret window, and Robert gazed through the icy filaments to see the orchard, its bare branches poking into the gray sky. The chill of the floor leached through his stockings. He drew on trousers and stood at the foot of the bed, where James had a blanket pulled up to his nose. This morning, Robert ached, but the ache made him smile.

Downstairs Van Tassel had the hearth blazing, banishing the cold to the corners of the room. Robert brought a plate of heavily buttered bread up to the garret, where James still slept, and then returned to the fireside to eat his own share and drink a cup of tea. "I'll split some wood today," he told his host. "Though first I must sharpen the maul."

"Is there aught I can do to help the invalid? A nourishing broth? More dressings?" Van Tassel perched by the fireside on a small stool, his bowed legs stretched toward the flames.

"If you have something that might serve as crutches, that would be a great aid."

"Indeed. I know just the branches." Van Tassel snapped his fingers. "I will set to carving this morning. Any chore that can be done by the fire is a chore I enjoy. You see that bowl by the mantel? I fashioned that last winter. A good piece of work, too. . . ."

Robert waited for the old man to draw breath and then interrupted his monologue. "It is a fine bowl, sir. I'm sure James will appreciate the crutches." He hurried out the door, chiding himself to patience. It must be lonely to be a widower in winter. This morning, a wanton laziness spread through him. He felt like a bird stuffed for the oven, full up, ready for nothing more than a languorous seat in the pan, soaking in the heat. Opening the door to the dusty dimness of the barn, Robert shook his head; such sloth wouldn't serve.

Robert sharpened the maul and then set up a block on which to split wood, for he'd found several stalls overflowing with already sawn sections of beech. The barn doors, propped open, let in sharp winter light and gusts of cold air. Swinging the maul and stacking the wood, Robert soon worked up a sweat. Now and then, he had to set the wedge into a tough piece and drive it deep to split the fibers apart. He paused to wipe his forehead, enjoying how his skin ran hot and cold with the clash of air and sweat. The lassitude of the morning had dissipated, replaced by a steady thrum of energy, as if he were a mill wheel turned by a rushing river.

He had not thought he would sleep with a man; he had not thought he would want it. And more, he had thought that the act would make him feel weak, overpowered, but instead he felt invigorated. Maybe the difference stemmed from the fact that James lay confined by his injuries. No, it was more than that. Robert raised the maul, swung it high, and hit the wedge on the downstroke. The ring of metal on metal echoed in the barn. James loved him. James loved Robert Shurtliff. He had not whispered Deborah's name. He loved a man who was a soldier.

There were girls in Middleborough, girls who served other families, girls in the Baptist Worship or the Congregational meetinghouse, who spoke of love, who fluttered and fancied and fainted over men. Maybe, back then, Deborah had never allowed herself to be open to those feelings, or maybe those girls were wrong, love was not like that, not like a butterfly or a sunny day, quick and passing, a trilling delight. Robert traded the maul for the ax, split the round into shards of kindling. He could trust James with anything. With his own body, uncovered, with his stories, the truth of him. There was nothing he wouldn't gladly share. That was love.

His shoulder grew tired before he had split all the wood. Still, he'd made a good start. He gathered up an armload and walked back to the house, dumping the logs into the box by the door. He shook the splinters from his coat and went inside, nodding to Van Tassel. The old man's cheeks glowed ruddy as he perched next to the fireplace, working his knife over a branch and smoothing the wood. "Not ready yet, lad, but soon," he called.

"He won't need them for a few days. I had best check on him." He climbed the ladder and found James sitting up on the bed, working on some whittling of his own.

"Another spoon?" Robert asked.

"It's all I know how to fashion," James said. "Besides buttons, and I have no need of those."

"How do you feel?"

"Much better today, Bob." He set the spoon down and lifted his hand as if he might reach for Robert, but then let it fall. Full daylight wavered through the windows, and Van Tassel sat below; better not to say too much.

Robert knelt at the foot of the mattress and gently undid the splint from James's left leg. The wrenched knee bloomed purple, but today it looked more like a knee and less like a sausage. "Does it hurt if I touch it?" Robert asked, running his fingers over the red-and-blue flesh.

"No, your touch does not hurt." James bit his lip and seemed to be thinking. "It might even bend."

Robert pushed slowly, feeling the joint creak and resist, but it flexed a little. He carefully tied the splints back on. "Maybe tomorrow you can try to stand on that leg, see if it will bear any weight. Van Tassel is making crutches for you."

"It would be good to move about, even a little. It's tiresome to sit and stare at a wall all day."

"Bored, are you? Missing the drill?" he asked sarcastically.

"Not quite. Are you, Bob? I bet you are."

Robert shook his head. "No, James. I'd rather be with you." He picked up the plate left from breakfast, surprised by his own words, and climbed down the ladder. He hadn't known until he had spoken, but it was true.

TIME AT VAN TASSEL'S FARM soon fell into a pattern. By day, Robert worked at various chores and nursed James, who limped across the garret floor as soon as his crutches were finished, tentatively putting weight on one leg. In the evenings, Robert joined his host for supper by the fire and then, after conversation and washing, went to the garret and curled up with James. He found that their bodies fitted together, both of them a mixture of hard and soft, both of them giving and taking. Some nights they lay on their sides, fingers exploring each other's flesh. James found the pucker of scar high on Robert's thigh, its surface still scabbed. When Robert told him of the wound, of hiding it and removing the ball himself at the French hospital, James pulled him close, kissed his mouth. They spoke in whispers, mouths close to ears, tried to move without making the house's timbers creak, slow and gentle.

On a day of bone-cracking cold, Robert hurried through the outdoor chores and, after warming himself by the fire with Van

Tassel—he listened to a long tale about trees bursting in the cold, years ago—withdrew to the garret.

James sat up in bed, his splints untied, and worked at bending his legs. Robert took out his letter box and sat near James, his back propped against the stones of the chimney. He withdrew the last letters he had received from Jennie and read them through again.

Giving up on his exercises, James leaned close. "Who are these letters from, Bob? All of us were quite curious."

"I expect Tobias satisfied that curiosity, but I'm glad to know he didn't share the information around. . . ." Robert wondered where to begin, what James would think of his past, of who he really was. "Let's see. Picture me as young Deborah going off to serve as a helpmeet for an aged widow."

James shook his head. "I cannot picture you as a little girl."

"Good," said Robert. "Another girl came to live with the widow as well, Jennie, and for several years, until the widow died, we were like sisters. Closer, even. Then we both went to serve families, but as luck would have it, those families resided near to each other, and we stayed close, often working side by side. That is who writes to me."

"What does she think of you being a soldier?"

"If you had known me then, known me as well as she does, you wouldn't be so surprised. If you could make my old master, Mr. Thomas, speak truly, he would say the same: Deborah Samson would make a good soldier. Certainly, a far better soldier than a servant. But he wouldn't mean it kindly."

"Were you not a good servant?"

"I hated every minute of it, James. It isn't fair, you know, that men can come and go as they please. . . . I know you were indentured, but even so, after your term, you knew you'd be free."

James touched the scar on Robert's forehead. "Things are fair between us."

"What do you mean, James?"

"I mean that I know you are able and smart, that if, after the war, we . . ." He let his voice trail off.

Robert lifted a page of Jennie's letter. "Here's a line she wrote: *But when the war is done, you will no longer be a soldier. You can be yourself again.* You asked me that as well, James, if I could live as a woman again. I like being a soldier. I like being free. Jennie isn't often wrong about me, but she is wrong here. This is who I am."

"I like who you are, Robert Shurtliff."

Robert put the letters away—he would write to Jennie later. For now, he let James hold him. While the cold winter light scratched its way across the floor, he held within himself the suggestion of James's words: that the two of them might be together after the war.

THE CHRISTMAS SEASON PASSED WITH little to mark the days except Van Tassel roasting chestnuts and waxing eloquent about a dessert his grandmother used to make, a Dutch treat with almond paste.

Up in the garret, the winter nights stretched long, and often both of them awoke in the deep darkness. Robert whispered stories he had never voiced before: how he had fled from Middleborough, how those first weeks on the road felt, how Shaw had found him out and tried to blackmail him.

One night as they lay together, Robert pressed up to James's side, they recalled the early days of training. "I hated the drill. Every time I lifted a leg, Munn would scream at me," whispered James.

"I liked it. . . ."

"Well, you were good at it. I can only recall a time or two that you misstepped."

"I made my share of errors. But drill was the first time that I could shed my worries about whether I was walking right or standing right, whether I moved like a man."

James shifted on the mattress, the husks rustling. "I never thought of men standing a particular way."

"That's because you were born to it. It is natural for you."

They rested quietly for a time, and then James turned over, rolling onto his side as much as his injured legs would allow. He reached out his arm, ran his hand down Robert's chest, his fingers grazing breasts, nipples, the soft skin of his belly. "All this was hidden beneath." Robert could hear disbelief in his hushed tones. "You seldom fell behind, no more than any one of us might. You never complained, even on long marches, but it must have been twice as hard for you."

Robert didn't know how to respond. "It wasn't easy for any of us."

"But harder for you. . . . Robert, if you could, would you wish to have a man's body?"

"I often wished I had been born a man. But there is no purpose now in wishing to have a man's body. I might as well wish to fly." He reached out a hand to James's cheek, felt the roughness of stubble there. "I have often envied your whiskers," he whispered. "Though mostly for the good disguise they would give. No one would doubt a bearded cheek."

"It's a chore to shave before roll call. Especially to Munn's standards."

Robert let his hand travel down James's chest, felt the muscle there. James ran his fingers, the lightest of touches, as if he were brushing away a fallen eyelash, along Robert's stomach, near the crest of his hips. "I am happy in this body, I think," Robert whispered. "I know I am happy now."

"Good," said James. For a time they didn't speak, letting their hands explore each other gently, patiently. He had never thought he would want to be a wife or a mother—those were roles for other women to inhabit. Yet he would not trade this body, would not exchange this tenderness between him and James, even if the act made him in some sense a wife or, on some future day, a mother.

AFTER ROBERT AND JAMES HAD been at the farm for several weeks, Van Tassel declared he would head into town, purchase some sundries, and find out the news. Hearing this, Robert resolved to send a letter with him and so settled himself in the hayloft of Van Tassel's barn, wanting a little solitude in which to respond to Jennie.

Dear Jennie,

Your happy news reached me a few weeks ago, and I have been remiss in my correspondence. You feared I might be angry, but I am overjoyed that you are free and in love.

I am still in the field and cannot easily write of what has lately happened. The autumn brought skirmishes, and I was wounded in the head and shoulder, which required that I recuperate in a field hospital. Rest assured that I am now healthy and well, as well as could be. Life is odd sometimes in its ebbs and tides, the way it brings together and pushes apart. After so many months of trials and after the loss of a friend, I find myself on an island of peace and contentment. I wish I could write you more fully of all that has transpired.

Tell me all about your married life and new husband and house. What is his favorite dish? How is the land laid out? I want to be able to picture you. I need to send this off as soon as possible with good tidings and best wishes to you, Missus Howe, so you do not worry about me. But I promise a longer note soon.

Love from Robert

Robert saddled up the mare for Van Tassel and gave him the letter to Jennie, along with a short note to Sergeant Munn, stating that James made good recovery but could not yet walk. He let the sergeant know that they would await either a wagon from the regiment to ferry James to New Windsor or James's full healing, in which case they would make the journey on foot. From the door of the barn, he watched the mare plod away and then went inside the house.

In the garret, he lolled with James for a while, enjoying the novelty of intimacy during daylight hours, the clear sight of the bodies they had known only in the dark. Unused to being able to speak aloud, they found themselves returning to hushed tones, then laughing.

"It will be hard to go to New Windsor," James said.

Robert nodded. He had tried not to think of this. "We will have to act as we were before . . . as if this had not happened."

"What if . . ." James began.

"What?"

"What if we didn't . . ."

"We have to go back. We cannot be deserters." The very word curled his tongue.

"I know. You are right. But, Bob, when our term of service is over, we will both be free. We could go back to Massachusetts or try a new territory. Would you do that? Would you start a life with me, after the war?"

"Yes, I would, James." He felt within him a burgeoning, the sense that some plant had taken root and begun to grow, reaching its tendrils into the corners of him. "I would go with you. There has never been a place where I felt right before. Even in my own family. But with you . . . I trust you, James. I belong with you." He reached out and took James's hand.

James squeezed his fingers. "We could manage a farm, the two of us. In a new town, we could tell folks we were cousins and none would bother about it."

"And what if I got with child? What then? I'd be your portly cousin, would I?" He tried to make it a joke, but the possibility of it rubbed at him, threatening and promising.

"Well, then I suppose we'd . . ." He trailed off, a fuddled look coming over him. "I guess that wouldn't work. The neighbors would wonder where the child came from. We could tell them it was dropped off from a sister and we were fostering it."

"James." Robert shook his head. "That is a terrible plan."

"You're the clever one, then. You sort it out. Or better yet, let's worry about it later." James brought Robert's fingers to his lips.

Robert paused, this dream of James's hovering in his mind. Might he be able to live as a woman with James? With all that they had been through together, Robert knew James would treat him as an equal, would respect him and his strength. And wasn't that what had been missing when he'd lived as a woman? But James was right: Why worry about it now? These were discussions to be had when their service had concluded. "We'll figure some way out. First, though, we have to go back to our company. Will it be difficult for you to think of me as a soldier again?" Robert watched James's face closely.

"I've never thought of you as anything but, Bob. Does that seem odd?"

It did; it didn't. Robert didn't know what he thought of himself. But no path led forward except through New Windsor. "All this is idle talk. I haven't seen you take more than a few steps."

"Is that a challenge, Robert Shurtliff?"

"Aye."

James pushed himself up from the bed and set the crutches under his arms. He hobbled the length of the garret, away and back, away and back again. Robert laughed at the sight of him, naked but for one splint. "Think that's funny, eh?" James lunged for Robert, but he easily ducked away, scooping up his clothes.

"I should feed the fire and work at feeding us too. And you should rest after that lengthy trip." He pulled on shirt and trousers and, before James could protest, clattered down the ladder.

He hauled water, set it to boil, filled the woodbox, and kneaded some dough for bread, placing it to rise on the hearth. Then he settled on a stool with his letter box. He had long been thinking of how to compose this letter. Now, a moment had arrived when he could safely write to Jennie as Deborah. He wanted to reveal to her his relationship with James, something he could not tell her in the words of Robert, not when a letter might be read by any who took it in hand. But if he wrote as Deborah, he could explain his love for a man. He could take the letter to town and post it there, say he sent it on another's behalf, and none would be the wiser.

Dear Jennie,

You'll find this letter odd after my long spell of silence. Here it is, January. I am at a private house, I will leave it at that, nursing someone who is wounded back to health. Our lives seem to have followed an oddly similar pattern. You fell in love and got married. And I have fallen in love too, with the man I am nursing. I know this must make little sense, but I have known this man for a while. This is just the first time we are alone, the first we can be open with each other.

I do not know another man like him. With him I feel strong. He treats me as I wish to be treated. He takes me as I am. I do not know what the future will bring, but I hope it is a future with him. We have spoken of trying our hand at a farm, perhaps in new territory. It is a dream that is much on my mind. He is the first man I have met that I can imagine being content with. More than content, happy. But I also dream I might come to visit you, and the four of us will meet. May that happen soon!

With love,
Deborah

How disconcerting to sign that name. His hand formed the *D* slowly, and he stared at each letter as it emerged from his quill. He had been Deborah. He was Deborah still, some part of him. And yet he was Robert—how could he be both? How could he not be? It made no sense, and yet it felt right. He folded the letter up and tucked it in his coat—he would post it himself before they rejoined the troops at New Windsor. He didn't want to risk handing it over to Van Tassel. Back at the hearth, he formed the dough into loaves.

Van Tassel returned before sunset, and Robert helped him unload his horse. Robert brushed down the mare and fed her in her stall before settling himself at the fireside. He had made a soup to go with the bread he had baked, so he brought some up to James, who sat near the opening to the garret so he could listen in on the news while Robert went down to sit with Van Tassel. "No treaty yet, of course. The British sit in Manhattan and they don't act as though they seek peace. The farms just south of here still have Cow-Boys ranging about." Van Tassel dipped his bread in the soup. "The raiders know you Continentals are busy building and settling into your winter cantonment. But maybe you could write to your colonel, tell him to send some lads down this way."

"That sounds wise. I am sure the army can spare men to protect this area." The army, the Cow-Boys, they all seemed so distant to Robert. All of his world sheltered in this little farmhouse; they'd been here almost a month and a half, yet it seemed far longer. Van Tassel prattled on about news from neighboring farms; Robert heard James rise and clunk about the garret on his crutches, wished he could join him upstairs, but he sat, his face a polite mask.

A FEW DAYS LATER THE sky grew heavy, then loosed its load of flakes, wet and thick. As if in celebration, James made this his first day to leave the garret, getting down the ladder by swinging his splint from rung to rung. As he tottered, aglow with happiness, around Van Tassel's hearth, Robert watched him, pleased until he realized that the sooner James could walk, the sooner they would leave for New Windsor.

Robert dashed off another note to Munn conveying Van Tassel's request for additional patrols in the area, and once the snow had stopped, Van Tassel posted it, this time by riding to a neighboring farm whose owner made more frequent trips into town. His mare left fresh tracks across the smooth snow of the yard. Robert cleaned the stall while it stood empty and wondered when he'd have a chance to post his other letter, the one to Jennie. When he returned to the house, he found James going up and down the ladder on his own. The swelling on James's knee had shrunk, while the other leg bore a cavity where the gash had mostly healed over. Above this was a bump, still tender to the touch, and James could only manage a few steps without pain; Robert worried that something hadn't gone right in the healing, but he still held hope that with more time, James would walk normally. He boiled pots of water, and James took a bath by the fireside. While James washed, Robert shook out their coats, and then he cleaned and oiled the muskets and set his field kit in order. "Expecting an invasion?" James asked, his skin pink and soft from the hot water.

"Expecting to leave soon," Robert replied. "With that note heading to New Windsor, I imagine they will send a wagon to fetch us. Or in another couple of weeks, you might be able to walk the distance."

A day of sunshine and bitter cold chased away another snowfall, and then the wind blew in, spinning the icy particles around the yard. Robert trudged a narrow trail through the snow in order to feed the livestock, and when at last the wind dropped, he shoveled the snow from the barn doors. He wondered whether the regiment would send men down in response to his message, whether tomorrow might bring a squad of soldiers, their return to army life. A shout from the house broke his train of thought.

"Bob! Come quick!"

James stood in the doorway, half-dressed. Robert ran over. "What is it?"

"There are men on the road. I saw them from the garret window. Four or five men. They are raiders, I am sure of it."

"How can you be sure?"

"They carry muskets, and . . . don't argue. Come on!"

Robert ran inside past Van Tassel—the old man pressed himself against the wall—and clambered up the ladder. From the garret, he tossed down James's knapsack and handed him his musket and cartridge box. Grabbing his own equipment, he rattled down the rungs. "Get your coat on, James. It's freezing." He glanced through the window at the yard. "Let's defend from the barn," he said. "The hayloft has a good vantage."

They could have fired from the garret windows, but he hoped that he might keep the Cow-Boys from harming Van Tassel. He paused long enough to load his piece; James did the same. Then he dashed out the door and headed across the barnyard. James came as quickly as he could, with a hopping gait as he tried to keep weight off his weak leg. Before they'd made it to the barn, the men appeared, three of them, coming up off the road, dark coats against the white snow. One of them pointed and yelled, "Regimentals!" Robert saw him reach to his belt. That gave all the sign he needed. Dropping to a knee, he fired—the musket sounded impossibly loud, shattering the silence of this world. Another report: James had shot. Robert reloaded, ramming down the rod, and sighted along the barrel. Two men still stood, and he saw one aiming back at him. He fell flat in the snow. The pop of a sidearm, then another. He waited a moment, lifted himself, aimed, shot again. The men were too close. He reached up, fixed his bayonet. He cast a sideways glance at James to make sure he was doing the same, but he was loading again, sprinkling powder in the pan, kneeling in the snow, his leg at an awkward angle beneath him.

Now mere steps separated them from the Cow-Boys; the two men came with swords drawn. One, in a green coat, stepped out toward Robert, while the other, clad in black, moved toward James. The blast from James's musket opened up a hole in the green coat, though the man took one more step. And Robert, thinking that James would fire on the black-coated man, had begun his charge toward the green coat, only to lodge his bayonet in an already punctured chest. He yanked his musket back, spinning, to see black coat raise his sword. James tried to stand and swung his musket like a club, as if to parry. The motion unbalanced him so that he staggered on his bad leg, stumbled to his knees. Black coat's sword thrust toward James, and the point of the sword disappeared for a moment, sheathed in James's body. Robert saw the blade emerge from the blue wool before he could plunge his bayonet into the black coat, deep but too late.

For a moment, he was the only one standing in that farmyard, four fallen around him. Then he flung himself to the ground, grabbing hold of James's shoulders, the warmth yet in him, so easy to believe that if Robert just shook him, just gently touched his cheek, he'd awake with a yawn or a groan. How could he not?

It felt as though he lay a long time in the snow before he stood up and let go of the body—admitted to himself that it was just a body, the dead body of James, lying in bloody snow that he couldn't bear to look at. Three of them, one of James. Robert lurched to the farmhouse door; Van Tassel, pale and shaking, pressed a sack into his hands. "Food and drink. I watched it all. Oh God. You should go, you should go." He ran his hands over his bald pate. "There may be more of them. Others may come. I'll ride to a neighbor's. But I will see his body properly buried."

Robert stared at the ground, "His name was James Snow."

"Now go. To the road, take the left turning, and always follow the downhill. That will bring you to the Hudson."

Back outside, Robert shoved the food into his knapsack, packed his few possessions, and picked up his cartridge box. His musket lay next to James, and he lifted it up, cold and heavy. His chin trembled; his eyes burned. He had to go.

CHAPTER TWENTY-ONE

Twice he heard hoofbeats behind him; the sound carried across the quiet landscape so he had enough time to leap into the woods and ready himself. Both times it was a single rider, scanning the trees. Robert thought of shooting or stepping out and allowing himself to be shot, but he stayed hidden, crouching low to the ground.

He arrived at the Hudson River late in the afternoon. Luckily these roads had been traveled by horse and man and bore other tracks, else he'd have been easily followed. He knew that if he walked along the river, it would take him to the ferry, and the ferry would bring him to the road to West Point, and then . . .

The water rolled past. Ice skinned the river's surface at the edges but not in the middle, where the current writhed, allowing nothing to take hold. He dared not sit, not yet, but he did pause for a moment. He reached a hand inside his coat and drew out the letter he had written to Jennie, the one he had signed Deborah. He wouldn't be sending it now. He tore it again and again, into pieces as small as snowflakes, and cast these out over the river. Then he headed north.

By sunset he still had not reached the ferry, so he climbed into the woods and found spruce trees whose thickly needled boughs held up the snow. The ground below was almost dry: cold, but dry. He had no stomach for food and just wrapped himself in his blanket, pulling his knees to his chest. The darkness held him, and he listened to the river's rush—on and on and on. It would last forever. He thought of James, ached for him—James, who had fired for Robert's protection rather than save himself. He wept for the sacrifice, for the stupidity of love, for the waste, and for the gift of that time, so unexpected.

As soon as he could distinguish a hint of gray in the sky, Robert rose, his legs stiff from the cold, and rolled up his blanket. His joints ached, even his teeth hurt; everything about him felt frozen. His toes tingled, and, dimly, he thought that walking would warm them up, but that didn't really matter. He shuffled his feet along the road, the river a roar that filled his head. The sun rose in a sky that turned robin's-egg blue, and light bounced off the snow, the ice, the rushing water. He squinted, sometimes closing his eyes against the glare, shuffling and stumbling along. His nose dribbled liquid that froze above his lip. At the crest of a hill, he spotted the tower and stout walls of the ferry landing. The ferry. He registered that. Neither bad nor good, just ahead of him. At the bottom of the hill, a guard in a blue coat stepped out, eyeing him warily.

"Who goes there?"

Robert shrugged his shoulders. "Fourth Massachusetts."

"Commanding officer?"

"Captain Webb."

The ferry took him across the river, and Robert stared into the dark water. He leaned on his musket. It would have been better to defend the house, not go out in the open. He should have stayed with James and brought his body back. Oh, what use is a body? The ferry bumped up against the bank, and Robert stepped to shore. The ferryman called after him, "Where are you heading, then?"

"West Point," Robert mumbled, half-turning to face the man.

The soldier shook his head. "No one there. There'll be a wagon going to New Windsor. Best you take that when it comes through."

When the wagon rolled up the track some time later, the driver nodded at him, and Robert slung his gear over the rails before taking his seat. A gray muffler swaddled the driver's head, with just a tip of red nose protruding. "Gee-up." He snapped the reins. The packed snow squeaked beneath them as the wagon skewed and skated before lurching forward.

The wind made Robert's eyes sting, and he tucked his chin to his chest. Soon he'd be back with his company. No more James. No more gentle touch, no more reassurance that someone knew and cared about him. He'd have to stand up straight and go back to being hard. He shoved his hands into his sleeves and pulled his arms across his body, hugging himself. When he had come to West Point, all had been simple. Not easy, but simple. Survive. Fit in. Learn the drill, keep out of trouble, measure up to the other men. But this simplicity had been stripped away. Robert recalled a dog he'd once found in the woods of Middleborough, just a typical mongrel, lying on its side in the dirt. As he approached, the dog appeared to be asleep, fur ruffled by the breeze, happy in the sun. But when it didn't stir, he nudged it with the toe of one shoe and turned over the body, now revealed to be a corpse, exposing the other side, the ragged hole out of which vermin poured, the hollowness within. How could he go on living as if the dog were just asleep, as if all was well?

"New Windsor," the driver said, pointing down the lane.

Robert stepped down from the wagon, still hugging his arms across his chest in a futile attempt to keep some warmth. From a snug stone hut a corporal appeared. "What's your business, then?"

"Fourth Massachusetts. Light infantry. Sergeant Munn . . ." His voice sounded like a frog's croaking, distant even in his own ears, and he felt his body give a violent shiver, a spasm almost, as if trying to throw off the cold all at once.

"Munn!" The corporal had stepped down the slope, cupped his hands to his mouth, and bellowed. "Munn!"

Robert watched a burly figure detach himself from the dark-coated group of men occupied in peeling the bark off logs. Even as he recognized the form of his sergeant, he felt himself slip further away from this moment and place. He stared down at the encampment, which seemed to waver before him with every breath he took. Here and there a tree had been left standing, but otherwise the slope was forested only by huts, along with raw logs and stone chimneys; many huts remained unfinished. Men moved about, and smoke rose from dozens of fires. The sounds of hammers and saws floated up; he waited but could not hear the commands of the drill.

Then Munn appeared before him, swaddled in a muffler, the tips of his ears gone white with cold. Robert lifted one of his arms to salute, but the sergeant seized Robert's hand. "Lad, look at your fingers!" They were blue and white, white as snow, blue as his coat. He nodded. Munn pushed Robert into the guard's hut, where a fire blazed in the hearth, and chafed Robert's hands between his own before settling him on a stool near the fire. From a kettle, Munn poured out a bowl of hot water, added a ladle of water from a bucket, and lifted Robert's hands, dunking them into the bowl and holding them there. They burned, a cold fire; he jerked and tried to draw them out. "Steady. They must thaw, or you'll lose them." Robert's arms trembled, but he kept his hands still. "Now," said Munn, pointing at Robert's coat. "Tell me what happened."

Robert gazed down at his chest, saw the wool matted brown with dried blood. He closed his eyes. "I was at Van Tassel's." He swallowed. "Some Cow-Boys came." His fingers itched in the warm water. But he could feel life returning now, painful. His eyes stung, and he blinked fiercely.

"Are you whole, Shurtliff?" Munn said, his hoarse voice full of worry.

Robert reeled, his own emotions softened by Munn's unexpected concern. He swallowed in a sticky throat. "I am not wounded," he said at last. "We were attacked. James was killed."

Munn bowed his head. "May the Good Lord have mercy on his soul. He was a fine soldier, a good man, and he's gone to his peace now." Munn paused, as if waiting for some response, but Robert could think of nothing to say. "We've been worried about you, lad. You've been gone so long." Munn signaled to a corporal. "Warm some cider for this soldier, eh?"

How long had it been? Robert curled and uncurled his fingers in the cooling water. "What day is it, sir?"

"It is the twenty-fourth of January."

"But I sent word. Twice. Messages to you about irregulars in the area." Robert frowned at how muffled and dim his memory felt. He was sure he had sent messages. He lifted his hands from the water and dried them on his trousers.

"I received nothing. It's possible that they were lost or misdirected. Or intercepted. Where did you post them, and with whom?"

"Our host took them to town, once to his near neighbor. . . ."

"The captain must know of this." Munn wrapped the muffler about his head again, took the steaming mug of cider the corporal had brought, and thrust it into Robert's hands. "Drink this. I reckon I'll be back from headquarters before you're finished."

A flash of cold air made the fire shiver as Munn departed. Robert stared into the flames and sipped the cider. He could not bring himself to wonder about what would happen next.

He was standing with his back to the fire and tipping the last of the now-cool cider down his throat when Munn returned, bursting through the hut's door. "Well, Shurtliff," the sergeant said, "the captain is sending squads down to Crom Pond now, you'll be glad to know."

"Sir, I'd like to volun—"

"No." Munn looked at him flatly. "I don't doubt your valor, but no. You've been given the position of—"

"I want to go out and fight." He clenched his teeth shut against saying more, against the wish that welled up in him for revenge or, barring that, for the chance to be killed, to let his pain be extinguished.

"No." Munn's voice rang with finality. "It is not a question of your courage or your ability. Not at all. But no. You've been out of the company for too long. You need to settle in to New Windsor. And the regiment needs a waiter on staff to serve General Paterson and to help out at headquarters. You can read and write, you are neat and clean. I just convinced the captain to give you the job, and so you will take it."

"Yes, sir," said Robert.

"Let's get you equipped."

THE SERGEANT BROUGHT HIM TO the commissary, where he was issued the trousers, coat, and waistcoat of the general's staff. "You'll meet Paterson today or tomorrow," Munn said. "You'll like him. He's a gentleman, a lawyer of Yale University before this war set in. But he's a soldier too, been in the army since seventy-seven." He picked a heavy winter coat from a trunk and passed it to Robert. "You need that coat fitted?"

"I'll manage it myself," Robert replied. The thought of a needle and thread and a simple task comforted him.

Robert followed the sergeant outside. The buildings and pathways flowed past him, and he fought to keep his vision from blurring; it felt to him as though he was still in Van Tassel's yard, as if he might return to that house at any moment. Munn showed him to his quarters. For the household staff, this meant a cottage behind the farmhouse where Paterson was staying. Robert was assigned a small room much like Jennie's chamber at the Leonards'. A bed, a washstand, a cupboard, a window: luxury beyond what he expected. But he would have slept in a frozen ditch if it had meant he could sleep next to James again.

"A bell will summon you to the main house. Lieutenant Walden runs the staff. He'll explain your duties."

"Thank you, sir."

Munn put his hand on Robert's shoulder. "I am sorry about Snow. I know you two were close. But don't dwell on it, Shurtliff. No good comes of that. He is with the Good Lord now. Let that be a comfort to you." He let his hand drop and buttoned up his overcoat. "Come and visit us in the huts, will you?"

Robert nodded, and the sergeant closed the door behind him. He stripped off his filthy coat, pulled off his boots, and let it all settle into a pile on the floor. He lay facedown on the bed, scrunched his eyes, and opened his mouth against the wool of the blanket. He knew Munn's advice was proper; he knew he should follow that course. Men pushed their emotions aside, denying them or stuffing them far away, but Robert couldn't ignore this pain, as real to him as the pain of being shot. If Jennie were here, they would throw their arms around each other and weep. But Robert had no one.

He howled into the wool, letting the blanket muffle his sound. He wailed for James, for himself. He cried to God. He saw again James's face in the garret, the hopeful lift of his voice as he spoke about a future for the two of them. "Robert, we could . . ."

Why hadn't he let one of the Cow-Boys finish him too? It would have been easier to die than to go on, one day after the other, here in the army without James—to have been so open, so understood, and now to have no one. His tears slowed, until he hiccuped and sniffed and struggled to catch his breath. There would never be another James. Lying there, he felt certain that he had been changed, that the month in the garret had shifted and shaped him as surely as the drill had in the months before. Where he had been hard, he felt soft; where he had wanted to prove himself, he now wanted to be understood. James's voice echoed in his head: *Bob, I don't want to be apart from you. . . .* It had felt so good to be joined to James. How could it be that he had lost it all, that he was, once more, alone?

LIEUTENANT WALDEN, A BOSTON NATIVE who looked young and fresh beside veterans such as Munn—a lily among turnips—outlined Robert's duties that evening while they walked through General Paterson's house. Serve the general at table, deliver messages, tend fires—the list went on and on. As Robert listened, he realized he would be part manservant, part aide. But that was fine. This job required steady activity, responsibility, and personal attention but asked nothing of life and death. A mere month ago the thought of such duties would have chafed at him, but now they were welcome. A simple world of order. He marveled at his change—that he found it a pleasure to serve in a house once more.

The general had reached his middle years, plain face but strong eyes, with brows that overhung and deepened his gaze. He took dinner with his colonels, and Robert brought him meat and bread, then stood along the wall with the other waiters. The officers dined with silver and porcelain at a table draped in linen. He had not known this world existed in the army, a world that exceeded the luxury of any house he had served or visited in Middleborough. He listened and watched, trying to anticipate Paterson's needs. In this setting, he could fade into the background—a virtue he hadn't cherished when he'd served in Middleborough but which he now enjoyed. No more drawing attention to himself through valor and distinction. He could leave the glory for others to pursue; he wanted quiet, time to mourn, space in which to re-collect the pieces of himself, which felt now scattered and moribund.

That first night Paterson dismissed him after dinner, and he went to the kitchen, set to the rear of the house, to eat. As he pressed in between other servants, the space grew as hot—and as odoriferous—as his tent at West Point, and Robert soon excused himself to go to bed. Before curling up under the blankets, he knelt on the floor. "Guide me, God," he whispered. "I am lost. Everywhere I turn, I think of James. Lord, what am I to do?" He pressed his hands together over his heart, then moved them lower to his stomach. How he longed for James's touch. Was there any chance that their lying together had left him with child? Did he dare to pray for it? He stood and pulled back the covers on his bed. What did it mean that he wanted this? These could not be the desires of Robert Shurtliff.

ROBERT TAILORED HIS TROUSERS AND waistcoat, and became familiar with the stables: which horse was Paterson's and which one Robert could ride on errands. Some of the schedule felt familiar from West Point, like the roll call just after dawn, when Lieutenant Walden inspected arms and uniforms before calling out the day's assignments. Still, he missed James, an aching absence, as when a tooth has been pulled and the tongue can't resist seeking out the gaping hole. It pressed on him, but the daily chores and errands pressed back, and somehow he found a balance. It felt as though he was perched on the edge of a steep cliff, but as long as he didn't look down, he could maintain his footing. It helped not to think too deeply, just work hard and fall asleep quickly.

On the first day that his schedule allowed him reprieve—about a week after he had arrived at New Windsor—he went down the slope to the huts, hoping that a reunion with his comrades would return him to his right mind. A few inquiries led him to his old company. Munn, clad in a heavy coat, watched as Matthew worked at a sawhorse with Corporal Booth, but they ceased their labor to greet him.

"Hey-ho! Bob's back."

"Fair as ever!"

"Let's welcome him proper!"

Munn clapped his hands and they fell silent. "A moment to

remember James Snow." The company bowed their heads. Robert closed his eyes. "Amen," said the sergeant. "We are glad to have you back, Shurtliff."

Matthew showed Robert the hut they were building. They had constructed a fireplace at each end, and though the roof sat low, the building possessed generous width. "We need to finish the bunks . . ." said Matthew, pointing to the far end. Two rows of bunks, one above the other, lined each side. Robert quickly counted: sixteen; and more to be built. The space would be packed full of men. ". . . And seal the stones of the hearth," Matthew continued. Robert nodded, trying to imagine four months here, from February to May. Now it smelled of fresh-sawn wood; within a week it would reek of smoke and piss and unwashed wool. Gratitude swirled through him at the thought that he would not pass the winter in these quarters.

Standing in a tight circle around a fire, the others inquired after Robert's new role and told him about life at New Windsor. They shared the news of the war, though they knew nothing more than what Van Tassel had told him: reports of grumblings from New York, the sporadic raids in Westchester. But still everyone agreed that peace grew close. He listened to their talk of treaties and skirmishes and found that he did not care. The hopelessness he'd held at bay through work threatened to rise up and overwhelm him, and he knew he had better return to headquarters and find something to occupy his hands and his mind.

"Once the huts are done, we are to start on a meetinghouse, what they're calling the Temple of Virtue," Booth said, his words cutting into Robert's thoughts.

"Making work to keep us busy," complained Matthew. "Break our backs so we don't have strength to complain." He paused a moment, then added quietly, "Or rebel."

An undercurrent flowed through New Windsor, and already Robert had sensed it. Officers were riding out to Newburgh—where

Washington was spending the winter—and General Knox's headquarters daily, coming back unsettled, displeased.

"All those fancy gents want to know is what'll happen to their commission," Matthew said. "You know we haven't been paid since we got in, and we better get paid before we get out."

"That's enough of that," Munn said.

"Have you stayed out of fights, Matthew?" Robert asked.

"He has," Booth interjected. "We've been keeping him as busy as possible."

Matthew kicked at the dirty snow. "Busy helps. I haven't had a fight since Peekskill."

"You've grown up, is what. Both of you," Munn said. "When I marched you to West Point, you were both pups. Now, Shurtliff still might not have a whisker to show, but still, I wager you're not the same lad you were when you arrived."

"That is the truth, sir," said Robert.

"Aye. It's hard to take a loss, and you've had injuries to bear as well. Still, you're alive, thanks be to God, and healthy. So lend your hands or stand aside. We have work to do."

Robert stepped back. Seeing again these familiar faces, hearing the bark of Munn's voice, he missed not the drill but James. He should have been here with them, thumping floorboards into place and making a snug home for the winter. The longer Robert stayed with the others, the more the ache of absence grew, so he raised his hand in farewell and walked back to headquarters. He was no longer part of their world. He had come to be Robert Shurtliff in their midst, and he no longer wanted to be in their midst. So what would become of him?

CHAPTER TWENTY-TWO

As minor scuffles broke out with frequency—products of the cold and confinement of February—Paterson served as the justice of the peace, hearing cases from the camp. When the court was in session, Robert took the role of body servant to Paterson, polishing his shoes, brushing his coats, and helping the general to dress. Although the intimacy of this office embarrassed Robert at times, and he could have laughed at the ridiculousness of the scene as he helped the general to powder his hair and do up his buttons, nevertheless, the job afforded an opportunity to talk to the great man about matters of justice and military practice.

At month's end, a group of soldiers from the regiment came to trial on the charge of desertion. They had quite simply walked away from their guard posts and were found several days later making their way upriver. Robert attended the trial in service to Paterson, stoking the room's fire, carrying messages, bringing fresh paper and ink. The accused were five scruffy men, their uniforms stained with soot and grease, pants torn and ill-patched. They spat out their stories in sorry bursts: how they were tired, how they were bored, how none had been paid in a year. Paterson pressed each one: "What were you seeking?" and Robert knew he suspected treason, that the men might have been trying to pass information to the British even in these waning hours of the war. "Home," the men replied. "Just home." They spoke of wives, of fields, of children, of two or three years spent in the army. As Paterson heard the case over the course of several days, Robert began to feel sorry for the men, for their simplicity and their stupidity; in the end, Paterson sentenced two—those he believed to be the instigators—to death by hanging and the rest to fifty lashes each. Robert carried the sentence to the sergeant-at-arms.

That evening, as he helped the general with his coat and boots, Paterson remained silent. At last, just as Robert was putting away the general's shirt and preparing to withdraw from the chamber, Paterson spoke. "I imagine you think me a monster for my judgment today, Robert."

"No, sir," he replied. He didn't think him a monster, but he did wonder if the hangings were necessary.

Paterson grimaced as if he sensed the deception. "I feel myself to be a monster. Yet I warrant that I saved lives and spared many from pain today."

"How is that, sir?"

"To hang two and flog the rest will serve as a warning to those who are tired of winter at New Windsor. Perhaps we will see fewer desertions and have no more cause for executions."

Robert closed the door on the wardrobe. "It is just that . . . they seemed to be simple fellows, and . . ."

"Men just like you?"

Robert nodded, though he would not have phrased it as such.

"When I was a younger officer, serving at the start of the war, soldiers deserted by the dozen in the winter. We had no food, no blankets, and very little hope." Paterson crossed the room to stand by the fire. "Deserters then were punished by worse than death, worse than floggings. The devices that some thought of . . . running a gauntlet or riding a wooden horse . . ." The general paused, stared into the flames. "Death or lashes are preferable. There must be honor in the matter. A man must be respected as a man."

"Aye, sir," said Robert.

Paterson looked at him for a long moment, his eyes shadowed under his prominent brow. "Speak your mind freely, Robert. You are ever inclined to hold your tongue."

"So I was taught, sir."

"Restraint is often called for, it is true. But you ought not to lose your faculty to speak, to articulate your own opinions. Nor should you feel that you cannot speak them in front of me."

Robert finished brushing the general's frock coat and hung it in the wardrobe. "Before I joined the army, I served a master who always bade me to keep silent. It is a hard lesson to unlearn."

"Ah, but that is why we have fought this war. For the British were like your master and told us that we had no voice. But I tell you that we have. Not just me, not just officers, but you as well. Speak your mind on the matter, Robert."

"I say that sometimes the law falls harder on those who have less. On the poor, on women, on the lower ranks of the army. For those who have less, a lashing that takes away a few days' labor, or a fine that costs a week's pay, why, these are punishments that cut to the marrow. Those who have less live within a smaller margin, sir."

"But their crimes are the same, are they not?"

"No, sir. The crimes of those in power hurt all those beneath them, but the crimes of the lesser folk, well, they hurt only themselves, or only a few."

Paterson nodded, holding his hands to the fire. "This is why our new country needs to hear the voices of all, not just the aristocratic few. I wish that those with whom I studied law at Yale University could hear your claims."

"Yes, sir." Robert sensed the air of dismissal and picked up the general's boots, retreating to the drafty hallway to clean and polish them. He had never thought that a great man would attend so closely to his opinion. Pride suffused him at Paterson's words, and amusement, too—he could no more imagine speaking to students at Yale University than he could imagine preaching a sermon at the Congregationalist church in Middleborough. In truth, despite Paterson's encouragement, he felt akin to the enlisted men and had a deep sympathy for the deserters and their simple desire to go home. He gave a last swipe to the boot leather, packed away the rags and oil, and began to make his own way to bed.

His footsteps were light on the floor, and he felt himself the only soul still astir in this great house. What if Paterson would sponsor him when the war was ended? What could he make of himself then? He imagined the world, this new country, vaster and darker than the corridors in which he now walked, and Paterson a gleaming lamp that illumined but one corner. The real matter was not about Paterson though; the real matter was what Robert himself wanted. Here, in the hallway, cold and dark as the night outside, Robert felt again that deep-seated wish—that he might be carrying a child within him. A month had passed since he'd left Van Tassel's. It could be possible. He wanted it, even as he knew it would bring about an end to his life as a waiter, as a soldier, as Robert Shurtliff. But it would prove that he had been loved. More, it would bring him someone to love, a something to answer this nothingness that resounded around him. He could picture the babe in his arms—what a promise that would feel like, a gift to give hope for the future.

As WAS HIS WEEKLY CUSTOM, Robert attended Sunday chapel in the Temple of Virtue, which had been completed in the middle of March. This Sunday, Munn sought him out, and the two sat side by side through the service. When the congregation had been dismissed, Munn turned to Robert.

"Spring will come soon, and when the wagons can pass the roads, we'll return to West Point. Will you come back to the lights, Bob?"

The question surprised Robert, and an old desire leapt in him for action, for a clear sense of purpose. But even as he started to say yes, he knew that what he wanted was a return to the past. "I hadn't thought that was possible, sir."

"I could ask that you be made corporal. There'll be plenty of work to clear every last loyalist out of Westchester."

What would it feel like to be back on the parade ground, to be back in a tent? He remembered the feel of shot flying past his face; he remembered the thrust of his bayonet into another man's chest. He remembered how the sword angled out of James's body. "I will think on it, sir." He found he could not meet Munn's eyes, fearing that he would see disappointment in them.

"A few months ago, you would have jumped at the chance to fight again, Shurtliff." The sergeant paused, looked at his hands, the broad spread of fingers, the cracked and swollen knuckles. "Do you recall what you said to me of fate, all those months ago? Are you wrestling with angels now, Robert?"

"I do. I am. Sir . . . I don't know who I would be if not for the lights. But you are correct. I have been wrestling, for weeks and weeks. I don't know if it's with angels or my own shadow or . . ."

"It is with God. We are always wrestling with God. Fight hard, then, and get your blessing from Him."

"Thank you, sir." His stomach gave a queasy turn. He wished he could tell Munn more, but the sergeant was not one for emotion, would not understand the torrent of feeling that Robert felt within himself, certainly would not understand the bond he felt with James. Not without letting all loose, and there was no chance of doing that. They stood, and Robert offered the sergeant a salute.

He went to the necessary behind the house where he quartered. When he unbuttoned his front fall and slid the buff trousers down, he saw a few rust-brown stains dotting the crotch. His menses. He stared at them as he urinated. Rising, he did up his pants and walked across the yard and up the stairs to his room. He closed the door behind him and sank to the floor. He could hear footsteps, the creak of floorboards as others walked past, so he kept his sobs silent. He shouldn't have hoped that he could be carrying James's child.

He sat on the floor of his room and tilted his tear-stained face to the ceiling. Perhaps he sought only a way out; perhaps he, like the attempted deserters, simply wanted to leave. No, he told himself. He had not come all this way to quit. He had not endured the fights and the training, the close quarters and poor rations, to have it end in humiliation and defeat. He had arrived on his own terms and he would depart on them. No more light infantry, but there was no shame in continuing as Paterson's waiter. He brought his knees to his chest, hugged himself close, and the tears tapered off. Unbidden, he thought of Israel Wood's clerk and the morning—so long ago—when he'd greeted his menses with utter relief. What did it mean that he now wanted to be with child? Nothing more than that he loved James and missed him, that he wanted proof of something that threatened to slip away as if it had never happened. No, the truth held more. He could see himself with a babe in his arms, or an older child—he could see a daughter, the two of them churning butter or kneading dough side by side, and the daughter turning to her and saying, "Mother, what was it like to be a soldier?" And Deborah would push the heel of her hand into the dough and remember James and say, "It was terrible and lovely all at once."

Tears blurred her vision again. She had signed on for a term and she would fulfill her duty. She had not been wrong to think that she was Robert Shurtliff. But she was also Deborah Samson. To be one, she had to be the other; she could deny neither. Deborah pushed herself up from the floor, drew out the old bundle from beneath her cot, and removed two strips of fabric—what had once formed the skirt of her dress. One she soaked in water and scrubbed the tears from her face. The other she folded up and placed inside her trousers, to catch the hope that flowed out of her.

Then, in the quiet of Sunday afternoon, she took out her letter box and began to write.

Dear Jennie,

I am writing to you now from New Windsor, our winter cantonment. It is already the middle of March, and you must believe me that I meant to write sooner. I am sure you have written to me as well, but I know that this season provides little chance for travel and post. Still, I need to write. More, I need to speak with you, but that cannot happen.

I was, for a time, nursing another soldier, a dear friend, but he died, and this left me alone and troubled. I remember long ago sitting beside you and hearing the reverend preach about the silver cord of being. Jennie, my silver cord nearly broke that day. Losing him, I fear I lost myself for a time. Now I can begin to piece things together again, but it is not easy, and though I pray for guidance, I am often unsure of the way.

I am serving an officer in our regiment. The chores are familiar: laundry and waiting table and tidying chambers. But would you believe that I take comfort in these tasks? You will be glad to know that there is not much fighting going on. All talk is of peace. I wonder what that peace will mean for me and what I will do when I am not a soldier. There was a time when I spoke with other soldiers of going to Ohio, if that territory should be opened, and trying our hand at farming. That seems impossible since I have lost my friend. I do not feel capable of starting over alone.

You know well that Middleborough was no easy place for me. Aside from you, there were none who understood me. These months as a soldier, I have felt myself to be understood. Our actions, even the most minor chores, carry a sense of importance and service. I will miss the fastness, the close sense of the company. Is Easton better than Middleborough? If I came to that town, would there be aught for me? There would be you, but you belong to another now. Oh, Jennie, I fear I am a lost soul.

I'd like to hear your news, to learn how married life is suiting you. The snow is thick on the ground here, but spring will come eventually, as it always does.

Love,
Robert

Word came that Congress intended to declare an official end to the war. The treaties were signed, England had proclaimed a cessation of hostilities, and everyone in New Windsor awaited Congress's next move. And so in mid-April, when Washington came to the Temple of Virtue to read the declaration and toast the new peace, the camp ran wild with revels. Matthew and Booth sought out Deborah, who let herself get caught up in the spirit of the day and found herself singing at the top of her lungs with the rest of her old company—a whole host of bawdy songs advertising the glory of the army and the not-so-glorious character of the king. She caught a fleeting glimpse of what she had loved about being a soldier, a reminder that chafed raw the spot that missed James.

In the wake of these festivities, as the roads became dry enough for travel, the true meaning of the war's end hit New Windsor. Each morning, after inspection and roll call, a captain read the list of furloughed soldiers and sent them on their way. With a formal discharge, soldiers could collect payment for service—years' worth of wages. But with furlough, they collected nothing, and there were grumblings throughout the camp. Over the course of April and May, the army shrank around Deborah. The huts emptied out, and company after company marched away. By June, when the remaining army—mostly three-year men like Deborah, who had time left on their enlistment—moved back to summer quarters at West Point, the once-full post felt like the lost colony of Roanoke. With buildings gaping empty, an air of despondency and abandonment permeated the place, though perhaps Deborah's mood added that color to the scene. It came as a surprise when Matthew appeared one morning at Paterson's headquarters.

"What news?" Deborah called when she saw him approach.

"Back to Mendon for me," said Matthew, his mouth lifted in a half smile.

"Truly? You are discharged?"

Matthew took Deborah's hand and shook it firmly. "Do you recall, Bob, those days last year when we talked of going to the Ohio territories?"

"I do." What a futile hope it had been. She let his hand drop.

"Wish we'd done it. But still, we made it through, didn't we? Earned that bounty, I reckon."

"Safe travels," she said. All the other words stuck in her throat. Yes, she'd made it through . . . and the bounty, which had started her on this long journey, what was it worth? How could she know her value, what all this had cost her?

She watched Matthew walk across to the barracks. The news of his departure left her feeling marooned on an island like Robinson Crusoe. Though they had not spent much time together throughout the winter and spring, Matthew nonetheless represented some substantial part of her, the last link to their tent in West Point and their training, to Tobias and his card games, to James and his dancing. Now she was by herself again—stronger and within the circle of Paterson's protection, but even there, still alone.

As all of West Point bloomed, Deborah settled the general into his summerhouse. Rooms were aired, handsome rugs shaken out, the heavy winter drapes replaced with light curtains. Deborah marveled at this fine mansion with its arbor and veranda, which the general called a piazza, amazed that she had alternately frozen and sweltered beneath musty canvas when this world sat mere yards away.

At last a letter came from Jennie. She received the missive at roll call and brought it back to her room.

Dear Robert,

It was a relief to hear that you are safe, though terrible to read of your loss. I know you are no stranger to death and have always possessed a strong constitution, so to hear that this loss so unseated you is troubling indeed. I hope spring and your new station have brought ease into your life.

I hope, too, that my own good tidings will cheer you, for I am with child and should be delivered in August. All the old wives of the village are clucking at me and trying to feed me horrible dishes. If you were here, you would chase them off with a broom!

Do come back, Robert. Somehow, we would manage. Haven't we always? We could once again work at our former chores side by side, or if it is more to your preference, you could work in the fields. I think of you often and have told Charles your story, which he thinks is a daring adventure worthy of a chapbook. There is always room in our house for you. Do write and be well.

Love,
Jennie

Jennie with child. Those were good tidings; Jennie had always loved small children and delighted in helping Mrs. Thomas with the youngest boys whenever the Leonards could spare her. Deborah read the letter through again and this time focused on the last section, the invitation to come and stay. Could she go back? Should she ask Paterson to be furloughed? Would he allow her? And if she did return, would it be as Deborah or as Robert? Here at West Point, the two tangled together inextricably. She would not be happy, she knew, if her fellow soldiers discovered she was female. She would not be happy to work here as Deborah—she would be shunted aside, ignored, and dismissed. The trust and faith that the general and others placed in her would evaporate. Yet she no longer felt that she was, once and for all, Robert Shurtliff. Deep within, she could not deny the feeling that had first risen back in New Windsor or even in Van Tassel's garret, the regret over not conceiving a child, the thought that she and James might have lived together after the war. That she might have been his wife and in doing so, somehow managed to find her place, not-quite-Deborah and no-longer-Robert.

Over the next few days, Deborah tried to imagine Jennie large with child and Jennie with an infant. She tried to feel happy for her friend and not jealous that she was so clearly settled while Deborah drifted, her future unmoored. Evenings, when the household staff had been dismissed, she often lit a candle with the intention to write, but she always turned to a book from Paterson's library or to the window, finding solace in the moon or the stars, something far away.

Deborah crouched in the yard, fixing loose paving stones in the front path. The June morning unfolded with cool sunshine, and she could see one of the few remaining companies run through the drill on the parade ground. She recalled the clarity of those exercises and the excitement that had flooded her when she'd mastered the maneuvers. It had been a little over a year ago that she had first learned the drill, but it felt like more than a century.

"Do you miss the manual exercise?"

Deborah spun around; the voice was Paterson's; the general had emerged from his house. Before she could salute, Paterson said, "At ease." He, too, watched the drill for a moment.

"No, sir," she said. "I don't miss it. There are moments when I watch them out there, and I can feel my arms twitch as if they want to follow along."

"That is the body, then, but not the spirit?"

"Yes, sir."

"And where does your spirit move you, Robert? When this regiment is dissolved, how will you seek your fortune?" He spoke in the voice of father to son, and Deborah didn't know how to answer. "Think on it—what you wish to do. Then come talk to me."

"Aye, sir." She watched Paterson walk toward the field and considered his words: more and more she thought of Jennie and Easton. She thought she might take one last trip as Robert Shurtliff and see the city of Boston, from which so much of the news sprang in her childhood. So often had she spoken of this trip with Tobias and with James that she felt she owed it to them to see the city. She thought she might give herself one more chance to belong somewhere else. But if there did not seem to be a place for her—a bench in a weaver's workshop, perhaps—in Boston, then she would return to Jennie, at least for a time. Maybe in the company of her friend she'd be able to regain the desire and the courage that had made her embark on this journey.

Before the front walk was repaired, before the company had run through its drills, Deborah watched a messenger gallop past and turn in at General Knox's house, and Paterson soon received summons. She abandoned her chore and readied Paterson for the meeting. Inside his chamber, she brushed the general's coat vigorously before laying it over a chair, then turned her attention to the shoes. "Trouble afoot," murmured Paterson as he buttoned his waistcoat.

"Where, sir? I thought the British had withdrawn." She lifted the coat and helped the general slide his arms in, then brushed at the epaulets to make them lie straight.

"There are more enemies than the British, Robert. Any new country must first go through the birth pangs and then the growing pains."

Within an hour the word came out about a mutiny of the Pennsylvania line. The waiters caught snippets of news: a hundred enlisted men had decried their condition as furloughed without pay and demanded a settlement, marching to Philadelphia and gaining hundreds of supporters along the way. Some said they occupied the State House, while others claimed they terrorized the city at large. One truth emerged clearly: Washington had ordered most of the army at West Point down to suppress the uprising. Paterson emerged from his meeting with Knox and summoned the regimental and company commanders. Deborah and the other household staff stopped their domestic duties and attended to the officers, bringing refreshment, stabling horses, carrying messages, and hoping to overhear a tidbit of news.

At midday the meeting with the commanders broke up, and the officers hastened to carry out their orders. Deborah saw Captain Webb with his lieutenants moving across the parade ground. How different this moment must feel; they no longer rode out to battle the British but to fight troops of their own country, poor men who petitioned only for what the nation owed them. She stood for a long while at the window, until a bell summoned her. In the largest sitting room, Paterson assembled all his staff: majors and captains, aides-de-camp, many lieutenants, and at the back, those who waited upon each officer. Sheets of papers were scattered over the table, with the general's hat at one corner; Deborah saw that only a few streaks of powder remained in his hair, for Paterson, when vexed, had a habit of running a hand through his locks.

"Gentlemen. We must make all haste to Philadelphia. Today we will provision the companies and plan the march. Tomorrow we depart."

With those words, all of West Point turned upside down. Wagons were loaded, tents folded. Deborah repacked what she had unpacked just days before. That night, she mindlessly loaded her own knapsack without the strength to consider what this march might bring.

All mustered, ready to venture out. The companies departed without fanfare. Deborah rode in the midst of the troop, somewhere between the vanguard and the supply wagons. It was the privilege of the household staff to ride instead of march, and though she had spent much time on horseback in the past few months on errands for Paterson, it felt odd not to be trudging on foot with the soldiers of the infantry. Still, it was a pleasant way to travel; the roads were firm, the sky clear; it did not feel like war.

The march to Philadelphia took more than a week. Paterson billeted in houses along the way, sitting down to sumptuous dinners with former officers and resting in four-poster beds. Deborah slept in the stables and peered briefly into worlds she had never imagined.

They were slowed one day by rain, and Lieutenant Walden, who was in charge of Paterson's waiters and aides, rode alongside Deborah and kept up a stream of commentary as steady as the raindrops.

"Just wait until you see Philadelphia, Robert. It is a wondrous city."

"I have never even been to Boston."

Walden waved his hand dismissively. "I was raised in Boston, but compared to Philadelphia, it is provincial." Walden now prattled on about streets and halls and theaters, and Deborah half-listened, unable to imagine it. She missed the easy banter of James and Tobias, even Matthew's surly comments. They had shared a wonder for the world, while Walden's boasts felt jaded and condescending.

"We'll have the mutiny to contend with before we can enjoy the city, sir," Deborah said.

"True. But Paterson will put them down. Some ill-assorted rabble, I am sure."

Deborah thought it best not to correct Walden, not to assert that she—perhaps more than anyone—was from the ill-assorted rabble. She couldn't help but think of her companions in Webb's company, many of them marching back to tiny, meager farms in eastern Massachusetts with only a well-worn uniform to show for their efforts.

THE HOUSES OF THE CITY grew thick about them, and they traded the dirt roads for cobblestone streets with close-pressed buildings. The army billeted in barracks and an empty armory, sprawling out into stables and a storehouse as well. General Paterson took quarters in a grand house near the armory, and as Deborah unloaded the supply wagons, she noticed other households busily stacking their goods into carts to flee the approaching tide of soldiers. As she watched servants and grooms bustle about, she repressed a smirk: the people of the city wanted protection but they didn't really want soldiers about.

The next morning, Paterson himself led two companies to the sections of the city that the mutineers had lately occupied. Deborah stayed at the barracks, awaiting messages and the arrival of the final supply wagons. She studied maps of Philadelphia, knowing she would need to be familiar with the streets, and half-listened to the talk of the aides and waiters around her. Most of the soldiers mocked the Congress, which had fled the city as the mutineers arrived. Deborah shared their disdain; to flee, in her mind, was synonymous with cowardice. Yet the tension in the army was palpable. She felt it herself and supposed every soldier must be pulled between pride for the country, this new country for which he had fought, and anger, no, even more than anger, fear, that they might be treated like the Pennsylvania line: denied pay, denied recognition, cut adrift.

In two short days Paterson had routed the mutineers. He arrested the ringleaders, those who had seized arms, but sent the rank and file home with half pay and certificates for the remainder. Some grumbled at headquarters and in the camp, disagreements that Deborah overheard as she delivered messages: Was this fair? Was half pay enough? Would the soldiers ever receive the compensation owed to them?

At last, after rounds of disputes and contentious demands from all sides, Paterson called Robert in to deliver his orders to the officers. She found Paterson in the parlor with pages scattered across his desk. He nodded to her and began to seal up the missives. "Well, Robert, I am to preside over the courts-martial of several perpetrators of this mutiny, so we shall be here for a time. I do believe some of the city fathers feel more comfortable with a general and half an army at their doorstep."

"Yes, sir."

"I had thought to be back to West Point by this time. We are an army, after all, not a traveling court." He ran his hand across his hair, sweeping the stray strands from his forehead. "However, there is no room for frustration. Justice should not be made to wait, and to my mind, there is no greater sin than treason. It is the worst of all deception to pretend to be loyal but truly to belong to another side. Mutiny is not far behind. . . ."

"There are those who would name our revolution a mutiny," Deborah said.

"There are, indeed. But a mutiny, like treason, happens from within, a revolution, from without. Those now on trial swore an oath to be faithful and to serve a cause. When we rose up against the British it was because we had no such understanding of faith between us."

"And our army, our new country, is built on such faith, I hope."

"It must be," said Paterson. "What have you learned of faith during your time of service, Robert?"

His question opened a floodgate in her mind. "There have been moments, sir, without faith. A corporal who deceived our company, then deserted. A good friend turned traitor, who would have let us all be killed so that he might gain money." Her thoughts tumbled over Tobias and his blond hair, Shaw and his bulbous eyes. "But these seem fleeting compared to . . ." Her voice caught a bit in her throat. "Compared to the sergeant who taught me the drill. Sergeant Munn. Would that I could ever meet his standard. But he believed in his soldiers and trusted us. There were nights on guard duty and days on patrol when he set me to watch his back. I cannot think of greater trust than that." She thought then of James, of his final sacrifice for her, but could not voice that, not to Paterson.

"There are times you are as thoughtful as a man twice your age, Robert."

She nodded. "Thank you, sir. This year in the army has seemed a lifetime. Certainly I have gained from it as much as one does in a lifetime—have gained brothers and fathers, in a sense." And a lover, an almost-husband.

"And faith in yourself?" Paterson asked. "Have you gained that, too?"

"At times. I have both gained and lost it and fought to gain it again."

Paterson nodded, riffling through a pile of papers. "As any honest man must."

THE COURTS-MARTIAL DRAGGED ON THROUGH June. Deborah attended Paterson or carried messages into Philadelphia. On the Fourth of July, the city fathers threw a tremendous celebration with Paterson as the guest of honor. The following day, the general ordered four of the mutineer privates sentenced to a hundred lashes each, and even as the trials of the sergeants continued, several companies were sent back to West Point. A small part of the brigade remained with Paterson. Word came from New York that more men had been sent home, and the garrison of West Point now numbered only in the hundreds.

During the weeks that followed, Paterson dined with politicians and former officers of the army; Deborah served and cleaned, delivered messages, and now and then helped in the stables. Lieutenant Walden urged her to come into the city, but Deborah did not like the narrow streets or the smells that wafted from every corner.

She found Philadelphia hot and confusing and she longed for open farmland, the vista over the Hudson, trees and quiet.

At last, she found a peaceful Sunday afternoon to write. She could not hope that post from Jennie would ever reach her in her travels, but her own missive could easily be sent from the metropolis.

Dear Jennie,

My regiment—what remains of it—has lately been called to Philadelphia. You may have heard of the mutiny down here, which has now been all but settled. Not a shot was fired, but the trials drag on. I think that our officers have fallen in love with this city after the seclusion of West Point and don't intend to leave for a while!

Indeed, the city is beyond imagining. Streets upon streets, each packed with shops. The wharves teem with ships and cargo. A year ago, I think I would have rejoiced at any work that would allow me to sojourn in such a metropolis. But I have learned that cities aren't for me and though I have delighted at seeing new sights, I am ready to settle down and rest. I miss the ponds and tracks, the woodlots and orchards. Even on days when I was cramped from sitting at the loom or tired from chores, such places comforted me. There is no comfort in the city; all is a bustle, a rush of people. Of late, I find myself tired, distracted. I hope and expect that General Paterson will release me in short order.

I do not want to intrude upon you in your married life, and you with a child soon to be delivered, but I wish to see you. Only the Lord knows when I will have that chance. I hope you're having an easy time of it. What name will you give to the babe?

Love,
Robert

Yes, she wanted to go back. She wanted to see Jennie, and she wanted a different kind of freedom, the freedom to let her guard down and to be herself. No more pretense, no more hiding. She longed for the frank conversation she would share with Jennie. Perhaps she could even return in the guise of Robert Shurtliff, to keep her future course open. For a few days, a week, maybe, she could stay as Robert with Jennie. Just a visit to refresh her and help her regain her confidence. She would not tie herself down; she would not be imprisoned again. She just wanted a respite from the demands of this world—the need to keep close, to guard her emotions carefully—and a chance to unburden her soul to her friend. They would sit by the hearth, Jennie with the babe at her breast, and Deborah would tell her all that had happened. Jennie would help her make sense of it; Jennie would know what to do.

CHAPTER TWENTY-THREE

All of Philadelphia sweltered under a blanket of thick air. On most days the sun hid behind a scum of cloud, but the gray film did nothing to diminish the sensation of being baked in an oven. On one such morning at the end of July, two gentlemen rode up to headquarters as Deborah readied the general's parlor for the day's business. She hastened to greet them, taking their riding cloaks and shaking the dust out at the back door. When she returned, Paterson had ushered the men to their chairs—one was Mr. Moore, a prominent public servant of the city, with bushy eyebrows and cheeks that showed the flush of good living, and the other, in a dark suit styled in the military manner, was Dr. Barnabas Binney, the head of the army hospital. A slip of a man, pale and thin, his eyes darted quickly and brightly across Deborah's face. Deborah passed into and out of the room bringing food and drink, waiting for the general's word. The three talked for almost an hour, the doctor's hands flying with forceful gesticulations. As the conversation wound up, she brought the men their cloaks and helped them mount.

Back inside, Paterson put his signature on a series of hastily drawn-up documents. "Well, Robert, out of one blaze and into another bonfire . . ." He sighed, running a hand through his hair.

"What's afoot, sir?"

"Dr. Binney brought word of an outbreak of smallpox and measles in the city. He fears that with the heat the pestilence will spread like wildfire. I am signing orders to remove the army from the city and set up camp farther afield." He shuffled more papers and looked at a map. "I hope they won't quarantine the city, but Binney said they've done so in the past." He ran his hand through his hair again, taking away the last trace of powder. "If they do, I suppose we will all return to West Point. . . ." He handed Deborah a stack of papers. "Take these, first to the docks to see that a full load of supplies is delivered in all haste—we need rations in the event the city is closed up, and then to report the new location of the camp. . . ." He turned to a map on the table and tapped his finger on it, muttering to himself. Deborah understood this as a sign of dismissal and, settling the papers carefully within her coat, took her leave.

Mounting her horse, she headed into the city. The houses closed in, and the humid air licked at her. Men working in shirtsleeves, kerchiefs around their necks soaked through with sweat, freight wagons straining to gain passage, the crowds pressing and pushing—she rode past them all with her nose wrinkled against the stench. The few ladies she saw swirled the air in front of them with vigorous fanning motions: a gesture of futility, for a paltry fan could scarcely stir the odors of Philadelphia. In front of a row of stately houses, carriages took on cargo, human and otherwise, and Deborah sensed from the haste and the jumble of crates that the city's gentry were fleeing the rumors of disease, just as some had fled the army. She lifted her hat and wiped at her own sweaty brow, wishing she could ride somewhere with enough space to allow a breeze. She turned her horse toward the river docks, where the wharves teemed with men stripped to the waist, heaving bales and bags, emptying carts, filling wagons, groaning from the heat and their burdens.

It looked to Deborah like a scene from hell, with so many souls damned to labor in the flames.

The crowds became impassable, so she dismounted and tied her horse to a hitching post, better to make her way through the throng. Boys were selling apples and pastries; men pushed their way through with laden handcarts. From the docks she heard shouts and crashes. A harbor crane swung across the deck of a ship, and sailors hollered, waving their arms at the operator. Deborah worked her way through, feeling that she moved more by means of her elbows than of her feet. She could just see through the crush of people the dockside office she sought. With everyone cheek by jowl, she thought, it was no wonder the doctor feared an outbreak of disease. Just then a stick caught her across the chest, none too lightly, and a bulky man pressed her backward to make room for a herd of goats bleating in distress. The closeness of the crowd was unbearable, and Deborah edged away from them and closer to the wharf's edge, to the hulks of the ships. Outside the main stream of traffic, she found a little breathing room. She stepped over a coil of rope and around a wooden post and heard shouts near to her: "Look out!" "You there!" She turned to ascertain the trouble, saw the arm of the crane pivot, and heard a crash so loud that it seemed to come from within her own head.

Cool, dark. Pressing down—heavy and tight—she was asleep. No, she was on the docks. She had to wake up. But how? Something pulled at her, tugged her coat, like an insistent child, and she wanted to shake it loose, be free, but it kept pulling. So heavy; she could not tell if she heard anything, though her ears seemed to roar, and it was hot, liquid hot. Someone opened her up; she could feel the blood flowing; she could see herself laid bare, felt cold air against her skin, then hot again. She could see nothing. She struggled, compelled by the need to keep close, the need to wake up, the need to shout, to speak, "Not here, not here," but all fell silent, and she was gone.

Scenes crowded in on Deborah, some assuredly phantasms of imagination, a dreamlike view of her own body piled onto a heap of corpses, her own efforts to prove herself alive. Oppressive darkness all about, a hand peeling back her eyelid, forcing it open to sudden harsh light, and a face before her, someone she knew, concerned, saying, "Robert?" Gone. That hand, in darkness once more, thrust now into her bosom, as if feeling for a heartbeat or to desperately bang against the organ itself, for everything had shivered to a stop. That cold, clean hand against her feverish chest. Gone. She felt a tube, metallic and smooth, the tang of silver down her throat, some liquid, medicinal and bitter, flowing into her.

The same face before her, thin and sharp, small, quick eyes. The doctor. "Robert?" She nodded, or tried to. "Good. Feeling better?" The hand, promising a cool touch, came toward her, and she edged away from it to darkness.

Flies beat against the windows, and the heat could make you mad, send you out of the house, out to the fathomless night, to seek the cold embrace of a pond. That's where she floated now, a pond, murky water without end. Swimming up from the bottom, slick and weightless, the water pressing against her ears, flooding out sight until finally she broke the surface gasping for air, and there came sound again, the sound of her name, "Robert?"

And she could say, "Yes?"

It was not a pond after all, but a room with the blinds pulled tight over the windows, only edges of light slivering in. She sprawled in bed, a damp tangle of linen about her, vinelike. In the cool dusk of the chamber she focused on the person before her, a woman, who offered her a cup. "Would you like water?" She drank, and in drinking realized the scale of her emptiness. "I'll be back in a moment. I'm glad you're awake." The woman left, and details coalesced, floated, and focused before her. Philadelphia. The summer. By the docks. Deborah did not recognize the chamber—at the top of a house, for the roof slanted over her. She rubbed a hand against her face, felt a sleeve fall back from her arm. Sitting up, she saw that she wore a loose shirt, a tunic or chemise—not a garment she had ever possessed or worn before. More than where it came from, she wondered how she came to be wearing it, where her uniform had gone, who took it from her . . . what they knew, and whom they had told. She could not properly lift her leg, but she shoved it out of the bed and was just trying to slide the other leg over when the woman returned, a bowl and cup on a tray before her. "Robert! Lie down." She set the tray on a table and helped her back into bed. Exhausted by this mere effort, Deborah let the woman lift her legs and tuck her in as if she were a child.

"Where am I?" Deborah asked. "And who are you?"

"I am Mary Parker—matron of the army hospital here in Philadelphia. And you are in the house of Dr. Barnabas Binney." Mary spooned soup for her. "You've been quite sick. It was a blow to the head that brought you to the hospital, and before you came properly around from that, you fell ill with fever." She put the soup down to offer her water; Deborah took the mug in both hands. It seemed unduly heavy, and she labored to bring it to her lips. "After a short stay in the hospital, the doctor thought you'd have a better chance of recovering here. He and his own family have nursed you, and I am here now as it is a Sunday morning and they are at chapel."

She put the mug down. "Does General Paterson know I am here?"

"The doctor will be able to tell you once he is back. He has been in contact with your officers. But I daresay the general knows some manner of what's befallen you. It has been the better part of two weeks that you battled the fever."

"Two weeks!"

"You've been very sick." Mary picked up the bowl. "Everyone will be most relieved to see you awake and restored to your senses." Leaving the water by the bedside, she retreated from the chamber.

Two weeks. Then all was known. Deborah collapsed against the pillow. If the doctor knew, and he must, then Paterson knew. What would happen to her? A court-martial? Prison? She had not the energy to succumb to the full weight of despair but could only close her eyes. Completely enervated, she sank into the pillows and slept again until the sound of the door awakened her, and she saw a man enter. He wore a dark suit and was pale with bright eyes: the face of her dreams—Dr. Binney.

"Robert," he said, sitting down by the bed. "I am glad you are awake." He took Deborah's wrist, felt for the pulse there, then put his hand to Deborah's forehead. "You feel less damp. I think the fever has broken. No doubt you're weak."

She wondered at the fact that both the matron and the doctor called her Robert—but perhaps they didn't know another name for her or merely wanted to keep her calm. "Yes," said Deborah, trying to figure what to say next. "I thank you for your care, but . . ."

"It has been a trying month in the city. Be glad you did not catch the pox." He cast a professional look over her and stood up. "Now then, you should stay in bed for at least a week. Though your spirit might be improved, your body remains weak. My wife will be most happy to feed you. It is her great pleasure to have a young man under her roof."

Deborah could contain herself no longer. "Sir, I must ask . . ."

Binney held up a hand. "It is a secret. Not my wife. Not the general. Just me and the matron, and you, of course. Now, save your strength for recovery. Sleep and eat."

Sleep and eat. Deborah did nothing else for the next week. Except wonder: Why had Dr. Binney kept her secret? Mrs. Binney came to the attic regularly during the day, bringing food and drink and often staying to talk. Some days she brought her sewing up and sat at her bedside, asking Deborah about the fighting she'd seen and what she planned to do next. She replied that she yet owed almost two years of service, and that though the war had ended, the army might be sent to fight Indians or defend new territory. But all the while, Deborah churned over what she really planned to do next or, more likely, what would be done to her. Mrs. Binney clucked about dangers and foolishness and how there had to be a better way to conduct the affairs of men, and Deborah found she liked to watch her sew, to watch the gradual appearance of a vest or a shirt, one stitch at a time. Mrs. Binney's presence demanded nothing and calmed her, and she realized that in the past year she had missed the company of women. This realization made her long even more to see Jennie: she should have asked for furlough and gone to Easton months ago. Whenever doubt or regret seized her, she answered it with prayer—a simple request for deliverance. She had to trust that God would make things right. After all, the initial journey that brought her to the army had been one of terror and doubt, but it ended with success. She had to hope that this journey might yield the same result.

While she was confined to bed, dreams provided her escape. Sometimes Robert rode on horseback over familiar roads in West Point; then, in a flowered dress, she was weaving at her loom at Sproat Tavern. As she dreamed, these lives merged, before and after; one moment he marched as a soldier, the next, Deborah again, shaking her apron at some chickens. She awoke disoriented, fearful, unsure of which was the future, which was the past.

At the end of the week, Dr. Binney checked on her and pronounced her ready to rise. "No vigorous activity. No riding." He raised a finger at Deborah. "I'll return your clothes to you on the condition that you recuperate here a further week."

Deborah nodded. Binney brought her regimentals. The sight of the uniform elicited relief, as satisfying and reassuring as a pile of coins might feel in her hand. "I trust this is the suit you prefer? I am happy to provide other garments. . . ."

Deborah shook her head. "These are my choice. Though if I might inquire . . ." She struggled to form the question, why? Why had Binney kept her secret? Why was he letting her carry on what must appear to him to be a masquerade?

The doctor laid the uniform over a chair, turned to Deborah, and seemed to read the emotions playing across her face. "As a doctor I have known humans inside and out." He walked across the room to the window. "We are all so much flesh. The mind and the soul, these I know nothing of. In this war, I have pulled soldiers from piles of corpses, men with their intestines hanging out, that others thought were dead, and sewed them up, seen them live." He looked back at Deborah. "Nothing surprises me anymore. I am glad you are alive, and I will return you to your commander in the same condition you came—though in better health, I trust. The rest I leave to you and to God to judge as right or wrong." He gave Deborah a wink, the slightest flick of an eye, as he left the room.

She rose from the bed and put on the breeches and leggings, the shirt and coat. Now she felt safe; now she felt comfortable.

The doctor had properly gauged Deborah's physical health and her need to recuperate. The stairs left her winded, and helping with simple chores exhausted her. Each day, after she watched the doctor leave for the hospital, she tried to sweep, to wash, to add one more chore, a little walk around the garden, before she felt she had to sit down.

At dinner one night, Binney returned with Walden, now promoted to captain. At first, the shock of seeing Walden in his crisp uniform and the thought that Binney might say something kept Deborah silent. But Walden held forth, voluble as always, telling stories about the doings in Philadelphia and the end of the courts-martial.

"That, in fact, is why I'm here, Robert. With the court cases completed and all quiet in the city, Paterson plans to decamp. He's leaving me in charge of a small squad." Walden swallowed a sip of wine and turned to address the doctor. "We will ride to Baltimore to provide escort for some dignitaries coming to Philadelphia and then rejoin the regiment at West Point. It was the general's thought that Robert might recuperate here while we travel to and from Baltimore and then accompany us to West Point."

"A capital idea." The doctor refilled everyone's wineglass. "A drink, then, to the success of your mission and to Robert's health." They drank, and he poured again. "This time," he said, "we drink to freedom, to liberty, to the end of human bondage."

Deborah drained her glass and felt the sweet wine uncoil within her. There was small talk and brandy before Walden took his leave. Then, for a time, the doctor sat with Deborah in silence. She studied his hands, the long, slim fingers, the paleness of his skin, feeling his eyes upon her. Finally he said, "Your story must be fascinating. I cannot imagine how you managed all this time in the army without exposure. I watched you at dinner this evening, and you seem every bit the man."

"I have been a man for over a year now," Deborah replied. "Perhaps it is because I have felt myself so that others have believed it as well."

"Perhaps. When I first discovered your true nature, I thought it was a mere pretense, a disguise, but tonight I see it is not. This is who you are."

Deborah felt a rush of gratitude. "It is. I am . . . I feel . . . when I think of how I want to live, I want to live as a man." She shook her head, knowing she wasn't explaining it well. "Perhaps if society treated women differently, I wouldn't mind being a woman." After all, there were people with whom she did not mind being a woman or having them know that she had been a woman.

Binney's eyes ranged over her face, bearing no trace of harshness but only curiosity. "Would you live as a man the rest of your days?"

"That question has plagued me for many months now. I didn't like being a woman before the war. I resented the way I was treated, how I was held in so constrained a sphere."

"Many women live in a depressing servitude, it is true."

A rush of gratitude for these words, for this understanding, swept through Deborah, adding fuel to her thoughts. "Now I know that what matters is not whether I live as a man or woman but whether I live without letting others confine or restrict me. If I can abide by my own rules and live as I wish, then I believe I can live as a woman. But I must say, it is easier to do so as a man."

Binney held his hands together, fingers touching, before his face. "You must have felt—you must still feel—terribly divided."

"At first, I did. But believe me, sir, this is who I am. It is no division to live as I want. Rather, it feels as though I am . . . together for the first time in my life."

"You possess a remarkable strength of character, Robert. Few would have the fortitude and perseverance to believe such a life possible, let alone live it. And I think you will find your way. If you live as a man, if you live as a woman, you have fought for liberty and you have earned it for yourself."

"Thank you, sir."

Binney refilled both of their glasses. Deborah took a sip and gazed at her own hands and the long scar on her index finger. She had not realized how good it might feel to talk to someone of these matters. Since losing James, she had closed herself off. How she longed to be open. Binney was the second person to know and understand her secret. Perhaps others like him existed, ready to share compassion, ready to accept her, however she might be. She sipped her brandy and thought about the doctor's words. She had earned her liberty.

When the time came for Deborah to depart, Binney gave her a small bundle wrapped up tightly with a letter on top. "The letter is for Paterson. It discloses the truth of your nature." Deborah blanched. "You are honest, Robert, and I put it in your hands. One should never be ashamed of one's true nature. Bear in mind that there are worse ways the general could find out than from your own hand. This too is freedom." He handed the bundle over. "The package is for you, a simple dress, if you wish it. One never knows."

"I cannot thank you enough, sir."

Binney shook her hand. "Good luck and Godspeed."

It felt odd to be on horseback once more, and even with the long recuperation, the exertion of riding quickly exhausted her. Walden led their small company at a leisurely pace, and—using Deborah's health as an excuse—turned the journey into a lengthy one. Their route from the city to West Point wound across the countryside as they made stops at the houses of former officers, a long string of dinners and gatherings where those of rank drank toasts and swapped war stories, and Deborah escaped into the autumn evenings to contemplate the letter stowed in her coat pocket, close to her chest. By day, she stayed to the rear of the squad and kept her thoughts to herself. The others were officers all, save a corporal serving as a waiter, a handsome young fellow who rode practically upon his captain's heel.

The bundle from Binney rested, unopened, deep in her saddlebags, and at times she wished to consign both the bundle and the letter in her coat pocket to flames: she would leave the army as Robert Shurtliff. But Binney's words stayed with her. How did the letter, the declaration of herself as a woman, equate with freedom? She puzzled over this question as she rode. Freedom to choose, to deliver the news herself, to say, this is who I am.

It would be honest; it would be satisfying. To say to Paterson or Munn: Robert Shurtliff is a woman. You have judged me strong and capable and diligent and brave, and I am. And I am a woman. But the cost, the cost. They would call her liar and deceiver, and they would be right. She prayed over the matter, but even as she asked God for guidance, she knew the decision rested within her power.

THE SQUAD CAME TO THE Hudson in late September. Autumn had already arrived in the highlands, a cool that matched the emptiness of the fort. A bare minimum of sentries guarded the gate; smoke rose from the chimney of headquarters and just one of the barracks. When they dismounted, Deborah helped the grooms with the horses, knowing that she only postponed the inevitable. But she wanted to be in this place that had meant so much to her, around soldiers—and be one of them—for another moment. Paterson might drum her out within the hour. But at least she would stand before him, this man who had been almost a father, and say, this is who I am, this is who I have been. I am not ashamed.

At last, she unpacked her saddlebags and walked into Paterson's headquarters. Walden and his lieutenants stood by the door, and the captain waved her over, saying, "Shurtliff, the general was asking after you."

Deborah knocked at the parlor and waited for the general's summons. As she entered, Paterson stood and ushered her closer to the fire. The impulse to take the letter and toss it upon the flaming logs seized her, but she resisted, gave the general a salute. "You seem hale, Robert, a bit drawn perhaps, but Walden tells me you held up on the trip."

Deborah nodded, feeling a terrible clump stuck in her throat. Paterson looked at her with concern. "Is all well?"

Deborah thrust her hand inside her coat and drew out the letter that Doctor Binney had written. "The doctor bade me give this to you. He disclosed some of its contents to me." She extended the letter to Paterson. "He said I should give it to you from my own hand if I wished. And so I wish."

Paterson took the letter, slipped his knife under the seal, and opened it. Deborah found she could not watch the general as he read; instead, she gazed at the flames, the liquid fury of them. When she glanced up, she saw the letter fall from Paterson's fingers and land silently on the desk.

"I cannot believe it," the general said, his face showing not anger or horror or disgust, but simple disbelief, like one who has seen a ghost or a miracle. "This letter tells me you are a woman."

"Aye, sir."

"That the doctor discovered your true form while you lay ill."

"Aye, sir."

He pushed his fingers through his hair, that gesture so familiar to Deborah that it touched her with longing, a sort of incipient nostalgia. Already she wished the letter back to her hand, to undo this revelation, to have things between her and the general as they had been. But he stared at her openly, no trace of fondness. "Am I to understand that your time in the army as Robert Shurtliff has been but a masquerade?"

"No, sir. I am Robert Shurtliff." She looked to the fire, to the general's face. "But I am also Deborah Samson."

"How can it be?"

Deborah stood still, for she knew not what to say except: it is my life; how else can it be?

Sinking into his chair, he waved for Deborah to do likewise. Paterson stared at Deborah as if he would see through her. "Tell me your story."

Slowly, starting where it began, her unfortunate family, her term of service to the Thomas household, Deborah tried to explain how she had been formed. She spoke of always being strong, of how, as a woman, that strength had been a detriment. She explained that she had always wanted to work hard, to do according to her abilities, to watch and to learn, but such behavior had been discouraged. "Is it any wonder," she asked the general, "that I wanted to be a man?" She explained how she first tried to enlist as Timothy Thayer, how she had been detected. "I wanted to serve, sir, I wanted to be of use. And, yes, I wanted to be free too, so I ran away and enlisted at Bellingham. The rest is in your regiment's logbooks."

"That it is," Paterson said slowly. "The fine service of one Robert Shurtliff." He rubbed his hair. "You truly are female?"

"Aye." And, delicately, she explained how she bound up her chest, how she minded her use of the necessary or the pot, how she had learned to walk and move and talk, and how she had scrupulously avoided horseplay. She left out so much—did not mention Shaw or James, her own struggles to become and be—that it scarcely seemed like her story. But Paterson appeared satisfied. "Indeed, the caution and careful observation are part of the habits that make you a good soldier. It is an unbelievable feat." He picked up the letter and read it again, frowning and nodding, then said, "I do not know what to say further. Had I not this letter before me, and your word of its truth, you would be just Robert Shurtliff, my trusted waiter and a soldier of good merit. But now you are much more, and I cannot fathom how you managed all these months of service."

Deborah could not help but smile. "I cannot say it was always a pleasure, but I am glad to have served."

"And what am I to do with you now?" Paterson stood abruptly and began to pace the length of the room.

"I remain your servant, and a soldier, too."

"But your term of service has come to a close." Deborah opened her mouth to protest, but Paterson spoke first. "It has naught to do with this letter. Congress has ordered the standing army drawn down to a few hundred men. In the next week, you will be discharged. Those are the orders." His eyes searched her head to toe, and Deborah knew he sought a glimpse of the young woman he now knew sat before him.

"I will follow orders, of course, and I will make my own way."

"I cannot know what is right, having never dreamed, let alone faced such a circumstance as this. It seems wrong to deprive you of your uniform, given that you have served faithfully and without blemish. But it also seems wrong to treat you as a man, since you are, by your own admission, not."

Deborah almost leapt to her feet, wanting to grab Paterson and reason with him. How could he think to deny her this after she had explained herself to him? After she had been honest and laid herself open, how was it just for him to decide who and what she should be? "Sir, I assure you. I prefer to keep my guise as a man."

"Yet I would not endanger you . . . Deborah." The name stalled on the general's lips, and he licked them, as if to brush the word away or, perhaps, to taste it better. "It cannot be safe to be a lone woman among all these men. Indeed, there is no place for a woman here. You must go home."

"I have been unharmed all these months, sir." To her horror, she found that her chin trembled, her throat tightened, that tears threatened to creep into the corners of her eyes. She clenched her jaw, pushed them back. "If I may be bold, sir?"

"You have been bold already, I daresay."

She managed to smile at that. "Then if I may continue to be bold, sir, I would like to choose my own course. As a woman, I was never allowed. You must know, sir, what women are told: that they are weak of mind and inferior of spirit. But have I not proven myself otherwise?"

"You have, that you have."

"Then allow me to make my own way. I will be happy to return to the area from which I came, but I would leave the army as Robert Shurtliff."

Paterson stared long into Deborah's eyes and said, "I believe you have earned that right." For a while, the room heard only the pop and hiss from the logs in the fireplace. Paterson scuffed at a cinder with his boot. "I will ask Captain Walden to accompany you home, to see you safely delivered. It is a courtesy I would extend to any faithful servant."

Deborah doubted this, but she said only, "Thank you, sir."

"It is most remarkable. Once you are home, I hope that you will disclose yourself to your officers in the light infantry. When I dismissed them, months ago, they all spoke highly of Robert Shurtliff, and I am certain they would like to know what happened to him."

She had not thought what she might write to Munn or Booth. But perhaps they should know, perhaps they should understand who she was and what was possible. "I will think on it, sir."

"Think on it, then. And in the meantime, I tell you this: the country needs strong women as much as it needs strong men. Perhaps more."

"I am glad, then, to say that I have been both."

The general fixed his gaze on her, and if Deborah was not mistaken, that gaze held pride and approval. "You are dismissed to your quarters."

THAT EVENING, DEBORAH SCRAWLED A hasty note to Jennie, knowing she might arrive before her letter did. Her fingers trembled with relief as she wrote, "I am coming to you, Jennie. I will be by your side shortly." Perhaps she would not like Easton; perhaps it would have nothing to offer her. But she would see Jennie, and she knew that in seeing her, some piece that had been missing would fall into place. It had always been so. And if Easton proved not to be the home she desired, she knew now that she could make her own way in the world. She had learned this and much else.

Within a week, Deborah rode beside Captain Walden, retracing the same journey she had taken on the way to West Point, only now the maples flamed red and the birches fluttered gold. Paterson had released her a few days before the rest of the men were discharged, telling Walden that she required early release and an escort home, so ordered by the doctor in Philadelphia. When the groom brought mounts for the lieutenant and Deborah, the general himself came out to bid farewell. "Take this soldier home, Captain," he told Walden, handing him a few letters to deliver on the journey.

"Are you excited to see your family, then, Robert?" Walden asked as they mounted up.

"I've no family to speak of. But I'm going to the closest thing I have, better than family, even." She raised her hand to salute the general. She would leave as a soldier; he had granted her that.

Walden, true to his earlier habits, prattled on about Boston, his destination after seeing Deborah safely to hers. So she would not see that great city. At least she had seen Philadelphia. Perhaps, she told herself, her mind plodding along with her horse, she would yet make it to Boston; she must keep hope of that. As they rode, the air held the rich culmination of autumn, a sweet smell that bordered on decay. When Deborah had taken leave from headquarters, Paterson had pressed upon her a small bag of money—to cover the journey, he said—and she and Walden stayed at modest inns as they made their way north. She would have preferred to sleep in barns and stables amid the hay newly brought in from the fields, but the captain insisted on keeping his charge warm and dry, and himself in a feather bed, no doubt. Miles passed, geese flew far above, cackling their departure for the winter. Nearer, crows landed in the orchards and fields; Deborah left them uncounted.

The surrounding countryside took on familiar contours. The walls of piled-up stones marking out each farm's boundaries, the kettle ponds glinting through the bare branches. Some part of the landscape whispered to Deborah, *this is home*. She saw herself in these fields as a little girl, as a young woman. It seemed natural now that she should return, a soldier come home after months at war, come back to the place that had forged her.

They passed through Mansfield, where Walden inquired for directions at an inn. From Mansfield to Easton was an easy ride, and soon they crossed paths with a traveler who knew Charles Howe and pointed them to his farm, near Shovel Pond. A turn from the main road to a smaller track. Woodlots and fields. A small farmhouse, chimney running down the center. Walden and Deborah tied their horses to the fence and walked up to the door. It was Walden who knocked, while Deborah stood to the side. The young woman who opened the door had pushed her sleeves above her elbows, with forearms red and face flushed, and threads of hair lay stickily on her brow, the signs of a woman who had been attending the wash. Her eyes flicked from Walden to Deborah. Then her mouth opened, and she let out a soft scream and threw herself into Deborah's arms with such force that Deborah staggered back as she caught her. Wrapping her arms around her—she had forgotten how slight Jennie was—they stood speechless for a moment. Silently soaking in this reunion, this happiness, Deborah knew she had been right to return.

EPILOGUE

"Charge—bayonet!"

Mrs. Gannett brought the butt of the musket tight under her armpit, the barrel landing heavily in her left palm, and took two quick steps toward the front of the stage. Perhaps she imagined it, in the glare of the theater lights, but the crowd seemed to shrink from her, as if fearing she would leap into their midst and skewer someone.

"Shoulder—firelock!" The clerk of the theater read his lines loudly but with a flourish that would have set Corporal Booth laughing. Nonetheless, Mrs. Gannett slid the musket neatly, bracing it against her right side. She gave a slight grimace as she gripped the stock with her left hand, that stiff finger flaring up in pain as she willed it to bend and grasp. It wouldn't. Her heels clicked together sharply as she snapped to rigid attention.

The clerk stepped out beside her. "The celebrated Mrs. Deborah Samson Gannett!"

With that, the audience leapt from its seats, and the theater shook with the thumping of feet and resounding applause.

Mrs. Gannett passed her musket to the clerk who'd played her sergeant-at-arms and withdrew backstage, letting the clapping and stamping echo on. She took a little kerchief from her coat pocket and wiped her sweaty brow. It had been a long week of travel in the coach, with a lecture and performance two nights ago in Springfield, and then again tonight in Albany. But at twenty-five cents a head, she'd turn a profit, especially if her next show drew a similar crowd.

At the rear of the building, she opened the door to a dusky dressing room, and, shutting herself in, began to unbutton the coat. "Tarnished," she muttered to herself as she fingered the buttons. "Munn would never have stood for it."

It was just as well her old sergeant wasn't in the audience. What would he think of her up onstage, delivering a lecture on her exploits, arguing for the rights and abilities of women? She hadn't been able to ascertain the whereabouts of Munn, though she had written to Paterson, who lived in these parts. No reply from him had reached her—the general was a busy man—but, oh, to see him again. To hear from his own mouth that she had served him well, that she had done a man's job. She longed for that affirmation, even as she cringed at the thought of the encounter. Some part of her wanted Paterson to know her only as she had been and not see her grown older, a mother and a wife rather than the soldier he knew.

She undid the front fall of her pants, pulled them off, and slung them over a chair. From a peg on the wall, she retrieved her shift and pulled it over her head before beginning to button up her dress. She felt some numbness in the tips of her fingers and blew on them before trying the buttons again. She was ill and tired. Bone-weary. How had she ever done that drill so readily? How had she kept up with those young boys? More even than the physical tiredness was the mental fatigue: the performance brought everything rushing back; her mind crowded with memories of Shaw that made her wince, thoughts of James that washed her in sadness.

Mrs. Gannett sat to fasten on her shoes. In a moment, the clerk would be coming with the evening's take, and together they'd count it out, portion her share from the theater's. Her husband, Benjamin, had made a mess of the farm, taken on too much debt, lost some land, never listening to her advice. She'd tried to bring in money, hoping to pay off some of his loans; back in 1792, she'd filed for wages owed to her, but the Commonwealth of Massachusetts had paid her only thirty-four dollars for her service in the army. Two dollars for each month she'd served. Still, that was better than the reception she'd received from Congress, who had rejected her petition for back pay and a pension. No money for a veteran with three children to feed, not to mention a ne'er-do-well husband to support.

She'd hoped that General Paterson, recently elected to Congress himself, would help her make another appeal. But even though she'd sent along a handbill announcing her performance this evening, she hadn't seen him in the audience. Well, he was a great man now, with a big landholding on the New York frontier and service in the courts; no doubt he had little time for a misfortunate woman. Still, it would have been nice. . . .

She rose and smoothed the coat, its blue wool a comfort to her but also something of an annoyance. Had she been wrong ever to take it off? All those years ago in Easton, could she have reveled in her reunion with Jennie and then gone away, continued to live as Robert Shurtliff? She imagined that somehow that possible future lived on without her—a ghostly Robert Shurtliff managing an existence on a farm in the Berkshires or Ohio. What happened to all the lives she hadn't led?

No sense in mulling it over. She'd let Robert Shurtliff go. There had been an aunt and uncle in nearby Sharon, and her brothers soon had word that she'd returned and came to see her. Jennie's old masters, the Leonards, even came up to visit, bringing along little grandchildren to meet the woman soldier. It had felt so good to be welcomed that she didn't want to disappear again, and Jennie had been so happy, so satisfied in her life with her husband, that when Benjamin Gannett had shown an interest in Deborah . . . and when she'd learned he was an eldest son, poised to inherit a sizable farm . . . it had seemed a good match.

"Hey-ho," she said tiredly. She folded the uniform and stowed it in her traveling case. Tomorrow, she'd give one more show in Albany, and then . . .

There was a knock at the door, then the barest pause for her to say, "Come in," and wearily brush back her still-sweaty hair, expecting to hear the reassuring clink of the till.

"Well, Robert?"

She gaped at the figure in the doorway. A face and voice she knew so well, though it had been almost twenty years since she'd encountered him last. "General Paterson!" She stepped toward him and offered her hand.

He shook it, as he would shake a man's, his grip firm about her fingers. "I had your letter two weeks ago, saying you'd be here. My apologies for not replying. It has been a busy season."

"And did you care for the presentation?"

"I'd say so. Your old sergeant would be happy with your drill, too."

Deborah could not keep from smiling, all vestige of weariness now dissipated. How good Paterson looked. His hair was receding a bit from his temples, but he was still sturdy and hale. It was odd to see him in civilian clothes, with a cravat about his neck and his coat of velvet broadcloth well brushed. But then, it must be even stranger for him to see her thus attired in a dress.

"Did you bring your children with you on this trip?"

"No, sir. They remained at home. It's easier that way."

He nodded. "A shame though. I wanted to tell them what a fine soldier their mother was. But I expect they know, and by the time you have finished this tour, I expect the world will know as well."

He offered her his arm. "May I take you away in my coach? I left orders for a late supper at the hotel."

"Yes," Deborah said. "Supper would be most welcome."

"I won't keep you long, I promise. But I've spent years wondering whatever happened to Robert Shurtliff."

"So have I," Deborah murmured, taking his arm. "So have I."

ACKNOWLEDGMENTS

A brief historical note: astute readers will note that I have spelled Deborah's surname "Samson" while many sources list it as "Sampson." There is no known record of Deborah signing her maiden name, so we will never know how she spelled it (though, interestingly, the signature of Robert Shurtliff is preserved). However, it is clear that her father and other family members spelled it "Samson." I have hewed to this spelling as the more accurate.

I have been fortunate to have had wonderful supporters for this novel from all parts of my life, and there is no sufficient way to thank the people who have helped make *Revolutionary* possible, nor is it feasible to list everyone who influenced the work, but I do want to express my gratitude to the following people.

My agent, Alison Fargis, and the others at Stonesong offered timely advice, had boundless patience, and possessed amazing enthusiasm throughout the process. It is no exaggeration to say that the novel wouldn't exist without Alison.

The same could be said of Anjali Singh, whose expertise and faith guided the editing of the novel through several drafts. Fair and focused, she helped me to shape the story and get the manuscript off the ground.

Millicent Bennett offered the final word in editing; she was insightful and positive, and I am grateful for her influence and suggestions. There are myriad others at Simon & Schuster who fielded my e-mails and answered my questions with patience and pleasant efficiency.

I owe much to the faculty at Vermont College of Fine Arts—whether in workshop or casual conversation, I was encouraged by many. In particular, my advisers Nance Van Winckel, Ellen Lesser, and Clint McCown were truly inspiring and endlessly helpful. My classmates, in all their robust zaniness, helped me to have not only faith in but also fun with this project.

Subsequent to VCFA, I relied on willing early readers, whose advice was immeasurably useful. Lexi Adams was the first to wade through it and tell me what she thought; she has been terrifically supportive. The next was Patricia Lothrop, who patiently helped me sort out the beginning. My parents also read the manuscript and returned it with advice both loving and instructive, as their advice always is. In this and so many other ways, I am grateful for their wisdom and nurturing.

Others aided along the path: my brother, Seth, who put me in touch with Deb; Bob Weston and other colleagues at St. George's School, who were always willing to chat; Alfred Young, whose own volume on Deborah is extraordinary and who corresponded energetically with me.

And, of course, the person to whom this book is dedicated: my wife, Ilona, who read and talked, asked and suggested, and always offered both insight and guidance.

ABOUT THE AUTHOR

Alex Myers is a writer, teacher, speaker, and activist. Since high school, Alex has campaigned for transgender rights. As a female-to-male transgender person, Alex began his transition at Phillips Exeter Academy (returning his senior year as a man after attending for three years as a woman) and was the first transgender student in that academy's history. Alex was also the first openly transgender student at Harvard, and worked to change the university's nondiscrimination clause to include gender identity. He lives with his wife and two cats.